There are very few novels which deal with the issues of contemporary medical ethics in the lively and intensely readable way which Hazel McHaffie's books do. She uses her undoubted skill as a storyteller to weave tales of moral quandary, showing us with subtlety and sympathy how we might tackle some of the ethical issues which modern medicine has thrown up. ALEXANDER MCCALL SMITH

From Tolstoy to Cronin, writers have raided medicine in search of the raw material of literature. How appropriate that Hazel McHaffie should be repaying the compliment by using fiction to grapple with the ethical dilemmas so often and so effortlessly conjured up by modern medicine. GEOFF WATTS, WRITER, JOURNALIST AND BBC PRESENTER

... skilfully written to bring out the complex ethical issues we as doctors, nurses, patients, or relatives, may face in dealing with difficult issues. THE BRITISH MEDICAL JOURNAL

... illuminates the novel moral complexities of the modern world with dramatic insight ... a great read. JAMES LE FANU, GP, WRITER AND MEDICAL COLUMNIST

Hazel McHaffie has woven together authentic clinical details and ethical dilemmas with a lightness of touch that transports the reader effortlessly into the world of scientific medicine ... these novels are accessible and compelling. BRIAN HURWITZ, PROFESSOR OF MEDICINE AND THE ARTS

... well written and researched ... presents issues of medicine, law and ethics in a very human and readily understandable manner. BRITISH MEDICAL ASSOCIATION

... accomplishes something of great value for the reader – something deep within the ethical and far away from the bio-ethical. She exposes the potential for authenticity within intimate human relationships. THE LANCET

By the same author

Fiction

Listen (a novella)
Inside of Me
Over my Dead Body
Saving Sebastian
Remember Remember
Right to Die
Double Trouble
Paternity
Vacant Possession

Non-fiction

Crucial Decisions at the Beginning of Life
Life, Death and Decisions

HAZEL MCHAFFIE trained as a nurse and midwife, gained a PhD in Social Sciences and was Deputy Director of Research in the Institute of Medical Ethics. She is the author of over one hundred published articles and books. *Crucial Decisions at the Beginning of Life* won the British Medical Association book of the Year Award in 2002. *Right to Die* was shortlisted for the BMA Popular Medicine prize in 2008. *Killing Me Gently* is her eleventh published novel set in the world of medical ethics.

KILLING ME GENTLY

HAZEL McHAFFIE

First published 2019

ISBN: 978-0-9926231-5-9

References to medical and scientific matters in this publication are believed to be accurate at the time of publication; however all characters and events are fictitious and any resemblance to real persons, living or dead, is purely coincidental.

The author's right to be identified as author of this book under the Copyright, Designs and Patents Act 1988 has been asserted.

British Library Cataloguing in Publication Data. A catalogue record for this book is available from the British Library.

Published by VelvetEthics Press
12 Mayburn Terrace, Loanhead, Scotland EH20 9EJ

CHAPTER 1

M ud sucked greedily at her boots, branches tangled in her hair, exposed roots snaked across her path. The viscous swirl of the river drew her like a magnet down into the thick darkness, the dank odour of slowly decomposing vegetation.

Anya had no notion of time, only an all-consuming compulsion to get as far away as possible from her tormentor. Several times she skidded wildly, once finding herself at the very brink, one false move away from those unforgiving rocks.

A rudimentary fence gave way to a low stone wall, and she paused for long enough to peer over the edge, letting the roar of mini-waterfalls drown out the memory of that demonic shrieking, then plunged on, the noise increasing as she ran. She craned her neck forward, straining to make sense of what was happening below her ... a crescent of white foam ... ahh, a weir. Magnetised by the unceasing movement, she crowded closer. *Oh, to block out every thought, every sound, but this!* She climbed up until she was sitting astride the cold stone ... swung her other leg over ... stared down into the depths ... *What bliss to let the force sweep her away to eternal silence.*

Slowly, slowly, she leaned ... further ... further ... her eye caught a glimpse of something to her right beyond the dam ... moonlight glinting momentarily on a calm surface ... a path running at right angles to the one she'd been on. Of course. Above the weir, the river would widen out. It would be deeper there. She swung her legs back. Leaves squelched beneath her boots as she stumbled towards firmer ground. She swung left, through trees, her footsteps now just inches from the water. *Yes ... yes ... this would be much more effective.* A viaduct loomed ahead; a sliver of moon winking far above her.

Persistent cramp forced her to a standstill and she let a fallen tree take her weight till the pain eased. Sudden blackness enveloped her as a cloud veiled the moon, and immediately the river took on a far more sinister edge. With every minute of immobility, the frozen fingers of the night increased their stranglehold, sapping both energy and sensation. Impatiently she brushed the tears from her aching cheeks with the back of one wrist. It made no difference; the darkness remained impenetrable.

Her brain began clutching at the returning memories like a sinking man grabbing one last chance to make peace with life.

Not a living soul knew where she was.

Or the car.

What if no one found her?

What if Leon woke?

What if he found her gone ... and the car ... and his daughter?

What if the baby ...?

Anguish tore an unholy cry from her, and she turned so suddenly the world spun. She clung to a nearby trunk until the dizziness passed, and then began staggering back the way she'd come, every intake of breath slicing into her raw throat.

Somehow she felt her way to the broader path without mishap ... along to the weir ... Keeping the sound of rushing water to her right, she felt her way inch by inch through the tangled undergrowth ... only ... she had no idea how far she'd come, no recollection of parking the car. Terror and darkness disorientated her. Twice she tracked back, away from the river, searching, pleading; twice she drew a blank.

'Please, please, *please* ... Let me find it ... *Please* ... Let her be safe.'

She ploughed on and on, keening as she ran.

Where could she have left it?

What if she was too late?

What if she never found it?

Every now and again she stopped to listen. Nothing. Only the susurration of the swirling water.

Had she already gone too far? Should she retrace her steps?

There was nothing to guide her. Only the dim memory of something snapping ... of crunching the car to an abrupt stop, heedless of where she was ... leaping out ... running running running .... away from that relentless screaming.

It could be anywhere.

She darted this way, that, searching, searching.

When she eventually stumbled upon the outline of the Peugeot on rough grass, she could only sink to her knees, sobbing her relief.

'Thank you, God! Thank you, thank you, thank you.'

But ... it felt all wrong. The darkness was holding its breath.

'No! No! No! No! *Please,* no!'

She wrenched open the back door. The car seat was still in position, just as she'd left it. She climbed in, eyes straining. The silhouette was absolutely still ... silent ...

One shaking hand reached towards it. A faint puff of air momentarily whispered across her fingers ... or ... was it ... wishful thinking?

She closed her eyes, waited till the world settled back on its axis. Tentatively she stretched again; yes, there it was, faint but unmistakeable, the elemental sign of life. But how cold the skin felt. Grabbing the car rug, she tucked it around the unmoving shape, and slowly, painfully, forced her own legs out of the mud-caked boots, and into the driving seat. The engine responded immediately, and she instantly ratcheted up the heat, turned on the fans. Massaging her calves brought a return of some sensation, and somehow, she managed to slide the car into gear and, after two abortive attempts, inch out from the wasteland's tentacles.

Some visceral sense made her leave the baby in the car seat when she reached the house, disturbing her as little as possible. Such a fragile hold on sanity would never cope with a repeat performance of that mind-altering screaming. No, she must concentrate now on thawing out her physical body, leave the mental effort till daybreak. A hot soak restored her circulation, and she curled herself into the chair beside the Aga, pulled two rugs over her body, and fell into the sleep of exhaustion, the car seat in the farthermost corner of the kitchen.

It seemed like only minutes until Gypsy awoke for a feed ... Leon appeared for breakfast ... he left for three days. Only when the front door clicked shut behind him did Anya finally let her shoulders relax. For once ignoring the detritus on the kitchen counter, she collapsed back into her chair, closing her eyes.

But instantly she was jolted upright as the door was thrown open.

'Anya?'

Every nerve jangled.

'What the hell's going on? I've just seen your car ...'

'I ... Gypsy wouldn't stop crying. I took her for a drive.'

'In the *middle of the night*? In *February*?'

One staccato nod.

'Where?'

'Down by the river.'

'The *river*? You must have known it'd be like a quagmire down there after all this rain.'

'I didn't sit down and analyse a route! I was desperate. I just drove. Anywhere. The bypass, the hills, the woods, the river ... what does it matter?'

Leon was always a rather commanding presence, now he was positively intimidating as he faced her, hazel eyes narrowed, incredulity personified.

'"What does it *matter?*"! This is *my daughter* you're talking about! I have a right to know if you're putting her in danger. You didn't even leave a note ... a text. What if you'd had an accident? I wouldn't have known where to start looking.'

'I'm telling you now.'

'Only because I found your car plastered in mud. And what a time to drop this little bombshell! When I'm on the point of leaving the house for three days. You *know* this meeting's important.'

'Work's *always* important. It was never the right time.'

'And you think this *is?*' He spread his hands in despair, knocking a breakfast mug flying, splattering coffee onto the new Amtico flooring. He grabbed a handful of kitchen towel, cursing as he mopped furiously.

'I'll sort it. You get off.'

He shouldered her out of the way. 'We're on the verge of clinching a really big deal; I *have* to be away. Thomas is *relying* on me to negotiate things with these clients.'

'It was *you* who brought it up, not me!' she flashed back.

'Well, I could hardly ignore the state of your car, could I? What d'you take me for?'

Anya felt the fury travelling through her entire body. And something more primal.

'That is so typical! Wrong if I tell you; wrong if I don't. You want to know why I was out driving the streets at 3am while you were fast asleep? Well, I'll tell you. Because *your daughter* was screaming … on and on and on and on … I felt I was going to … *explode!*' She punched the sides of her head with clenched fists. 'I just *had* to do … *something.*'

'Right. That's it. You've got to stop these damn night feeds. The sooner the better, for all of us. I don't personally believe it would kill her to get some formula, but express milk if you have to. And when I get back, *I'll* get up in the night. But look, I haven't got time for this. Not now. I *have* to go.' He was gathering his coat and briefcase and papers together again. 'I'll talk to Thomas.' He moved to give her the customary kiss goodbye. 'And if I can't work from home more, I'll ask my mother …'

Anya held him off, shaking her head vigorously. 'No, Leon, no! Please! I absolutely could *not* cope with anybody staying here. But I know I need help. I've already made an appointment.'

'Appointment? Who with?'

'The GP.'

'I thought you saw her last week?'

'This is a second opinion. Dr Jones wasn't really interested. This is the most senior one.'

'When?'

'Wednesday. Wednesday morning.'

Leon studied her face, doubt scrawled across his eyes. 'Are you sure? Wouldn't it be better …?'

'I'm absolutely sure. And this has been a wake-up call. I'll be extra, extra careful from now on. Promise.'

She saw his eyes flick to the kitchen clock.

'Yes. Go! You concentrate on persuading Mr Brandybutter, or whatever his name is, to siphon all his gold into the Morgan coffers.'

'There's no call for sarcasm. And his name's Braithwaite not Brandybutter. Giles Braithwaite.'

She shrugged. 'Whatever. You won't impress him if you're late.'

'Well, you call me if things start getting on top of you. *Before* they do! Promise me? If I can't take your call at the time, I'll ring you back first chance I get.'

'I hear you.'

He kissed her cheek.

She waited several minutes after his brake lights had vanished from sight to be sure he'd gone this time. Then she hunched a coat around her shoulders and slipped out to retrieve the plastic bag from the boot of her car. The mud caking her boots was still wet and easily sluiced off; in three days she'd have them thoroughly dried out, polished and back in the closet. No one would ever know they'd paced the bank of the River Esk, while an eight-week-old baby screamed herself to sleep alone in the darkness.

And in the meantime …

She returned to the kitchen, opened the drawer, lifted out the placemats, and removed two boxes. Forcing herself to concentrate, she drew out a blister pack from each box. She counted out loud: one from the first ... two from the second ... dropping them into the milky white liquid stored during another long night.

A quick swirl.

They dissolved without trace.

Slowly, carefully, she carried the glass upstairs.

CHAPTER 2

The surgery door swung open yet again, another blast of cold air reached her. Perched on a chair just inside the waiting room, Anya felt the temperature drop another degree, but it was worth it; anything to avoid inhaling the lethal cocktail of second-hand germs and second-hand breath and second-hand angst. With each new patient she gulped in the freshness, holding it in until her desperate lungs insisted she exhale again. Thirty-seven seconds, her best effort to date.

From time to time she peered inside the white cocoon on her lap.

Please, please, please, stay asleep. Stay asleep. Stay asleep. Please.

Rock, rock, rock; pat, pat, pat. The steady rhythm soothed her too.

It was a full twenty-three minutes before a deep voice called her name. 'Anya Morgan?'

A muted peacefulness pervaded Consulting Room 1.

'Chilly morning to be out this early, huh?' the doctor said pleasantly, gesturing towards a chair. A full head of wavy grey hair, bushy eyebrows, crisp shirt and matching tie, slight paunch, immaculate nails, polished black shoes – reminded her of her Grandpa Joe: always well turned out even at home.

'I like it frosty,' she said.

'Some of my more seasoned patients assure me it takes a sharp snap to kill off the bugs; if it's a mild winter they pay for it health-wise.' Lovely mellow voice, soft Scottish accent. He was smiling, deep creases corrugating the tanned-even-in-winter skin. 'Robert Brownlee. I don't think we've met before, have we?'

'No. It's always been one of the others.'

His hand was large and warm and dry. She wiped her own surreptitiously on her coat before resuming the pat, pat, pat on Gypsy's quilted sleepsuit.

'So, may I call you Anya, or do you prefer to be Mrs Morgan?'

A first – consulting her. Courteous too – like Grandpa Joe.

'Anya's fine.'

'And this must be Gypsy Lysette.' He leaned forward to peek inside the bundle in her arms. 'Pretty name for a pretty baby, huh, Gypsy?'

His glance slid towards the screen on his desk.

'I understand you asked for a second ... or is it third, opinion?'

'Someone more senior, yes.'

'I see. Although, I can reassure you, both Drs Brocklehurst and Jones, the doctors you saw, are very experienced.'

'But Dr Jones is only part-time.'

'Technically, yes, but she was a much-respected partner here for many, many years. It's only circumstances that have made it necessary for her to reduce her hours.'

'Oh.'

'So, how can I help you now, Anya?'

'There's something wrong with my baby.'

'What kind of a something?'

It was so much easier to explain to this kindly man with his unhurried manner and his total attention. Sympathetic nods said yes, he'd been round the block a few times, he knew all about fretful babies who refused to be pacified, who screamed inconsolably every night, who went rigid if you tried to cuddle them, who held their breath until they went blue.

'You're shattered. New babies are demanding little people. And the more upset you get the more it conveys itself to the baby. A vicious circle.'

'The health visitor said that; it's making my milk like fizzy pop, she said. But it's more than that. There's something wrong. I *know* there is. I'm her mum, I can tell.'

'So ... you've been seeing the health visitor ... and the practice nurse ... as well as the doctors.' His eyes were scanning the records, the dates.

'Nobody's really listening.'

'Well, let's start with examining baby, shall we?' he said.

He'd be a shoo-in for the diplomatic service.

Gypsy stared up at him as he kept up a steady coo of baby talk all the while his practised hands moved over her body, checking, testing, listening. Even stark naked she was relaxed.

'Well, you're a little stunner, aren't you, poppet?' He laughed as her fingers closed over his stethoscope, her mouth curving into a toothless smile. 'Yes, you are.'

'Not at 2am, she's not,' Anya said tightly.

Where else has that same instrument been?

'That I can well believe. Are you giving Mummy a hard time, little one?'

The traitor actually gurgled as she reflected his smile.

'Right, you can pop her nappy back on again,' he said. 'And we'll have a wee chat about what your days look like. And your nights.' He was washing his hands so thoroughly now ... she felt resentment rising inside her.

It didn't take long to describe the relentlessness, and his eyes remained focused on her throughout. Cool grey eyes. Kind eyes.

Only when she'd quite finished did he lean back and steeple his fingers. He hadn't found anything that concerned him, he said; baby Gypsy was exactly where she should be at this age. But it's natural to worry. The responsibility of a new life can be overwhelming. And remember, the health visitors are there for you. They'll keep an eye on things. Catch naps while the baby sleeps ... try not to worry if there's dust on the piano ... your husband doesn't need a cordon bleu meal every day ...

Same old, same old.

They just don't get it ...

'Could you tell … if there was something … damaged … inside?'

'Well, that depends.' Now he was a guard dog hearing something sinister in the attic in the dead of night. 'What sort of damage are we talking about?'

'If maybe she'd twisted badly … or hit something …'

He leaned forward.

'Tell me what's bothering you, Anya. You're quite safe here. Everything you say is in confidence.'

'I … it's a gut feeling. The screaming …'

'But look at her. The picture of health. If she'd sustained any kind of injury, she wouldn't be lying there beaming up at you, now would she? And she wouldn't like me prodding her.'

Anya stared down at the baby, brushing away a solitary tear.

Dr Brownlee laid a hand on her arm. 'Could your husband take a turn during the night?'

'He's away a lot. For his job.'

'Which is?'

'Sales and marketing. He goes all over the country, seeing clients, visiting retail outlets, drumming up new business for the family company. Morgan & Sons? Luxury leather goods? No?'

The doctor shook his head apologetically. 'Sorry. Not much call for expensive calfskin briefcases or handbags in my line of work.'

'Headquarters are in the Newcastle area, so Leon needs to go south a lot.'

'Does he know how desperate you feel at times?'

'Sort of.'

'And how does he respond?'

'He says I need to stop being such a perfectionist.'

'Ouch.' Dr Brownlee grimaced. 'And how is he with Gypsy?'

'When he's home he does his bit. And I have to admit, Gypsy's much more settled when *he* puts her down.'

'I guess nobody ever promised us life would be fair,' the

17

doctor said lightly.

He slid into the familiar groove … anyone else available to give you a break? … go to relatives? … meet other mums … share the load. And finally, with a wry smile, 'You know, you mothers today have such high expectations. You've grown up through a system of grading and measuring success in everything. And I think that sometimes spills over into parenting. But babies haven't read the textbooks – or should I say apps? – or been on the courses, or read the list of targeted outcomes. My advice? Just forget all the professional stuff. Concentrate on enjoying the miracle of an individual little person emerging from this baby shell. It goes by all too quickly.'

Anya managed a strangled, 'Thank you' as she gathered Gypsy's paraphernalia up in her arms.

'Come back and see me again if you're still worried. We could maybe think about something to help you relax.'

Another wasted visit. But how could she drag this kindly man into her nightmare, burden him with knowledge he couldn't ignore? The horror that had brought her here today.

04:16. The luminous numbers reproach her in the darkness of the bedroom. For three and a half hours Gypsy has paused only long enough to take another breath, her shrill shrieking piercing through Anya's maternal instincts to the raw need for self-preservation known only to the terrified and the tormented.

She changes the nappy … tepid sponges the hot face and neck … offers her breast again. The back arches, the face turns away, the screaming continues unabated.

Next moment the child is flying through the air, propelled by sheer force.

Silence.

Without a backward glance, Anya flings herself out of the room. The door slams behind her. She stumbles blindly down the stairs, grabs the first jacket her fingers encounter, and next moment she's outside, running down the deserted street, tears whipping from her eyes before they can touch her cheeks, her leather slippers flap flap flapping noisily on the pavement. Down Eskbank Road, past the park, towards the church ... her legs cave in ... she slumps to the ground.

When she can finally breathe normally, she rolls into a ball and surrenders to exhaustion. In the tranquillity of the night, time, place, identity, responsibility, lose all consequence ...

The street is still shrouded in dusky anonymity when she comes to with a jolt. Where ...? What ...? Paralysing numbness has claimed her body from toe to waist.

Her bleary gaze falls on imposing Gothic architecture ... a massive doorway ... stained glass windows ... an ugly rectangular noticeboard looming above her ...

St David's Roman Catholic Church
Confessions: Saturday 11am, 5-5:50pm
Confession ...? What day is it ...? When ...?

She leaps to her feet, only to collapse again when her numb leg refuses to support her. Desperately she scrabbles her way up the church gate, clutching the railings until some sensation returns. She stumbles ... limps ... hurtles back through the deserted streets, raw panic constricting her heart.

Through the half-open front door ... up the stairs ... into her own bedroom ...

Gypsy is lying, half-hidden, in the middle of the king-size duvet.

Anya drops onto the bed, pulls the rag-doll child into her arms, her own breath escaping in a long shuddering sigh.

The green luminous figures chastise her: 06:59.

It's two hours later when her eyes next open and she dares to look down at the face pressed up against her chest, lips slack around the nipple.

Back in the waiting room, Anya concentrated on dressing the baby.

'What a little bobby-dazzler.' From two seats away a

tall woman with a streak of purple through her neat black bob and striking amber eyes leaned closer. 'What's her name?'

'Gypsy. Gypsy Lysette.'

'Oh, I love it. So unusual. Gypsy. How old is she?'

Before Anya could reply, a voice called, 'Janet Barker?'

The woman jumped up. 'That's for me. Better not keep them waiting.'

They almost collided a few minutes later, but the older woman gave a little bow and held the door while Anya manoeuvred the pram outside. She caught up with them again at the busy crossroads.

'Looks like we're neighbours. I'm in the new houses off Abbey Road. St David's Avenue? Know it?'

'Where the school used to be?' Anya kept it neutral.

'I believe so, but before my time.'

'I'm just over there.' Anya waved in the direction of an elegant detached stone house with steep pitched roofs highlighted by ornate woodwork, set back from the road and framed by mature silver birches and a high wall.

'Oh wow! What a stunning place. Top or bottom flat?'

'Uhhh … both.'

'Really? Wow, again! Lived here long?'

'Just over four years. We're still doing it up. And you?'

'Only eighteen months. Foreigners to this part of the country. And we're in a new-build modern box; nothing to do up.'

A lull in the traffic allowed them to cross swiftly.

'Well, nice to meet you … Janet, isn't it?'

The woman managed to laugh and grimace simultaneously.

'Thankfully not! Janet's my mother. I was collecting a prescription for her. My name's Tiffany. Tiffany Corrigan. And you are?'

'Anya Morgan.'

'Listen, I couldn't help noticing you'd been crying. If you need a shoulder any time, don't hesitate. Here's my mobile number. I mean it. New motherhood can be a lonely place.'

'That's kind, thank you.'

'Maybe meet up some time, yeah?' Tiffany called cheerfully.

'Maybe. Bye.'

Not if she could help it.

CHAPTER 3

I must let Leon help more. I must let Leon help more. I must let Leon help more. She repeated the mantra as the time of his return approached.

His key in the lock was enough to rouse her from a fitful dose. She hastily smoothed her hair, picked up her knitting, adopted an engrossed air, before he entered the room in a familiar waft of leather and spearmint.

'Sorry, love. Hellish traffic on the A696. Some tractor-trailer combo shed its load just north of Belsay. Had to take a diversion – but of course, the world and his wife's uncle were doing the same thing. And then some idiot left a broken-down Volvo stuck in the middle of the road at Alnwick, so we were all snarled up for miles back there.'

His moustache grazed her forehead briefly before, dropping his briefcase and jacket onto the floor, he slumped into the chair opposite, with a weary sigh.

She rolled up her knitting.

'You must be knackered. What d'you fancy? Cold beer? Glass of wine? Cup of tea?'

'I'll get it ...'

'No. Let me. What's it to be?'

'Tea, thanks. Need a clear head. Early start tomorrow, so I'm going to hit the hay early tonight. Get well up the A9 before the morning rush hour.'

He leaned back, closing his eyes. She stole a glance at him. Since when did he acquire such heavy creases along his brow, so much silver in his dark hair? He was only thirty. She slipped out quietly, taking his case and coat to their rightful places. That was the thing with these big solid houses, you couldn't converse between rooms. That Tiffany woman would

22

probably be able to chat to her partner while she made the tea. She popped her head back round the door.

'Why don't you come to the kitchen, we can keep talking.'

He dragged himself up and followed her, only to drop into his soft chair on one side of the Aga. He wriggled back into the cushions and sighed. 'It's so good to be home.'

'You wouldn't think so! The neighbours must imagine you're a casual acquaintance.'

'Who cares what they think? As long as *you* know I'm not the Betterware man.' He yawned expansively. 'Work's frenetic at the moment, but I promise you …'

She stilled him with a raised hand. 'Don't, Leon. Don't promise what you can't deliver.'

A long silence fell. His voice sounded stiff when he eventually broke it. 'What kind of a week have you had then? Tell me more about the GP visit.'

'He was lovely. You feel he's got time to listen.'

'And Gypsy's fine?'

'He says so. And he gave her a thorough examination.'

'Good. And will you take his advice? Get together with other mums? Share the load?'

'I had a chat with another mum on Wednesday as it happens. Somebody called Tiffany. She lives down in those new houses off Abbey Road.'

'*Tiffany*? Heck! Imagine calling your kid Tiffany. Sounds like a Laura Ashley lampshade!'

'Some people might think we're mad calling ours Gypsy. If you've grown up locking your doors and warning your kids about "tinkers", like my great aunt!'

All too soon the grandmother clock chimed the hour.

'I'll pop in and see the sprog, and then crash in the back bedroom tonight so I don't wake you when I crawl out of the sheets at silly-o'clock.'

'You don't need to.'

He shot her a look. 'Much as I like the invitation in that comment, I fear I must take a rain check. You wouldn't believe the crazy schedule Thomas has lined up for me.'

23

'Doing what?'

'A big meeting in Fort William, with the director of a really prestigious company. This guy's doing the rounds, coming across from Belfast tomorrow apparently, very keen to discuss possibilities, so it's looking promising. And then back down to Newcastle to thrash through some forward-planning stuff with the guys.'

'He pushes you too hard.'

'Keeps the roof over our heads and food on the table. Sorry not to be better company tonight, though. Make it up to you at the weekend, promise. Keep it free. Don't let the lampshade monopolise you!'

His kiss was short and undemanding, and she felt a wave of disappointment when he released her after a moment, to vanish upstairs. Had they come to this after only four years of living together? She was left alone to contemplate yet another white lie. Well, she *might* get to know this Tiffany woman.

She sighed. It was so easy for men. Nothing much had changed in Leon's life. He could escape all day, every day, days together even. He could meet normal intelligent adults, speak coherent business language, negotiate complex deals, sleep soundly in smart hotels, eat uninterrupted proper meals. Except ... things *had* changed. He was no longer the ardent Leon who would never have considered separate beds never mind different rooms, the spontaneous Leon who would whisk her away to some romantic resort for a long weekend, the solicitous Leon who would know instinctively when all was not well.

Gypsy had changed everything.

Her thoughts strayed as they so often did these days to her sister, Claire.

Was this why Ronnie had left her? Because babies change everything? Was this how the unravelling started?

CHAPTER 4

A productive meeting with the Irish director under his belt, Leon was fired up, eager to share the detail with the management team. At times like this he was acutely aware that he owed his seniority in the firm to his birth; any other company would have required a far longer apprenticeship. Thomas and Roger could be relied on to be as frank as brothers can be, but the approval he really craved was that of the most senior manager on the factory floor.

Bill Broadbent had been working for the firm since their father, Douglas Herbert Morgan, had taken over from his father, Jerome Charles Stanley, the entrepreneur who'd first conceived a plan to create a company that would keep their only son in the style to which his mother aspired. Bill's sound common sense was legendary, justification alone for an extra trip down to Northumberland. Leon had never voiced his suspicion that Bill resented some of the changes he and Thomas had made, but he was well aware they were still 'nowt but lads' to him, his allegiance still firmly with the two men who had founded and established Morgan & Sons – the kind of loyalty Leon aspired to.

But Bill was not overseeing production that day. Away sorting out 'some staffing issue', according to the note he'd left on Thomas' desk.

'Good work, Leo,' Thomas managed, as they strode down the corridor to the first big meeting of the day, before their paths diverged and they were swallowed up in the plethora of responsibilities executive status brought with it. 'Your biggest contract yet. Braithwaite was singing your praises, too. "Astute business head" on your shoulders apparently.'

Thomas and he were cast in the Morgan mould, same lean frame, same familial stoop, same cracking smile, same reticence when it came to emotional matters. Roger took after their mother, shorter, softer, more intuitive. Thomas was the big brother in both senses, at six foot five a good three inches taller, and his tight red curls, darkening over the years to a rich auburn, eclipsed Leon's own more sombre dark hair, fast greying at the temples and nape. It was the harelip that had been his most memorable feature ... well, until seven years ago, when his sister-in-law, Juliette, had casually commented on how facial hair suited him. Anya had never known him clean-shaven.

Juliette and the au pair, Solange, were clearing away the debris left by the children when the brothers strolled into the kitchen that evening.

'Kids in bed?' Thomas said, sliding an arm around his wife and giving her a lingering kiss. Leon averted his gaze.

'You might just catch Rowan before he nods off, but Xanthe's already dead to the world.'

Thomas vanished, a rapid staccato on the polished wooden staircase.

'Help yourself to a drink, Leo,' Juliette said, turning to the vegetables she'd tipped into the sink. 'We'll be eating in half an hour or so.'

'Something smells yummy.'

It was after ten before the two men were alone and Leon finally broached the subject preying on his mind all day.

'I might live to regret this, and maybe it's your excellent coffee using its power for evil, but ... any chance I could do a bit less travelling, d'you think?'

Thomas shot him a hard look. 'Something wrong? You ill?'

'No, I'm fine. But it's Anya. New baby, sleepless nights, you know how it is.'

'I must admit, those days are a bit hazy. But I do remember Juliette wasn't that keen on the tiny baby stage, when they just eat and sleep and shit. That's why we took on

Solange, so Juliette could go back to work part-time.'

'Well, we don't have a Solange. So, I was wondering if I could operate from home more, maybe ...?'

'Give it a few more weeks, huh? With these big contracts in the pipeline, not the best time to take our main field man out of the equation.'

'Oh, I don't want to be taken out of anything. I know exactly how important this stage of the negotiations is.'

'A few more months and the way you're going, you'll be able to hire in three Solanges!'

'If only! But Anya won't even consider it. You know what she's like.'

'Makes Juliette feel like a slob!' Thomas laughed.

'I suggested Mother – interim measure – but she's adamant she couldn't cope with anybody else in the house.'

'What about her sister?'

'Claire? Just what I thought, but I got a flea in my ear for *that* one. Claire's baby died, remember? Cot death. Anya reckons it'd be the height of tactless to even ask her. And besides, she works in this hotel, crazy hours; the owner seems to be some sort of old-school slave driver. She'd have difficulty getting time off. She does come out to visit occasionally, and I'd have said she dotes on Gypsy, but what do I know? Anya's her sister, and she reckons it just rubs salt in the wound for Claire.'

'So, she *wants* to do it all herself, really.'

'Kind of.'

'And she wants to keep the place immaculate and ...'

'Actually, it's more than the tidiness thing. Since we had Gypsy, she's ... I don't know ... different. Obsessed is too strong a word for it. But she's hyper-anxious, seems to me. She's convinced herself there's something wrong with the baby. She's gone through three of the doctors in our local practice already. *And* she's seen the health visitor umpteen times. That's not normal, is it?'

'Blimey, don't ask me! Best chat to Juliette. She's a mum, and she's in HR. Much better at this touchy-feely stuff than me. And, for pity's sake, use this place more. Don't go tanking back home when you've been driving all day. You're always welcome here, you know that. The kids think all their Christmasses have come at once. And Juliette's always had a soft spot for you. Bring Anya and Gypsy too, if that'd help. But just don't get my wife broody, that's all I ask! Two's our lot.'

'And that's final! But thanks, Thomas.'

'No problem. And don't worry too much, the baby stage zips by. It gets better when the little blighters sleep at night; that much I do remember. Juliette was like a zombie early on. And they're definitely passion-killers!'

'Roll on adolescence, huh?'

Thomas groaned theatrically, but then slapped one hand on the arm of the chair. 'Speaking of which ... want to see my latest teenage fantasy?'

Leon was only too ready to drool over his brother's most recent investment, a 1974 Jaguar E-type, and forget the gnawing doubts that had plagued his day.

Breakfast at The Old Manse in Draycourt Lane was normally a rather frenetic affair, but on this occasion Juliette was taking a couple of hours off in lieu of the evening she'd spent working on a case of alleged racial discrimination, Solange had driven the children to school, Thomas had left for work absurdly early – some kind of emergency meeting Bill Broadbent had as good as demanded, Juliette reported. Peace descended on the kitchen.

Leon shot his sister-in-law a wry smile.

'I guess Thomas set this up, huh?'

'He reckons you might welcome a listening ear.'

Leon kept the catalogue short.

'She's always been a bit OTT – as you know. Fitness, food, additives, pesticides, she tends to go overboard about things. That's just Anya. But this time ... she seems ... kind of ... terrified?'

'It *is* different this time. Nothing really prepares you for the awful responsibility of a new little life. I was convinced on a daily basis I'd somehow kill Rowan!'

'Were you? You always come across as totally calm and together.'

'Pphh! You didn't see me in the wee small hours! It's a nightmare. They can't tell you what's wrong. Dirty nappy, empty tummy, lonely, too many blankets, pin sticking in them, twisted intestine, lethal infection, inoperable tumour, meningitis – they just shriek. And it feels like you're failing if you can't get them to stop.'

'And Gypsy can scream for Britain when she puts her mind to it! You don't think it's anything out of the ordinary, then?'

'Well, if the professionals are happy, I'd tend to believe them. Concentrate instead on getting Anya to relax.'

'Try telling her that! She says she *can't* switch off knowing the house is a tip and the washing's piling up.'

Juliette grimaced. 'I can't imagine your lovely home is *ever* a tip! It's easier for me, not having her high standards.'

'So, you'd agree, she needs more help, huh?'

'If she'll accept it. Thomas mentioned your mother; Anya said no to that, I believe? Which I can kind of understand. We daughters-in-law have our pride to think of, you know!'

Leon grinned at her. 'You know Mother adores you!'

'Flattery will get you everywhere. Seriously though, you're more than welcome to bring her here. Xanthe would *love* having a baby to play with. Me too, come to that!'

'Thanks. But she reckons going away is more hassle than it's worth, what with all the paraphernalia and the disruption to their routine.'

'Can I trade on our long friendship and say something, Leo?'

''Course.'

'It's pretty hard for somebody like your uber-smart wife to accept everything that goes with new motherhood. Crumpled clothes, puke on your shoulders, milk leaking from your boobs, hair and make-up optional extras … she probably needs more than the usual amount of reassurance she's still a desirable woman.'

'Well, if we're going down that track, I can tell you, I actually rather like seeing her more natural and ... kind of vulnerable. The totally-perfect Anya's a tad intimidating sometimes!'

'It's also tough going from being a successful career woman to a novice stuck at home with very little intellectual challenge. Heavens! Here's a woman with a first-class honours, a PhD! She's been used to feeling totally to grips with high-powered statistics, holding her own in research meetings, being completely sure of her role in the team. She'll miss the external confirmation of her worth and abilities. And she's probably channelling all that drive and striving for perfection into being the best mum ever. But the goalposts for mother-of-the-year aren't so clearly defined. A screaming kiddie certainly isn't one of them, though, so if she can't pacify Gypsy she'll feel a failure. The more she screams, the more knackered Anya gets ... you can see how the insecurity, the doubt, spiral, can't you?'

Leon nodded, looking steadily at his sister-in-law. 'You're a wise woman, Juliette Morgan.'

'Must be my white hair creating the illusion.'

It was an in-house joke. Juliette's long glossy dark mane had started to go grey at the age of twenty-two. Horrified, she initially dyed it weekly. Then at twenty-eight she'd decided to let it return to its natural state and within two years she was snow white. It proved a winning combination. Dark blue eyes, flawless skin, alabaster hair cut in a neat bob which framed her heart-shaped face perfectly. Add to that a curvaceous body and absurdly long legs – she stood at five-feet-eleven – and you had the poise and beauty of a successful model. Another Maye Musk.

'No,' Juliette said now, instantly serious again, 'it's just that I'm a mum. Should I ring Anya, d'you think? Give her a chance to offload?'

'She'd smell a rat. Suspect we're talking about her behind her back.'

'So, how about booking a break somewhere? A bit down the track. So she has something to look forward to?'

'Thomas permitting!'

She shot him a hard look.

'Only joking,' he said quickly. 'What d'you suggest?'

'Something totally relaxing. Lazy, sexy...'

He closed his eyes, seeing the scene ... sun-kissed beach, turquoise sea stretching to the horizon, tall glasses of something cool and sparkling, white bikini, tanned limbs, floppy sunhat ...

He gave an exaggerated start as he consulted his watch.

Damn. He didn't need any more complications in his life right now. And certainly not this one.

Because the face below that sunhat hadn't been his wife's ... it had been Juliette's.

'Bugger! – excuse my language. Is that the time? Thomas'll be champing at the bit.'

As if on cue his mobile rang.

'Leon. Get your sorry ass here pronto. Bill's just been to see me, and you've got some serious explaining to do.'

Bill?

His thanks were perfunctory.

Her 'Good luck!' followed him.

CHAPTER 5

Both men looked up when Leon arrived. Neither smiled.

'What's up? Sounded urgent.'

'Sit down, Leon.' *Sunday name!*

Leon slid onto the seat opposite his brother. Bill kept his gaze somewhere on the far wall.

'You remember Frank Fowler?' Thomas started.

'Yep. One of our drivers.'

'For twenty-two years.'

'And?'

'He's about to lodge a formal complaint against us. Citing you in particular.'

Leon startled. '*Me?*'

'Bill's been to see him and he's insisting he was unfairly dismissed. I want you to hear what Bill's got to say, and then you and I have some serious talking to do. Fire away, Bill.'

The Geordie accent was dulled today, all the usual exuberance gone from this man who'd devoted his life to Morgan & Sons. He kept his gaze steadily averted from his employers, glancing periodically at a piece of paper for direct quotes.

'It's Fowler's story I'm reporting, sir, I weren't there meself. But seemingly, back in December he were "forced to come in on a weekend" to prepare a new truck ready for an early start Monday morning. Christmas deliveries. He protested. They had words. According to him, Mr Leon said ...,' – he peered closer at the paper – 'Mr Leon said, "If that's your attitude, don't bother coming back tomorrow," ... and "You know where the door is." Amongst other things. Fowler says he were so angry he took Mr Leon at his word. Reckoned it were "a poor return for all those years of service"

– mostly under Mr Douglas, of course. He didn't come in to work next day. Not been back since. And according to him, nobody even asked after him. He just got his P45 in the post.'

'But I ...'

Thomas held up a hand. 'You'll get your chance, Leon. Let Bill finish.'

'Fowler took advice. He contacted ACAS, notified them he'd be making a claim. They wanted to try reconciliation, but Fowler's having none of it. He's just submitted his ET1 – that's the Employment Tribunal form, sir, but I daresay you know that. Mr Thomas got the notification four days ago. He asked me to follow it up. I went to see Fowler yesterday – first day he reckoned he were available. We ... that's to say, the firm has twenty-eight days to submit a response. That'll be the ET3 form, sir.'

Bill folded the piece of paper over and over and over again until it was hidden in his palm.

'And *you* didn't follow up Fowler's absence because ...?' Thomas prompted.

'I were told Mr Leon were dealing with it himself.'

'Thank you, Bill,' Thomas said quietly. 'And again, I can only apologise. Had I known the accusations, I'd have seen the man myself.'

'No apology needed, Mr Thomas, sir; it's my job. But thanks anyway.'

'It wasn't ...' Leon began, but Thomas stopped him again. 'An apology to Bill for dragging him into this mess will suffice, at this point. We'll discuss the rights and wrongs later.'

Bill listened to the forced apology, looking to the side of Leon's head. He briefly inclined his head, before Thomas opened the door and the floor manager walked stiffly from the room.

As soon as his brother had taken his seat again, Leon let rip.

'The guy was insufferable, Thomas! Insolent. Always quick to take umbrage.'

'And you discussed this with who exactly? Certainly not me. Nor Bill, from his account.'

'I can't be always running to you with problems. This was something I could handle. I was the one he was outright disrespecting.'

'But when he left …'

'I thought he was just in a huff. Give him time to cool off and he'd come crawling back with his tail between his legs. He'd been with us for yonks; he'd know which side his bread was buttered. So, I let him stew.'

'But he didn't come back.'

'And when he didn't, I dealt with it. I arranged cover. And eventually I got his P45 sent to him.'

'Did you attempt any kind of reconciliation? Any sort of negotiations?'

'No point. The guy'd made it perfectly clear he didn't respect my authority.'

'Respect has to be earned, Leon. It's not a birthright. And just for the record, I did a bit of digging and there's considerable doubt about the reasonableness of Fowler's dismissal. What's more, at his age – fifty-seven – it might be difficult to get another job commensurate with his position here. He hasn't found one as yet anyway.'

'How much are we talking to settle this?'

'Compensation? Out of court? Up to a year's salary.'

'Peanuts, huh?'

'According to Bill, Fowler's not interested in a few thousand. He's gunning for our reputation.'

CHAPTER 6

Anya was on the point of putting the phone down when her sister's breathless voice spoke.

'Hello. Claire Gilchrist.'

'I've caught you at a bad time. I'll ring back later.'

'No, don't be daft. I'm never too busy for you. I was downstairs helping my neighbour, Mabel, with her online shop, and I've just run up two flights. That's all.'

'This can wait.'

'No. Fire away. Smokey, get down! You know Mummy doesn't like you climbing on the kitchen surfaces.'

Anya envisaged the blue-grey Korat turning to stare at his human and mewling a protest when she scooped him off the surface into her lap, where she would instantly smother him in love. Claire had no idea of discipline. But Korats were considered to be good luck in their native Thailand and her sister lived in hope.

'When did you first start suspecting Ronnie was going to leave you?'

A long pause.

'Why? Don't tell me Leon's ...'

'No! I don't know. It's just ... he seems to be losing interest in ... home.'

'But you've got Gypsy. Surely he's spending time with her.'

'When he's here.'

'Well, there you are then. Look, it's totally different, Anya. This is just a phase you're going through, adjusting to being three instead of two. Gypsy will grow up. You'll get more sleep. Leon will be more interested in a toddler who responds to him. It was completely different for Ronnie and me. All those months looking forward to being a family, the baby being born, Kelly being a real little person, and suddenly, ppff, she's gone. And it's never ever going to get better. We were both grieving but in different ways. And ...'

'Claire, I'm sorry. I should never have raked it all up again. Forget I said anything.'

'Listen, I'm more than happy to come over and give you a hand, but, don't make this into something it's not. You're just exhausted. Once you start getting proper nights' sleep it'll all come right. Just you wait and see.'

'You're right, of course. How's Jim?'

'On a bit of a downer at the moment, but the medication's definitely helping and the new psychiatrist is much more on the ball. She's got him on some different antidepressants. She reckons a bit of sunshine would do wonders for morale too, so we're off to Tenerife next month – just for a week – I can't get more time off than that. But the break should do us both good.'

Anya had never understood the attraction. At fifty-eight Jim had the bearing of a man weighed down by care. Shoulders hunched, unable to maintain eye contact, slowed down by his pharmacy of pills, with the vague aroma of neglect, he shuffled through life, apologetically listing to the left, only becoming animated when he was with animals.

'Only ...' Claire hesitated. 'I'm afraid he's going to propose again, when we get there.'

'And?'

'I'm happy just jogging along as we are. We might go through all the wedding malarkey and then everything could go pear-shaped, and what a waste of time and money that would be. My thinking is: if it ain't broke don't fix it.'

'But Jim's still keen?'

'Sort of, though he'd never push it. He wants kids, of course, and I can see why marriage would be a good idea if we went down that route ... but ... what if it happened again? I really could not bear it.'

'And does Jim get that?'

'He does and he doesn't. We talked about this early on

– well, we did meet at a bereavement group, after all, as you know. But it's a totally different thing, grieving for your wife and grieving for a baby. He had a happy marriage with Olive; I had a devastating experience of being a mother.'

'And he sees that?'

'He thinks having another one would heal some of the hurt. And, as he kindly points out, I'm forty-four now; clock's ticking. Can't keep procrastinating. Oh, glory be! I've just seen the time. I really must go. My shift starts in thirty minutes and the bus is due any second.'

Anya was still mulling over her sister's advice when the doorbell rang.

The woman from the surgery, Tiffany Corrigan, stood on the doorstep with a covered dish and a wide smile.

'Cottage pie,' she said, handing it over. 'Nothing exotic, but it might help to have one less thing to do.'

Anya could feel the warmth through the teacloth.

Couldn't get much fresher than that.

'That's so kind of you,' she said.

'How's Gypsy Lysette?'

'She's fine, thanks. Probably going to start shouting for a feed any minute now.'

Now you've woken her with the doorbell.

'Fair enough. Fancy some adult company just till she does?'

Not really.

Anya stood aside to let her in and led the way to the kitchen.

'Oh wow! This is sooo lush.' Tiffany's eyes were instantly roaming over the rich warm hues of chestnut wood, the muted terracotta walls, the neat rows of matching utensils, the huge family table Anya had chosen with such care, picturing children's parties, family get-togethers, Leon's mates filling the house with raucous laughter. Her fingers skimmed the gleaming marble surface, her shoes clip-clopping around the polished floor.

'Can I offer you a coffee? Tea? What d'you fancy?'

'A good old cuppa would be just the ticket if you're making one. But you probably go for something much more exotic, huh?' Tiffany sank into one of the deep chairs beside the Aga and reached out to feel the warmth. 'I've always hankered after one of these machines, but no chance in the kind of houses we can afford. Did you put this in or was it here when you came?'

'We put it in. Leon – my husband – grew up with them, but it's my first one and I must confess, it took me a while to get used to cooking with it. You have to think ahead a bit and modify cooking times. And it's a moist kind of heat, great for bread and cakes, not so good for things like meringues.'

'Blimey!' Tiffany stared at her as if she'd just admitted to sunbathing nude in the front garden. 'You don't ... you surely *don't* make your own bread and meringues? Do you? Seriously?'

Anya smiled crookedly. 'Sorry! I've always enjoyed baking. It's a kind of hobby. I find it therapeutic.'

'And you manage to keep a figure like *that*?!'

'Oh, it's mostly for coffee mornings, charities. And Leon takes things in for the staff.'

Tiffany shook her head. 'You're something else.'

'Not at all. I love cooking so I get to indulge my hobby, but we prefer healthy foods ourselves. You probably do a million other things I don't do.'

'I doubt it. You must be super-mum. My home would never look like this in a month of Sundays.'

Anya poured hot water into the teapot, her back to her uninvited guest. 'I'm certainly not that. I don't think I'm a very good mum at all, actually.'

'You're kidding me?'

'No.'

'Heck! What kind of planet do you come from? I turn up unexpectedly in the middle of the morning, and what do I find? You, your home, everything, immaculate. Peace reigns, you're being the perfect hostess. How d'you *do* it? My place looks like a bombsite. If it wasn't for my mother, it would be.'

'She comes in to help?'

'No, she lives with us. That's how we can afford the house we live in. We sold our flat, she sold her cottage, and we bought St David's Avenue together. She's the one who clears up the stuff everybody else strews around the place and I'm too darned knackered or lazy to bother.'

'I'm sure you're just being modest.'

'Nah, just honest. But hey, what makes you think you're not a good mum?'

Anya concentrated on arranging a neat circle of home-made chocolate chip cookies.

'Because she screams and screams for no reason at all, she goes rigid and fights against being cuddled ...'

Her fingers clenched as she spoke; a biscuit crumbled over the plate. She took down a fresh one and started again.

As if on cue, a wail came from an adjacent room. Anya was instantly taut, willing her guest to take the hint.

'Shall I get her for you, while you finish that?' Tiffany was on her feet.

'No. It's fine, thanks. I'll go.'

Gypsy had become far too hot in the swaddling blanket and stopped crying as soon as Anya released her, so she was alert and curious when she found another face cooing and bobbing in front of her.

'You're simply gorgeous, aren't you? Gorgeous, gorgeous, gorgeous.' The soft highland accent was more pronounced in the baby-talk. And somehow within minutes the baby was on Tiffany's lap, kicking her legs in delight.

'Any time you want a break, I'd be happy to have *this* little sweetie to look after. Yes, I would, wouldn't I?'

'And I can see you're a natural,' Anya conceded.

'Well, I have got three of my own at home.'

'How old?'

'Sam – Samantha – she's eleven going on forty-one. Maribel's nine, and Jude, he's seven. I just love the softness of them at this age, the smell, the trust – the whole baby-ness, you know? I'd have had more but Dan drew the line at three.'

'Are they still needing you full-time, or d'you go out to work?'

Please, please, let there be a deadline to meet before feed-time.

'I'm a part-time receptionist at Sick Kids, three days a week. In a former life, before the kids, I was a nurse, but that's too demanding. Unsocial hours, nights, all that stuff. This job suits the family much better.'

'A nurse – that must come in handy when the children get sick. I don't know how you can tell if it's serious or not.'

Tiffany laughed. 'Well, there's a well-worn saying: nurses make bossy wives and unimaginative mothers. And my kids would probably tell you that I have no imagination whatever. Unless they're actually vomiting or have a temperature in the hundreds, off to school they go! I can't be doing with giving in to every little niggle.'

'See, there you are. You're a much more confident mother than I am. Even Gypsy can sense that. Look at her. She's totally relaxed with you.'

'Pphh. Novelty value. You'll be fine. Believe me, they're much tougher little beggars than you think. But, if you ever need a weather-eye cast over this gorgeous small person, don't hesitate to give me a shout. Nothing too trivial for yours truly. You've got my number. I mean it. Save you bothering busy health visitors and doctors.'

'Thank you, that's kind. And thanks again for the pie.' Anya scooped the baby out of her arms and remained standing.

'I'd better be off then. But lovely to see you, and your super-delicious little one, and your super-splendid home.'

When her sister appeared that evening with a bean casserole, a lemon meringue pie, and renewed offers of help, Anya knew she was giving out way too many distress signals. And her diet really couldn't take too many of these calorie-laden gifts.

She watched Claire closely as she cuddled a sleeping Gypsy. Her face, normally strained and weary, reminded Anya of those classic pictures of the Madonna and child.

What must it feel like, burying your own child?
Listening to your over-privileged sister wailing about

tiredness and trivial complaints?

Holding your baby niece, remembering ... comparing ... mourning all over again?

Claire would never whinge about a sleepless night.

She would never throw a child.

She would never leave one alone in a car in the dead of night.

She would never contemplate ending it all.

CHAPTER 7

It was a routine house call, prompted by a team meeting. Four consultations with three different doctors within seven weeks? Warning bells.

Vulnerable new mother.

Lucinda Devonshire parked her Clio on the gravel drive and sat for a moment looking at the elegant building ahead of her. She had a thing about angles and roofs. This one was exactly the kind of architecture that ticked all her boxes, but how loaded would you need to be to afford something like this? A million miles away from a flat-share with a university friend which was all she could manage at the moment.

She swung her legs out, reaching for her bag at the same time, an appreciative whistle from the road making her drag her skirt further down her thighs.

At only five feet two, Lucinda was used to feeling disadvantaged, but here she was eye to eye with the client. And they were almost the same age; Anya just six months younger. But there the similarity ended. Lucinda's nut-brown hair was caught up in a loose twist when she was in professional mode, only the highlights betraying off-duty glamour. As a new mum at home Anya's naturally-blonde curls could be loose and feminine all the time. A small nose and button mouth gave Lucinda a doll-like look which she did her best to toughen up with tailored navy and white outfits. Anya's more casual attire sat well on her more rounded lactating contours, although nothing could disguise the tone of a scrupulous fitness enthusiast. Lucinda knew all about the home-grown organic produce, the home-cooked balanced meals, the gym in the annex.

Guarded blue eyes met her.

42

'I'm sorry, there's someone here at the moment ... but do come in. It's only a neighbour.'

The baby lay on a fleece on the sitting room carpet, thrashing her little arms and legs in excitement as the visitor tickled and sang baby songs to her. A shaft of light lit up the glossy black bob, the eloquent purple streak.

Someone with a statement to make, huh?

'Tiffany, this is the health visitor, Lucinda Devonshire.'

'Hi.'

She blew a raspberry into Gypsy's hand evoking a happy gurgle, making everyone smile.

'I should get going. Nice meeting you, Lucinda. Unusual name.'

'Dad wanted Lucy; Mum wanted Linda. This was their compromise.' She grimaced. 'Pleasing nobody, I fear.'

'Including you?' Tiffany quirked one eyebrow.

'Definitely including me.'

'Too bad.'

'And I even sometimes get Luce – makes me sound like a prostitute!'

Tiffany laughed. A small smile lifted one corner of Anya's mouth.

Lucinda watched Anya ushering her visitor off the premises.

Flat thanks. No animation.

Her mind darted through the past history: confident control of pregnancy, long labour, difficult birth, forceps, insistence on no formula feeds in spite of an irritable baby. Where was that assurance now? Superficial perfection, but ... haunted eyes, fingers constantly fidgeting with a silicone wristband, twisting a lock of hair, adjusting earrings.

Lucinda broke her own rules and accepted a scone, but shook her head at the jam and cream. 'Better not. But this scone looks perfect. You go ahead though, you have every reason to tuck in, eating for two. How's feeding going?'

She segued into her role effortlessly, and they soon hit the kernel of Anya's problems: being woken by an inconsolable baby from 2 to 6 every night had to take its toll.

43

'Could I see the nursery?'

It was an exquisitely decorated room, the palest of pale pink drapes, white walls, white furniture, delicate tracery of silver leaves etched above the cot. Spotlessly clean, a faint aroma of baby lotion lingering in the air. Not an item out of place. More like an ideal home exhibit, than a working nursery.

Anya's tension was palpable and she soon led the way back downstairs. Lucinda did her best to make the routine questions unthreatening, neutral, friendly. Bedtime routines? number of layers? nightlight? music? pacifier? response time?

'You say you wake her for the last feed before you go to bed, have you tried leaving her to wake naturally when she's ready?'

'I'd never get to sleep.'

'Why's that?'

'My sister did that and she was so tired she went into a really deep sleep. When she woke up next morning her baby was dead.'

Now *we're getting somewhere.*

'How tragic. Must have been a terrible shock – for all of you.'

'My sister's never really got over it. It took her years to get pregnant in the first place, and then that happened. Her present partner's keen to try for another baby now, before it's too late. She's forty-four, he's closer to sixty. But Claire says she couldn't take the chance on history repeating itself.'

'Most unlikely it would. The incidence of unexplained Sudden Infant Deaths in the UK is less than one in three thousand births. And only a miniscule number of these families lose a second one the same way.'

'Maybe. But statistics can be used to prove anything. I should know, I was a medical statistician myself! Besides, we might be the one family to buck the trend.'

'I'd forgotten you were a statistician. Goodness, I'd better be extra careful what I say, huh?'

No answering smile.

'That was before Gypsy.'

'I guess you miss the cut and thrust of such a challenging job.'

A brief shrug.

Lucinda smiled. 'We had to learn the basics of research in our training, but I have to confess, the statistics bamboozle me. I tend to read the methods, then skip to the findings and conclusions, and hope the publishing journal has reported only bona fide work that's been through the vetting process.'

'You're not alone there!'

'So, were you always interested in numbers and statistics and everything?'

'I always loved maths but I kind of fell into statistics. The job came up, I applied, and that was that. My husband always says I must have a kink in my brain to enjoy that kind of stuff.'

'Remind me again, what does he do in the family business?'

Lucinda watched Anya gradually relaxing as they chatted. How much prettier she looked when those anxious lines melted away.

'Gypsy's doing well. Do your best to relax and switch off yourself when she's asleep. Maybe your friend, Tiffany, could give you a break sometimes? Give you an opportunity to catch up on sleep?'

Anya gave her a sharp look. 'Just out of interest, d'you have kids?'

'Well, no.'

'I thought not. But thanks for coming.'

'Thank *you* for the delicious scone. And don't hesitate to pop in to the medical centre or give us a call if you're worried about anything. That's what we're here for.'

CHAPTER 8

Leon lay absolutely still, feigning sleep, his restless mind surging over the events of the past few days. He felt horribly conflicted. The unpleasantness at work had cast a long shadow and he wanted – no, he *needed* – to shoulder his fair share of the load, prove his mettle. But only he could offer Anya the support she clearly needed.

Gypsy's cry pulsed through the monitor.

02:15.

He felt Anya slide out of bed.

Peace. He drifted off.

03:06.

She slid back in again, hunched up on the far side of the bed.

03:21.

The persistent wailing increased in volume and urgency. Anya scrabbled in the drawer of her bedside table.

'Leave her. She has to learn,' he muttered.

She didn't reply … but at least she didn't get up. He could see the faint glint of an earplug as she lay down again. Fair enough.

The demands gained momentum … turned into a piercing scream … ending abruptly in a strangled choke. He was instantly on his feet.

The baby lay on her back, purple in the face, arms flailing, hands clutching, breath suspended. He grabbed her, threw her over his shoulder, and patted her back vigorously.

'Come on, honey, come on. Breathe. You can do it. Breathe.'

The child took an enormous gulp and instantly resumed a high-pitched shriek.

'That's it. Good girl. Daddy's got you. Just you tell me all about it.'

He closed the door, switched off the monitor and began pacing up and down the room, rocking, soothing. She was sweating. He stripped off two layers. The cries turned to a muffled whimper. He tepid-sponged her flushed face, her neck, her hands. She quieted, taking short hiccupping breaths. He changed her nappy and Babygro. He laid her along his lap and took her head in his hands. She stared up at him.

'Now listen to me, Gypsy Lysette Morgan. I'm your father and what I say goes, right? And I can tell you now, no daughter of mine is going to turn into a spoilt little brat. No sir. No way. So, you can cut out the tantrums right now. You hear me? You're fine. Mummy's fed you. I've changed you. There are no bogey men under the bed. So just you hush up and go to sleep. When it's dark, we sleep. Got that? Mummy *and* Daddy will be much less crotchety in the morning if you give them a break, OK? So, it's in your own best interests to quit shrieking like a banshee. You listening?'

Baby and father held each other's gaze. Both were absolutely still.

It started slowly, grew tentatively, then blossomed … a beautiful wide smile, the more heart-stopping because of the tears still sparkling on the baby lashes. Leon felt something melt inside.

'*That's* more like it.'

He beamed back.

She gurgled.

'Fair enough. You win. Twisting me round your little finger already, huh? That's what little girls do. But here's the deal. I'll play with you as much as you like in the daytime, if you cut the cackle and sleep when it's dark. Fair dos?'

He caressed the soft downy head gently with the tips of his fingers.

'One more Daddy-cuddle and then sleep time. Got that? Just one.'

He lingered long over that single concession, savouring the feel of her head nestling in the dip under his chin, the soft pant of her warm milky breath against his bare skin, the gentle scratch of her fingernails against his arm. As he laid her carefully back in the cot, her lip quivered, but he placed a firm hand on her heaving chest and made soft shushing noises. After a while, maintaining that steady restraint, he lowered himself onto the nursing chair so she could still see him, and gradually, gradually, dimmed the night-light.

My mother's right: night-lights only encourage babies to think it's wake time.

But Anya's got a valid point: I need to be able to see her colour and check she's breathing.

Quite when he drifted off to sleep himself he didn't know, but his hand had remained on his baby daughter and she was soundly asleep when he woke. He arched his back and rose stiffly.

There was no movement from the mound in the middle of his own bed when he slipped beneath the quilt, careful to keep his cold feet firmly on his side.

But sleep eluded him. His disobedient mind roamed over all the niggling doubts he'd been pushing into the background of late.

He missed the old Anya. The warm affection. The animated conversation. The easy banter. The shared passion. The fun. This new listless Anya, always anxious, homebound, bewildered him. Her world was confined to the baby.

He gave himself a mental shake. As Juliette said, it was just a phase. Once Gypsy started sleeping longer, once the business settled down after this crazy period, they'd do more together, they'd be a real family.

He loved them. Of course he did. From the first moment he'd been introduced to her, he'd been totally smitten by this vivacious, clever, stimulating woman. Even now, with her obsessive tendencies, her critical tongue, her stubborn independence. They were as much the real Anya as the gap between her front teeth, her sibilant speech, the tiny tattoo on her ankle acquired in response to a dare when she was a teenager.

And Gypsy? She'd leapt straight to number two in his affections the second she was placed in his arms, a slippery, bawling bundle of squirming babyhood. He'd cried; he, a natural stoic, a Morgan, had actually wept, overwhelmed by the miracle they'd created together, the lifetime of responsibility he'd just accepted. Sometimes he crept into her room just to watch her sleeping, marvelling at every tiny bit of her, perfectly formed, in the right place. And sometimes too, he prayed, silently, fervently, that he'd never, ever, let this precious little human being down.

Of course he wouldn't. Certainly not at the first hint of trouble.

OK, so Juliette was attractive. Any fully paid-up man would think so. Bright engaging personality, emotional confidence, ready smile, calm attitude, ridiculously long legs, indecent cleavage ... He couldn't stop going to Newcastle, nor staying in her house, but he could avoid being alone with her. And in a few months' time, Anya wouldn't be feeding Gypsy; her body would be his again. Temptation would be back in its proper box. Off limits ...

He didn't even hear Gypsy's early morning cry. It was Anya's shake that aroused him.

'Hey, sleepy head ... Leon ... Leon ... It's eight o'clock. You said you needed to be away by quarter to nine.'

'What time did the banshee wake this morning?'

'Seven.'

He grinned at her. 'Good show.'

'Did you slip her a sedative or something?'

'Nope. A strict paternal talking-to did the trick. She just needs firm discipline.'

She turned away but not before he saw the look on her face. Typical; she had to interpret every blessed thing as criticism these days.

Visits to his parents' house in Alnmouth had been less frequent since Gypsy. Moving into the country represented an outward demonstration of Douglas Morgan's commitment to passing on the baton to his three sons, and at the age of sixty-eight, he'd poured his energy into creating a stunning garden out of a building site; the barren soil was nurtured and coaxed into self-sufficiency and the ageing couple grew back together through their shared ambitions. Maintaining a healthy distance suited both generations, but the bonds between them remained strong.

Hannah Morgan's style was as relaxed as her husband's was forceful, a combination that had maintained the balance within the business as well as the family while the boys were growing up. It felt particularly good today to shed the years and responsibilities and Anya-constraints, and accept his mother's unconditional love, her particular brand of homespun wisdom.

Bohemian skirt swirling, white hair glinting, she darted around him.

'This is such a treat. Not often I get you all to myself, nowadays.'

'Don't tell my wife about this,' he laughed, as he accepted a second slice of Devil's cake. 'I should be on lettuce and celery rations for a month! And an extra hour on the treadmill for good measure!'

'What she doesn't know, won't hurt her, huh?' Hannah smiled.

'Mother! I'm shocked. I thought you didn't believe in secrets between husbands and wives.'

'Whatever gave you that idea? Goodness me! If I'd told your father everything I got up to, I doubt we'd still be together after forty years.'

'So that's your magic ingredient, eh? Secrecy!'

'One of many. All marriages have to be worked at, love.'

He threw her a sharp look, but she was brushing crumbs off the tablecloth, her face expressionless.

What has she seen? How much does she know?

'It was lovely to see Gypsy last week.'

'I didn't know ...'

'We were on our way to St Andrews to meet Dad's old

golfing friend. Victor Burrington. Remember? Victor and Mavis?'

'Do I ever! Victor used to give us boys a lift on the tailgate of his pickup truck when we were nippers.'

'Did he, indeed? Good thing I didn't know about *that* at the time.'

He grinned at her. 'What you didn't know didn't hurt you, huh?'

'Touché. Gypsy's such a dainty little soul. Very much like Anya – I think, anyway. And we both got lots of cuddles, which was a real bonus.'

'Funny, Anya didn't say.'

'Probably slipped her mind. She'd had a friend over that morning, so I guess it had been a pretty busy day.'

'A friend?'

'Yes. She was just leaving as we arrived. Tall, purple flash in her hair?'

'Ah, yeah. That'll be Tiffany Corrigan. Lives along the road from us. Anya accepts help from her better than … Listen, I know you're more than willing to help, Mother, but Anya seems to feel that's an admission of failure. Tiffany's just another mum who pops in for coffee and a chat. I guess they can talk babies without boring each other.'

'That's perfectly understandable, dear. As long as she's got some company. It can get lonely when you're on your own with a new baby.'

'Speaking of which, I must try ringing her again. She hasn't answered the last four times I've rung. Not like her. She always has her phone on.'

'Well, maybe that's a sign that she's starting to get her own life back again.'

Maybe.

But …

His mother didn't know about the paranoia … about Gypsy being driven to the river in the dead of night … about Anya leaving her to cry till she choked … about the switched off monitor … the pills in the kitchen drawer. Ahh, the pills … he'd come across them by accident, hunting for the leaflet that told him how much it cost to send a letter to China. Vitamins, she'd assured him. *So why were they tucked under placemats and serviettes?*

He kept his foot hard down on the road home.

CHAPTER 9

Dr Robert Brownlee's words set the tone for the briefest of reports.

'Right. Time's marching on. Next up, Anya Morgan. twenty-nine years old; first baby. I think most of us have seen her at one point or another. Not sure why she's on the list. Lucinda? You seem to be the one with worries here.'

Lucinda felt a wave of annoyance, fuelled by the vagueness of her own misgivings.

'It's nothing I can pinpoint exactly. More a hunch really. The baby's well cared for, but Mum's tense and anxious. I'm concerned about her.'

'Anybody else?'

'Neurotic, *I'd* say. Just within these four walls.' Dr Simon Brocklehurst rarely made even a remotely pejorative comment, so all eyes turned to him. He was looking more than usually dishevelled today, a 'paperwork' day for him, and somehow less authoritative in his sloppy pullover, unruly hair tamped down by his glasses. He shrugged. 'Just saying.'

'I agree.' Dr Coral Jones pursed her lips, kept her back ramrod straight.

And we all know why you both say that!

'Look,' Robert said, 'I know it feels uncomfortable to have a patient seeking another opinion when you've already done a thorough job. Been there, done that. I agree, Anya Morgan's anxieties aren't problems to *us*, but I guess they're real enough to her, and she needs to know somebody's listening. Any insights, Lucinda?'

'Sleep deprivation's the main issue, basically.' Lucinda sensibly ignored Coral's sniff.

'Show me the first-time mum who's up half the night

who *isn't* knackered!' Robert said, raising hands and eyes to the ceiling. 'Specially the breast-feeders.'

'Plus, she's a perfectionist,' Lucinda ploughed on. 'Home. Person. Everything. No baby's going to conform to her ideals.'

Robert sighed. 'And she's a high-flier. These types can't get out of the habit of measuring everything ... performance indicators, targets, outcomes, in their DNA ... and just settle back, be ordinary mothers doing what comes naturally. That's what I said to her.'

Like mums did in my day, Lucinda finished in her head.

'She needs to get out more, meet other mothers, get a grip on reality. See how the other half live.' Coral sounded dismissive, but everybody made allowances. They all knew her circumstances – ageing parents with dementia; teenage daughter with learning difficulties going through a particularly difficult transition from the protected environment of a special school to the challenges of being in a regular college.

'Any progress on that front, Lucinda?'

'Possibly. I did find another mum there one morning I called.'

'But ...?'

'Well, I sensed Anya wasn't altogether welcoming the woman's visit.'

'What kind of family support network do we have here?'

'Dad's away from home a lot. There's a sister, but her baby was a Sudden Infant Death. Anya was actually staying in the house when that happened.'

'Was she indeed? How old was that kiddie?'

A glimmer of interest at last!

'I don't know.'

Damn. I should have asked.

'Anybody any real worries about the Morgan *baby*?' Robert clarified.

Shaken heads all round.

'Could we be talking puerperal psychosis, here?' Simon

chipped in. 'I'm hearing mania, anxiety, agitation, unsociable, not sleeping, fearful ...'

'No.' Robert shook his head. 'She's just a tired first-time mum.'

Silence.

'Thanks, Lucinda. We'll leave her in your capable hands.'

Thanks for nothing!

CHAPTER 10

Anya stretched lazily. What bliss; seven hours' unbroken sleep. Leon had kept his promise and attended to Gypsy when she woke in the night. They'd even made love – so gently it didn't hurt as much as it had ever since the birth.

The ring of his mobile roused her. *Strange, he always kept it with him ... 'in case it was a client'.* She could hear the faint sound of Leon whistling under his breath in the shower. He wouldn't hear it.

'Hello?'

'Oh, hi. This is Sonya ... at the Tillmouth Park Country House Hotel? I'm just ringing to confirm the reservation you made with my colleague last night? That's a de-luxe suite and spa from Friday 4th to Sunday 6th for Mr and Mrs Frobisher?'

Anya held her breath.

'Hello? ... Are you there? ...'

'Thanks.'

She ended the call abruptly.

By the time Leon emerged, damp and smelling of sandalwood, she was sitting in her dressing gown brushing her hair. Her eyes flicked from her own image to his in the mirror. Firm muscles rippled as he vigorously dried his hair. How lucky men were. No sagging, no expanding, no dripping, no stretch marks, only pride in their virility. She hunched the honeycomb waffle closer.

Could he see her brush hand shaking? She applied herself to the task with more energy.

'I was thinking of asking Claire to come the weekend after next. That all right with you?'

'What date would that be?' He tossed the towel aside and raked his fingers through the dark strands, as he walked stark naked across the room.

'5th and 6th.'

'No can do, I'm afraid. Fully booked on the 5th *and* 6th. Sorry, but we really need to firm up our new contracts with the House of Bruar that weekend. Too late to reschedule now.'

Was she imagining a sudden tension, a shifty avoidance of her gaze? He hadn't even needed to consult his diary. He'd known instantly. Special dates. Important reservations.

'Oh.'

His eyes were averted as he started to dress. 'Could you make it the next weekend?'

'I'll see.'

In the space of seconds, the colour had left her day.

Normally it did her good to visit her sister. The tired flat in Trinity, the second-hand furniture, the prominent photo of a dead child, the synthetic fabrics, the puffy ankles ... everything made her count her own many blessings. Today she could only envy Claire's capacity to make the best of what she had.

The cat hissed from a distance when she sat down, one hand protectively over Gypsy's bonneted head.

'Can I hold her?' Claire was already reaching out.

''Course you can. Smokey won't ...?'

'No. He's far too much of a scaredy cat to come anywhere near her. He's just staking out his territory and letting you know he's the boss around here. From a distance. Aren't you, petal?' She reached across to fondle the cat's ears, stroke his beautiful grey coat. 'You're just jealous because Mummy's got a new baby, aren't you?'

Anya gritted her teeth as Claire used the same hand to take off Gypsy's outer wrappings.

She'd intended to confide in her sister but somehow her own suspected betrayal paled into insignificance against the yardstick of Claire's everyday reality. Gypsy's routines gave her all the excuse she needed to keep her visit short and return to the security of her own standards.

In the event Leon wasn't away all weekend after all.

'Rubbish timing,' he said, when three days of diarrhoea and vomiting left Gypsy miserably whining day and night. 'Think I'll take out shares in Pampers. This kid is single-handedly keeping them afloat!'

'The poor wee mite. Sore tummy. Raw bottom. Bad enough when you *understand* what's happening. Must be so frightening when you haven't a clue.'

'Bollocks. You're anthropomorphising. *She*'s not lying there analysing what's going on. Fair enough, she probably isn't feeling too chipper, but she's used to being soggy in the nether regions, and you whisk the sheets away the second she's been sick, so she hardly even gets a whiff of it. But it *is* pretty dramatic stuff, I grant you. You wouldn't think a little dot of a creature could produce quite so much gubbins.'

'I dread to think what it's doing to her weight.'

'What did the health visitor say about that?'

'They record she's had this bug, and make allowances on her weight chart. As long as we keep her properly hydrated, she'll pick up.'

'So, no black marks. No inquisition. No maybe-we-should-take-this kid-away-from-its-inadequate-parents.'

'Don't even joke about it!'

'Lighten up, Anya. The doc says she'll be fine. It's just one of those things.'

'But that was Dr Jones. I'd sooner have seen Dr Brownlee.'

'In all probability, Dr Jones has dealt with a shedload more D&V than Dr Brownlee.'

'She didn't even want to know where we'd been, what might have triggered it. Beyond a cursory question or two.'

'Ach, these bugs are everywhere. But I take it you have a theory?'

'Well ... no, I probably shouldn't ...'

'No, go on.'

'Well, you remember on Tuesday, Tiffany persuaded me to leave the baby with her while I went for my dental appointment? It was straight after that the vomiting started.

That afternoon her wee tummy was so bloated. I just wonder if Tiffany slipped her some regular milk or something. Maybe Gypsy was crying, she couldn't pacify her. I was away longer than I expected.'

'Did she *say* Gypsy'd been crying?'

'No. She said she'd been as good as gold.'

'There you are then.'

'Or maybe her kids brought home a bug and she carried it here. You can do that without getting any symptoms yourself.'

'Which means you or I could just as easily have brought it into the house. And we're with Gypsy much more than the lampshade. I could have picked it up from Juliette and Thomas's kids. They were all over me just before this started. Stop fretting about it. It's a done deal. Gypsy'll soon be back to her old self. But good for you, finding the courage to leave her with somebody else apart from me.'

'Oh. Well, I don't intend to make a habit of it. And I think Claire's a bit miffed I didn't ask her, being my sister. But I must admit, I feel more confident about Tiffany. She's so good with babies, plus she's a qualified nurse, plus she's got three of her own. And ... well, I hate it when Claire doesn't wash her hands after petting that cat.'

'Each to their own. But listen, you look all in. Off you go, get some sleep. I'll look after Gypsy this weekend.'

'What about the House of Bruar?'

'Huh?'

'You said you had to firm up contracts or something this weekend.'

'Ochh, that. I'll give them a ring. Re-schedule. It can wait.'

So, he could re-schedule now, but not when she'd suggested a visit from Claire? What had he really intended doing this weekend? Just who was he planning to take to that country house?

CHAPTER 11

The study door was ajar when she popped her head in to tell him lunch was ready.

Tillmouth Park Country House Hotel

The scrolling letters jumped out at her. Same hotel; same luxury room pictured.

Leon instantly switched off his screen, and followed her to the kitchen. He seemed his usual self over the meal, but she knew in her gut: he was hiding something. It continued to prey on her mind. Was this anything to do with his vague 'Just down at HQ' explanation for another two days away this week?

With her imagination in overdrive, Tiffany proved a welcome distraction in his absence.

'Da-daaaa!' She threw her arms out theatrically. 'Come to sniff those fragrant stools!'

'Help yourself, although it beats me how you can tell the bug's out of her system just from the smell of her poo.'

'Did I, or did I not, predict three days?'

'You did.'

'And was it, or was it not, three days?'

'It was.'

'The power of a nurse's highly-trained intuition!' Tiffany tapped the side of her nose and made a beeline for the baby. 'I don't think I get enough credit for being so brilliant un-medicated!'

'You should go on the stage,' Anya laughed.

'Didn't I tell you? I'm a star member of the local am dram society.'

'You're kidding.'

'No. Scouts' honour. Well, maybe not *star* exactly, but

been going a couple of years. It's great fun. We even go public on occasion. You should come and see us in action some time.'

Drama queen she might be at times, but it had certainly made a difference having Tiffany's confidence and experience behind her. Anya felt more secure with her assessment than with Lucinda's.

'Don't judge her too harshly,' Tiffany said. 'It's not her fault she doesn't have kids of her own. Fair enough, the professionals learn all the milestones and the statistics and the *theory*, at university, but I agree, there's no substitute for real experience.'

'I'm really grateful. I hope I'm not taking liberties.'

'Never. I love coming here. And with mine away at school it's nice to have baby cuddles again. Fairly puts the sparkle in my humdrum days.'

'Can I take advantage of your nursing experience to ask you something else?'

'Sure. Fire away.'

'See this mark at the nape of her neck. What causes that? Will it go away or is she stuck with it?'

'The old stork bite! Two of mine had – still have – one. Jude and Sam. It's really, really common. It's a little birthmark, made by the stork's beak!' Tiffany gave her a broad grin.

'Pull the other one.'

'No, seriously, that's what it's called. However, sadly, as both you and I have learned the painful way, babies are not delivered washed and brushed and beaming in beautiful white triangular sheets in the beak of a tame stork. So, my money's on the alternative.'

'Which is?'

'The kiss of an angel. Or so my granny maintained to her dying day. Cool idea, huh?'

'Mmmh. Well, I wish I believed in guardian angels. So, what is it medically speaking?'

'Just a few irregular blood vessels under the skin. Much less poetic, huh? But perfectly harmless.'

How good it was to be able to ask these trivial questions and not be made to feel neurotic.

So, the following week, when Gypsy had a further bout of explosive stools, and Tiffany said, 'Get your coat, lass. This one's above my pay grade,' Anya didn't hesitate.

Dr Brownlee agreed this was more worrying and referred Gypsy to the Royal Hospital for Sick Children, just to 'be on the safe side'. Tiffany insisted on chauffeuring them.

The paediatrician, Dr George Hooper, seemed much younger than his fifty-six years. Floppy fair hair and pale blue eyes with almost invisible eyelashes and brows, gave him a kind of watery look as if he wasn't quite in focus. A slight overbite contributed to a rather goofy look when he smiled and this, coupled with his Mickey Mouse bow tie and bright red shirt, gave him the air of a children's entertainer rather than a serious medic.

But there was nothing comical about his expert examination of Gypsy. Totally focused; utterly professional.

He perched on the couch beside Gypsy.

'Are you happy for me to talk in front of your friend, Mrs Morgan?'

Anya nodded, heart sinking. This sounded serious.

'She's a nurse. It'd be useful to have somebody else listening.'

Tiffany moved in closer as if she'd been awaiting this endorsement, and both pairs of eyes turned to the doctor. He pushed his heavy-rimmed glasses up his nose and began questioning Anya. It felt like a tick-list of all the errors and bad practices an uninitiated mother might fall into.

Even his attempts at reassurance had barbed ends.

He 'didn't think' (*not know for sure, then*) it was 'anything serious';

'Make sure you keep her well hydrated' (*her milk wasn't good enough*);

'Hand-washing's the most important thing' (*she was being too slip-shod*);

'Go back to your GP if it recurs and we'll get her in for

some tests' (*no confidence she'd get it right from now on*).

She left feeling crushed. He had judged her sub-standard. But Tiffany dismissed her dejection.

'You're being far too sensitive, Anya. It's routine stuff. The runs can be caused by loads of things. He's just going through the motions, so he can say hand on heart he told you about hand washing and hydration and going back to the GP and all the rest of it. So, if things were to go pear-shaped he could defend himself in a court of law.'

'What kind of things?'

'Say Gypsy was found to have something more serious that he didn't find at this stage, but she presented later and it was too late and you sued him or the hospital. But for goodness' sake, don't start imagining anything like that's going to happen. It's just a simple case of her getting a tummy bug. And him watching his back. Like as not you'll never darken his doors again. So, come on, girl, relax! How about you feed Gypsy, and then I'll make you a nice cup of tea and you can get some shut-eye. You must be shattered.'

She was. She fell into a sound sleep the minute her head hit the pillow.

CHAPTER 12

Leon was well on the road back to Edinburgh when his phone rang.

'Yo, Thomas. What's up?'

'I've just had a call from somebody called … Tiffany … Tiffany Corrigan. Mean anything to you?'

'Yeah, she's a neighbour, but why the devil would she be phoning you?'

'Apparently, she doesn't have your mobile number, so she looked up the main company website. Rang here to see if we could pass on a message.'

'Saying?'

'Seems she was round at your house earlier today. She left something or other behind, so she called back about twenty minutes ago to collect it. Only she can't get an answer. But she can hear Gypsy crying.'

'For Pete's sake, what now?! OK, I'll try to ring Anya. Can you tell her, I'm about forty minutes away?'

His foot hit the accelerator.

He rang … landline … mobile … landline … mobile … landline …

'*Please leave your message after the tone.*'

Gypsy's cries combined with Tiffany's calls were loud enough to have attracted the attention of several passers-by, and by the time Leon arrived, a small crowd had gathered.

He ignored them all, unlocked the door and raced inside. Tiffany followed, making a beeline for the distraught baby.

Leon dived into the kitchen … sitting room … den … dining room … conservatory … playroom. He raced upstairs

... burst into the first bedroom ... second ...

Anya lay on their bed, dead to the world. Heart in his mouth, he felt her skin ... warm.

He spoke her name urgently, shook her shoulder. She stirred but merely turned her face the other way.

He shouted in her ear. She muttered his name ... *slurred speech*.

He smelt her breath; no alcohol.

He called Tiffany. She came at once, still pacifying a hiccupping Gypsy, who instantly resumed fresh wailing when she saw her mother.

'You're a nurse, aren't you? Can you ... is she all right? Is it a stroke or something?'

Tiffany handed him the baby and checked Anya's forehead ... pulse ... breath ... neck ... muscle tone ... reflexes ... pupils ... ability to smile.

'Anya, can you sit forward, swing your legs off the bed for me a minute, pet?'

Anya slowly obeyed.

'How many fingers am I holding up?'

'Three.'

'Can you follow my finger?'

She did.

'Have you taken anything?'

'Whatdyamean?'

'Pills or ... drugs ... or anything? Anything that might have made you sleepy?'

'Na.' The eyes were drooping again.

Leon glanced across at Tiffany. 'Should we call an ambulance?'

'Not sure. Maybe ...'

But Anya was clutching his arm. 'Naa. Donwannago anywhere,' she slurred. 'Jusneed tosleep.'

'How about calling the GP?'

'Naaa.'

'What about Lucinda?' Tiffany chipped in. 'Shall we just call her – ask her advice. For Gypsy's sake.'

Anya gave a small nod, her eyes still shut. ''Kay.'

Lucinda was there in ten minutes.

She listened, watched, examined Anya. She rang the surgery, returned with a set face.

'Dr Jones is on her way.'

Coral Jones did all the same checks, asked all the same questions, gestured to Leon to accompany her downstairs.

'As you can see, she's adamant she doesn't want to go to hospital for a check.'

'D'you think she needs to? Can you overrule her? Should *I*?'

'Well, I can't find anything amiss apart from the drowsiness. And I know she's been extremely tired since the baby. So, I think it's probably best not to upset her further. But it's imperative that she's not left alone in the house.'

Leon's response was immediate. 'I'm going nowhere till I know she's all right.'

'Right. That's good.'

'And what about feeding the baby? She's entirely breastfed at the moment. Is it all right to continue with that while ...?'

'Probably best to keep the routines as normal as possible at the moment. Maybe express the milk this time and discard it. You've got a pump, have you?' Leon nodded. *Good job Anya always kept a bottle in reserve.* 'After that, I'd suggest she sits or lies somewhere soft ... the bed, a large armchair ... and you remain with her just to make sure everybody's safe. Until she's slept off whatever this is. If you're worried at all, if her condition deteriorates, don't hesitate. Ring 999. And I think you should start introducing the baby to solids.'

'You said "slept off whatever it is". What d'you mean?'

'Well, it looks to me as if she's taken something – a light sedative or something with drowsiness as a side effect. Is she on any kind of medication?'

'Nothing! She's obsessive about everything being natural. Vitamins and herbal supplements only.'

'Well, in that case she's probably just so exhausted that she's fallen into a deeper sleep than usual. And that being so, more sleep's the solution.'

A quick consultation with Lucinda and Dr Jones was gone.

'Are you all right with this, Leon?' Lucinda asked, one eyebrow raised.

'I think so. But, since you're here ... would you mind just checking Anya's vitamin supplements? She sends away for them, and ... I was just wondering ...'

Leon fished out the tablets from the kitchen drawer.

Lucinda examined the fine print.

'Seems legit. Certainly nothing untoward *listed*.'

Tiffany hesitated before following Lucinda out of the house.

'I hate to mention this, but it might be a good idea to speak to your neighbours when you get a minute. Apparently, Gypsy's crying night after night's disturbing their beauty sleep.'

Leon glared at her. 'You're kidding! Bloody hell! They should try living in a high rise flat! Then they'd know about noise.'

He'd be damned if he'd pander to their nonsense.

Alone again, Leon stared down at his sleeping wife, his thoughts churning.

CHAPTER 13

The café was pleasantly buzzing.

'Go on. Push the boat out! I dare you,' Tiffany laughed. 'You make me feel such a glutton.'

'We just have different tastes. Salad's my thing; hearty soup's yours. Each to their own.'

'Hearty soup *and* a slice of cheesecake!' Tiffany blew out her cheeks and spread her hands wide. 'Well, I wish I had your will power, but cheesecake's one of my weaknesses. That and crème brulée. Can't walk past them.'

The meal took far longer than Anya had anticipated; Gypsy's food must be totally fresh and homemade, so by the time they got back to the house, the child was starting to protest. Tiffany scooped her up and walked around the house playing baby games to keep her quiet, periodically checking on progress in the kitchen.

Then, precisely as the cooker-alarm buzzed, the doorbell chimed.

'Claire!' Her sister *never* appeared unannounced. 'Something wrong?'

'No. I just thought I'd come and see if you were all right. I tried ringing but didn't get an answer ...' Her voice tailed off as she caught sight of Tiffany jiggling Gypsy up and down in the background.

'I've only been out to lunch,' Anya said sharply.

What was it with everyone wanting instant access to her?

'Want me to change Gypsy, while you talk to your sister?' Tiffany asked.

Anya swallowed hard. *Don't think about the hand-washing technique, the cleansing of the skin ...* But gut instinct won.

'Actually, I wondered if *you'd* like to change her nappy, Claire?'

The shadow instantly lifted. 'Oh, *please*!'

'Of course,' Tiffany said flatly. 'You're her *real* aunty. There you go, sugar plum. Be good for Aunty Claire now.'

Claire took the child with infinite care. She blew a raspberry into Gypsy's exploring hand and laughed at the answering gurgle.

'Sorry, Tiffany,' Anya said. 'I know I'm too possessive. D'you want to stay and feed her instead?'

'Love to. Although I'm not sure I should be party to shovelling *spinach* into a helpless infant! Foul stuff!'

Claire vanished upstairs; Tiffany went to wash her hands; Anya switched on the liquidiser.

'*Anya!*'

She leaped up the stairs. Claire was staring down at her half-naked niece.

'Is that ... normal?'

'What did you do?'

'I didn't "do" anything. I just took off her nappy and there it was.'

'Tiffany!' Anya's shout made Gypsy's lip tremble, and she instantly moved to soothe her, muscling her sister out of the way without a second's thought.

'Ah, you're repentant! You want me to take pity on her and rustle up something decent ...' Tiffany stopped when she caught sight of Anya's face. 'What on earth's the matter?'

'Look!'

Tiffany peered closer.

'Have you maybe got a wee cut on your finger or something?'

Claire turned her hands. 'No.'

'Could you have nicked her skin maybe?'

'I hadn't even *touched* her skin. I only just opened up the nappy.'

'Right. Let's think.' Tiffany said slowly, staring down at the child.

'It is blood, isn't it?' *Please say it's a mirage.*

'Yeah. It's blood.'

'Shall I change her anyway?' Anya asked.

'Yeah. Get her freshened up.'

'Could you have a wee look first? Check her for me.'

'Sure. ... Nothing visible.'

Anya cleansed the skin with trembling hands, put on a fresh nappy and held her baby close, rocking, patting, shushing.

'Let's not panic here,' Tiffany said calmly. 'There's probably a perfectly innocent explanation. So, while we think, I suggest you feed Gypsy and keep her calm.'

By the time Gypsy was sated, Tiffany had arranged to chauffeur mother and baby to the clinic.

'Makes sense for Tiffany to come with me, she's a nurse. She'll know what to say, where to go, what to do. I'll ring you as soon as I know anything, Claire. '

The health visitor on duty at the clinic was new to Anya.

'Did you bring the nappy with you?'

'Sorry. I should have thought of that,' Tiffany said. 'But I can vouch for it; there was blood in it.'

'And she's a nurse,' Anya chipped in.

'Ex-nurse,' Tiffany clarified.

'Well, it's probably nothing to worry about, but I'm going to see if the doctor can see you, just to be on the safe side.'

Anya knew a moment of acute disappointment when she was ushered in to Dr Jones' room. But the GP was gentle with the baby and listened attentively to Anya's account.

'There's nothing obvious, but it could be due to a number of things.'

'Like what?'

'A urinary tract infection maybe. A little polyp. A fissure in her anus – a tiny crack. Has she had any hard stools or been constipated at all?'

'Never. If anything, it's the opposite.'

'Was the blood at all mucoussy? Like red currant jelly?'

'I'm not sure. I don't think so but … My friend saw it and she's a nurse. She's in the waiting room. Could she maybe come in and tell you what she thinks?'

Tiffany seemed somehow to fill the consulting room.

'It was a little bit slimy,' she nodded.

'Is that important?' Anya's eyes were fixed on the doctor's impassive face.

'Well, it might be indicative of something.'

'You're thinking intussusception?' Tiffany said. 'That's the first thing I thought of.'

'Maybe. It can spontaneously resolve itself.'

'What's intussus… whatever?' Anya looked from one to the other.

'It's where the bowel folds back inside itself,' Dr Jones said, miming the effect.

'Is that serious?'

'It *can* be, but your baby seems perfectly comfortable, so, try not to worry. I would like to get it checked out though, so I'll refer you to Sick Children's just to be on the safe side.'

'I'll run you up,' Tiffany said instantly. 'We'll be back before you know it.'

She was right. The paediatrician asked all the same questions, offered all the same alternatives, gave the same reassurance. Nothing to worry about.

'If it happens again, save the nappy, and come back.'

Anya's first instinct was to text Leon.

Tiffany's face said it all.

'It's your decision, of course, but I'm not sure why you would want to worry him when he's at work. If it was me, I'd want to prove to him, I can cope. I've dealt with it. I stayed calm. Got expert advice. You can safely leave me to take care of the baby.'

'I see what you mean. But I was only semi-calm because you were there.'

'Nonsense. You'd have got there on your own if I hadn't been here.'

Buoyed up by this commendation, Anya rang her sister, but resisted the temptation to contact her husband.

Six hours after the event, Leon was not amused.

'Of *course* I want to know if there's anything wrong! I'm her father, for heaven's sake. Seems to me the lampshade's taking over my role these days.'

'Don't be silly, Leon. I was glad she happened to be there. I didn't have to faff about parking.'

He pursed his lips but said no more.

CHAPTER 14

The phone call splintered his concentration, and Leon swore under his breath. He'd have to start the calculation all over again. *Dammit. Dammit. Dammit.*

'Leon Morgan speaking.'

'Gypsy's been … stolen!' Hysteria shrieked through Anya's voice.

'*What?*'

'Somebody's … kidnapped Gypsy!'

'Where are you?'

'In the park.'

'Which park?'

'Dalkeith Country Park.'

'Calm down, Anya. Calm down! Tell me what's happened.'

The words raced each other for the finishing line. 'I took her for a walk in the pram I was watching some goldfinches and when I turned around … she'd *gone!*'

'OK. Listen. Stay exactly where you are in case somebody comes back with her. Maybe it was just kids mucking around. Have you rung the police?'

'No.'

'I'll ring them and get them to come to the park. Where exactly are you?'

'In the park!'

'*Whereabouts* in the park?'

'I don't know.'

'Think, Anya, think! Did you go to the Restoration Courtyard thingy, or to the kiddies' adventure playground, or on one of the walks, or what?

'One of the walks.'

'Which one?'

'I don't know what it's called!'

'Does it have a made-up road suitable for buggies and bikes or ...'

'Yes. It's one of the easy trails. The one where you can see bluebells in the spring. Remember?'

'Gotcha. Stay exactly where you are then. Keep your phone switched on. I'll ring the police, get them to come to you. OK?'

Mercifully there were no patrol cars on the bypass and he sliced a good ten minutes off his best drive-time from office to home. His hand shook so badly when he tried to fit the key in the lock that he had to stand still and consciously steady his breathing.

Anya would be distraught all alone ... Gypsy would be beside herself ... with strangers ...

The house felt eerily silent.

No bleeping answerphone. No demands with menace.

He kept the phone glued to his ear.

'Anya?'

'Yes.' A quivering whisper.

'I'm at the house now. The police are on their way. They want an up-to-date photo, but I'll be with you as soon as I can.'

All he could hear was her sobbing breaths. 'What if they've already taken pictures ... sold her ...'

The tiptoe of his feet sounded thunderous as he crept through the house, eyes alert for any hint of intrusion.

No graffiti dripping from the walls ... No gun pointing at his head ... No ominous parcels waiting to explode or cover him in excrement ... No ransom note ...

Nothing.

He took the stairs two at a time. He'd collect a spare comforter for Gypsy ... or at worst, for Anya ...

After the bright light everywhere else, it took a moment for his eyes to adjust to the gloom in the baby's nursery.

Odd. Anya always opened all the curtains and blinds first thing. He sidled in cautiously, eyes darting, muscles tense.

Silence, darkness, total order.

A shrine to a lost baby.

Get a grip, Morgan!

He flung open the curtains; sunshine instantly flooded the room.

He stooped to lift Mr Rabbit from the end of the cot and ...

He blinked rapidly.

He reached down with a shaking finger and touched the smooth cover.

It was no illusion.

One arm thrown up, face half-covered by the sheet, lay a ... *doll? ... body? ....*

A finger moved involuntarily. *A real baby.*

Soft rhythmic breathing. A gentle grunt. A sound asleep baby.

In slow motion, he gently peeled the cover back.

Yes, it was. It really was ... a warm, living, sleeping *Gypsy.*

'Anya?' His voice came out as a hoarse whisper.

'The police are here ...'

He could hear deep voices in the background: 'Mrs Morgan?'

'Anya, listen. She's safe. She's here. At home.'

'*What?!*'

'Gypsy's here. Asleep in her cot.'

'But ... I don't understand ...'

'Can you pass your phone to one of the policemen? We need to stop them instigating a search.'

Someone called Constable Bryn Forsyth listened. He kept his voice perfectly even.

'Thank you, sir. Someone will be with you shortly. We'll bring your wife.'

His eyes darted everywhere. From room to room he stalked, searching – cupboards, wardrobes, en suites – alert for the tiniest sound, the merest flicker of movement ... house ... annex ... garden ...

Not a single hint of intrusion or of any alien presence.

The three police officers dominated the room.

Anya clutched a protesting Gypsy close, smothering her with kisses, rocking fiercely, her face still ashen. Leon had to prise his daughter from her clutches and prowl up and down within eyesight before the police could gain the information only Anya could supply.

Did she remember going to the park today? Yes.

Could she describe events that morning? She could. And did.

So, she'd taken the pram? Yes.

Did she remember putting the baby in the pram? Yes.

Did she remember seeing the baby in the pram? Yes.

So, how had the baby got back into her cot? She had no idea.

What had she done in the park? She'd walked around for a while and then sat on a bench – the one she was on when they'd found her – watching some goldfinches.

Was she extra tired this morning? No more than usual.

Had she ever sleep-walked? No.

Had the baby had a screaming match that morning? No.

Had she walked out of the house and left the baby before?

Leon had his gaze fixed on her now.

Well, yes, she had … once … maybe twice … just to cool down.

And was that what happened this morning? No. Look, she'd admitted it, hadn't she? But things were different now. Gypsy didn't scream all night any more.

How did she really feel about her baby? She adored her. Ask anyone.

Leon gritted his teeth. They'd be sure to ask him. Lies wouldn't help. They might even look for confirmation from the professionals. It was routine stuff. The mother's mental state was material to the whole business of what had happened in the park. They had to rule out the perfectly possible before they contemplated the highly implausible.

A someone who would steal a baby and tuck it back snuggly into its own cot? You're kidding, right?

Anya needed help, and she needed it right now. The sooner he reassured the police this was a domestic issue and no crime had been committed, the better.

'Well, sir. Seems to be no doubt that your wife went to the park and that she took the pram with her. Question is, did she take the baby too? Or not?'

Leon laid it on thick. Gypsy had been securely and tidily in her cot. The room had even been darkened. She was obviously fully fed. There was absolutely no sign of frenzy or desertion or panic. Gypsy was perfectly safe.

Fair enough, things *had* been tense in the early months, but Anya had had enough insight to seek help, and she had come through it.

Yes, today's incident was odd, but he'd personally make sure a doctor checked them both over. And he'd make sure she had more help. No need to waste any more expensive police time.

The eyes Anya fixed on him when he returned to the room after seeing the officers out, were wide and staring.

'What did you tell them?'

'The truth.'

He sat on the arm of the chair and slipped an arm around her shoulders, but she shrank away from him.

'You don't believe me either, do you?'

'I don't know what to think.'

'*They* don't know me. *You* do. Or at least I thought you did.'

'What's your explanation, then? How *did* Gypsy get back here and into her cot?'

'I don't know.'

He stared her down. 'So, we've got two choices here as I see it. Either someone took her, brought her back here, and somehow got into the house without breaking or disturbing anything. Or she wasn't in the pram in the first place.'

Anya sank her head into her hands and said in a dull voice, 'I know I *did* take her out. I did.'

'Look, Anya, I don't know what happened, but the main thing is she's safe. Thank God. But you've had a terrible fright today, so we'll get Dr Brownlee to check you over.'

'To see if I need locking up, you mean.'

'No. That's not what I mean at all. Hell, Anya, I'm trying to help here. I'm not the enemy.'

'But you think I'm going crazy, don't you?'

'Not crazy, but I think maybe your mind might be playing tricks. It happens after birth sometimes. And remember how you walked out on her before.'

'That was different. I was exhausted. She wouldn't stop crying. I walked away so I wouldn't harm her.'

'I know. But it's a constant pattern, isn't it? This inability to settle her.'

'"Inability" ...' she broke off, shoulders slumping.

'She's picking up on your anxiety. She isn't like that with ... other people, is she?'

'You mean, you.'

'Well, she isn't, is she?'

She lifted her head to stare up at him.

'How do I know *you* didn't follow us, snatch her out of the pram, bring her back here and then go off to the office?'

'Why the devil would I do something like that?'

'To make me out to be losing the plot.'

'What on earth *for*?'

'To get me out of the way.'

Leon felt his face close, and bit back a sharp retort. He worked to keep his voice unemotional.

'Look, I have absolutely no idea where you're coming from here, but you've had one hell of a fright. I'll take care of Gypsy; you go and get some rest.'

Anya stared into his eyes, her own cold and unblinking.

'If they take my baby away, I will never forgive you. Never.'

And with that she got to her feet and left the room.

When the doorbell rang twenty minutes later, Leon felt

a flash of annoyance. What *now*?!

'Is Anya all right?' Tiffany had that universal look of concern on her face.

'Yes, why wouldn't she be?'

'The lady down at the newspaper shop said there'd been a police car at your door. I just thought …'

'It was a misunderstanding. She's fine, but she's tired, so I don't want her disturbed right now.'

'Fair enough. Give her my love.'

'Sorry for your wasted journey.'

He felt mean, but the Corrigan woman's finer feelings were the least of his concerns.

CHAPTER 15

Leon stared at his brother.

'I don't have a choice, Thomas. The doctor insists. Anya must get more rest and support.'

'Look, you can't *keep* letting your domestic affairs encroach on work. Time off, neighbours ringing ... you need to get this sorted, Leo. Get Mother to come up. Your place is here.'

'Anya refuses ...'

'"Anya refuses ...", "Anya insists ...", "Anya won't ...", ... for heaven's sake, Leo, grow some balls! You can't keep mincing around letting your wife pull your strings. You can't expect other people to keep sorting out the shite you've created.'

'I know ... but I can't leave ...'

'I don't think you heard me,' Thomas said, his mouth set in a grim line. 'When I say shite, I mean capital letters SHITE; major-league cock-up.'

Leon frowned. 'You mean ... Fowler?'

'Not only Fowler. Remember the Irish deal?' Thomas was staring straight at him.

'What about it? You said it was sweet. Biggest contract I've bagged. You said ...'

'That was before I knew the facts. But you've guffed up ... big time, Leo.'

'What? How?'

'That's why I called you in this morning. That company – how much did you research them?'

Leon didn't answer.

'You *know* how important due diligence is. Father always stressed it. Check 'em out. Any doubt at all, test them with a small order first. Make sure they pay up. On time. You *know* all that.'

Leon felt a wave of nausea sweep over him.

'But did you do that? No, you did not. And we're not just talking mega bucks, here, it's a matter of credibility, reputation too. If this leaks out ...'

Leon sank down onto the nearest seat.

'How come?'

'They've gone into liquidation, that's how come. Before we've had even a farthing out of them.'

'No. Please tell me, our guys can sort it out.'

'Nope. They're looking for loopholes as we speak, but they aren't holding out much hope.'

Leon felt all the energy drain from his body. He dropped his head in his hands, fingers clawing through his hair. How *could* he have made such a monumental error?

'But ... we'll get the stock back, huh?'

'Possibly.'

A long pause fell before Thomas spoke again.

'And what about the guys on the floor, huh? We've had them working flat out to honour that order. They're due a fortune in overtime. Where's it coming from, huh? You've just squandered it. How are you going to sort *that* one out, Leo?' He paused but Leon had no answers. 'You're firing on half a cylinder, that's your trouble. Even when you're physically here, your mind's not properly on the job. Something's got to change. We can't afford to carry you. And we certainly can't afford losses like this one!'

'Are you ...?'

'I'm giving you a strong warning. A *very* strong warning.'

'Who else knows?'

'The guys in accounting, of course. And Roger. And Bill.'

Leon screwed his eyes shut.

'And while we're on the subject of our esteemed senior manager ... you do realise, don't you, that Bill Broadbent is seriously considering his position in the company at this precise moment?'

'*No!* You don't mean it ...?'

'Oh, I do. I do. While you've been playing happy families, our most trusted employee has been releasing the full barrage of his pent-up wrath, no holes barred, and I'm the sole target.'

'*Bill?*'

'The very same. Mild-mannered, loyal Bill. In a nutshell, it goes something like this. It was the blood, sweat and tears of Mr Jerome and Mr Douglas that built this firm up from nothing. *They* were gentlemen; always courteous, respectful and supportive of their staff. We privileged youngsters swan in by virtue of our parentage, and in no time, have executive status. We were lucky – Mr Douglas wasn't like many CEOs who actually own companies, clinging to his earned position; he was committed to a plan of succession as soon as we left school. He even ensured an orderly transition, then backed away to give us space to develop things in today's world. And how do we repay him? By doing our damnedest to destroy everything he slaved to build up: reputation, trust, integrity, future. OK, my interpretation but his thoughts. And as an honourable man himself, Bill's not at all sure he can continue to serve in a company that has so little regard for its employees.'

Waves of nausea forced Leon to drop his head below his knees.

'What d'you think Father would make of us losing Bill Broadbent?' Thomas said.

'Does he know ...?'

'No. And I'm doing my damnedest to keep it from him. But if Bill walks ...'

'I'll ring Mother. Get her to help with Gypsy.'

'And you'd better be fully back in harness on Monday, or ... you don't need me to spell it out.'

Physically in Newcastle he might be, absorbing some of the ramifications of the Fowler case, and the colossal business error, but his own domestic problems still haunted every waking hour.

Staying with Thomas and Juliette held new tensions these days too. He did his best to avoid being alone with his sister-in-law, but she was completely innocently relaxed in her own home, wandering around in her pyjamas, answering the phone in a leotard when disturbed during a workout, reclining along a settee watching the news ... oblivious to the effect.

He worked in the office till late but it was imperative that he give a semblance of normality. Thomas could vanish to his study or take his Jaguar out for a spin, but Leon had no such escape routes. And what's more, Juliette was obviously watching him.

'Want to share?'

He hesitated. At least she was fully clothed; still in her professional formality.

'You're no good to anyone else if you're in pieces yourself, Leo,' she persisted.

The story spilled out in staccato responses in the gloom of evening, fragmented, incoherent, even contradictory at times, but the overall picture was unmistakeable.

'I simply ... can't do right for doing wrong ...

'She panics over nothing. Totsy bits and pieces that all kids get from time to time, in our house, they're major-league crises ...

'She doesn't trust the professionals ...

'She won't listen to their advice ...

'She's still mad at me because I can't swallow her story of someone stealing the baby in the park ...

'Things are pretty bad between the two of us.'

Juliette sat perfectly still, listening, giving nothing away.

'Do *you* trust Anya with Gypsy, Leo?'

'Yes ... no ... I don't know.' He raked his fingers through his hair, head slumped. 'She's ... I think she's near her edge. I'm worried sick about what's going on all the time I'm away.'

'Are you worried about Gypsy's *safety*?'

'My brain says I should be; my heart says no. She

wouldn't *deliberately* harm her own child ... but abandoning her, forgetting her ... it could lead to putting her in danger. Unintentionally.'

'Have you told anybody about your misgivings?'

'Yes. I had to. When we found the baby alone in the house.'

'And they said?'

'Make sure Anya gets more support. But I *can't* be there all the time ... with the best will in the world. Especially not now, with all this bloody mess hanging over us at work. And besides, what if I take steps to protect Gypsy, and Anya does something ... terrible ... to herself? I'd never forgive myself.'

'Has she ever shown signs of being suicidal?'

'Not that I *know* of! But she's never been out of gear like this before.'

A long silence fell.

'Listen, Juliette, I know you're not into doling out advice. Your job's to help people work out their own solutions. But just as a matter of interest, what *would* you advise?'

'Accept help. It's not an admission of failure, Leo.'

Try telling Anya that!

'Look, I try to stay out of the business, but I can't help knowing that Thomas is on your back, and I'm sorry. But in his defence, I have to say, he's under a fiendish amount of pressure at the moment. He needs you. My advice? Either get an au pair, or let your mother be more involved. She's lovely. Practical but not interfering. I'm sure, once she gets to know her better, Anya wouldn't find it nearly as intimidating as she fears. And it's only till she gets properly on her feet and puts all this anxiety behind her.'

Thomas chose that precise moment to return. Leon left them some privacy and went to his room to ring his wife for the third time that day.

His call went to voicemail. Again.

CHAPTER 16

It wasn't that Hannah Morgan was bossy or intrusive or domineering – she was none of those things. It was what she represented … control, mistrust, suspicion. After tiptoeing around her mother-in-law for five days, it was something of a relief to have Leon back for the weekend. A chance to start re-building his confidence in her. She had to. She absolutely *had* to.

But all her good intentions evaporated the instant she took his shirts out of the plastic bag. He always brought his used clothes home for washing; this time … they'd already been laundered. The scent of someone else's fabric conditioner mocked her.

Why? Who? Exactly where had *he been?*

And suddenly the signs were luminous. Whatever the subject, he was tight-lipped – work? family? Newcastle? – any reference to his week and he quickly changed the subject to hers.

How could she have been so naïve?

Thomas and Juliette had been married for much longer, had two children together … Tiffany and her husband had three children … and they still shared everything. Fair enough, Claire's marriage had foundered … and that had been because of a baby.

But her own relationship … after one baby …? The more she thought about it the more sense it made. Vague suspicion about that country house hotel solidified painfully.

Her own husband was having an affair.

It had been Tiffany who'd offered her an opportunity to escape from the surreptitious scrutiny for a couple of hours, leaving Hannah with Gypsy.

It felt odd, with no baby to focus their attention, and Anya realised how little she knew of this woman who'd done her best to be a friend. General chit-chat felt strained.

'Your mum-in-law seems nice,' Tiffany said, exaggeratedly surveying a large slice of carrot cake from every angle. 'What's it like having her staying?'

'She *is* nice. But ... well, I like my own space.'

Tiffany savoured a mouthful of cake.

'But you have your mother living with you all the time,' Anya said. 'How does *that* work?'

'Fine. But I'm not one for my own company like you. Ma's the reason Dan and I can get out so much, follow our own interests.'

'And she's your own mother. Must be different. I presume you learned your mothering skills from her, she'd do things the same way?'

'Never really thought about it. But I guess she's the reason I've been around babies all my life.'

'How come?'

'Catholic,' – Tiffany crossed herself irreverently – 'hair-shirt variety; no bending the rules. Five kids. Could have been worse though; my pal's one of *nine*! Imagine. Ma was still only in her fifties when my dad died. Suddenly. Undetected aneurysm. Meant I had to grow up in a hurry.'

'Where d'you come in the family?'

'Eldest. Only thirteen when we lost him. And I very nearly sent *her* into an early grave soon after!'

'How come?'

'Pregnant at fifteen.'

Anya couldn't help herself; her eyes widened.

'I know,' Tiffany said, her gaze in the past. 'I can still remember ... dreading telling her, the shame – disappointing her big time.'

'So, what did you do?'

'No brainer; had to be adoption. I absolutely couldn't expect Ma to bring my baby up as well. Abortion was a no-no. Thou shalt not kill; drummed into me from the cradle. So,

Ma arranged it. Sent me away to my aunt in County Fermanagh, Northern Ireland, and nobody locally knew I'd even been pregnant.' Her voice softened. 'They let me name her, though. Holly Justine.'

'Oh, you poor thing.'

'Yep, but it worked out for the best – as Ma always says. Just after that my kid sister, Isla, got sick. Ma had these part-time jobs. Spencer, Alastair and Murray were typical boys – living for football, off out as soon as the bare minimum of homework was done. Tremaine was only four, and Isla was barely two when we lost Dad. Which left me. The kid was poorly for years. Everything revolved around her.'

'That must have been tough.'

'Yep. Boy, did I resent all the attention she got!'

'Does Dan know – about baby Holly, I mean?'

'Always has. But he's cool about it. Reckons he'd rather know and deal with it, than be wondering what else I'm keeping from him. Besides, he could have been a teenage dad and just not know about it, so who's he to judge.' She smiled. 'I remember exactly what he said. "Just think, that little soul will have given some couple somewhere a wonderful life."'

'That's a positive way to look at it.'

'Typical Dan. Live and let live ... Strange thought, huh? – she'd be twenty-three now. Old enough to have made me a grandmother several times over! Blimey O'Riley! Imagine! *Me*, a *nana*.'

'Old enough to trace you if she wanted to, as well. How would you feel if she just turned up on your doorstep?'

'I hope she doesn't need to. I'd rather she thinks of her adopted mother as her real one and there's no gap to fill. But if she *did* come looking? It wouldn't destabilise us. Even Ma's reconciled to what happened; she'd take it in her stride now. I think.'

'How did you and Dan meet?' Anya scooped the remaining crema from her espresso.

'In a cold and draughty village hall. My pal Leila – the nine kids one – her disabled brother was a cloud in this play about ... well, I've no idea what it was about. I just went along for moral support. It was all pretty shambolic, going nowhere. Then all of a sudden, this young bloke – six foot three, fourteen stone – long hair, rings, tattoos, leather, studs, the whole shebang, was up there on stage with them, arsing around, being the wind, then a bird, then an elephant, and making everybody laugh. And the more he entered into the action the more the disabled kids got involved, taking their cue from him. The audience went wild. He completely turned the evening around. I was intrigued: who was this fit guy, and what made him tick?'

'And that was Dan.'

'Yep. He was studying for a degree in the performing arts, and somehow, he heard about this college that put on plays involving folk with learning difficulties, so he offered to help out in his spare time. Wanted to "do something useful for society". And long story short, after he'd got his degree, he went off and did a course in special needs and put both qualifications to good use. He's a natural with these kids. Patience of a saint. They love him to bits.'

'He sounds like a very special man.'

'Drives me up the wall sometimes, looks like a train wreck, and the world's worst memory, but yep, he's not a bad old stick, my bloke. I've got a lot to be thankful for.'

'He must make a really fun dad.'

Tiffany grinned. 'Always dreaming up some mad caper or other. Not just with our three; the nieces and nephews spend half their time round at ours, too. We've got hordes of them, of course. Dan's one of four, I'm one of five, and everybody's got several sprogs. Dan's the draw. He's there at the centre of everything, egging 'em on, encouraging 'em to get the best out of life. But like I say, looks like a tramp most of the time at home. Not like your Leon, always so immaculate.'

Don't go there.

'Different kind of life. So, how long have you been together now?'

'Thirteen, going on fourteen years, all told. Married for

twelve. Our Sam was on the way when we got spliced. And you know what? He's still my best buddy. But hey, enough about us. Your mum still alive?'

'No. Ovarian cancer when she was forty-six. And my father's got a new family now. Lives in South Africa. There's just my sister Claire and me.'

'Sad that. Gypsy's missing out on the cousins' thingy. You'll just need to have a dozen brothers and sisters for her to make up.'

Anya felt something tighten in her gut.

Tiffany's eyes narrowed momentarily, and she quickly added in a lighter tone, 'You can't be as intense when you have a whole tribe of them. But always remember, I'd be perfectly happy to come and take care of Gypsy. I know you don't want her exposed to the snotty noses and dirty fingers and general grot of our mad household. But maybe when she's older and developed a bit of immunity ... Plenty of little mothers and sisters and cousins there to give her a high old time.'

'Thank you.'

'Glory Alleluiah! Look at the time! Must rush. I promised Maribel I'd take her swimming when she got in from school today. She's just learned to do backstroke and wants to show me how far she can travel without colliding with anybody. She's really into beating her own personal records, is our Maribel. Latest craze is staying underwater *for ever*. Scares me rigid the time she can hold her breath. I have to be in the pool with her just so I'm on hand to haul her up if she loses consciousness.'

'Could she do that?'

'No idea. But that's what it feels like when she's crouching there in the corner not moving. Every second feels like an hour!'

'So, you *do* worry about some things,' Anya said.

''Course I do. Doesn't every mother worry? Goes with the job description.'

'Well, compared to me you seem to be completely unflappable.'

'Been at it longer, that's all. Come to believe in their survival. Speaking of which, mind if I mention something?'

'By all means.'

'Your mother-in-law might have said already, but I'd go easy on the solids. I made the same mistake myself with our first, Samantha. Kept shovelling it in until the kiddie pushed it away. Better to decide yourself how much is a reasonable portion for her age, and give a little bit less rather than too much at this stage, while you're still topping her up with milk. Hope you don't mind me saying.'

And she was gone, leaving Anya to deal with another sense of failure and the bill.

CHAPTER 17

Tiffany's advice soon proved spot on.

Gypsy woke at 5am whining pitifully and refused to settle after her early morning feed. She was still fretful when Tiffany arrived, her crying so distracting that Anya took her outside to watch a light breeze spin the tiny foil windmill Claire had brought her, leaving Tiffany to finish off two tasty concoctions: one vegetable-, one fruit-based.

'Baby cordon-bleu ... I don't think! But she should sleep more comfortably if her stomach isn't over-extended.'

Gypsy promptly fell asleep after her lunch and had still not surfaced when Leon got in at 7 that evening.

Anya toyed with the thought of using the unexpected opportunity to have a civilised adult meal with her husband, but no sooner had the idea entered her head than she dismissed it. How could she sit there alone with him, all the while suspecting his mind was straying to some other woman? Someone who not only was familiar enough to do his laundry, but who openly left her scent. His permanently distracted air, his secrecy about his days away, evenings spent in his study, hastily ended phone calls ... the evidence was mounting daily. And tonight, the doubts were compounded by a growing sense of unease as the hours passed and the baby did not waken.

Her restlessness and tension affected Leon, and when Gypsy still hadn't roused at 10 that night, it was his suggestion she should ring Tiffany.

'Sorry to bother you, but should we be worried? We've tried waking her but she's dead to the world. I know you said she'd sleep more soundly, but is this OK? It's what, ten hours now since she fed. She's never gone that long before.'

Tiffany rattled off a catalogue of questions.

'What's her colour like? ...

'Is she floppy? ...

'Is her breathing normal? ...

'Is she hot? ...

'Does her mouth look dry? ...

'Is there any kind of a rash? ...

'Does she protest when you move her head? ...

'Want me to pop over?'

Both Leon and Anya hovered nearby while she examined the baby, who remained unresponsive throughout.

Her voice was textbook professional: 'Sit down a minute, Anya.'

Anya backed into a chair, eyes never leaving Tiffany's face.

'Listen, don't take this the wrong way, but have you given her anything – anything at all, done anything, that might account for this sleepiness?'

'Nothing. I haven't given her *anything*, full stop. Not even a drink. She hasn't woken up. Not since I gave her lunch just after you left.'

'And you said she was irritable this morning, wasn't she?'

'Yes.' It came out as a hoarse whisper.

'And you can't think of any explanation for her lethargy now.'

Anya shook her head, eyes wide.

'Then no question, we need to get her to the hospital – now!'

'What d'you *think* it could be?' Leon said, his hand gripping Anya's so tightly, his wedding ring cut into her fingers.

'Not sure. But ... it could be the start of something.'

'Like?'

'Maybe ... an infection ... meningitis.'

'Bloody hell!' Leon spat out. 'What are we waiting for?'

He drove furiously, Anya's eyes glued to the baby on the back seat, Tiffany doing her best to backtrack on her tentative suggestion.

But the paediatrician, hearing the story, seeing the baby, was taking no chances.

'We'll just pop a needle in her spine.'

CHAPTER 18

Irritation smouldered in spite of Lucinda's best efforts to stay calm. No one was taking her concerns seriously here.

Fair enough, nothing conclusive had been found by either the clinic or the hospital, but on top of all the little crises, this baby was now losing weight, not reaching the normal centiles. And the mother was ... well, what was she?

Something wasn't right.

A fresh eye might help, someone to share the responsibility.

Robert Brownlee had been uncharacteristically brusque. 'You're reading way too much into this, Lucinda. Back off. She'll get there in the end.'

She'd dug in her heels. This was exactly why the referral system had been set up; to make sure no single agency – no near-retirement doctor wanting a peaceful life – could overrule a colleague's legitimate qualms.

Robert avoided her gaze, leaned back in his chair, his usual bonhomie nowhere to be seen.

'The kid's fine. She's been checked out by the paeds at Sick Kids as well as us.'

'Where are you going with this, Lucinda?' Coral Jones sniffed. 'Next you'll be telling us it's a case of child abuse!'

'Why not make it Munchausen's by Proxy!' Robert chipped in. 'Just what I need to end my working days in this community. Go out in a blaze of glory. Or ignominy, more like.'

'Philistine! At least give it its proper modern name! Fabricated or Induced Illness,' Simon Brocklehurst grinned.

Lucinda felt her jaw clench.

'I know it all seems far-fetched. The family don't fit the

usual kind of profile. But … I don't like it. And I don't think this mother is a reliable witness.'

'So, this hunch you've got … I presume it means you want to involve Social Work?'

'I don't *want* to. Anya would be furious. But I think we *ought* to.'

Robert surveyed the faces around the table.

'Anybody?'

'You tried offering practical assistance?' Coral said.

'Yes.'

'And?'

'She categorically refused. And to be honest, I'm not surprised. She's super-organised. Super-efficient.'

'So, where's the problem?'

'The baby's not thriving and the mum's still hyper-anxious. She's … sort of haunted.'

'Poltergeisty, kind of haunted, or disturbed, kind of haunted?' Simon asked.

'You might think this is all faintly amusing, Simon,' Lucinda snapped, 'but one thing's for sure: we've got a duty of care here. If we don't go with the approved process and something happens to this child … I, for one, would never forgive myself.'

'And if a social worker ticks the boxes, you'll let it go?' Robert asked. 'Or are you wanting to go the whole hog and bring in the police too?'

'At this stage I'd be happy with just Social Work. As long as I'm satisfied they've done a thorough check.'

'Well, if it means you'll sleep easy in your bed, I suppose we can't deny you the right to an independent opinion. But I can't pretend I'm happy about wasting resources here, when we've got a hundred and one underprivileged families much more deserving of support on our caseload.'

The tension felt decidedly uncomfortable in spite of the grudging agreement.

Jane Carver had a stillness about her that was immensely

reassuring. Lucinda was struck again by the loveliness of this woman who saw so much of the seamy side of life. The luxuriant fair hair was swept up in a neat French pleat; the translucent skin, full lips, perfect teeth, owed more to heredity than cosmetics; her commanding height and excellent posture gave her an air of quiet authority that inspired respect. And at thirty-nine she had plenty of experience under her belt – exactly what Lucinda needed.

She nodded slowly. 'If there's a possibility of abuse, even in its mildest form, then it's a child protection issue. We *need* to be involved.'

'I've given this some thought,' Lucinda said cautiously. 'The last thing I want to do is antagonise Anya. I'm wondering if we could say that it's standard practice to draft in extra support after a certain number of trips to hospital, and with some evidence of a baby not reaching their milestones. Just as a precaution. To monitor things, make sure there's nothing underlying these blips that we ought to be taking steps to address. Better to err on the side of caution, rather than wait till there's a real problem. Play it by ear and plead time-constraints or different areas of expertise, maybe. If she knows it's because we want the very best for Gypsy, I think she might ... *might* just buy it.'

'Sounds good to me. Might be useful if we go together for the first visit, if you can spare the time.'

'I agree. If I could introduce you as my friend, it could soften things a bit. And thanks, Jane. I know you guys are horrifically overstretched, and this must sound like a storm in a teacup compared with all the horrors you deal with.'

'Well, I wouldn't say no to half an hour in a lovely clean house with a woman who isn't shouting and cussing, with no necessity to run for my life from a violent bloke who threatens to massacre our entire department if I dare to lay a finger on his property, aka his horde of feral kids. What's not to like?'

'Great. I really like this mum. But just in the short time I've been seeing her, I can see she's changed. Something's bugging her. But whatever it is, I couldn't bear the thought of taking her baby away. She adores Gypsy, that's abundantly plain.'

'Let's hope it won't come to that. And you know me, splitting up families is definitely a very last resort.'

'I know. Last thing we need here is a gung-ho novice frightened to death of litigation, seizing the kiddie at the first suggestion of trouble.'

'Although, the boss hasn't chosen me for this case because she thinks I've got special sensitivity; she's just shuffling papers. As long as she's got a name on the dotted line, she's not asking if there're enough hours in my day.'

'Still as overworked and understaffed as ever then?'

'Yep. And we're another man down right now. Sohier Kartoum walked out earlier this month. Just couldn't hack it any longer.'

'It must really take its toll, the kind of problems you deal with. I wouldn't last a week.'

'It's an acquired taste, I guess. And it can be pretty thankless.' .

'Damned if you do; damned if you don't.'

'Something like that. But for every case where the press lynch us, there's a thousand little triumphs where we rescue kids and put families back together again. All unseen, but so rewarding. Just working with a dysfunctional family, supporting them, encouraging them, seeing them stick together. But I do hate, hate, hate, the ones where we've run out of options and have to take the kids away for their own safety. Kills me every time.'

'And you have to live with the consequences.'

Jane nodded.

'Is it still Sharon Vine at the helm?'

'The very same.' Jane pulled a face.

'How much longer has she got to go?'

'Couple of years max ... if she sees out her full time, that is. Lots of them retire early. Wouldn't want her job for all the chocolate in Africa.'

'Wouldn't you? I was about to say, you'd make a great boss. All that empathy with the crew and all your hands-on experience and your lovely way with people.'

'Well, I'm not so sure about that. I guess when the buck stops with you, and all these demands keep piling in, your hands are pretty much tied. But anyway, it's not going to happen. My boyfriend – correction, fiancé – would never want me doing admin. I'd be an absolute pain in the backside to live with, and he's got enough hassles with his job without me burdening him with mine.'

'What's he do?'

'Jeremy? He's a police officer.'

'Oh wow! You two must have some crazy conversations.'

'He reckons he's locking up the guys our lot failed in their youth.'

'Charming!'

'So, if your Anya Morgan's hubby comes baying for my blood, just you make sure Detective Sergeant Jeremy Tait doesn't find out you referred the case …!'

'The protective kind, is he?'

'You could say. Which is rather sweet given I'm three inches taller and probably got more enemies than he has.'

'You two set a date yet?'

'If we both survive, sometime next year; autumn probably.'

'Well, it won't be Leon Morgan wot does yer in. He's a perfect gentleman.'

'So's Jeremy, but if he found out some busybody – no offence – was trying to blame me for hurting our baby, there's no telling what he might or might not do. Alpha male mentality kicks in, fighting for his mate and cubs, and all that jazz.'

Lucinda cowered in mock terror.

'Plus, we're into red flag territory here,' Jane added.

'Meaning?'

'He operates a zero-tolerance policy where all kids are concerned. Doesn't have to be an outsider harming them to get him rattled. Woe betide any *parent* who comes into his orbit if they've done anything to harm a baby. No mercy.'

Back in her flat Lucinda felt a chill run through her spine.

Was Leon Morgan a typical alpha male? What exactly was going on behind those expensive closed doors? Could he be ...?

There was most definitely *something* driving a wedge between this couple.

CHAPTER 19

These days Leon himself didn't feel like alpha anything, either at home or at work.

Thomas insisted he had to be a presence in the factory, show the staff he was up to the job, not running scared, but Leon knew there was talk. Staying at The Old Vicarage was fraught with tension, and Thomas was not best pleased by his reluctance to take up Juliette's offer of talking through the Fowler case informally with her. 'I don't think we should drag her into this,' met with 'The whole bloody family's going to be dragged into it if we don't reach some kind of resolution soon.'

His comfortable relationship with Bill Broadbent had been replaced with uneasy formality and stilted conversation. So, when he arrived early for a meeting and found Bill already there, Leon steeled himself for an uncomfortable wait.

The manager was as meticulous in his manners as he was in his dress – favouring sharply creased tweeds in muted colours, superior leather brogues, crisply ironed shirts, toning ties; he stood as Leon entered the room. They exchanged polite civilities and Leon was surprised when Bill soon broke the silence with, 'How's your young bairn these days, sir?'

'Growing like a mushroom. Thanks for asking, Bill.'

'Wee pet.'

A long pause.

'And Mrs Leon? Sorry to hear she's been under the weather.'

What did you tell him, Thomas?

'She's getting there. And I do feel bad about having to take time off.'

'We all knew it had to be an emergency.'

'Thank you for that.' Leon hesitated ... *should he* ... ?
'Thomas mentioned your good lady had a spot of trouble
when your youngest was born ...?'

'Wey aye, she did that. And I were glad of time off then.
Mr Douglas, he were champion. Even saw to it we got
temporary accommodation till the boiler were fixed.'

'I don't know the detail ... but I vaguely recall my
father mentioning poison – I was only a lad at the time, and it
rather scared me, actually. It *was* poison of some kind, wasn't
it?'

'Aye. Carbon monoxide.'

'Really? If you don't mind my asking, how did you find
out?'

'The wee lass, she were proper peeky, like, sleeping a
lot, fussing and fretting, upset tummy. Not a bit like her
sisters at that age. And Gertie – that's the missus – she were
right paggered, as we say down here; dizzy, nauseous, short of
breath, tummy upsets. Gertie, she put it down to three bairns
one after the other, but then she started to get confused, and I
don't mind telling you, that *did* put the wind up me, man, and
no mistake! She's never been one for fanciful notions. Straight
down the line plain speaking, plain acting, no frills, no add-
ons, that's our Gertie. So, when she started forgetting stuff,
wandering round in a dwam ... well, that's when I says, "No
arguments, you're seeing the doc, even if I have to drag you
their meself."

'And there it were, carbon monoxide. Turns out there
were a faulty boiler in this flat we were renting, in the
cupboard in the bairn's room, like. Gertie were feeding her in
that wee bedroom, so they were both exposed to the fumes
more'n the rest of us. Give him his due, the landlord were
onto it quick smart soon's he knew. Right apologetic and
everything. But I don't mind telling you, Mr Leon, it give us
all a mighty scare.'

'I'm sure it did! And now? Are they ...?'

'Aye. They're champion. I looked it up on the computer,
and it says it can impair intellectual function long term, so
we've a lot to be thankful for.'

'Did you ever pursue it ... seek compensation?'

Bill gave him a hard look.

'Gertie and me, we aren't the kind to dwell on what cannot be changed.'

The shutters were down again.

'You're a good man, Bill. We're lucky to have you in the company. I know my father and grandfather valued you hugely. As do we.'

Bill's chair scraped back as he stood again in deference to the other Morgan brothers.

The sudden change in mood niggled somewhere in the back of Leon's mind, but Bill's family were soon forgotten in the whirl of business and a difficult session with their lawyers who delivered a few unpalatable truths which left him smarting. He was appalled to realise he hadn't checked in with Anya for thirteen hours. There was no answer when he finally rang, so he left a brief message and went back to his client and one more strong coffee before he hit the road.

The Range Rover came out of nowhere and he wrenched the steering wheel violently to avoid a head-on collision. The sickening sound of his prized Audi scraping along a metal spike tore through his fatigue, and he pulled into the first layby with a hollow dread. It was every bit as bad as he'd imagined. He cursed the Range Rover. He cursed his own moment of inattention. He cursed that last customer. He cursed the deserted area. He cursed the absent signal which meant he couldn't let Anya know he'd be late.

What wouldn't he give for a drink! But a nap would have to suffice.

It was dark when he eventually came to and resumed his journey; too late to ring home even if he could find somewhere with a signal. Besides it'd all waste valuable time.

There were no welcoming lights to greet him. Good, she hadn't waited up. He crept upstairs, peeped in on Anya, then Gypsy, before tiptoeing into the spare bedroom for what was left of a wretched night.

CHAPTER 20

Anya was sorting laundry in the utility room when he surfaced next morning and startled when he spoke.

'I'm so, so sorry I was late last night, honey. I couldn't get a signal to let you know.'

No answer. She finished loading the machine and switched it on before turning, walking past him with her eyes averted.

'Hey. Am I in disgrace?'

'I don't know. Are you?'

Had she somehow heard ...?

'At least have the decency to look at me and tell me why you're mad.'

She filled the kettle. 'We're clearly not a priority anymore, so why should I be surprised by anything you do?'

'Good grief, Anya. What's got into you?'

'What's got into *me*? Well, that's rich, I must say.'

'And whatever gave you the idea that you and Gypsy aren't my priorities? Everything I do is for you.'

'Everything?!" The sarcasm, the sneering look, chilled his blood.

'Yes. Everything. The hours. The miles. The days away from home. The whole bloody thing. To give you and Gypsy a decent life.'

'Well, maybe your idea of decent isn't the same as mine.'

She stalked out of the kitchen without so much as a glance in his direction, his bewilderment lost in the sudden emptiness.

He heard her moving about upstairs, footsteps on the stairs, the sound of the pram wheels, the click of the front door, the silence of absence.

She had crossed a rubicon here; never before had either left the house in anger.

What was he supposed to do now? Go to work as if nothing had happened? Stay at home and risk Thomas' exasperation?

He was no clearer in his mind after breakfast. His phone calls went straight to voicemail, his texts were ignored.

He shot home at lunch time in the Vauxhall the garage had loaned him. Still no sign of habitation. The lilies and roses he left on the kitchen table with a note felt clichéd:

I'm sorry. You are my world. XXX

It was impossible to concentrate on anything and by 4:30 he abandoned the attempt.

Erratic heartbeats filled his throat as he opened the door …

What if … ?

The pram was back in its customary spot.

He let out his breath in a shudder of visceral relief.

Classic FM played softly in the kitchen. A bag of fresh vegetables lay beside the sink. The Aga was turned up high. Normal, everyday life chez the Morgans.

The flowers and note looked untouched.

Leon slipped off his shoes, put them neatly in the rack, hung his jacket up on a hanger, stowed his briefcase in his study. No point in inviting trouble.

He was peeling potatoes when Anya came into the kitchen.

'Roast? Mashed? Chips? Boiled?' He kept it neutral.

'Dauphinoise.'

'OK.'

She left without another word.

Leon sliced the vegetables, crushed the garlic, with venom. For the first time, he understood his mother's words: *Chopping things fine gets rid of a lot of tension.* He'd seen her absolutely killing an onion! What would she advise now?

104

Always be ready to take the blame, even when you're right.

He popped the dauphinoise in the Aga and went in search of his wife. She was kneeling on the floor in their bedroom, surrounded by piles of scarves, folding each one meticulously and re-stacking them in neat piles.

Leon crouched beside her.

'I'm sorry I've upset you. Please, talk to me.'

She continued to separate the silky fabric from the fine wool, the patterned from the plain, creating a lovely rainbow of colours, but he saw the sparkle of tears. He moved in and slipped an arm around her shoulders. She didn't resist. He stroked the fragrant hair.

Not until the silent sobs subsided did he risk speaking.

'Look, Anya, I'm completely at sea here. But I'm going nowhere till we get to the bottom of this. I need to know what's wrong, at the very least.'

Anya seemed to struggle with herself before she managed, 'Thanks to you we're now a family who need a social worker watching our every move.'

'*What?!*'

'Apparently, I'm an unfit mother. Can't be trusted to look after my own baby.'

'What's it got to do with *me*? *I* didn't call in any social worker.'

'Not directly, maybe.'

'Hey, stop right there. Rewind. Tell me what's happened – from the beginning.'

'One: Gypsy's been in and out of the surgery and the hospital too many times. Two: she's not gaining weight like she should. Three: you're never here. Conclusion: it's all down to me, and apparently I'm an inadequate mother.'

'Inadequate? *You*? Don't be silly.'

'I'm the kind of mother who can't remember what she's done with her baby. Remember? The kind who does things that give her the runs, or make her lethargic. I'm a hideous kind of mother. A mother who's a danger to her own child. Even my own husband thinks so.'

'When did I ever give you that impression?'

'When you didn't believe me that day in the park. When you said as much to the police. I *did* take Gypsy with me. I did. I *know* I did. And when we took her to the hospital that day when she wouldn't wake up. You told them you were worried I might have given her something. I know you did.'

'Who told you that?'

'Tiffany.'

'Damn that bloody interfering woman.'

'Because she told it like it really is.'

'It wasn't like that.'

'So, what *was* it like?' She turned her eyes to him at last.

'They were going over every conceivable cause for her being so sleepy. And they wanted to know if there was any possibility she might have been given something she shouldn't have at her age. Routine kinds of questions. And they asked me how you'd been recently. I couldn't in all conscience say you'd been fine. You *haven't* been yourself for ages, have you? Not since you had the baby really. It's not a criticism, it's just a fact. But I laid it on thick that you loved Gypsy to bits; you'd never in a million years do anything *deliberately* to harm her. Not if you were thinking straight. I said that. I swear, I did.'

'Qualified loyalty, then. If I'm "thinking straight." So, you think I'm not.'

'I don't know. I just don't understand what's going on.'

'Well, they – the professionals – they aren't convinced that I love my baby more than anything in the world. They think I'm some kind of a monster. Doesn't seem to occur to them that it might not be *me* ... doing things.' The look she gave him froze him in his tracks.

'What does *that* mean?'

She fixed him with a cold glare.

'It's a whole different ball game when *you're* on the other end of the suspicion, isn't it?'

He recoiled. '*Me?!* You aren't serious ... Are you actually suggesting ...?'

'You've changed, Leon. Don't think I haven't noticed.'

What could he say?

She spared him the necessity of defending the indefensible. 'You could be doing, saying, just enough to make it look like I'm losing the plot. You hear about people doing that.'

Leon stared at his wife in horror.

'So, you'd better watch out.' Anya's voice had dropped to a sinister hiss. 'There's an extra pair of eyes watching us now. Keeping notes. Looking for the least sign.'

'A *social worker*? Hell, Anya ... what *is* going on? This is like some ruddy nightmare.'

'Tell me about it.'

'Have you told them you suspect me?'

'Maybe I have. Maybe I haven't.'

He clutched his head in his hands and swore eloquently. 'That's all I need!'

When he eventually lifted his gaze, she was staring at him without expression.

'What's happening to us, Anya? None of this makes a blind bit of sense.'

'Doesn't it?'

'You mean ... it makes sense to you?'

'I can think of a certain logic.'

'Well, for Pete's sake, explain it to me.'

'You want out of this marriage.'

'You are kidding, right?'

'Do I look like I'm in the mood for jest?'

'Why on earth would I want out of our marriage?'

'Because you've fallen for somebody else.'

'Now you're being ridiculous.'

'There you go again. Turning this around onto me. It's always my fault.'

And with that she rose to her feet and walked stiffly out of the room.

Not until she was on her way to bed did Leon attempt to make further contact.

'For what it's worth, I'm getting the Aga tested this week.'

'Why? It's not due till July.'

'I'm suspicious it's malfunctioning. There could be a blockage in the flue or … something.'

She frowned. 'What makes you suddenly think that?'

'Carbon monoxide poisoning can make you feel generally unwell, confused …'

She stood like a statue.

'Since Gypsy … you're spending much more time in the kitchen and utility room …'

She turned without a word and headed up the stairs.

CHAPTER 21

No social worker was going to judge Anya Kathryn Morgan deficient on any yardstick in her armamentarium. Leon was spending less and less time at home, so with any luck, the professionals wouldn't even meet him, never mind hear his doubts about her mental stability.

If only he hadn't driven her beyond endurance, forced her to blurt out her suspicions before she had real proof, giving him more ammunition to use against her. But, sitting there, being all reasonable, the patient husband soothing his crazy wife ... what a hypocrite! ... it had simply spilled out.

But who would believe her? Leon was out there in the real world, handsome, debonair, together, successful, coherent, logical. Proving his impeccable credentials over and over again. No one else saw the shifty behaviour, the avoided looks, the sneaking into the spare room, the excuses. They didn't detect the foreign scent, note the absence of phone calls, the flimsy excuses, the illogical reasoning.

Three nights later her suspicions were confirmed.

She'd tossed and turned until 2:30, then crept downstairs to make a hot drink. A light still shone below the door of Leon's study and she padded towards it. His voice was low and intimate but enough to stop her in her tracks.

'I could really use that hug right now.'

...

'We'll talk again tomorrow – if that's all right your end?'

...

'Bless you.'

...

'Night night. Sleep well.'

...

'Same to you.' The unmistakeable sound of a blown kiss.

Exhausted from lack of sleep, on high alert, Anya startled when her own phone rang at lunchtime the following day. But it was only her sister-in-law, Juliette. She was on annual leave and fancied a trip to Edinburgh. Was Anya free on Friday? It'd be good to meet up, see Gypsy.

Persistent rain put paid to their plans and an afternoon at the house seemed preferable to sloshing through the streets with sodden feet and a baby invisible behind plastic. The two women had always been at ease in each other's company, grumbling mildly together about the Morgan men, the family business.

Anya knew a great sense of relief when Gypsy behaved impeccably for her aunt. For one glorious day she was a normal mother, proudly sharing her normal baby, safe and secure in her normal home, enjoying normal companionship.

In spite of the weather, Juliette could not be persuaded to stay overnight. Nor would she share an evening meal. She 'wasn't too keen' on these driving conditions in the dark. She'd wait just long enough to say hi to Leon when he returned home, and then make tracks.

'Back to the madness we in Newcastle call wur hame!'

Leon had only been in ten minutes when Juliette began to take her leave. Quite what made her glance at her husband, Anya didn't know, but the look on his face was unmistakeable. And he was staring at Juliette.

Burying her face in Gypsy's neck, pretend-eating her skin until the child gurgled and thrashed with delight, Juliette looked stunning. Her shiny white hair was lit from behind, creating a halo effect, her dark eyes were alive with laughter, her skin glowed with health, a rose-pink low-cut cashmere jumper emphasised her generous curves, black skinny jeans outlined her long slim legs.

No wonder Leon was mesmerised. What red-blooded male wouldn't be?

But there was no such rational explanation for what happened when Juliette moved to take her leave of him. He held up a hand to ward her off.

'I'll see you out, make sure you don't dissolve between here and the car,' he said lightly.

Under one umbrella the two figures suddenly seemed absurdly close. The black canopy masked their faces but Anya saw Juliette pass something to Leon which he immediately slipped into his jacket pocket, before they leaned in for a farewell kiss. A brief contact, no more, even to her feverish imagination. Heedless of the downpour, Leon remained in the drive, watching until the rear lights vanished. One final wave and she was gone.

Anya was in the nursery preparing Gypsy for bed by the time he found her.

'Foul night for driving,' he said. 'She should have stayed.'

'We'll ring later. Check she's safely back.'

'She promised to let us know .... whatever the hour. I'll stay up.'

Anya said nothing.

'Want me to finish off here?' he asked.

'If you like.'

She left the room without a backward glance, the low rumble of his singing to Gypsy following her:

'Row, row, row your boat
Gently down the stream.
Merrily, merrily, merrily, merrily.
Life is but a dream.
Row, row, row your boat ...'

His jacket hung in the hall. Left hand pocket ... A tissue ... rubber band ... small folded piece of paper.

She hesitated. There would be no going back if she opened it ...

> **01890 882255**
> **Booked. Usual name.**
> **J X**

111

It took only seconds to enter the number in her phone.

Tillmouth Park Country House Hotel.

Google supplied the detail.

Nestled in the Secret Kingdom of North Northumberland midway between Edinburgh and Newcastle, Tillmouth Park is one of the region's very best kept secrets ...

A place to escape ...

A perfect hideaway for a secret assignation ....

Leon ... and *Juliette*?

'Usual name' – how long had this been going on?

CHAPTER 22

It was clearly not a good day to appear unannounced. Lucinda's heart sank. She'd never seen this Anya before. Hair scraped back in a ragged pony tail, face devoid of makeup, jeans and tee shirt spattered with cleaning fluids. Dishevelled. Wired.

Strong smell of bleach in the air as if someone was removing all trace of a crime. Contents of the kitchen cupboards strewn across the surfaces, rice scattered over the floor where someone had dropped ... *or thrown?* ... a packet. Washing machine, dishwasher, tumble dryer, all competing for pre-eminence, piles of bedding heaped on the floor as if the entire house was being purged.

'I'm afraid we've called at a bad time,' Lucinda said, backing away.

'Did you just want to check up on Gypsy?' Anya's voice was hard. 'She's still alive. See for yourself.'

She strode across to the playroom, opened the door with a flourish.

Gypsy lay fast asleep in her playpen.

'I'm sorry, Anya ...' Lucinda began.

'Oh, don't be. I'm getting rather inured to criticism by now. Feel free to wake her and do your worst. I daresay she'll go back to sleep eventually. And if not, well, you already know I'm a lousy mother.'

'Anya ... Anya ... what's going on?'

'Just when I think things can't get any worse ...'

Lucinda approached Anya and put a firm hand on each arm. 'Sit down a minute. Please. Tell me what's happened.'

But Anya flounced out of her hold.

'I don't have to tell *anybody anything*. This is *my* life.

113

My home. And if I want to spring clean the entire place, I can. It's not a crime, is it?'

'No, of course it's not. But this is more than you spring cleaning. And I can't just walk away when I can see how upset you are.'

'Why not? Doesn't everybody get upset? I'm entitled to have a rubbish day, aren't I, without my performance being recorded on some stupid scale or other?'

'Yes, of course, but …'

'Look, say what you came to say and then leave me be, OK? That's all I want. Just to be left alone.'

Lucinda hesitated.

'Well, remember I told you about the protocols we have to follow? That I was bringing a friend of mine …'

'The social worker. Yes, I remember. I didn't believe your lame excuses then, and I don't now, but go ahead, what about her?'

'I'm so sorry, I know this is dreadful timing, but she's outside in the car …'

'What, now? Here? Today?' Anya was casting wild looks around her chaotic kitchen.

'Listen, it doesn't matter about the … Everybody's house looks a bit messy when they're doing a big clean …'

'But *everybody* doesn't have professional snoopers poking around looking for trouble.'

'I promise you, she's not. She just wants to help. And to do that she needs to see for herself you're all right, Gypsy's all right …'

'Can't she come back another day? I'm not usually in a state like …'

'I know. I *know*, Anya. I've seen you loads of times, remember? But it's all right. She isn't here to see you dressed in your Sunday best, embroidering a sampler, crooking your pinkie over a cup of Earl Grey in a bone china cup and saucer.' Lucinda mimed each action, doing her best to coax a smile. 'She wants to see real life, and real life for you today is being Mrs Super-housewife. She'll probably want to employ you to sort her place out!'

Anya's shoulders relaxed a fraction.

'Can you give me five minutes …?'

'Of course.'

The Anya who returned was a close approximation to the one Lucinda knew. To a casual observer, the picture of a serene, confident, well-off woman. Only the glittering eyes, restless fingers twitching at the silicone wristband, betrayed her.

Lucinda took a deep breath. 'All right if I invite Jane to come in now?'

'Yes.'

Anya was watching from the doorway so there was no opportunity for anything more than a murmured, 'Go cannily', under her breath. But Jane was impressive to watch. Her approach was natural and measured, her smile wide and friendly, her voice low and soothing.

'Hi, Anya. I'm Jane Carver. Thank you so much for allowing me to visit you at home.'

Anya offered a hand, the instinctive hostess.

'Nice to meet you. Excuse the mess. Lucinda probably told you, you've caught me on a bad day. I'm having a bit of a spring clean. Making the most of a lovely sunny day. Shows up all the dust and cobwebs, doesn't it, the sun?'

'Don't worry about that. And I know exactly what you mean about the sun. I had no idea my windows were so disgustingly filthy until this better weather started. But I'm way behind you with my catch up.'

Anya had closed the door on the noise and chaos, and the sitting room felt restful. She calmly offered her guests coffee, produced home-made chocolate muffins.

'Wow, you are some cook. That was delicious.' No outward sign yet of Jane's professional antennae.

'Thanks.'

'Now, I should just explain, Anya. My role isn't to interfere, or pass judgement, or make life difficult. My job is to help. So, all I'm needing to do today, is to check you're coping all right, and if you *could* use some help, find out how best we can supply that support. I'm your friend not your enemy, you understand?'

Anya gave a half-hearted nod.

'So, a few basic questions, a quick check or two, and we'll be done. You can get back to restoring order in your fab kitchen. Sorry, I'm nosey. I caught a wee glimpse when you went for the coffee. Looks new. Did you put it in or was it here when you came?'

'We put it in.'

'You've obviously got a real eye.' Jane's gesture embraced the whole house. 'Your colours are fantastic – like something out of an ideal home catalogue.'

'Thanks. Apart from the chaos in the kitchen.'

'That just shows me you're a busy mum, doing ordinary everyday things, fastidious about cleanliness. We don't care about a temporary guddle.'

By the time Jane began her formal questions, Anya was a model of composure and reasonableness. Birth family, career, marriage, social network, interests ... nothing gave Lucinda so much as a passing qualm. Inspection of Gypsy's room ... the parents' bedroom ... the bathrooms ... Anya took it all in her stride. Even questions about the medical emergencies were recounted with calm precision, almost as if she'd learned the detail off by heart. Chapter and verse. Textbook correct. And Gypsy herself was displayed without a moment's hesitation.

Not until they were driving away from the house, waved off by a smiling mother, holding a contented baby, did Lucinda slump in her seat and let her breath out in a whoosh.

'That woman is one hell of an actor.'

'Hmmm. Tell me more.'

CHAPTER 23

Nine in the morning? You have to be kidding! Did social workers call unannounced before a body could even clear up the evidence of breakfast? Anya pushed the plates and mugs into the dishwasher, bundled the washing into the machine and slammed the door on it.

Best smile firmly pinned on, she opened the door … She felt her whole body sag with relief.

'You all right?' Tiffany's face was wreathed in concern.

'Yep. I'm fine. Come in.'

'Sorry I've not been for ages. Didn't want to bring you any unwelcome guests.'

Anya spun round. 'What unwelcome guests?'

Could Tiffany Corrigan be part of the surveillance too? A spy in cuddly-toy clothing.

'Bugs. The dreaded norovirus to be precise.'

Anya shrank away from her friend.

'Oh, don't worry, we're totally clear. By a country mile. What *is* a country mile? I've never understood that expression, but hey, who cares? We're absolutely squeaky clean. Even using Miss Hannigan's OTT measures.'

'Who's Miss Hannigan?'

'Head teacher at the primary school where our kids go.'

'I'm getting a bit lost here.'

'Sorry.' Tiffany sank onto a stool at the central island. 'Our Jude's had the old norovirus. Been galloping through the school apparently. In my day, they reckoned people were only contagious for three days after recovery, but this head's a stickler for health and safety. We got letters telling us to keep them off school for two weeks. *Two weeks!* I ask you. Apparently, she read somewhere, folk can occasionally remain

117

contagious that long – extreme end of the bell curve and all that jazz. But can you imagine what an energetic seven-year-old's like after being cooped up indoors for *fourteen days*? Typical though. From a number-crunching autocrat who's never had kids herself.'

'What about the girls? Did they get it too?'

'Nah. Fit as fleas. Mind you, we went into overdrive with the hand-washing and antibacterial lotions and potions, the whole shebang. House stinks of antiseptic! You could eat your lunch off our bathroom floor!'

'So, Jude, is he fine again now? Was he really poorly with it?'

'Well, he was for a day or two, but kids soon bob up again.'

'Remind me again, what are the symptoms?'

'Nausea and generally yucky feeling, initially. Then vomiting, diarrhoea, abdo pain. Same as gastroenteritis, really. But it's pretty contagious, which is why you get these waves of it, usually at winter time, that hit the headlines and play havoc with hospital admissions and waiting times. I took time off as a precaution simply because of where I work.'

'And how long after you come in contact with it does it manifest itself, if you do catch it?'

'Twelve to forty-eight hours … but listen, Anya, don't start thinking Gypsy's going down with it if she gets the squits in the next few days. We're totally out of the infectious stage. And I'm a nurse, I know all about hygiene and infection control. Heck! I even stopped the rest of the family getting it, and we're all living in the same house, touching the same door handles, using the same loos and wash hand basins. The neighbours must think everybody's birthday's in April! We've been singing *Happy Birthday to You* umpteen times a day, while they sanitised every milli-milli-milli-millimetre of their hands and nails!'

Anya was lost again.

'That's how long it should take; as long as it takes to sing that dratted ditty all the way through.'

'Oh.'

'But I know you're extra, ultra, uber-protective of Gypsy – and I don't blame you – so I stayed well away from you.'

'I appreciate that, but I wasn't thinking about *you* bringing it here. It's just that Gypsy started with watery stools this morning. She does get loose movements occasionally but well, I'm just wondering, hearing what you just said, could she …'

'Is she out of sorts in herself?'

'No. Not that I've noticed.'

'Whingey?'

'No.'

'Off her food?'

'No.'

'Then she isn't going down with this virus. Probably a surfeit of figs and curly kale, if I know you!'

Anya smiled wryly.

'You look peaky, Anya. You well yourself?'

'Just tired.'

The response sounded more terse than she intended, but Anya kept her eyes on the coffee pot as she filled two mugs, and offered a plate of date and walnut cake.

'Mmmhmm. I've missed your scrumptious cooking.' Tiffany settled herself more firmly on the stool, closed her eyes, and took a large bite. 'Delish. So, what's been happening in your world while I've been in germ-assassination mode?'

'Not a lot.'

'You still worried about Gypsy's bowels?'

'A bit.'

'Have you been to see about it? Asked the health visitor or GP or anybody?'

'No. They all think I'm over-anxious already. No point in giving them ammunition.'

'Eeeh dear. Well, *I* sympathise. And if I were you, I wouldn't care tuppence what they think. If you're worried, you get some advice. And if I can help, I'm happy to back you. Some of these people are too full of themselves in my opinion. Lost sight of what the service is there for. Heck, it's a health visitor's *job* to take care of the nought to fives. It's the very reason for her existence. And they jolly well *ought* to listen. Nobody's as tuned in to a kiddie's health and welfare as the mum is.'

Anya felt the tears well and turned away to busy herself with a second coffee.

'Hey, what's up?' Tiffany was on her feet, arm around Anya. 'Was it something I said?'

'No. I'm fine. It's just ... nobody else seems to understand.'

'You poor love. Let it out. A good old cry'll do you good.'

Three tissues later Anya felt able to speak.

'Sorry.'

'Don't be. Things must be pretty awful for a kind word to reduce you to this. What on earth's going on here?'

'Gypsy's not up to where she should be on the centiles. And they think I'm neurotic, and pestering the medical people too often. More times than I'm allowed apparently. So now they've drafted in a *social worker*!'

'You're joking!' Tiffany spluttered on her coffee.

Anya shook her head.

'They must be out of their tiny minds,' Tiffany said. 'Flipping heck, if *you* need a social worker, heaven help the rest of the population! I mean to say. Look at you ... your house ... everything. You're A-star material.'

'Not in their judgement. I feel so ... such a failure.'

Tiffany turned to face Anya squarely. 'Listen to me, Anya Morgan. You are *not* a failure. I repeat: *you are not a failure*. You hear me? Right enough, you *are* a tad obsessive sometimes, I grant you, but that's only because your standards are higher than everybody else's. That doesn't make you a poor mother. I can't believe this! What a ridiculous waste of scarce resources to draft in a social worker *here*! Absolutely takes the biscuit. I never heard such a crazy notion in all my life.'

'Thanks, Tiffany. I just ... I'm so wound up, expecting the social worker to call any minute, all the time worrying what she'd make of what she sees if she does. It's a complete nightmare.'

'*Has* she called unannounced?'

'Just the once so far.'

'But it's always hanging over you. Blimey O'Riley, I'd be going mental.'

'Well, they think I'm already there!'

'Don't be silly. You're as sane as anybody I know.'

'Try telling them that.'

'What does Leon make of all this nonsense?'

'He thinks I'm losing the plot too.'

'You're kidding! You sure you haven't been reading too many novels?'

'If only!'

'Men can be such morons at times. Even the best of them. They ought to go through some of the hormonal stuff we do, the sheer chaos of childbearing. They'd soon show a bit more understanding. I reckon it's a design fault, everything dumped on the woman. Although my mother would tell me to wash my mouth out and do six days of penance for daring to criticise the great Creator!'

'I even question my own sanity sometimes. *Did* I take the baby into the park that day? Did she *really* have blood in her nappy? Am I *imagining* the pile of dirty nappies? I took a photo of her diarrhoea last week just in case …'

'Look, the last thing you need is to doubt yourself. If you want outside corroboration, you send for me, yes? I'll tell you if you're imagining things. Although I'm sure you're not. I was there when she had blood in her nappy, remember. And I've seen the loose stools. I'll back you. Don't let them mess with your head.'

'Thanks, Tiffany. I feel better for having told somebody – somebody who actually believes me.'

'It's agreed, then. You aren't on your own. But where's that gorgeous bundle of babyhood of yours? I've missed my cuddles.'

It was a turning point. At last, someone indisputably on her side; someone whose knowledge and experience she respected. Somewhere to turn for advice, with no fear of reprisals. Although …

No, strictly baby-related matters. The state of her marriage was her own affair.

CHAPTER 24

Why did men always have to assume they knew best? Why did they have to be in control all the time?

She'd held her irritation in check even as she confronted Leon directly. 'I thought you were going to be away at the trade fair at the NEC in Birmingham tomorrow?'

There really *was* a trade fair at the NEC – she'd checked. And Juliette was in Boston, USA, at a conference. Leon's passport was still in the drawer. It was safe to persist.

'I was. But I'm not now.' Terse.

'Why not? You're always saying you have to pull your weight.'

'Roger can take care of it.'

'He doesn't have your contacts. You said so yourself.'

'He'll make new ones. I should be here.'

'Why?'

He spread his hands in exasperation. 'There's no winning with you, is there? You accuse me of not helping enough, then when I *try* to be here, in case …'

'In case what?'

'You need me.'

'*If* I need anybody, there's always Claire. And Tiffany.'

She could see he was swithering. Time for her last ace.

'Besides I've made plans. You go. If there *is* any kind of emergency I'll keep you posted.'

'Definitely? Not like before.'

'No, I promise.'

Much as she might dislike being dictated to by Leon, she was grateful for Tiffany's motherly wisdom, natural, unthreatening, non-judgemental, and based on real experience and knowledge.

So, when she commented on the nappy rash, Anya listened.

'It's probably all these loose stools. Look, I admire your determination to keep Gypsy's diet wholesome and healthy, I really do, but I'd back off with the fibre for a few days, if I were you. And some soothing cream'd be good. Why don't you shoot along to the pharmacy, get the guy there to recommend something. He's really good, Vic. I'd go but he's sure to want details and you can answer all his questions better than I could.'

Anya recoiled.

'I don't fancy showing Gypsy's bottom to ...'

'Don't. Take a photo of the rash. I'll stay with her ladyship till you get back. It'll only take you fifteen, twenty minutes, tops.'

The pharmacist proved every bit as helpful as Tiffany had foretold, and joy of joys, he didn't criticise or doubt or call in reinforcements. No social worker suddenly appeared with probing eyes and tick-list questions.

The rash cleared quickly. But the diarrhoea continued unabated.

By the Saturday Tiffany voiced a new concern: dehydration.

'Push the fluids. That should help. Plenty of water.'

Anya pushed. Gypsy vomited. And vomited.

'Get your coat, Anya, we're going to A&E. To hang with them all. I'll drive you. I'll make sure they know it was *my* suggestion. Surgery's closed on Saturday so it has to be the hospital. This kid's poorly. I'll get her dressed and into her seat, while you get your bits and pieces together. Promise I won't take my eyes off her. Quick as you like.'

Trembling hands threw basic provisions into a bag. She half-ran, half-fell down the stairs.

Tiffany was leaning over Gypsy, now strapped in her car-seat, tension in every line.

'Now, don't panic, right? I ought to tell you – you're her mum, but stay calm, OK?'

'What? What's happened?'

'She's just had what looked to me like a mini-convulsion, so the sooner we go the better. I'll drive, you sit in the back with the baby. Shout if you need me to pull over.'

Anya's eyes remained glued to her daughter's face. Would she recognise a convulsion if she saw one? Should they change places? No, she was in no state to drive.

Oh please God! Hurry, hurry, hurry. Please God, please, please, please.

It was Tiffany who assumed control once they reached the hospital. She raced up to the reception desk, hard heels rapping out an urgent message.

'This is Gypsy Morgan, seven months. History of several days of loose stools, now dehydrated, had a convulsion … what?... thirty minutes ago. This is her mum, Anya. She'll fill you in on the details, but can you get a paed pronto, please?'

The receptionist instantly swung around on her seat and hailed a nurse.

'Gloria, you free to take this one? Convulsions.'

Staff Nurse Gloria Armitrading strode forward and took the child, her oversized ebony frame dwarfing the tiny figure in the car seat. She glanced briefly from Anya to Tiffany. 'Who's the mum?'

'Me.'

'So, Mum, come with me, your friend can wait in reception.'

The curtains swept around them and Anya entered a new phase of terror.

'What exactly happened?'

The salvo of questions came thick and fast, while the nurse expertly undressed Gypsy. In spite of her size she was both nimble-fingered and quick. She listened, felt, sounded, peered, probed, rechecked.

'Can you tell me about the convulsion? Has she had one before?'

'I didn't see it. You'd need to ask my friend.'

Enter Tiffany. Instant reassurance. The epitome of calm and authority.

'It only lasted ... less than twenty secs, I'd say. She suddenly went rigid, eyes rolled back so you could just see the white, blue around the mouth. It was over almost before I'd registered what was happening. She went all floppy afterwards, unresponsive. She didn't feel particularly hot, and she hasn't had a temperature recently, has she, Anya?'

'No.'

'So, how long has she had loose stools?'

As if to confirm her mother's veracity, Gypsy let loose an explosive jet of ochre slime. Gloria jumped out of range keeping one hand firmly on the child's torso.

The couch was still stained, the smell still pungent, when the curtain parted and a disembodied freckled face with close-cropped dark hair, and a chipped front incisor, asked in a beautifully modulated voice, 'Ready for me, Gloria?'

Anya desperately wanted to clear up the mess first, but Tiffany laid a restraining hand on her arm and shook her head imperceptibly.

Gloria slipped a clean incontinence pad under Gypsy. 'Yep. All yours.'

The tanned face was reconnected with a stocky body in dark green scrubs, the faint aura of deodorant momentarily overriding Gypsy's acrid emission.

'Hi. I'm Karl Vurtmeyer, one of the doctors.' He gave a nod, but his attention was instantly all on the baby. 'So, what have we got here?'

Gloria gave a rapid inventory and did her best to facilitate his examination of the wriggling form on the couch.

'Well, you're a bundle of energy, aren't you, Miss Gypsy?'

He doesn't think she's ill enough to be in hospital.

'So, Mum, what made you bring baby to the ED on a lovely sunny Saturday morning?'

Anya took a deep quivering breath before launching into an account.

Concentrate. The detail's important. The sequence.

'Any problems in the past?'

What exactly would constitute a problem to an Emergency doctor?

'Riiiight. Give me a moment, would you? I'd like to have a quick chat with my colleagues'

It's serious.

The wait felt like forever. Gypsy was fretful by now, hungry and tired. She refused to be cuddled, rejected all attempts at comfort.

By the time Dr Vurtmeyer reappeared, both mother and baby were sweating and fractious. He stood for a moment surveying the scene with a passive expression. When he spoke, his tone seemed more measured.

'Well, Mrs Morgan, I can't immediately see any reason for the convulsion on physical examination, but I note that Gypsy's been in before. I've had a look at her notes, and it seems you've been worried about her bowel habits for some time. I think given the history and today's events, we should keep her under observation for a bit, just to be on the safe side.'

'Observation? How long for?'

'Let's just see how we go. She's a bit dehydrated anyway – nothing unusual about that if she's had diarrhoea for a few days. We'll pop in a little needle and top up her fluids; she should feel better after that. And then we'll transfer her to the ward so we can run some tests.'

'So, what d'you *think* is wrong with her?'

'I can't say at this stage. It could be nothing. Best wait till she's settled and got some fluids into her, and the ward staff have had her under observation for a bit.'

Anya stared up at him. He didn't know what was wrong, but he was worried enough to admit Gypsy. They didn't fill expensive cots in a cash-strapped NHS unless it was really necessary.

As the curtain swished shut behind him, she looked wildly at Tiffany.

'It's just to be on the safe side,' Tiffany said

127

immediately. 'Don't instantly start imagining the worst.'

'I must let Leon know.'

'Of course, but ... well, no point in putting the fear of God into him.' She moved in close and whispered, 'Don't read too much into this. These medics hate to admit they haven't a clue. I worked with a professor of paediatrics years ago who reckoned every child was allowed one convulsion. Just keep calm. Don't let Gypsy sense you're upset. Breathe ... in .... and out ... and in ... and out ...'

Anya concentrated on the soothing voice.

'I guess you want to stay with her, yes?' Tiffany said.

'Of course. I *must*! She'd be so frightened all alone amongst strangers.'

'Then maybe just check you can get a signal from inside the hospital. So you can text Leon.'

Anya checked. Excellent reception.

'So, d'you need anything brought in from the house? Happy to whip across and get things. Or, if you prefer, I can stay with the baby while you go. She knows me.'

'I'm fine at the moment. Will they let her go home tonight, d'you think? If they keep her in, I'll need some of my stuff.'

'Let's see what they say when you get to the ward. They'll probably have a completely different take on it. Best to take your cue from them rather than these guys in A&E.'

But the paediatrician who admitted Gypsy to the ward was adamant.

'We'll be keeping her in meantime, certainly overnight. For observation. Maybe a few tests. Don't worry, as soon as there's anything to tell, you'll be the first to know, Mrs Morgan. We'll keep you fully in the picture.'

It was a picture that terrified her.

If there was something seriously wrong ...

She'd never forgive all those people who'd doubted her. A pyrrhic victory.

CHAPTER 25

By the time Leon got to the hospital, it was almost midnight. He tiptoed through the corridors catching a heart-stopping glimpse of a floodlit crisis, crowded figures hunched over an invisible child.

A whispered exchange with a nurse who was expecting him, and he was in. All was peaceful within the ward. He let his breath out carefully and crept forward.

Gypsy was fast asleep, wispy hair plastered to her head with sweat, a snail-trail of tears silver on her flushed cheeks, her tiny arm bandaged to a splint securing the intravenous infusion. She looked so small and vulnerable in the enormous institutional cot, a pearl in a massive oyster shell.

Anya, dozing in the chair beside her, somehow sensed his presence, startled upright, promptly burst into muffled tears.

'Not exactly a rapturous reception.' He handed her a wad of tissues.

'I thought you weren't coming.'

'Give me a break, Anya! I was in *Birmingham*! I came as soon as I got your text. It was you who insisted I went in the first place, remember? I *told* you I should have stayed.'

She blew her nose vigorously.

'But I'm here now, so off you go and get a proper sleep.'

She shook her head. 'I need to stay. But ... since it's the weekend, could you stay too ... just in case ... it's bad news.'

'Yep. Good to know I'm useful for something.' He dropped into a chair and massaged his aching shoulders. 'I see you've got your night things. You suspected she'd be kept in, then?'

'No. Tiffany went to get them for me, so I didn't have to leave Gypsy.'

'Your ace organisation would pay off there! Second drawer on the left, four inches down, white nightie. Cupboard in bathroom, middle shelf, plum coloured toilet bag, already filled with essentials. Third cupboard from the left in the nursery, fourth shelf, second pile, three quarters of the way down, three night-time babygros ...' He grinned as he said it but she merely shrugged. 'Let's just hope she didn't rootle through the place, find your stash of leather handbags.'

'She already knows they're out-of-date stock.'

He sighed. 'Another black mark. Is nothing sacred?'

'Wait ...' – she extended a hand – 'while I remember, there's one thing I *do* need you to sort out. The social worker called while Tiffany was at the house.'

'Surely not.'

'What d'you mean?'

'A social worker came ... on a *Saturday*?!'

'I suppose they try to catch people when they're in. Or maybe she was just out our way seeing some other family and called in on the off chance. Anyway ... Tiffany wasn't sure what to say to her. She didn't think it was her place to tell them that Gypsy was in hospital.'

'So, what *did* she say?'

'Apparently, she mumbled something vague about house-sitting while I was out.'

'Which probably sounded highly suspicious. OK, we'll sort it out on Monday.'

But Gypsy was not home for Monday.

Fair enough, weekends were dead; none of the routine tests would be carried out then, but ...

Anya kept asking. And gradually an answer took shape. There was no doubt about it: Gypsy was under close observation. Unremitting.

This had to be something horribly serious.

What weren't they telling her?

She couldn't even concentrate on reading. Constant

interruptions, nurses wandering by, lingering, vigilant from their central station, doctors hovering over the baby.

'Hospitals are one of the worst places to get any rest,' the night nurse said lightly. 'But *you* don't need to stay all the time. We're here twenty-four seven. We'll keep an eye on her if you want to go out and do other things.'

But there was no way Gypsy was being exposed to the trauma of being alone among strangers. Anya gritted her teeth and bit her tongue. She willed the baby to wake up to play. Only when she could safely leave Leon, Claire or Tiffany in attendance would she pop out for a short walk, or a seat in the sunshine, or a trip to the canteen. And twice, while Leon sat with Gypsy, she shot home for a vigorous session in the gym, a shower, a change of clothes, a catch up with the mail and a quick tidy of the house.

CHAPTER 26

Quite deliberately she avoided the other parents. She had no appetite for stories of chronic illnesses or dire prognoses, and too many of the children looked frighteningly pale and lethargic. She'd never allowed herself to consider quite how many ailments lay in wait for her precious child, not to mention germs ... resistant strains ...

Would her wipes and sprays be effective ...?

Getting to know the staff was different. They were potential allies in this battle, sharing responsibility for Gypsy's wellbeing; their attitudes, backgrounds, home lives, career pathways, all keys to open doors. Some nurses grated, some annoyed, others ingratiated themselves with their confidences. She grew to know when to leave the ward, whose vigilance she could trust.

Auburn-haired Senior Staff Nurse Rosemary Stewart soon became a favourite. She oozed compassion and understanding. Her seniority, her impeccable techniques, her bright personality, her comfortable conversation, her reassuring touch, endeared her to Anya.

'I remember, you came in once before. From Dalkeith, Eskbank, that area, yes?' Rosemary said, cornflower-blue eyes crinkled behind ridiculously long eyelashes. 'My aunt's a doctor there, that's why it registered.'

'Of course. I remember. Dr Coral Jones.'

'She's an amazing woman, Aunt Coral. So much on her plate, but she still manages to hold down a responsible job. Don't know how she does it.'

'I've heard she used to be a senior partner in the practice.'

'She did. Until the family demands became too heavy.'

Anya raised an eyebrow.

'She's got a quite severely disabled daughter who leads her a merry old dance. And her parents are quite old. Her mum's got dementia too. Must be a nightmare juggling that little lot.'

'Goodness. I had no idea.' She paused. 'You don't look at all like her.'

'I'm not. She's my aunt by marriage. Uncle Sean – he was her husband – my mum's brother.'

So, she's not even got a husband to support her.

It was Rosemary who found her in tears on Wednesday morning. She slipped an arm around the trembling shoulders and simply waited till Anya regained control.

'Why are you keeping her in so long? Is there something you're not telling me? She hasn't had any symptoms since she came in, has she?'

'No.'

'Nobody's doing *anything*, as far as I can see. What are we waiting for?'

'That's the nature of observation. Just watching how things go. You've been worried about her before, I'd have thought you'd be glad the doctors are taking this seriously.'

'Well, of course I *was* in the beginning. But it's going on and on. And she's fine now. Everything's settled down – bowels, fluid levels, convulsions, rash. You've reassured me.'

'Well, that's good. That's a result in itself, isn't it?' Rosemary gave her a strange look and then said levelly, 'Have you got a theory?'

'I don't want to admit this, but I think … it could be … a question of diet.'

'Why don't you want to admit that?'

'Because I don't want her to get used to stodgy food. I think you establish habits and sow the seeds for future health from the beginning. Lots of fruit and veg are good for them.'

'Within reason, yes. And I admire your efforts to give Gypsy the best possible start in life. But it's possible to be over-zealous in the pursuit of health. And an excess of dirty

133

nappies, painful rashes – they tell us something.'

'So, if I ease off on the fibre, can I take her home?'

'I'm not the one to authorise that; that's down to Dr Hooper. But, you know, if it was *my* baby I'd be glad to know people were being cautious, not bundling us off home at the earliest opportunity.'

'Should we be worried that Dr Hooper isn't coming up with any answers?'

'Oh, he *is* getting answers, believe me. Everything he sees is telling him something. He'll fill you in when he's good and ready.'

'Can she at least have the cannula taken out of her arm?'

'Not at the moment, but I think it won't be too long now.'

'D'you have any children of your own, Rosemary?'

Rosemary looked startled at the sudden change in direction.

'No,' she said slowly. 'Not yet. But my partner and I are thinking of adopting one.'

'Really? That's quite a step to take.'

'Yep. And please don't tell me all about it being a gruelling process. I *know*. But we're prepared to have our lives and motives put under scrutiny if that's what it takes. It'd be worth it to give some kiddie a good stable home life. We think so, anyway.'

Like baby Holly Justine.

'Good for you. And they'd surely look favourably on *you*, wouldn't they? All your experience with children, your background.'

'Time will tell. There are no shortcuts. No perks of the job where adoption is concerned. But I hope so.'

When Dr Hooper appeared the following morning without his usual entourage, it was obvious he meant business. Drawing up a chair, he hooked his feet around the legs as if he needed an anchor, the garish monsters on his socks somehow belying the gravity of his responsibilities.

'Hello, young lady, you're looking mischievous this morning,' he said, chucking Gypsy under her chin. She beamed up at him, mesmerised by the intermittent flashes from his bow tie.

He turned his attention to the parents, fingers fidgeting with the heavy glasses as if seeking perfect vision.

'I know you've been anxious to get this little girl home, but how are you feeling about things at the moment?'

'She seems fine to us,' Leon said. 'To be honest we don't know why you're still keeping her in hospital.'

'Given her history, we wanted to be quite sure there wasn't something triggering these incidents you've been concerned about. But she's been well while she's been with us, and we've found nothing to suggest there's anything sinister going on.' '

'So, can we take her home?'

'You certainly can. Tomorrow. We're waiting for one more blood test to come back and we might just want to repeat it. But thank you for your patience.'

'Thank *you* for taking such trouble to be sure she's all right,' Anya said. 'We were beginning to think it must be something serious.'

'That's understandable. Lots of little symptoms can be every bit as troubling as a big incident. But no, you're a fine healthy little girl, aren't you, sweetie?'

'Can I just ask …' Anya began.

The direct unblinking gaze was rather disconcerting.

'If she did happen to present with any of these things again, should we just come here, where you know her, or …?'

'The GP is your normal first port of call, but if, for any reason, it was an emergency, the ED's your best bet. They would refer anything that needs specialist attention.' He turned to Gypsy, 'But we hope we don't see you ever again, huh, Gypsy? You just stay well away from doctors and hospitals and tests till you're all grown up and having your own babies, yes?'

Gypsy rewarded him with a gurgle of delight and a huge belch that froze her in mid-smile. Her lip wobbled but

Anya scooped her up and held her close, while they repeated their thanks.

Anya was in the playroom, still buzzing, when Tiffany dropped in.

'She's getting out tomorrow! I'm going to pop home to do a few bits and pieces, once Leon gets back. I can't *wait* to get out of this place.'

'You happy with everything they've done in here?'

'More or less. Dr Hooper seems sure she's perfectly healthy. One more blood test this afternoon and that should be it. For ever, hopefully. I never want to go through this again. Being cooped up in here with all these really sick children ... how do these mums cope ...?' She shuddered.

Tiffany changed the subject adroitly.

'Dr Hooper does look a bit goofy, don't you think? But he's extremely thorough. He has a reputation for playing his cards close to his chest – annoys the heck out of the nurses sometimes. They're the ones the parents badger for information. If you don't know what's going on, it's fiendishly difficult to reassure them without risking giving false hope. But he's cautious. Some doctors bash on and then try to bury their mistakes. It's a well-known fact. But Dr Hooper doesn't want to make a mistake in the first place, so he takes his time. If he says Gypsy's fine, she will be.'

'It's such a relief, knowing for sure.'

'So, you'll lay off the artichokes and aubergines now, will you?' Tiffany grinned broadly at her friend, taking the sting out of the implied criticism. She glanced at her watch. 'But hey, never mind Gypsy's diet, what about you? You need fattening up and that's a fact. Off you go. Get yourself to the canteen and buy something tasty. I'll stay with Miss Gypsy till you get back or Leon arrives. Plenty of time before my meeting.'

She instantly lifted Gypsy off the mat and began to play *This little piggy* with her toes, ignoring Anya's moment of hesitation.

CHAPTER 27

By the time Leon found them in the playroom, Anya was dozing, back against the wall, Gypsy lying across her lap fast asleep.

Anya startled awake as she felt the baby being moved.

He bent to take Gypsy's weight. 'Off you go, and take your time. We'll be fine, won't we, sweetheart?'

Her head jerked back and Anya immediately reacted, reaching out to support it.

'Careful, Leon!'

'Whoops, sorry, angel,' he whispered, holding her more securely.

'*There* you are.' Morag, a shy nurse from Inverness, put her head round the door. 'Time for Gypsy's blood test. Could you bring her through, please?'

Leon laid the sleeping child on the freshly made bed, a limp rag doll, dead to the world.

Morag took two steps closer. She lifted Gypsy's arm and let it flop back on the bed.

'How long has she been like this?'

Neither parent answered. *Like what ...?*

Morag felt Gypsy's pulse, opened one of her eyes, touched her skin.

Leon's heart skipped a beat. No response ... grey ... beads of sweat fringing her forehead ...

Next moment the child's limbs splayed, her back arched, her head was thrown back, all four limbs started to thrash, the whole cot rattled.

Alarms rang. Red lights pulsed overhead. Someone dragged the curtains round them.

Four pairs of feet thundered up the ward. Five figures

went into action, blocking Gypsy from their view.

Staccato commands peppered the air, urgent, imperative.

'On her side.'

'Oxygen.'

'Airway clear.'

'Temp?'

'Get me the drug chart, someone.'

'Page the registrar, will you?'

'Dr Hooper's next door – shall I ...?'

'Yep, he'll want to know.'

Leon dragged his gaze away momentarily. Anya was the colour of parchment, eyes wide and staring, fists rammed against her mouth. A silent scream.

The rattling slowed ... the bent figures remained frozen like a human shield. Leon held his breath. Gradually, gradually, they unravelled, straightened up, all eyes on the tiny figure at the centre, now eerily still. The whole assembly ... waited ...

The comments were calmer now.

'OK. OK.'

'There you go, little lady. You're fine. We've got you.'

'Let's get FBC, blood glucose, Us&Es.'

'On it.'

'Start a saline drip.'

'And can we check her urine.'

It meant nothing to Leon. All he could focus on was the limp body on the bed. It was as if the Gypsy he knew had left her shell.

So much for the 'fine healthy little girl' of this morning. Fine healthy little girls didn't suddenly have full blown convulsions.

CHAPTER 28

Someone somewhere ushered the parents out of the clinical area into the relatives' room. Pale cream walls, muted plum furnishings, comfy chairs, soft lights ... kettle, real china cups, Rich Tea biscuits ...

Anya and Leon touched nothing, rigid in their shock.

Morag popped her head round the door. 'You all right? Can I make you a cuppa?'

They both shook their heads. 'No, thanks.'

'Help yourself to anything you fancy. One of the doctors will be with you shortly.'

As soon as the door shut behind her, Anya hissed, 'Dr Hooper said she was fine. He sat there and *told* us. He *assured* us.'

'So much for medical opinion, huh? No tablets of stone here; he's obviously not Moses.'

'After all that observation ...'

'Well, look on the bright side. Imagine if we'd got Gypsy home yesterday ...'

'I know.' She seemed to shrink into herself at the very prospect.

'I don't know what they shot into her, but it seemed to do the trick. Good thing she still had her cannula in, eh?'

The door opened and Rosemary Stewart entered, closely followed by George Hooper. Both parents sat up straighter. Rosemary perched close enough to lay a hand on Anya's arm fleetingly.

Clad in navy scrubs, without his trademark fun ties and cartoon characters, Dr Hooper looked grave and more impersonal.

'It can be very frightening to see your child having a

seizure.' His voice was as quietly authoritative as usual.

They simply stared.

'Can I just confirm … Gypsy's just had the one minor episode in the past, that you're aware of; is that correct?'

Leon nodded, but Anya put out a hand to stop him.

'It was my friend who saw that one and she said it was over really quickly. Not like this.'

'Ah yes. The neighbour who used to be a nurse.'

Anya nodded. 'It was that, on top of several days of loose stools, that brought us here in the first place. Tiffany thought it ought to be checked out.'

Looks like she got that right.

'Well, convulsions can be caused by a number of things, but essentially they're the outward manifestation of sudden abnormal electrical activity in the brain.'

'Is she going to be OK?' Anya whispered hoarsely.

'She's still very drowsy at the moment, and she'll probably sleep for some time after this one. That's perfectly usual. But we'll need to do some more investigations to see why she's had a second convulsion, especially in the absence of a high temperature. You probably know that febrile convulsions are very common in children; it's their way of bringing their temperature down.'

'I don't get it,' Leon began.

Stay calm. Stay in control.

He gripped his hands together tightly.

'This morning you gave her a clean bill of health. We were all set to get her *home*! How come, this afternoon – the very same day! – she has a convulsion?'

'Exactly what we're asking ourselves.' The doctor looked from one to the other. No smile. 'Can you talk me through what happened this afternoon prior to the convulsion?'

'We were playing in the playroom. And after a bit she just put her head down on my lap and drifted off to sleep.' Anya mimed the action.

'I'd popped out and when I got back, I picked her up and brought her through to the ward.'

140

Anya froze. 'Her head did jerk back with some force when you took her from me, didn't it? Remember?'

'That was nothing.'

Dr Hooper waited a beat. 'Was anybody else in the playroom with you?'

'A couple of other children, their parents. And various nurses came in and out briefly.'

'D'you remember who exactly?'

'Not really ... Rosemary, I know; Morag ... maybe ...'

'You were dozing, weren't you?' Leon clarified. 'I woke you when I arrived.'

'I was only resting my eyes.'

Dr Hooper shot a hard look at Leon before turning his attention to Anya. 'When did Gypsy last eat?'

'Lunchtime.'

'And did she finish her lunch?'

'Yes.'

'Did you give her anything else?'

'No. She's already getting more than I'd let her have at home.'

'You think we're over-feeding her in here?' The tone was mild but ...

'Well, not exactly *over-feeding*. But more stodgy stuff than I would give her normally.'

'So, since she came in, did you ever skip meals?'

'No.'

'Did you ever substitute your food for hospital food?'

'I did give her some pureed fruit a couple of times, to make sure she got some roughage.'

'What are you suggesting, Dr Hooper?' Leon felt himself bristling.

'I'm not suggesting anything, Mr Morgan. I'm simply trying to understand why Gypsy suddenly had a convulsion when there was no indication of anything which might precipitate one.'

'And you think it's something to do with her *food*?' Leon demanded.

'We don't know. But what we do know is that her

blood sugar was unusually low when she had the convulsion.'

'Her *blood sugar*? I thought you were looking into her bowels or her brain.'

'When blood sugar levels fall too low, the body releases the hormone adrenaline. Adrenaline helps get stored glucose into the bloodstream quickly. The early warning signs of adrenaline release are ... palor, clammy skin, sweating, shakiness, increased heart rate.'

'And she was showing these signs when we brought her back into the ward,' Leon said slowly, his mind roiling.

'Yes. We don't know how long she'd been going hypoglycaemic, but a seizure tells us that the brain isn't getting enough glucose to function normally.'

'Are you saying ... she'll be brain damaged?' Anya's voice was unrecognisable.

'No, no, no. That's not at all what I'm saying. There's nothing to suggest she'll be affected in any way long-term from this one incident. What we need to ascertain is, why did it happen?'

'Hence the questions about her meals ...' Leon felt a fool. 'What happens now, then?'

'Well, we've given Gypsy some sugar in a drip. We'll keep that running while we do some more tests.'

'What kind of tests?'

'Repeat blood tests to check that she's maintaining her sugar levels for long enough after she's eaten. She should be able to go at least four hours without her blood sugar dropping below three mmol per litre. And we'll do a lumbar puncture. That will allow us to compare the sugar levels in her blood and her CSF, the fluid in her spine. Those two measurements should be close.'

Leon felt Anya shudder and reached out to cover her hand with his.

Dr Hooper shot her a sympathetic look. 'I know. Just when you believed all the needles were a thing of the past. But she's still quite sleepy, and Dr Andersen is going to do the lumbar puncture now so we don't cause her any more distress than is necessary.'

'So, that means – she won't be coming home now …'
Anya's voice was lost in a sob.

'I'm afraid not. Not until we've established the cause of
her hypoglycaemia, and we're confident that she's able to
maintain appropriate safe levels of sugar.'

CHAPTER 29

Anya had insisted: there was no point three of them sitting around the cot with Gypsy fast asleep. The child was under close observation; there was nothing to suggest imminent problems. Claire would do the crossword with her. Far better that Leon should catch up with work so he could accrue time off for when they were all back at home again.

If only it worked like that!

But she knew nothing of the pressure he was under, the crisis facing the company, the imperative to prove his mettle now. And in all honesty, it'd probably be easier for her not to have the added pressure of maintaining a civilised front for the staff; the strains in their relationship were becoming more and more apparent.

He rang Thomas to fill him in. 'But I'm at home getting on with those reports. It won't hold anything up. I'll email each one as I complete it.'

Sorting out the disastrous Irish deal was proving far more complicated than Leon had ever imagined, and humiliating meetings with lawyers weighed heavily. Thomas had demanded full detailed reports at each stage so that he and Roger were fully in the picture – a perfectly reasonable response in the circumstances, Leon knew, nevertheless the erosion of trust cut deep.

He was fully immersed in the task, when the doorbell rang. Should he ignore it? Once again the spectre of the social worker loomed large.

But it was no official spy, only Tiffany standing in the shelter of the porch, bearing a gift basket festooned with yellow ribbons.

'You'll be extra busy tomorrow and I don't want to intrude on a family occasion, so I thought I'd pop across with this wee welcome-home gift for Gypsy. It's nothing much, but I'm just so delighted she's got a clean bill of health.'

'You'd better hang onto it meantime,' Leon said, gesturing her inside the porch.

'Something wrong?' Tiffany half-offered the basket and then, seeing his grim face, clutched it close against her body.

'Gypsy had another convulsion this afternoon so they're keeping her in.'

'Ohh no! Poor Anya. She'll be beside herself.'

'Her sister's with her at the moment and I'll be going in tomorrow morning ... sooner if anything changes. So, no offence, but it'd be best if you didn't visit at the moment.'

'Of course. I quite understand. But don't hesitate to shout if I can do anything. I'm back and forth anyway.'

Tiffany turned to leave but then hesitated.

'Listen. I don't want to speak out of turn, but ... since you're here on your own ... well, it's been bugging me ...'

'What has?'

'Well, you know Anya asked me to collect her night things.'

'Yeah.'

'It's just that, she gave me a bag of Gypsy's things to bring home and put in the laundry basket. Only ... I found a wee syringe in the bag; an insulin syringe. I don't want to cause any trouble, and I know Anya's been having a pretty hard time lately. But ...'

'It probably fell in when the nurses were clearing up. They use syringes all the time sticking stuff in Gypsy's cannula, taking blood, all that kind of thing.'

'Yeah, you're probably right. Sorry, maybe I'm just being paranoid. Forget I said anything. Oh, and please don't let her know I told you. I don't want her to think I have any doubts about her. She needs all the friends, all the support, she can get.'

'OK. Thanks.'

'No problem. Good night.'

Part of Leon brain was still distracted by what she'd said when Claire came in.

'You know Tiffany Corrigan, don't you? Anya's friend from along the road.'

'We've met,' Claire said stiffly.

'Eeuw. You don't sound keen!'

'I don't really know her.'

'And what you've seen you don't like.'

'She's Anya's friend, not mine. It just strikes me as odd the way she spends so much time here. She's even got her own key.'

'Ah, that's down to me, I'm afraid. When we had that spell where Anya was exhausted and sleeping through Gypsy's screaming, I gave keys to both you and Tiffany, so there was somebody who could get in if there was an emergency and I was away. Anya trusts her. And she respects her opinion – she's a nurse as well as having loads of experience with kids. And she's local. She can be here in minutes if the need arises.'

'Of course. It makes sense. Besides it's none of my business.'

'She called round this evening, with a welcome-home gift. And she said something ... Apparently, she found a syringe in the bag of Gypsy's clothes Anya sent home that day when she was admitted to hospital. Why would she feel the need to report it in that kind of this-could-be-serious kind of way? I mean, it must have just fallen in the bag, right? It's a perfectly reasonable explanation when you're in hospital and the nurses are doing things with syringes all the time. Isn't it?'

'Could be.' Claire's voice was guarded.

'You don't sound very sure.'

'Well, I hope you're right, Leon. I really do. But you must admit Anya's not been herself recently. She's not the old Anya, totally on the ball about everything, is she? Sometimes it's ... well, I hate to even say it, but it's as if she's kind of spaced out ... drugged up.'

Leon stared at her, thoughts racing. This was the second time someone had suggested Anya might be taking something.

Those pills ... She'd assured him they were only vitamin and herb supplements. Perfectly harmless. Lucinda had checked the ingredients ... But what if they were just a cover? What if she had other reserves ...?

She often nodded off these days. He'd put it down to sleep deprivation, but what if ...? And she was definitely *asleep when he found her in the playroom, Gypsy lying on her lap ... Could she be under the influence, not even aware of what she was doing?*

Claire's voice intruded on his thoughts.

'And lately... she's been asking me questions about Jim's psychiatric history.'

'What kind of questions?'

'How you can tell when someone's off balance. What do I notice first? Is Jim aware when he's not totally with it? That kind of thing.'

Leon stared off into the distance, questions clamouring in his brain. *The problems Anya'd had bonding with Gypsy from the outset ... the times she'd abandoned the baby ... that he knew of! ... all the trips to the surgery ... her wild accusations ... the deterioration in their relationship ...*

'And she doesn't *look* well, does she?'

'Should I mention all this to someone?' Leon mused. 'What d'you think?'

'She'd be furious if she knew *we* were doubting her.'

'Gordon Bennett! My life wouldn't be worth living!'

'I must admit, I'm getting really worried. Since she's had Gypsy, it's just been one crisis after another. I'd happily look after the baby for a weekend, but can you see Anya trusting her to anyone else after this? Not on your life. And I can't say as I blame her.'

'I'm afraid you're right, Claire. But don't take it personally. She won't let *me* do much and I'm Gypsy's *father*!'

'I guess I should be grateful she left her with me in hospital when there were umpteen nurses within hailing distance, huh?'

'Yep. You were one of the privileged few there.'

'I hated coming away tonight, leaving her scared witless

something terrible's going to happen to Gypsy, but she insisted.'

'She's her own worst enemy sometimes.'

CHAPTER 30

George Hooper sat immobile for a long time, his whole concentration on the sheaf of papers in front of him.

Lists.

Names. Dates. Incidents. Outcomes.

Medically speaking it simply didn't add up. What was he missing here?

A light tap startled him. He flipped a blank sheet of paper across the accumulating evidence.

'Come in.'

Magnus Andersen put his head round the door, a blond Viking, instinctively inclining his head in deference. George smiled, beckoning him in. The registrar was proving a sound team player, a natural with his juvenile patients, a methodical analyst.

'I've just re-sited Gypsy Morgan's drip – first one tissued. Hypoglycaemia's less profound but we've upped the dextrose. Put her on ten-minute obs. Sent off another batch of bloods.'

George leaned back in his chair. 'What d'you make of it, Magnus?'

'I'm baffled. Makes no sense. You?'

'I agree.'

'The nurses are restless. Mother keeps asking. Anything we can share at this stage?'

'I'll come and speak to her. Give me five minutes.'

Silence fell as he entered the cubicle. Good, Rosemary Stewart was on duty; safe pair of hands. He nodded to her, watched while Magnus's long fingers checked the baby yet again, surreptitiously observing the mother. Kwame Musawenkosi, the FY2, hovered behind Magnus, a file of notes clutched in his hands, face inscrutable as usual.

Everyone needed answers here, some kind of reassurance.

He crouched beside the cot and observed the sleeping child lying totally still, spread-eagled, face pale, chest movement shallow, occasionally fluttering. He reached out to caress the downy hair, soft to his touch. No reaction. He let one knee take his weight, remaining at her level, looking up at everyone else – a deliberate ploy.

'Well, this little lassie's certainly giving us a run for our money. As far as her present condition is concerned, I think she's stabilised for now. But as to why her blood sugar has suddenly plummeted, there are no simple answers.'

'She will be ... all right ... in the end ... won't she?' Anya's haunted eyes stared down at him, unblinking.

'Until we know what's causing this, it would be foolhardy to make rash promises, but one thing you can be sure of, we shall do our absolute utmost for your little girl.'

'So, what now?'

'I'm going to have a chat with my consultant colleagues. Sometimes a fresh pair of eyes helps. And in the meantime, we shall monitor Gypsy continuously, so we're going to move her out of the cubicle into an area where this is possible.'

'Can I ... stay with her still? She'd be so frightened if she ...'

Rosemary laid a hand on Anya's shoulder.

'Yes, of course,' George said. 'But I would advise you to take a proper break at night. Get all the sleep you can snatch, while you can. You won't be much use to her if you're exhausted.'

There was the sound of rapid heavy footsteps, and Leon Morgan not so much entered as exploded into the cubicle.

'Sorry. Phone call. What have I missed?'

'Dr Hooper's just said they're going to move Gypsy ...' Anya's voice was flat, her eyes dry, but she was clearly incapable of proceeding.

Leon's eyes darted from one person to another, his jaw tight.

'Will somebody please fill me in here?'

George unravelled slowly till he was at eye level with Gypsy's father.

'Perhaps we could have a chat somewhere quiet, Mr Morgan? I can tell you where we are so far, and you can ask any questions you might have.' To those gathered around this child it was a gentle suggestion; but George channelled all his authority into the look he directed at Leon Morgan. This was no place for aggression and naked fear.

He turned to Anya. 'I'll leave you in the very capable hands of Dr Andersen and Staff Nurse Stewart for now, but I'll be back in a bit to see how things are going.'

Pausing only to sign a drug chart a nurse put in front of him, he led the way out of the ward. Neither man spoke till the door shut behind them. Sunlight poured through the window, highlighting the tiny motes dancing in the air; a fridge hummed in the background. George gestured towards a chair and eased himself into his own high-backed one, fitting his spine deep against the rigid contour.

Only then did the floodgates open. Direct, forceful, challenging, even an edge of accusation. But George had seen too many frightened parents to be fazed by this father's bravado. He answered each question carefully and calmly.

Leon was not easily reassured.

'Look, from where I'm sitting, Dr Hooper, this looks ugly. My daughter comes in here after one little mini-convulsion that by all accounts was pretty much over before it began. You keep her here for five days, poke and prod and do God knows what to her, and then you tell us, hand on heart, she's A1. Totally healthy. That's what you said. Then just hours later – the very same *day*! – she has this major seizure and you're putting her onto high alert. And now, you're sitting there, telling me you have no clue as to what's wrong. What the hell's going on here? Do you have *any idea* what you're doing? Should I be getting a second opinion?'

'You are perfectly entitled to seek another opinion, if you wish, and in fact, that's exactly what I've done myself. A fresh pair of eyes can sometimes help. I'm happy for you to speak with the other paediatricians.'

'And in the meantime?'

'Sorry?'

'What else are you doing?'

'I'm in the process of talking with every member of staff who had anything to do with Gypsy in the hours leading up to the incident. There was a shift changeover so that's quite a number of people to get through. It could be, someone will remember some little indicator that at the time didn't register, but retrospectively could be significant.'

Leon nodded slowly.

'And we shall continue to monitor Gypsy. Her blood sugar levels, of course, and ketones. Pancreatic function, metabolic function, immune responses. Brain function. We'll also look into other autoimmune conditions – thyroid, coeliac disease ...' George broke off abruptly.

All the belligerence had evaporated.

'You think ... this is something ... really serious?'

'We simply don't know at this stage. It's a process of elimination. These are routine investigations in such circumstances. And the names sound much more alarming than they are. Some of these conditions at least will be easily eliminated.'

'But I thought ... you said ... it was not enough sugar in her blood. The kind of thing you get if you haven't eaten for ages.'

'That's correct. But the question we're asking is, *why* she ran out of sugar in the first place? Can I just check again, is there anything at all in the past or in the family history, you can think of that might be relevant here? Any diabetes? Kidney ... liver problems?

Leon shook his head.

'And in the case of the niece who died, was there a definitive reason given for her death?'

'Not that I know of, anyway. Claire just told Anya it

was sudden, unexplained. Cot death, they called it. SIDS.'

'Your wife's been anxious from the outset, hasn't she? Have you noticed anything unusual in her behaviour or … well, anything untoward, recently?'

'She's totally fixated on Gypsy. Paranoid. Exhausted. She *was* asleep in the playroom when this happened, only, half the time, I don't think she's aware of what she's doing. And she goes into orbit over the least little thing.'

'Would you describe the convulsion as a "little thing"?'

'No, of course not. I'm talking about odd bits and bobs like the runs, a speck of blood. But this … this latest thing … it was totally different. I was *with her* when *this* happened – in hospital too. You can't put that into the same category.'

'I understand. Sorry for all the seemingly unconnected questions, but we're in the process of amassing the evidence at the moment. It's not always apparent we're doing anything, so, let me reassure you, we are. And we shall continue to do everything in our power to get to the bottom of this mystery.'

'So … if you *had* to commit to a theory at this precise moment …?'

'No sleuth worth his salt puts his hard-earned reputation on the line prematurely, Mr Morgan.' George softened the words with a rueful smile.

'Fair enough. But … well, can you say … do you think Gypsy will, you know … be all right, in the end?'

'With all the caveats I've already outlined, if I *had* to say one way or the other, I'd say I'm fairly confident she will.'

'Thanks. And I promise I won't take you to court and hold you to that.'

'Goodness! I sincerely hope you aren't thinking in terms of court action already!' Dr Hooper laughed for the first time in their exchange.

'Best keep you on your toes anyway!'

Both men shook hands.

'And thanks for all you're doing for our baby. Sorry, I should have said that before.'

'It's my job.'

Leon was on the point of leaving when George put out

a hand and spoke again.

'One more thing, Mr Morgan. It's important that your wife doesn't completely exhaust herself at this stage. We've got Gypsy under close observation. She can safely go out, take breaks, get some sleep. We'd call you immediately if there was any change. I don't know if you could persuade her?'

'I'll try. And if she insists one of us must be here, I'm perfectly happy to do night shifts.'

'Good.'

CHAPTER 31

Anya listened in silence to Leon's report of this conversation. But she was adamant: she wouldn't sleep being far away from her baby.

'And by the time we got here, Gypsy could be hysterical, surrounded by strangers.'

'Fair enough. Then *I'll* stay here tonight. You do the day shift.'

'What about work?'

'They'll cope without me for a bit. Which reminds me … Juliette says, would you like her to come up for a few days? Just to keep things going at home and … anything that would help.'

And be alone with you in the house? I don't think so.

'No need. Claire's here. She'll do anything that needs doing.' She was acutely aware of the strange look Leon shot her.

'Mother offered too. And Gypsy's her *granddaughter*. It's only natural that she'd want to see her. Help.'

'Of course, she can *see* her. I've never said she couldn't.'

'I'll let her know.'

'But Claire's taking care of the washing and stuff. She's my sister: it makes sense. No disrespect to your family.'

Leon's voice was devoid of emotion. 'I hear what you're saying.'

It was impossible to concentrate. The buzz, the hum, the constant activity, inane comments – everything irritated her. Books were meaningless hieroglyphics; knitting futile; crosswords baffled her; codewords seemed bent on thwarting her; solitaire became mindlessly repetitive.

Nurses hovered endlessly. What should have been a comfort became irksome. Social etiquette demanded polite conversation; unequal status limited her repertoire. She closed her eyes, feigned sleep, simply to avoid the necessity of dredging up niceties. But inactivity left her mind unfettered in a wilderness of doubt.

What if the doctors suspected Gypsy was seriously ill? A tumour. Some terrible degenerative disease. Were they just waiting for the right moment to tell her?

What if they'd already told Leon? What if he was protecting her, knowing it would devastate her?

What if her baby never grew up? How could she bear it?

Claire had, but hers was a different temperament altogether. She didn't have the same aspirations ...

Claire! Was she being fair dragging her grieving sister into her problems?

What if she'd brought this whole business about with her ridiculously high standards of hygiene? They said children needed a healthy exposure to common or garden germs. Had she been single-handedly responsible for lowering Gypsy's immunity?

Was this terrible tiredness affecting her ability to look after her child?

Was she somehow making mistakes?

Would Leon care as much if they lost Gypsy?

Would he stay around if she was mourning, if she disintegrated, as Claire had done? Would that be his cue to go off with Juliette?

Dr Hooper said he was going to talk to all the nurses and doctors. Why? What was he suspecting?

Did the community staff liaise with the hospital staff? Did Dr Hooper already know how she'd struggled to bond with her baby in the early weeks?

Nothing made any sense ... but ... was it her fault?

CHAPTER 32

George Hooper's pale face was sombre as he went in search of his medical colleagues. The sooner he got to the bottom of what was happening the better for all concerned.

His wife was starting to issue veiled threats; a bad sign in the Hooper domain. He might be the top man at work, but at home Millie Hooper ruled the household. Indisputably. She hadn't juggled part-time work as a radiographer alongside raising four children, without learning exactly how to organise the whole household with military precision; and there were few concessions due simply to his position. Though the nurses laughed when he said things like, 'My life won't be worth living if I'm late for our evening appointment,' or 'my guts will be garters if I don't pick up the boys from school', there was a price to be paid for his ridiculous hours and overactive conscience.

But how could he relax into comfortable domesticity when some other father's child could be in danger? He'd always been a fiercely devoted parent to his own four. Indeed, he'd recently been shocked into increased vigilance where they were concerned; acutely aware of the fine line between control and independence. The girls, Shelby and Edwina, older than their brothers by several years, had lulled him into a false sense of security. Industrious, conforming, easy to guide, and even now, in their twenties, in regular touch, ready to share their worries and challenges out in the real world away from his protection. But the boys, Felton and Emmett? They had something else to prove, and their father's success was, if anything, more of a challenge than a cushion. Teenage rebellion mixed with high intelligence and a love of danger had now twice brought him to the headmaster's office.

But *this* father, Leon Morgan, had no idea what the hazards even were; whether indeed there were any. Or ... had he? He seemed to be pretty edgy about something.

Beth Maroney welcomed George warmly. A gentle, serene woman in her fifties, she had a wealth of experience to draw on and no apparent insecurities to raise her defences. She'd already listened attentively to George's dilemma and was quick to reassure him now: she knew of no suspicious anomalies in her caseload.

Hamza Hussein wandered in after twelve minutes and casually sat astride the chair normally reserved for a second parent, no excuse, no apology. Still in his late thirties, Hamza had been fast tracked to consultant status on the strength of an outstanding research portfolio and impeccable clinical credentials. There was a hint of arrogance in the younger man's attitude, an aggressive edge, that seemed to put him beyond the courtesies George respected and adhered to himself.

Now Hamza rocked back on two legs of the chair, stretching his arms and his listeners' patience. The extended movement served to accentuate the toned torso, the tailored shirt.

'Nothing untoward in my cases, and I say that with confidence. I monitor everything on my patch and I'd have been onto it straight away. Too bad if a rotten apple has sneaked into your basket, though. You have my sympathy.'

Supercilious prat!

'I'm not at all sure there are bad apples anywhere. It's just something I'm trying to rule out.'

'Any chance you've made an enemy somewhere along the line?'

George's startle was genuine. 'The idea never entered my head.'

'Sophisticated way of exacting revenge, huh? Set somebody up to fail.'

'We aren't talking failure, here, Hamza,' Beth slipped in firmly. 'George knows what's wrong with the baby. He's treating her appropriately. He's just asking why it happened, as any of us would. And of all of us in the team, George is probably the last one to make an enemy of anyone.'

Hamza shrugged, lifted an eyebrow.

'It's an interesting avenue of thinking, though,' George said slowly, his mind racing. 'Deliberately introducing medical conundrums. I'll add it to the mix.'

'So that takes us to new faces in the camp.' Hamza seemed to be pursuing his own tick list of possibilities.

'Kwame Musawenkosi's our new FY2.' George turned to Beth. 'You've worked with him for a bit, haven't you?'

'I have. I like him. Promising guy, I'd say. Conscientious to a fault. A bit gung-ho with ordering tests, but ready to listen and learn.'

'Gung-ho? Enough to experiment with drugs?'

'No!' Both seniors reacted instantly.

'And Magnus Andersen's taken him under his wing. He's exactly the chap to round off any jagged edges. Steady as a rock and completely unflappable with that inimitable Scandinavian calm.'

'What about the nurses?' Hamza actually yawned noisily as he spoke. George resisted a strong urge to jump on his rudeness.

'Four new ones in the last couple of months, but Sister Marchmont checked credentials – all very below the radar, of course – and there's nothing we can see in the records.'

'So, you're assuming innocence amongst the staff?' Beth asked softly.

'Well, of course, as we all know, it doesn't have to be somebody new. Could be someone who's been here some time but lain low, or something's happened to flip them over the edge. And I haven't spoken to Morven yet.' George glanced at his watch. 'I guess she's got held up, but I'll go and check with her after this. If she's had no unexplained incidents, and none of us have, I guess we'll need to look elsewhere, but I'm not exactly keen on that prospect either.'

'Indeedy. Shout if you need some support,' Beth said. Nobody liked going down that particularly delicate route alone.

'Bless you. But if we get to that point, it'll be over to Diane Moore and Child Protection.'

'What's the family like?' Hamza asked.

'Very pleasant. Well off. Well educated. Mum's a medical statistician. Dad's a businessman. First baby. Dad's away quite a bit, so Mum's on her own with Gypsy a lot. According to the notes, community staff describe her as rather neurotic, needing a lot of reassurance, exhausted.'

'Has anybody spoken to the primary care team?'

'Diane would do that.'

'Anything else unusual in the history before admission?'

'Social Work have been involved.'

'Hello? Did you say, Social Work? Ding, ding. Ding, ding. Alarm bells!'

Annoying git!

George took a deep breath.

'It's all in the file. But nothing really to make one suspect the kind of trouble we're considering.'

'But definite warning signs.'

'Yes, certainly. And duly flagged up.'

'And you've had this kid on the ward ... what? ... almost a week. Anything untoward before the convulsion?'

'Nothing. And of course, we've been keeping an extra vigilant eye on the parents, without being too obvious and arousing their suspicions.'

'Anything around the time of the convulsion?'

'Opportunity. Mum and baby were in the playroom unsupervised for part of the time at least ... a couple of the nurses went in and out. Gypsy was due for discharge the following morning so nothing wrong with that, but still ... opportunity. What's more Mr Morgan alleges the mum was asleep when he arrived. The babe was on her lap also asleep ... or going into a coma, as we now know. So technically *anyone* could have snuck in and administered the dose without Mum being aware of it. Gypsy had a cannula in so it'd be the work of seconds.'

'Thereby broadening the list of suspects yet again ... nurses, doctors, relatives, visitors.'

'Yep. Unlikely but *possible.*'

Silence fell.

'Unless ...' – George was thinking aloud – 'the perpetrator was canny enough to use slow-release insulin.'

'Jings, George, you've been reading too many trashy novels!'

'Running out of options, more like!'

'But who would have access to insulin?'

'Turns the spotlight back on the staff. Ward protocols and stocks all check out, I take it?'

'Yep. Checked and double checked.'

Brains whirred.

'I asked you to meet the parents, Beth; what's your assessment?'

'I agree. Lovely family. Not the kind to make you doubt their motives.'

'Who ever really knows what goes on behind closed doors?' Hamza said in the tones of an ancient sage.

Beth and George exchanged a quick look but said nothing. Decades of clinical experience counted.

The fourth consultant, paediatric surgeon, Ms Morven Strong, was still in her theatre scrubs when George finally tracked her down. She always reminded him of the actress Stefanie Powers, and even with her luxuriant chestnut hair caught up in a tight hat, a mask hanging lop-sidedly around her neck, she was arresting. But she was a down-to-earth person with no airs and graces, well-endowed with common sense.

'Hey, George. Abject apologies. I don't even believe myself when I say I'll be with you in ten minutes, nowadays! Two new admissions at exactly the same time. One needed emergency surgery; the other's on ventilation, sats in his boots, and writing's on the wall. Couldn't leave the chaps without a bit of moral support.'

'No problem. I knew you must be saving the world.'

'Only wish I could. This one'll be a black mark on my escutcheon, I very much fear, so forgive me if I rush you.'

161

They entered her room and she gestured to George to take a seat. He put down his file of notes and waved her aside.

'Sit down yourself, Morven. Take the weight off your feet if not your shoulders. I'll get *you* a coffee.'

Relieved of the burden of maintaining a façade, the surgeon's head slumped onto her chest and she massaged her neck rhythmically, suddenly looking more than her forty-three years. She accepted the strong black brew with a grateful smile.

'I did winkle out all our sudden hypos and unexplained incidents as you requested, George, but nothing there that we couldn't account for. Histories, reactions, eventual diagnoses, all added up. Sorry. Well, no, I don't know why I'm apologising! We none of us *want* to find a psycho skulking in the paediatric wards of this august establishment, do we?'

'Indeed not.'

'I confess, I was stumped. From the information you gave me, at least. Anything else come to light?'

'Nope. I've checked, and double-checked, and triple-checked. Magnus Andersen's been through the whole thing with a fine-tooth comb. Beth's seen Gypsy and the parents. You're welcome to do the same if you can spare the time.'

'So, in the absence of a Beverley Allitt ... or a Harold Shipman ... we're left with ...'

'Exactly.'

'Mum? Or Dad?'

'Mum more likely, given the track record of incidents over the six months since Gypsy was born. Dad's away most of the time and certainly at some of the critical times. He could *technically* have given the insulin, but ...'

'So, it'll be over to Child Protection? Psych department?'

''Fraid so. You were the last hope.'

'Bummer.'

'Indeed. But listen, thanks a lot for freeing up time for this, Morven. I know you've got a load of stuff on your own plate, so I'll leave you to it now. Any chance you could manage a nap?'

'A nap sounds so childish or geriatric, doesn't it? I prefer "a horizontal life pause"!'

George grinned. 'Whatever. Here's hoping your case *and* mine have a happy ending, huh?'

'I'd stake money on yours before mine!'

It took just one phone call to set in train the process George had been hoping against hope to avoid.

Dr Diane Moore was a paediatrician, lead paediatrician in fact, responsible for liaising with the Social Work Department and the police, when clinicians had grounds to fear for the safety of a child. She listened in silence to George's catalogue of facts and instantly drew up her own bullet points for action.

CHAPTER 33

Anya was aware of Dr Hooper appearing periodically in the ward during the day, occasionally glancing in their direction, but it was not until Leon arrived after work that he approached Gypsy's cot. He scanned the nursing charts and stood for a long moment looking down at the sleeping baby.

'Well, you'll be pleased to hear that nothing new has emerged to alarm us. All her observations are fine, test results so far all clear.'

Anya let out her breath noiselessly.

'But?' Leon sounded surprisingly abrupt. She turned to look at him. His face was taut, the silver scar above his lip glinting slightly as if with sweat.

'Sorry?'

'You haven't called in to say there's nothing to report, have you? So, what's the "but"?'

'Well, as you know, this is an unusual presentation. We're going to continue to watch Gypsy very closely, but we're also going to run more tests.'

'More? I thought you said ...' Anya began but Leon spoke over her, his tone harsh, his posture rigid. She could smell his fear.

'Look, this is our child. We have a right to know what you're thinking. So, give it to us straight, will you, Doctor?'

'Well, I reiterate, it's highly unlikely, but we can't rule out something rare going on here.'

'Like?'

'Possibly something called islet cell adenoma. A tumour producing insulin.'

'A tumour! You mean, *cancer*?'

George leaned forward to lay a hand on Anya's arm,

holding her gaze. 'It's an outside, outside chance, and extremely rare, and I honestly – really and truly – don't believe in my heart of hearts that's what we're dealing with here. But just in case, to be sure we're leaving no stone unturned, we're going to measure Gypsy's insulin levels, and I'm going to bring in my colleagues from endocrinology. I've already consulted them by phone, and they consider it highly unlikely too, but we want to be as confident as we can be that your little girl hasn't got anything sinister going on here.'

'You told us that yesterday.' Leon's voice was flat, colourless. He seemed to have deflated.

When Tiffany next popped in, Anya struggled to hold back the tears.

'Blimey, Anya! What will they dream up next? Look, it's far more likely that they're just covering their backs. Don't get yourself all het up over this nonsense. I mean, who was it who told you Gypsy was fine? Dr Hooper. Was he right? No. Who was it who suddenly starts talking about some rare tumour today? Dr Hooper. Funny coincidence, huh?'

'You think?'

'These hotshots never like to admit they're wrong. Believe me, I know. Nah. I bet you any money, all the tests'll come back negative. Look at her? Does she look like a kiddie with a serious condition? No. 'Course she doesn't. Put it out of your head.'

'But why did she have a convulsion, Tiffany? You can't deny she did. We saw it. Leon and I were *there* this time.'

'Well, I have no idea. But kids do have them, and they bob up again. Two out of three of mine did. And how often d'you ever hear they have some terminal condition?'

'But children *do* get cancer. We've seen them. In here.'

'These places are enough to give you the screaming abdabs, but honestly, my friend, the chances of Gypsy having something as rare as that are about a million trillion to one. Trust me, this'll be Dr Hooper watching his own back. But hey, we all make mistakes, we're all human, doctors too. So, we'll be magnanimous here, and give them the benefit of the doubt, huh? Bide your time, let them do their tests, and before you know it, he'll be telling you it was a false alarm. OK, maybe something isn't quite right, but it's not that.'

'This is like some nightmare. It just keeps getting worse.'

'I know. I feel for you, I really do.'

'I just want it to stop.'

''Course you do. Any mother would. And it's all the harder to bear when you've been told she's fine.'

Tiffany did her best to offer diversion with local gossip, her children's latest antics, and a greatly embellished account of her husband's attempts at DIY, and little by little the world began to right itself once more.

Left alone, Anya turned back to Gypsy and watched the baby chest rising and falling rhythmically, trying not to imagine what might be lurking under that translucent skin, how easily that little rib cage could be crushed, the heart stopped. When the images began to assume grotesque proportions, she wrenched her gaze away and scanned the window for Leon's return. She was surprised to see Tiffany still in the corridor laughing with the ward nurses. But of course, she knew lots of them; she worked here. *Oh to be as relaxed in a hospital as that!*

CHAPTER 34

George Hooper did indeed have to admit it had been a wild goose chase, and his feet felt leaden as he walked along the corridor. Even an invitation to the so-called 'bad news room', raised blood pressures; in this case, the consequences were much more significant.

Go cannily, George. One step at a time. Caution's the name of the game here.

He shut the door so carefully behind him it barely registered a click. The Morgans were seated side by side on the plum sofa, not touching, but undoubtedly a unit squaring up to an unknown enemy. They simultaneously put down their half-empty cups, visibly bracing themselves. He seated himself opposite them, allowing the light to illuminate their faces, leaving his slightly in shadow.

They listened in silence as he recapped the position before delivering his first arrow.

'The facts simply don't add up.'

'So, what's your latest theory?' Was that sarcasm in Leon Morgan's voice?

'Well, the next step is to draft in a colleague from outside this hospital. Her name is Dr Diane Moore. She's a very experienced paediatrician and she has a special responsibility for protecting children.'

Leon did a double take.

'What d'you mean?'

'She heads up a team who look into cases where families may need a bit of extra support.'

'So, what's that got to do with us?'

'Well, we've ruled out a *medical* cause for Gypsy's convulsion, so the next step, given the circumstances and the evidence, is to consider a different kind of approach.'

'Which is?'

'Let me get Dr Moore. She'll explain.'

He texted a message and almost immediately the door opened. As ever, Diane looked every inch the professional – elegant in her fifties, dark hair caught up in a neat bridal pleat, skinny frame accentuated by a plain black trouser suit. She advanced with a warm smile and shook hands with both parents.

'My name is Dr Moore, and my job, first and foremost, is to ensure your daughter's safety. OK?'

Both parents nodded, guarded looks on their faces.

'Dr Hooper's taken me and my team through the medical history and I've read through Gypsy's notes carefully – that means all the records from the primary care team, as well as during her hospital stays – and what jumps out at me is the number of minor ailments Gypsy has presented with.'

'I don't call a full-blown convulsion minor!' Leon said.

'Indeed. And it's this latest incident that's raised concerns about just what's going on, and that prompted Dr Hooper to consult me. Do either of you have a view on why these things are happening?'

'There's something wrong with her, I know there is,' Anya said flatly. 'Right from the beginning I've felt it. Only they aren't doing the right tests. That's why they haven't found anything to explain what's going on.'

'And d'you agree with that, Mr Morgan?'

George saw the hesitation, the swift glance at his wife.

'Well, Anya spends much more time with her than I do. I must admit, I thought it was her being a bit paranoid before, but this time – well, I agree, there must be some reason for the convulsion. Fair enough, they found a low blood sugar, but why?'

'Yes. Why?'

'So, are *you* going to take over? Do some new tests?'

'No. We're satisfied that Dr Hooper has done everything medically speaking that can be done at this stage and that Gypsy has made a good recovery. However, we feel that she'll need to be more closely monitored.'

'You mean … she has to stay in hospital …?' Anya was flicking her silicone wristband rapidly.

'Is that what you'd prefer?'

'No! I want her to come home.'

'You don't feel it's too big a responsibility for you?'

Anya shook her head vigorously.

'That being so, we've formulated a suggested plan which gives *you* more support, and *us* an opportunity to keep a closer eye on Gypsy.'

Both parents stared at her.

'Mr Morgan, I understand your work commitments necessitate you being away from home, often for several days at a time. Is that right?'

'Yes, but last time I looked, that wasn't a crime. Working hard? Providing for the family?'

'No, indeed. It wasn't a criticism. I'm simply establishing the scenario Gypsy would be returning to. I take it, you're not in a position to take time off from work?'

'No, I'm not.'

'Fair enough. So, in that case, here's our proposal.' She looked steadily from one to the other as she addressed each in turn. 'That you arrange for someone, perhaps more than one person – a relative, maybe, a good friend, an au pair? – a responsible adult, anyway, to help at home, take some of the pressure off you, Mrs Morgan. The health visitor and social worker will pop in and out, and monitor the situation to see if this is helpful for you. And we'll review things periodically to check that you're both happy with the way things are going, and that Gypsy's thriving. How does that sound for a plan?'

'I've been telling her for ages, she should accept help.' Leon sounded like a thwarted child.

'Mrs Morgan?' Dr Moore was looking directly at her.

'Are you saying, if I want to get Gypsy home, that's what I have to do?'

'It's what we strongly advise, yes.'

'Then, if that's what it takes, I'll do it.'

'And you do have relatives, friends, available …?'

'My sister, Leon's mother, my friend … yes.' The voice was hard, the eyes not meeting Dr Moore's.

'Our sister-in-law, too – she's offered to come up and help out,' Leon added.

'Good. I'll let the professionals who'll be responsible for monitoring things know to expect to see them at your house. Perhaps you could give me their names and contact details for our records.'

CHAPTER 35

Every day felt like an infinity, a disconnected sequence of checks, alarms, panics, a never-ending search for space and peace.

But realisation of a shameful truth caught Anya unawares: unjust and unequal it might be, but she was glad 'pressures at work' kept Leon away from home, far away from her unguarded tongue. He'd given that solemn undertaking to conform to their stipulations; he'd drawn up a month's rota of assistance and forwarded a copy to the professionals … and then he'd returned to his busy life. *She* was left with the daily expectation of an unannounced visit from someone with probing eyes and a suspicious mind hedging her about with restrictions, while *he* was free to be wherever, whenever, he pleased.

The first of the monitoring visits went badly.

Hannah Morgan was staying for the first two weeks and her gentle presence encouraged Anya to relax and let her be a hands-on grandmother. For the first time she'd allowed herself to leave Gypsy – albeit sleeping – for long enough to keep a dental appointment.

Sixty-nine minutes later she returned to the smell of fried mushrooms and the muted sound of conversation in the kitchen. Hannah was outside hanging sheets on the line, Tiffany was perched on a high stool, Gypsy on her knee happily drooling on a teething ring, the health visitor across the counter top, laughing at some joke Tiffany had just cracked.

'Ah, there you are, Super-woman!' Tiffany greeted her. 'I've just been telling Lucinda what a fiercely independent woman you are.'

'Hello, Lucinda. I'm sorry I wasn't here when you called.'

'No problem. Good to see you getting out.'

At that moment, Leon let himself into the house. He did a double take when he saw them all.

'Goodness. Party-time, huh? And something smells good. Hi, angel.' He chucked Gypsy under her chin and she rewarded him with a huge beam. 'You being a good girl, huh?'

'She's been brilliant,' Tiffany said, bouncing the baby high. 'Haven't you, darling? She let Mummy have some lovely free time, didn't you, honey?'

D'you need to rub it in in front of the health visitor?

'You're home early,' Anya said flatly, a stranger in her own kitchen.

'Just thought I'd check all was well here, before I head off for tonight's dinner with a client. But I see you've drafted in some extra back-up.'

Resentment flared.

'I didn't draft in anybody. Your mother's still here. Tiffany's just called in.'

'And is just about to leave,' Tiffany said, sliding off the stool. 'My three will have Ma swinging from the chandeliers by now.'

She passed Gypsy to Anya, who immediately took the teething ring out of the clenched fingers and dropped it in the sink. The child whimpered in disappointment. Anya gritted her teeth.

Please don't! Don't! Don't!

She wiped the sticky face and hands and then, propping Gypsy on her hip, turned to Tiffany. 'I'll see you out, and then you and I can have a chat, Lucinda.'

Gypsy was twisting and tugging at the suddenly-available blonde curls and Anya tossed her head to remove them from her grasp.

The inquisitive fingers seized a dangling earring; Anya removed it.

Gypsy poked a buttonhole and discovered part of her finger disappeared, she peered closer, banging her head sharply against her mother's jaw. Anya yelped, tears smarting in her eyes, and quickly transferred the child to her other hip.

Irritatingly Leon lingered in the kitchen, denying her the opportunity of a quiet session with the health visitor. What's more he even qualified her answers to the inevitable questions.

'Well, it wasn't quite like that, was it, Anya?'

'You're making it sound easier than it is.'

'You sure about that? As I recall, you were …'

'I have tried to tell her that …'

Two adults talking over the head of a recalcitrant child.

He left no chinks, no opportunity, for her to tell her own unvarnished story.

It took a super-human effort to clench her teeth, hang on to her façade, keep the screaming inside.

CHAPTER 36

Fingers clenched around a pen, a deep frown shadowing his eyes, Thomas looked more like their father than Leon had ever seen before.

'But they *promised* they'd return the stock,' Leon protested.

'Oh, they have.'

'So, what's the problem, *now*?'

'The problem, Leon, is that these precious Irish clients of yours are complete charlatans – not only in over their heads financially, but they can't even manage to protect their stock. Apparently, their warehouse was in such a rotten state it leaked like a sieve. Oh yes, they've kept their promise; they've returned the consignment – well, most of it anyway – but it's completely and utterly worthless. Ruined by water.'

Leon dropped heavily into a chair. 'I don't *believe* it.'

'A king's ransom ... down the proverbial swanny.' A long pause to let the enormity start to sink in.

'But ... we'll fight it ...'

'We will? ... With what, Leon? With. What?'

'What d'you mean?'

'Watch my lips. Elementary economics lesson coming up. a) Our Irish friends are bankrupt; they couldn't pay even if they wanted to. b) It takes money to file a case against a company in a situation like this – money we can't afford. c) Suing them would just add to our losses. A plus b plus c. There's not a snowball's chance in hell of us recouping a penny from Ireland.'

Waves of nausea washed over him.

'So, what happens now?'

'Our accountants have arranged a meeting for 4:15,

and I can tell you now, they won't be smiling, and neither will they be mincing their words. Nor will they be producing any magic wands any day soon. To put it in plain English: Morgan & Sons is in one helluva mess. And at this moment in time, apart from starting to sell assets, I have absolutely no idea where we go next.'

A groan escaped Leon. But Thomas hadn't finished yet.

'Oh, and in case you were thinking things can't get any worse, Frank Fowler is hell-bent on exacting *his* pound of flesh and – I quote – "bringing you fat cats to your knees". Fat cats, huh? If only!'

To Leon's horror, Thomas seemed to collapse inside.

Damn Frank Fowler. A fool and a hypocrite, a liar and a liability. But you couldn't fault his stubbornness. Flatly refusing to negotiate or settle, immune to persuasion and inducement through their solicitors. Single-minded about going to tribunal. Thomas was right: this news took Leon another rung below abject misery.

He hid in his office till 4:15.

If only he'd been less gung-ho.

If only he hadn't been so tired.

If only he hadn't been driving back to Scotland so frequently.

If only Anya had been in control at home.

And now, on top of that, cold fury filled the space around Anya when he *was* at home.

She'd been quietly submissive until the door closed behind Lucinda, then a veil had descended.

'Who needs enemies when they've got you?'

He'd never felt such ice before.

'What?'

'You heard.'

'I heard the words, but I have absolutely no idea what you're talking about.'

'And therein lies part of the problem.'

She'd stalked out of the room and flatly refused to explain. 'I'll only say too much.'

Try as he might to force the images to one side, they kept intruding. Not even the nightmare that was now 'work' could erase them.

It was three long days, three interminable nights, later, before he finally found the opportunity to sit down alone with his wife to talk seriously. Sobering to realise how much of their domestic agenda was determined by his work schedule, and at home there was no perceptive secretary to evaluate the crowded diary, winkle out the trivia, shoehorn in the big stuff, steer him in the right direction.

He entered the sitting room cautiously. Anya was already there, curled into a single armchair a distance from any other seat. No drinks. No nibbles. No music. No soft lights. Face inscrutable.

'Look, Anya, I know you're mad at me, and I'm sorry I've upset you, but I honestly don't know what I've done.'

'Not even after three days of analysing?'

'No. But whatever it was, it wasn't deliberate.'

'You constantly undermine me.'

He stared at her, at a loss.

'And Wednesday was the last straw. You breeze in all unexpectedly. You can *see* the health visitor is there, *and* Tiffany, *and* your mother. And from the second you step into the room, you do nothing but run me down. Imply I'm not coping, I'm not to grips with things, I can't speak for myself. Like I'm some sort of backward child, to be vaguely humoured. To the *health visitor* too! – the very person who's employed to check up on me.'

'I wasn't undermining you ...'

'Oh, you were, Leon. You most certainly were.'

'Well, I'm sorry if that's how it came across ...'

'It did. Loud and clear. And if you say things like that *in front* of me, who *knows* what you say behind my back?!'

'I don't talk about you behind your back.'

'No? You sure about that?' Her eyes bored into him.

He felt the colour rush into his neck.

'Well, I may have said I was worried about you ...'

'*May* have?' The acid stung, the question suspended between them. 'All these offers of help. Solicitous enquiries. Pitying looks. There's no "may have" about it. You did.'

'I've been desperately worried about you.'

'So, you thought disloyalty would shore me up.'

'It wasn't disloyalty …'

'I think your definition of loyalty comes out of a different dictionary from mine.'

A long silence, more hostile than any words. His brain tried one approach after another – all seemed calculated to inflame a volatile situation on her side of the room.

'Tell me, did your "loyalty" also extend to priming the professional staff? Did you tell *them* I was a nutter, unable to cope with one little baby? Is that why everybody's watching my every move?'

There was no smoothing this over, she needed to vent her wrath before he could attempt to explain and start to rebuild.

'Your silence says it all. While I've been doing my level best to get us back on track, you've been feeding them a totally different scenario. Well, thanks for nothing, Leon.'

Stung by her tone and the sneer on her face, he reacted before he'd thought through the consequences. 'Look, don't take this out on me. I'm not the one with the problem here!'

'Oh? Is that so? If you were here more, if *you'd* been dealing with all the symptoms, maybe you wouldn't be dismissing them so easily. But you *aren't* here, are you? You swan off to work, down to Newcastle, and bury yourself in your precious company. What's an extra dirty nappy or two, a little convulsion, when you're chatting over a civilised meal with a wealthy client, or drooling over the latest vintage car with Thomas?'

The incongruity cut deep. 'And worrying myself sick about what's happening to Gypsy the entire time I'm absent!'

'But you know *I'm* here. You know *I'm* taking care of her.'

'Depends on your definition of care, I guess. I don't personally include walking out leaving her unattended in the house; sleeping through her choking; forgetting to put her in the pram …'

'There! At last. It's finally out in the open. You don't trust me. Well, you know what, Leon? *I* don't trust *you* either. So that makes us quits.'

He frowned, genuinely lost.

'Don't think I don't know what's going on,' she spat out. 'I've seen enough evidence to know how the land lies.'

He gritted his teeth. 'I have absolutely no idea what you're talking about, Anya, but one thing I do know, this conversation is doing nobody any good. And we're both in danger of saying things we'll later regret. So, I'm going to go to my study now, to do some preparation for tomorrow. I'm supposed to be in Newcastle for the next three days, but it's up to you. I'm ready to cancel it – and incur Thomas' wrath yet again – and stay here for you, or I can go. You choose. Let me know when you've had time to think rationally.'

'I don't need time. I'm perfectly rational. You go. Enjoy watching your perfect sister-in-law manage her perfect kids and a perfect job and a perfect home.' As she spoke she unravelled herself from the chair and strode to the door.

Something primal flared. 'At least she listens and doesn't throw a hissy-fit at the drop of a hat!'

She turned and gave him a withering look.

'Of course.' – sarcasm was seared into every syllable – 'She *listens*. It's what Juliette does. And no doubt she'll swallow the misunderstood-and-unappreciated-husband act hook, line and sinker. What a pity you didn't marry her, huh?'

'Grow up, Anya. Some of us have bigger fish to fry.'

And she was gone.

Leon found he was shaking uncontrollably.

CHAPTER 37

It had taken every ounce of effort to make her exit without dissolving.

The second she reached the top of the stairs, Anya's legs buckled and control deserted her. She flung herself onto the bed, buried her face in the pillow and gave herself up to a full-blown fit of sobbing, stuffing the fabric into her mouth to mute the sound. How had they become a source of mutual reproach to each other? Where had love and sensitivity and warmth gone?

When there was still no sign of Leon at 11:30, she crept to the top of the stairs. The strip of illumination under his door suggested he was working ... should she ...?

No. It was down to him to take that first step now.

Her pillow was still damp in the morning and a crushing headache dominated and blurred her thinking.

Was she fit to carry Gypsy downstairs?

Was she capable of making the thousand and one tiny decisions that constituted mothering?

Hannah would be only too ready to take over ... No, she shouldn't be dragged into their disharmony. Besides, the sooner everyone agreed that Anya was perfectly competent to cope alone, the better. She just needed a little boost ... maybe a double dose under the circumstances ...

The moment Hannah went to the utility room to sort the laundry, Anya opened the drawer, lifted the napkins, slid four white tablets from her blister pack, added them to the painkillers she'd already tipped into her palm, and swallowed them without allowing herself another doubt. The day had to be survived somehow.

Gypsy seemed to sense her mother's preoccupation. She opened her mouth automatically for each new spoonful of cereal, blowing no raspberries, throwing no utensils. She made no fuss when she was put into her playpen but scrambled around, grinning at the squeaks and honks and rustles and jingles she generated as her body made contact with the sensory toys scattered all around her.

Only then did Anya start her search ...

... kitchen surfaces, hallway, living areas. Nothing.

... phone, inbox, answerphone. Nothing.

... Leon's study, spare bedroom. Nothing.

The conclusion seemed inescapable. He had left home without a word. Leaving no note. It was a new low.

She dropped onto the floor beside the playpen and stared into space, ignoring her daughter's upstretched arms.

Fury gathered in her breast. Betrayal. Disloyalty. Insensitivity. Now, walking away! Hot tears stung her eyes.

Was this the point of no return in their marriage? Neither willing to reach out across the yawning abyss of those accusations?

'Are you all right, Anya?' Hannah was hovering with a clean nappy, clearly unsure of her next step. 'I don't want to pry, but you don't seem yourself this morning. I'm happy to take care of Gypsy if ...'

'Would you? I'd be grateful. I've got such a headache.'

She must have dozed; she certainly hadn't heard the doorbell.

Hannah said nothing until Anya had brewed a pot of tea.

'The social worker called while you were upstairs – Jane? Jane Carver?'

Anya put down her cup of tea abruptly. 'Why didn't you wake me?'

'She insisted I shouldn't. Said your sleep was more important.'

'What did she want? What did she say? Did she do a full inspection? I should have been there.'

'Actually, no. And no! She just chatted, really. It was

quite obvious everything's fully in control, so she didn't need to inspect anything. And she was really happy to hear you were accepting a little bit of help, catching up on some rest when you could. I told her that you were coping brilliantly. I wasn't really needed at all, but we were following all the procedures to the letter.'

'Did Gypsy? ... Was she ...?"

'She behaved impeccably! And Jane declared herself entirely satisfied with everything she saw.' Hannah smiled.

'I think I owe you an enormous debt,' Anya said softly.

'Nonsense. It's an absolute pleasure to do what I can ... which isn't much.'

'It's everything. Without you here we wouldn't have been allowed to get Gypsy home.'

'Well, I'm sure you could see me far enough much of the time, but after today ... well, perhaps they'll relax soon, and stop this nonsense, and see for themselves what a wonderful mother you are.'

Anya felt the tears well. 'Thank you for that. It means more than ...'

Hannah reached out to lay a hand on her arm. 'You are. You've been through a tough time – and there'll be more ups and downs yet – but I have every confidence you'll come through this stronger and wiser.'

Anya shot her a shrewd glance but Hannah merely said, 'I'm not going to interfere. You're adults. But have patience, dear. Rome wasn't built in a day.'

There was something new and warmer between them.

'I feel I'm on a hiding to nothing. If I put Gypsy first, I'm a martyr. If I put myself first, I'm a monster. I can't win.'

'Welcome to motherhood!' Hannah said ruefully.

'How did you cope?'

'I muddled through like most mums do. Trial and error for the most part. But I remember reading about a doctor – Wonnacott ... Winnacott ... something like that ... who introduced the idea of "good-enough" parenting. Nobody gets it right all the time; you just need to get enough right for your baby to be safe and develop normally. I found that reassuring. Until Leon came along! And of course, that was much more of a struggle. It was a shock to start with – the harelip, I mean. People don't mean to be cruel, but the looks, the comments ... It hurts when it's your precious baby. Easy to feel you've failed somehow. Feeding was a nightmare, too, before the repair. And seeing that tiny little scrap, only three months old, going under the anaesthetic ... going into theatre ... all on his own ...'

Anya sat perfectly still.

'Thomas was almost five by then, remember, so he was running around causing mayhem at the same time. Not an easy time for us as a family. And Douglas wasn't much use at home, preoccupied with building up the firm.' She patted Anya's hand. 'Thomas was a real little hero, I will say. He was so protective of his kid brother. Wouldn't let anyone call him names, overlook him for a team, bully him. I suspect he still does that to some extent – shoulders the weight of things himself rather than give Leon too much worry. I might be wrong, maybe it's just a firstborn thing, nothing to do with the disfigurement.'

'Is that why Leon feels he *has* to be down in Newcastle now? All he said was, he has a responsibility to other people; he can't shirk that. But maybe he's repaying Thomas in some way.'

'I don't know about the specifics, dear. I stay well out of company business. Douglas tries to, I know, but it's harder for him. It was his life, his baby.'

'Must be really difficult, building something up and then handing it over to younger people. They're bound to do things differently.'

''Course they are. I say that to Douglas: the boys have to put their own mark on it, make it theirs, not keep it like some shrine to him.'

'I know Thomas and Leon have huge respect for what Douglas did. On his own. I don't know Roger so well so I can't speak for him, but I imagine he'd feel the same.'

'Roger's different. He's the artistic one, feels things deeply, cares about people's sensitivities. He's not competitive in the least; more likely just to go along with what Douglas used to do, not challenge things. There's always been this special connection between the older two; it excludes Roger sometimes, I know. It's not malicious, just the way things are. It was Thomas and Leon against the world when they were growing up. Roger was happy to read, paint, play at make-believe; the other two were into sport and bikes and computer games. I was never sure he really wanted to go into the family firm.

'But Huong Mai has been good for him. He's become more confident, more forceful, since she arrived on the scene. I guess steering her through all the vagaries of a completely different culture, introducing her into his milieu, has matured him. She's very sweet, but she still relies on him a lot. I think that's good for him. And now there's a baby on the way, it'll give him a greater sense of purpose which I hope spills over into the company.'

'Oh, is there? I hadn't heard. That's brilliant news. I must ring them.'

'Argggh. Maybe I'm not meant to have said. It's very early days. Can you forget I mentioned it? Wait till they tell you themselves. Sorry. It just slipped out.'

'Of course. I won't breathe a word till I hear officially. It's their news.'

Such affirmation from both Jane and Hannah softened Anya's mood, but Leon had still not made contact. With every hour the sense of impending trouble gained a stronger foothold.

The letterbox rattled. She dragged herself to the vestibule. The usual junk mail, catalogues, official transparent windows; only two personal items addressed to her.

It seemed like too much effort to bother. She stared out into the garden, still very much a work in progress. The rough ground in the far corner, overgrown with rampant raspberry suckers, mint and ivy, remained a dominant eyesore. Might do her good to get out there and hack away at that. Elsewhere the trees and shrubs had come alive while she was going through her own personal winter. Sun enhanced the strong colours of the burgeoning crab apple, the delicate tracery of the golden acer wafting in the slight breeze. The vivid plumage of three goldfinches attacking the seeds on the feeder was in sharp contrast with a single drab sparrow that vanished as soon as three pigeons ambushed the space, demolishing the falling grain as fast as it was dropped. She watched the over-stuffed creatures posturing and cooing. Yes, it would do Gypsy good to get some fresh air too.

The kitchen was full of the aroma of savoury chicken when she looked again at the post. The first envelope was a card from her cousin in New Zealand, congratulations on the birth of her baby. It looked odd, one belated card alone on the mantelpiece, as if she had no other friends or acquaintances to share this momentous event. She took it down, tucked it behind the jar of used postage stamps. Once Leon had seen it she'd put it into the scrap book ...

If Leon ever came back ...

She mashed stewed pears furiously, covered the dish carefully, set it aside to cool. Her hands were still damp when she picked up the second envelope.

A wave of unreasonable irritation flooded through her. The address was printed in an unexceptional font. *Why were people always in so much of a hurry?* There was something special about handwritten missives. You felt the connection immediately; envisaged the person as soon as you saw their distinctive hand, reaching out to you personally across the miles, sharing their news.

She slit the envelope crossly. Inside was a single sheet of white paper.

Just three measly sentences. *They couldn't even be bothered to pick up a pen ...*

I KNOW YOU'VE BEEN HARMING YOUR LITTLE GIRL.
PEOPLE LIKE YOU DESERVE TO BE LOCKED
UP IN PRISON.
I'M WATCHING YOU.

Anya froze. The paper dropped to the floor, partially

refolding as it went. The soft sounds of happy grandparenthood shrank to a vague murmur in the background. Mechanically she stooped to retrieve the note, stuffed it in her trouser pocket and returned to her task. By the time Gypsy's meal was ready she'd regained her outward composure and resolved not to give those cruel words the tiniest chink of head-space. She read Gypsy four bedtime stories, lingering long after the heavy eyes had closed, willing the tales of adventurous bunnies and beautiful princesses to soften the ugly thoughts that hovered somewhere above the pale pink covers.

But with Gypsy sound asleep, the evening stretched ahead of her like a wide canyon, ready to drag her down into a fathomless pit of doubt and fear. She went through the motions of watching a documentary with Hannah but her mind refused to concentrate.

Who could possibly have sent that venomous note?

Who hated her enough to turn her life into this hell? And why?

There was still no text or phone call from Leon. It was now almost twenty-four hours since they'd parted so heatedly. Uncharted waters.

The first stirrings of fear swirled into her anger.

CHAPTER 38

The phone rang and rang.

Please be in. Please, please, please.

Claire sounded as if she's just been wakened from a deep sleep, though she denied it.

Even to Anya's own ears, her theories seemed absurd. But the anonymous letter itself could not be dismissed. It was real. It was there, in her house, irrefutable.

'You're far better at decision making than me, Anya, but d'you think ... should you report it ... to the police? I mean, it's what they call a poison pen letter, isn't it? Like in Agatha Christie. Aren't they illegal or something?'

'I did wonder that, but you know what? I can just see them thinking: this crazy woman is sending poison pen letters to herself, now! I *know* I didn't send it, but I can't prove it. I can't prove any of it. That's what's so frustrating. Damn it, Claire, sometimes I even doubt myself! Am I in some parallel universe where I'm not responsible for my actions and too loony to even know what I'm doing? I just don't know.'

'Don't be silly, Anya! Sometimes you do talk a lot of rot. 'Course it's not your fault. Whoever sent it must have a screw loose. It's *their* problem. Anybody who does that kind of thing has to be seriously off their trolley. D'you hear me?'

'I hear you, but it's one thing to know something intellectually, a completely different thing to hang on to the idea when everything is conspiring to tell you you're wrong.'

'Know what I think? This'll be some creep who's envious of you. You're beautiful, clever, competent. Successful husband, lovely home, gorgeous baby. They've seen you wobble a wee bit recently, and they've latched on to this tiny little chink of weakness; an opportunity to get at you for

186

making them feel inferior the rest of the time.'

Anya interrupted her sister.

'Claire, don't make me something I'm not. You're worth ten of me. I may *look* as if I've got it all, but I know I'm not an easy person to be with. I know I'm hard to like. My ex-colleagues don't visit. I don't mix with the other mums – well, except Tiffany who practically forced herself on me. So, I reckon there'd be a queue of people who'd feel pretty smug seeing me brought down.'

'Rubbish. People don't go around writing malicious letters to folk just because they keep themselves to themselves. That's sleep-deprivation talking.'

'I keep going round and round and round with this, and none of it makes sense.'

'When's Leon due home?'

'I'm not sure. I can't remember if he even said. Friday, I think.'

'Couldn't you contact his brother?'

'No. He already thinks I'm a drag on Leon.'

'They're probably both caught up in something at work where they can't use their phones. What about your sister-in-law? See if she knows where he is?'

'No.'

'Shall I come over?'

'No need. Leon's mother's here. I'll be fine. But thanks for the offer, and thanks for listening.'

'Well, if you change your mind …'

'I know. You're there.'

But you're a constant reminder of how much damage babies can do to a marriage.

The thoughts circled relentlessly but Anya was determined not to let this horror get out of control. Nevertheless her voice clearly belied her resolve when Tiffany rang an hour later.

'You free for coffee tomorrow morning, Anya? You and the irresistible Gypsy Lysette, of course.'

'Maybe not this time. Sorry.'

'Have I annoyed you?'

'No.'

'So how come you aren't sure if you're free or not?'

'I'm just not in the mood ...'

'Is everything all right, Anya? You sound ... I don't know ... not yourself.'

'I'm ... I've got things on my mind.'

'Want to share them?'

'Not really.'

'OK.'

Another friend slipping away from her ...

'If you must know, I've had a letter.'

'And that's a cause for rejecting a friend's offer of coffee? Funny kind of letter.'

'It's an anonymous letter. Accusing me of ... stuff.'

'What?!'

The pernicious accusation sounded even worse spoken out loud. Anya flung the paper away from her the second she finished reading it out.

She heard Tiffany's swift intake of breath. 'Flaming Nora, Anya, no wonder you're rattled. Sorry I was snippy. I had no idea.'

'How could you? I was trying to ignore it, but I can't get it out of my head.'

'What kind of a loser writes something like that? And why?'

'I only wish I knew. My sister thinks I should take it to the police.'

'And what d'you think?'

'I'd rather wait till Leon's seen it. See what he thinks.'

'Good idea. Don't let this crackpot think they've got any kind of hold on you. Carry on as if nothing's happened.'

'Easy to say; not so easy to do.'

'Sure. I can quite see that. But ... '

'"But" what? What're you thinking? Am I missing something here?'

'No, it's nothing. Forget I spoke.'

'No, tell me.'

'Well, I was just wondering … who would even *think* you'd do something like that? Who knows Gypsy's been poorly? Who knows how much that particular accusation would get to you? It's weird.'

'That's exactly where I'm at. It's like somebody's been watching, waiting, looking for some way of getting to me.'

'D'you know anybody who might dislike you that much?'

'Not that I can *think* of.'

'What about Leon? Has *he* got any enemies? Somebody who's trying to get at him through you?'

'I don't know. And I can't get hold of him to even ask the question. He seems to have vanished off the face of the earth!'

With both Gypsy and Hannah in bed, Anya scoured the kitchen and the bathrooms, finished the ironing, and three times picked up the phone only to put it down again immediately.

But the thought of a night not knowing whether her husband was dead or alive was too much for her. She resolutely put all her reservations aside and dialled Juliette and Thomas' number.

'Hi. This is the home of Thomas and Juliette Morgan. I'm sorry we aren't available to take your call at the moment. Please leave your name and number and we'll get back to you as soon as we can.'

So Leon and Juliette were both *out of communication at the same time …*

And surely, surely, surely, someone, somewhere, would have contacted her if he'd been in an accident.

CHAPTER 39

Lucinda scanned the outside of the house, marvelling again that a young woman of her age, could actually own something as desirable as this property. It looked even more lovely than the last time she'd called, bathed as it now was in brilliant sunshine, framed by fresh unfurling leaves, bordered by a bed of fragrant hyacinths, daffodils and tulips.

'Beautiful, isn't it?'

'To die for,' Jane agreed.

'Let's just hope things are as serene on the inside.'

Distinctive chimes reverberated hollowly. Too bad if they'd missed her again. Lucinda was on the point of pressing a second time when the sound of a key turning stopped her. She stepped back so they were both on the path and not looming over Anya when she opened the door ... perfectly groomed, smartly dressed in monochrome maroon. But Lucinda's eyes lingered on the dark circles and drawn skin.

The steel frame seemed to give almost imperceptibly when she saw them.

'Oh, hi. Sorry. I was expecting ... someone else.' She rapidly pinned on a smile.

'Is it convenient for us to come in?' Lucinda kept it light, friendly. 'Sorry if we've come at an awkward time.'

'No, not at all. Please.' Anya opened the door wide.

'We're just calling to see how things are going for you and Gypsy.'

'Fine. We're doing just fine. Thank you.'

Anya led them through to the kitchen. A gleaming, immaculate expanse fit for a prospective buyer in a TV reality show. Who wouldn't fall in love with this perfection?

How did anyone avoid a single fingerprint on those

gleaming surfaces?

There was no sign of Anya having been engaged in any activity whatever.

Was she actually polishing everything – in that outfit?

'Do have a seat. Can I offer you tea, coffee?'

The perfect, composed hostess. She calmly and methodically made them drinks, steadying the kettle with two hands, pushed a plate of bourbon biscuits within range, Lucinda's personal favourites.

No home-made cakes this time? Signifying what?

Besides … *they* weren't the expected guest.

'Your garden's looking fabulous,' Jane said.

'It's a lovely time of year. But the trees and most of the shrubs were here when we came, so we can't claim much credit for them.'

'They set off the house perfectly, don't they?'

'I think so. Yes.'

'And how's Gypsy?'

'Sleeping well. Eating well. Playing well. Reaching all her milestones.'

'Good. Is she asleep now? Could we see her?' Lucinda asked gently.

'Of course. I'll get her for you.'

Did she not want them to venture beyond this showcase?

Anya put down her own cup again very carefully, using two hands as if she couldn't trust herself with one. Lucinda saw the tremor in the split second before they were thrust into the pockets of her trousers.

What was spooking her?

Was she on something?

As soon as she left the room Lucinda saw Jane's eyes roaming everywhere. Not a thing out of place. Unnervingly tidy even though their visit was unannounced. But of course … she'd been expecting someone else. *Who warranted this kind of preparation?*

Gypsy sat erect in her mother's hold, bright and alert, clearly not newly awoken, and looked from one face to the other with wide unblinking gaze as she was carried into the room. Anya's full attention was on the baby.

'Hello, Gypsy. My, look how grown up you are! And what fabulous curls!'

The solemn look was focused on her.

Nothing wrong with her hearing.

'Any problems at all?'

Lucinda rose from her seat and moved carefully towards mother and baby. She extended a finger and stroked the soft plump skin on the back of the child's hand. Gypsy snatched it away and leaned her head against her mother, but maintained her watchful stare.

Complete trust there then.

'None.'

'No more convulsions?'

'No.'

'And how about bowels? That settled down now?'

'Yes.'

'Jolly good.'

'She certainly looks the picture of health.'

A picture-perfect baby, a picture-perfect mum, a picture-perfect home. Hmmm.

'D'you need to see her undressed? Check her over?'

Aware of their possible concerns. Confident.

'Would that be all right with you?'

'Certainly.'

Anya handed the child to Lucinda, and offered her a clean soft cover still warm from the Aga to lay her on. She held out a soft toy in front of Gypsy and the eager fingers snatched it up, stuffed it into her mouth. There was no glimmer of protest as Lucinda deftly removed the layers of clothing until the little girl was in nothing more than her nappy, bouncing on her feet, back strong, head control excellent. It was methodical: skin, muscle tone, reflexes, fontanelle, weight, basic measurements, hearing, sight. She was very aware of Jane sitting passively beside her watching, but knew the trained eyes were roaming over the soft fair skin: no visible marks, no evidence of any kind of trauma.

192

And the child was clearly perfectly at ease, with her mother as well as these strange women.

Not a single sign of anything to alarm them.

Except Anya. She ticked all the boxes, said all the right things, but something didn't ring true. She responded perfectly politely to every topic of conversation introduced, but there was no vestige of the sparky, edgy woman they'd come to know.

Why wasn't she inwardly rebelling, injecting even a soupçon of sarcasm or resentment, letting them know that she wasn't fooled for one second?

'Is there anything at all you want to mention, ask, clarify?'

'Just, how long does this scrutiny go on for?' It was said without rancour; a simple enquiry.

'You mean the health visitor checks? Till Gypsy's five.'

'And the social worker? Needing to have my mother-in-law here. She *is* still here, in case you're wondering. But she didn't want to intrude.'

'I'm afraid that's completely outside my jurisdiction.'

The phone rang shrilly and Lucinda saw the reaction in Anya's rigid face and body.

'Excuse me.'

She positively raced to the hall.

When she returned minutes later, she seemed to have visibly deflated.

'Sorry about that.' Her tone was completely flat and colourless. 'Only I'm expecting a call.'

'Just one more question ... is your husband still away a lot?'

Lucinda watched the shutters close.

'Yes. Work's particularly demanding at the moment.'

Was she ... afraid? Could he be ...?

'You're clearly a busy lady. We'll leave you to it. I hope the call comes through soon,' Lucinda said softly.

Whoever she was expecting had to be extremely important to her to raise her hopes so high, to be dashed quite so spectacularly.

CHAPTER 40

Anya leaned against the door and let out her breath in painful jerks. She'd been so sure it would be the police at the door: *May we come in?* Bringing their standard platitudes, their false sympathy, their grotesque news, tainting her home forever.

There'd been no time to debrief from that certainty, to change her mind-set from new-widow to mother-under-suspicion. What had these two spies made of things this time? There were no yardsticks known to her.

Yes, her home was immaculate: Tick. Hadn't she just put every ounce of pent up stress into polishing it as her go-to therapy for a terror beyond belief.

Yes, she looked smart enough: Tick. On the outside anyway. Controlled enough to go through the usual social niceties. Could they detect the turmoil within? She'd hardly been able to lift the kettle, pass the biscuits. She couldn't risk undressing Gypsy with two pairs of professional eyes on her fingers. How much had they seen?

Yes, Gypsy had been a star: Tick. *Big* tick, bless her. Surely, surely, surely, she alone had convinced them of her safety, of her healthy development. Surely.

The morning seemed interminable. She'd tried ringing Leon again directly but there was no reply. What could possibly prevent him from contacting her now? She even rang his office once, but got some temp who said she had no idea where her boss was, and hadn't been told how to put the call through to someone who might have a clue. It sounded so improbable Anya would have smelt a rat had she not already entered a zone where nothing made sense any more.

Four times her landline rang – each time she was sharp

and short with the caller. She *had* to keep the line clear. Twice she felt the vibration of her mobile – and both times trivial messages drove her fear deeper with every silly syllable.

When the phone shrilled at midday, her first thought was to clutch this shred of hope to her breast for as long as was humanly possible. She dragged herself to the hallway like a lame salamander.

'Hello?'

'Anya, hi. It's me.'

'Where have you *been*?! Why didn't you ring? I've been out of my mind with ...'

'Look, don't start. Just don't start, huh? I've got five minutes. Is Gypsy all right?'

'Yes. You didn't even text ...'

'You knew where I was. It's on the calendar.'

'I know you were *supposed* to be in Newcastle. But you didn't pick up ...'

'I haven't had a chance ...'

'I even tried phoning Thomas.'

'He was in the same boat ...'

'And Juliette. She didn't answer either.'

'Oh.' A pause. *A significant pause?* Long enough for her mind to conjure vivid scenarios. 'Well, we've made contact now. And I think we're on target to be home on Friday. Give Gypsy a big hug and loads of kisses from Daddy.'

'I will.'

'I really *must* go. Big brother's lurking.'

There was no time to reply.

Not a word about their fight. No hint of an apology for the things he'd said. No interest whatever in *her* days.

Her mind was in turmoil. The prospect of him never returning had thrown into sharp relief the fragile state of their marriage. Now she knew he was at least alive, and furthermore intended coming back, the questions changed. *Just how important was he to them? To Gypsy ...?* She felt a strong need to get some distance from the stranglehold of unresolved conflict. A long walk would do both her and

Gypsy a power of good.

'Honestly, Hannah, you really don't need to come. I'll take full responsibility. We've just been inspected; they were totally happy with everything. You'll be here to see we return safely. And I'll keep my phone on.'

It felt wonderful, totally alone with her daughter.

She pointed out a squirrel playing Suicide Dash on the road; fluffy clouds pretending to be ducks; a row of sparrows – ninety-nine green bottles on the cables above their heads; multi-coloured animals masquerading as bouncy frames in a play park; a pristine bridal dress in a second-hand shop waiting for Cinderella; a lone royal-blue mitten in the gutter planning a big adventure before its owner returned to claim it; a forlorn white balloon tied by a pink ribbon to a rusting gate – a secret message to a little girl who'd never been to a party ... until Gypsy's eyes closed. With no incentive to divert her mind she stepped up her pace; at least she could get the benefit of some more vigorous exercise and fresh air.

When she found herself at the entrance to Dalkeith Country Park she hesitated. *Why not?* The memories might be exorcised if she overlaid them with healthier ones. She stuck to the properly made-up paths, it was no part of her plan to run into difficulties and require assistance this time. The easiest route – *who on earth had named this rural loveliness Wilderness Walk?* – offered no challenges. Buoyed up by the soothing effect of simply walking in peaceful surroundings, she braced her shoulders and resolved to lay the worst demons to rest.

She swung the pushchair into the Lugtonhaugh Walk, the very one she'd been on that fateful day when she'd found the pram empty beside her. Her heart thumped uncomfortably, her mouth felt dry, her muscles tense, but gradually, imperceptibly, the tranquillity soaked into her being, softening the dread, replacing the agitation. She even paused for a few minutes at the very seat where the police had found her. But not for a moment did she take her eyes off the sleeping child this time. No voices, no people, disturbed their passage throughout the second walk. Eerie. As if the whole park was holding its breath.

It was a relief to arrive back at the central area, and be amongst dog-walkers, families, retired couples, milling around, selecting activities, licking ice-creams. She indulged in a quick coffee before Gypsy woke, and then took her across to the adventure playground to watch the children at play.

Four families were already there and Gypsy sat bolt upright, eyes darting from one child to another as they screamed to each other from the fort, vanished into tunnels, coo-eed from the turreted treehouse, clambered up the rope netting, raced across the suspension bridge, scampered through the shadows of the trees. Her body remained perfectly still as her brain synthesised the kaleidoscope of vivid colours checkering her field of vision.

Occasional remonstrances came from the benches where two mothers of indeterminate age sat surrounded by buggies and bags. One bottle-blonde, one dyed-black. One easily a size twenty, the other somewhere shy of a size eight, harsh accents, disillusioned expressions, faded jeans, fake leather jackets in common. The only contact with their offspring shouted commands, not one followed up or enforced. And clearly the children were perfectly well aware the threats were idle; they scarcely paused in their pursuit of their own selfish ends.

'Jenny, let Alice have a turn.'

'Stop that, Davey. There's room for you both. No, stop it.'

'You do that once more and we're going home *now*!'

'Mikey, you're fine. Just hold on and come down one step at a time.'

'I can see you! Just you wait till I get you home.'

'Jenny! I told you before.'

Another girl, denim from neck to ankle, looking not a day above fifteen, sat alone and silent in sharp contrast, a screen inches from her nose, immersed in her messages, only occasionally checking the whereabouts of her charge, a flaxen-haired boy of about three, who approached each activity with extreme caution and never climbed above the first rung of anything. He looked to be totally absorbed in his own inner world.

'Maribel! Come up here. It's totally ace! You can see for ever!' a disembodied face draped in an untidy shock of mousey-brown hair, shrieked down from the turret window.

'Coming!'

A younger girl of about eight, long skinny legs brown beneath skimpy shorts, streaked across the ground and vanished from sight, only to appear in another window. Both waved furiously in Anya's direction. She tentatively raised a hand, only to realise her mistake when she heard the rapid-fire clicks from a camera immediately behind her. She glanced back with an apologetic smile. A tall, slightly stooped man, overweight, early forties, was following the two girls with his zoom lens, making adjustments, altering his angle, capturing childhood in all its spontaneity. His voice was low but carried clearly.

'Jude! Why don't you join the girls? Good to have you all in one shot.'

The tousle-headed boy, six feet from her, dismissed the idea with a shake of his head, not taking his eyes from the contraption he was contentedly trailing behind him. To Anya it was a long branch draped in a vivid red fleece; to the child who had concocted it, it was clearly exactly what he wanted it to be.

The man moved closer, crouching to capture the boy's rapt expression.

The girls had temporarily vanished from sight somewhere in the turret. *How long did it take to learn to be unconcerned when your beloved children were nowhere to be seen? How could you possibly watch three at once!*

The man dropped onto the end of her bench, camera at the ready, his fingers already in position for that moment of magic. His light brown hair was tied back in a ponytail and a row of silver rings studded his left ear. Khaki trousers, checked shirt, scuffed leather boots, gave him the appearance of an extra in a crowd scene for some bucolic film.

'He...llooo!' Deep, mellow, extended syllables.

He was leaning forward, beaming at Gypsy, who stared for a long moment and then grinned back, arms pumping, two brand new teeth glittering with saliva. Anya bent to wipe the wet mouth.

'You're a wee charmer, aren't you?' His smile revealed crooked teeth and a tongue piercing. 'What's her name?'

'Gypsy.'

'Gypsy?' He startled in an exaggerated way. 'Not … Gypsy Morgan?'

Anya felt something clench inside her.

'Why d'you ask?'

'My wife knows someone called Gypsy Morgan. Tiffany Corrigan?'

'You're Dan Corrigan?'

'As I live and breathe.'

'Well, hello. Lovely to meet you. I've heard a lot about you. Sorry, I was a bit … well, cautious, earlier.'

'No problem. Weird guy in a kiddies' park … can't be too careful. But I assure you, I'm perfectly harmless. Just here trying to exhaust our three. They've been hyper since a birthday party yesterday. Good place to let off steam.'

'It *is* a good play park, isn't it?'

'Did you know it before they revamped it?'

Anya shook her head.

'Apparently, it's changed out of all recognition. We come here a lot. And even Sam doesn't think this one is beneath her. You know what they're like when they're that age; image is everything. But here, she's just a kid again. I'm soppy enough to want to hang on to that innocent age as long as I can. They grow up far too quickly.'

'They certainly seem to be having fun today. It's nice that they've got each other too.'

'Yeah. They get on well for the most part.'

'Although Tiffany tells me they're all very different.'

'Chalk and cheese. But maybe that helps. Gypsy's your first, I think Tiff said?'

'Yes.'

'Enjoy the peace and quiet while you can, is all I can

say. Not much of it in our house!'

'All the more reason to thank you for sparing Tiffany to help me. She's been a lifesaver. With all the problems I've had, she's kept me sane – nurse, chauffeur, advisor, all rolled into one.'

'She hasn't mentioned any problems. Nothing serious, I hope.'

It suddenly felt too personal to discuss a small girl's bodily functions with a strange man.

'Oh, just bits and bobs ...'

'Dad! Dad! Look how high Sam's gone!'

He turned towards the voices and lifted the camera to catch the girls hanging from distant frames, focusing in on radiant faces.

'Better not neglect my paternal responsibilities. But nice to meet you, Anya, and I do hope Gypsy's fine now. She certainly *looks* the picture of health, don't you, sweetheart? I'd be snapping her twenty-four seven. Bye, precious.'

He twittered his fingers at the baby in farewell and strode over to catch his daughters' antics for posterity.

Weird to think Dan Corrigan had spent more time in the park with Gypsy than Leon had. But he wasn't running a company, raking in big bucks. She watched him revelling in the simple pleasures of his children's fun and felt a pang of envy. Tiffany might scoff at his casual approach to life and appearance, but there was a lot to be said for devotion to family. There was no one taking a thousand pictures of Gypsy.

She turned the pushchair in the direction of home, and the relentless questions began again.

Could she salvage her marriage?

Did she even want to?

It was several minutes before she remembered the anonymous letter.

Who could possibly want to derail her sanity?

Leon still didn't know about the note ... but Tiffany did.

Had she shared the information with her husband?

What had been going through his mind as he sat there beside her on the bench?

Was he pitying Gypsy saddled with such a neurotic parent?

The relief on Hannah's face when she returned smote her conscience.

'Sorry. I was just laying a few ghosts to rest. And I've decided ... it's totally unfair you putting your life on hold for us. If Leon can't be here, I'm going to appeal to the social worker. Gypsy's been absolutely fine all this time. They have to stop this nonsense now. And if not ...'

CHAPTER 41

Leon looked up with a frown. No disturbances: what part of that instruction did this wretched girl not understand?

Sally Ford had spoiled him. An exemplary personal assistant, she knew exactly how to protect him, and probably more than he did about the inner workings of Morgan & Sons. Thank goodness her two weeks leave was almost over; this temp was driving him stir crazy. She looked like a freak to start with, her unconvincing red hair permanently escaping from its clasp, her glasses never seeming to quite fit her needs, her idea of smart clothes defying logic but defined by clashing colours, and her high-pitched voice grating on his frayed nerves to such an extent that he had deliberately and quite unreasonably put himself outside her range by repeatedly issuing a do-not-disturb instruction. Of all the weeks to be without Sally ... but *of course* she had to be with her daughter for the birth of her very first grandchild. He'd insisted.

He glanced up at the vision in lime green and bilious yellow, and pursed his lips.

'What is it?'

He knew it was harsh, and he definitely wouldn't get a boss-of-the-year star from Flick (*whoever chose to abbreviate their name to Flick?!*) Reynolds. The only saving grace was she appeared completely oblivious to sarcasm, curtness and sudden rules. Probably thought it was par for the course. She'd never met the former Leon Morgan – the boss he'd been before his marriage disintegrated ... his daughter's safety was threatened ... he'd personally planted a ticking time-bomb underneath the company ... stared an uncertain future in the face.

He schooled his expression into something resembling bland. 'Is there something urgent? Only, I'm busy.'

'I just remembered. I forgot to tell you. Your wife phoned yesterday.'

'And?'

'I told her you weren't available.'

As per instructions.

'So?'

'She said to put her through to your brother.'

'And?'

'I said I don't know how to transfer calls. Nobody showed me. So, I couldn't put her through to Mr Morgan senior's PA.'

'Riiight.'

'If she rings again do I tell her you're at the hearing?'

'*No!*'

She looked like a kid who'd just been told how *not* to tackle a problematic algebraic equation, but given no guidance as to how to begin to apply basic principles. He had neither the time nor the patience to teach her in the few minutes he had left before he must leave for what promised to be one of the most gruelling days of his life so far. Besides, she'd soon be someone else's problem.

'I don't think she will, but were she to do so, say I'm not here.'

'What if she asks where you are?'

'Say you're new. Say you're only a temp, Sally will be back on Monday. Say I don't tell you anything. Say I'll ring her tonight.'

Give me strength!

She backed out with a look of concentration as if rehearsing the lines for an end of term play.

When the door opened almost immediately without so much as a knock, he slammed his hand on the desk and bellowed, 'For heaven's sake, will you …'

Are you always this imbecilic or is today a special occasion?

Thomas' frame filled the doorway. The sombre suit and

tie, crisp white shirt, slicked down hair, spoke volumes, but it was his frowning demeanour that made him look like a stranger. He put his Morgan-special briefcase down without taking his eyes from his brother.

'Steady as you go, Leo.' His voice low and calm, he slid forward closing the door with his person. 'We're all pretty uptight, but let's take ten here. No point in giving anyone ammunition against us before we even start.'

Leon felt a wave of shame wash over him.

'Sorry. And I will apologise to that wretched girl before we go. It's not her fault she isn't Sally, but honestly, Thomas.'

'I know. I've seen enough to know Ms Reynolds won't be coming back. But it's time to go, so say what you have to, and let's get going. And keep it brief. We can't be late today.'

Flick looked stupefied by his apology. 'It's OK. I'm sorry I don't know how to do stuff. And I know I'm not good at lying. Only ...'

What an indictment!

'Forget it. I shouldn't have spoken to you so sharply. I'm off now. Won't be back for the rest of the day, so if anyone rings I really am not here. That's the truth. Right? And you have no idea when I'll be back. Also the truth.'

She bent to write the message carefully on her notebook, her bitten nails gripping the pen hard enough to turn the tips white. Read out loud it would be too ludicrous to be credible.

In spite of the hours spent with their legal team preparing for every eventuality, Leon felt physically sick entering the building where Frank Fowler would drag his name into the mud. His first Employment Tribunal ever and he was at the epicentre.

On the face of it, Morgan & Sons held the whip hand – a sound track-record, established reputation, excellent representation, a raft of reliable witnesses. Frank Fowler was arrogant enough to have dispensed with agents of any kind (even those offered generously by the company), confident in his own ability to make a watertight case. But Leon knew the public could attend these hearings and Fowler's family and friends were sure to be noisily behind him. He'd even had nightmares about seeing his own father's sad face observing his humiliation.

Behind the scenes, the lawyers had duly gone through the final stages of attempted reconciliation, but it came as no surprise to anyone that Fowler rejected the offer of a last-minute settlement; no one was going to deny him his literal day in court.

There was to be no reprieve.

Everything seemed calculated to exacerbate Leon's inner terror – the imposing room, the unsmiling judge, the panel members' averted eyes, the silent waiting lawyers, the unknown faces in the public gallery, a brash Fowler centre-stage.

The formalities helped to steady his nerves, the reasoned language of the written statements taking something of the heat out of the dispute, cloaking the human frailties in legal niceties. But cross-examination was brutal. His heart bled for the men who were subjected to Fowler's vitriolic questions – Thomas, Bill Broadbent, three trusty employees who'd put their heads above the parapet and volunteered to be witnesses against their erst-while colleague. Even the two ex-drivers Fowler had co-opted to speak to a culture of bullying within the workplace earned his sympathy as the company lawyers set about demolishing their credibility brick by brick. But Fowler reserved his worst for Leon himself.

'Look at *his* track-record ...'

'Too busy tearing up and down to Scotland in his fancy car to notice ...'

'You'd think nobody else ever had a baby ...'

'Ask his wife ...'

Leon felt ice in his heart.

What exactly did Fowler know about his personal circumstances? And how did he know it?

The judge felt compelled to intervene several times, but the damage was already done. Leon felt the weight of guilt mounting. He knew a visceral urge to stand up and put an end to this destruction, shoulder the blame and take the consequences. But weeks of careful schooling denied him that relief. They'd drummed it into him: there was much more at stake than his personal comfort.

He held steady, maintained a dignified poise, a coherent story. Exactly as they'd rehearsed.

Fowler, without the benefit of such expertise, soon resorted to shouted invective, exaggerated claims, his façade eroded by the relentless barrage. Intellectually Leon knew that intimidation was the normal tactic in such circumstances, but it gave him no pleasure to see a man losing control against such a calculated system.

There but for the grace of God …

To everyone present this must look horribly like justice being determined by the depth of your pockets; deprivation pitched against privilege. By the time closing submissions were heard, Leon was beyond assessing the hearing dispassionately. All he could see was the trail of devastation left in its wake, the human cost, his role in it.

Nor could he seek solace in the verdict: after conferring briefly the panel decided they needed time to consider the evidence.

'A decision will be sent to both parties at a later date.'

The company must continue to operate, employees must continue to wonder, the owners of this family firm must continue to prepare for every eventuality.

CHAPTER 42

The sword of Damocles hanging over Morgan & Sons haunted him at every turn but Leon went through the motions of a normal day at headquarters – being seen by the troops; facing Bill Broadbent; meetings; phone calls; moving on. He swallowed his reservations and discussed the future briskly … prospective designs, new machinery, fresh advertising, potential outlets. He even found the superficial grace to wish the temp, Flick Reynolds, well in her future career, though he drew the line at rewarding complete incompetence with flowers.

Secretly, he'd been shocked by the toll recent experiences had taken on him, and Thomas' injunctions to break the journey rang insistently in his ears. A coffee stop and an extended doze in a layby near Ayton, meant it was well into the early hours when he let himself into the silent house.

Exhaustion overwhelmed him immediately, and it was almost 9am before he surfaced. He followed the sound of banging, and found Anya, sitting in a low chair, holding a tambourine for Gypsy to hit with a wooden spoon, the noise enough to mask his entry and give him space to stand and stare. Slumped posture, vague expression, no engagement with the child; everything spelled defeat.

'Well, I don't think you're quite ready for the Albert Hall yet, but good effort,' he said lightly, moving forward to drop a fleeting kiss on Anya's hair and stoop to pick up Gypsy. 'Look at yooouu!' He swept her high over his head.

She beamed down at him, a silver stream of saliva suspended from her lower lip. Anya reached up to mop it with a tissue, and he jiggled the child until she gurgled with delight, stuffing both hands into her mouth.

'I swear she's visibly bigger every time I come back,' he said, not taking his attention off his daughter. 'You'll soon be running away from me, and I'll have to *huff* ... and *puff* ... to catch up with you. Yes, I will.'

Out of the corner of his eye, he sensed Anya slipping out of the room. Propping Gypsy on his hip, he followed her into the kitchen.

'It's so good to be home. I've missed you two,' he said.

'It's been a long week here too.' She busied herself boiling his eggs.

'Sorry, contact was a bit erratic this time. Pretty hectic down there, closed meetings, out of range quite a bit of the time. I really need to get a better phone. Damn thing takes forever to recharge. So, what have I missed? Any news? Anything dramatic to report?'

He sensed her hesitation.

'Have your breakfast first and I'll fill you in.'

He watched her slim figure moving around, making toast, lifting out the eggs, the light glinting on her shining fair hair, the tailored shirt and trousers following her contours as she stretched and bent to her tasks.

'Have you been losing weight?'

'Not deliberately, but I have been exercising more. And before you criticise, I feel better for it.'

'Hey, I wasn't going to criticise. You look fabulous. You always look fabulous.'

Was he too critical?

She took Gypsy so that he could eat in peace.

'I'll just change her and put her back in her playpen.'

He sat in the wake of her distancing behaviours, sensing the tension, unsure of his next move, and she'd still not returned when he'd cleared everything away.

She had remained in the nursery, staring into the garden. He moved to stand beside her.

'Anya, I hate being at odds like this. Can't we put the past behind us, try again?'

'I don't know. Can we?'

'I'd like to try.'

'D'you still doubt my sanity?'

'Let's not rake over old scores. You only have to look at Gypsy to know she's totally cherished and loved and cared for. And that's down to you.'

'Me ... under constant surveillance.'

'We had no choice.'

She didn't reply.

He softened his tone. 'How did it go ... with Mother staying here?'

'She's been brilliant ... but it's just not fair. Why should she be stuck up here? She should be in her own home, doing her own thing.'

'I totally agree. And I think ...'

'I'm going to appeal. We had another inspection this week. The health visitor and the social worker came together. One distracts you while the other one checks things.'

'And?'

'They *seemed* satisfied ...'

'So I should hope! I mean, what more can they ask for?'

'Lucinda will still be doing the routine stuff – everybody gets that. Until they're five. I asked about the social worker side of things, how long they keep that up. She said it wasn't her call. So, I'm going to find out who's call it is.'

'Right.'

'And in the meantime, Tiffany and Claire will pop in and out. And your mother says she's happy to take her turn.'

'And me. Look, I'm not going to make excuses, Anya. I *should* have apologised before you went to bed. I *should* have said goodbye. I *should* have left a note explaining. I *should* have made sure I rang you. I really am sorry I didn't, and I promise to try to do better from here on in. Please don't shut me out.'

'There's something else.' He felt the sudden tension. 'I've had a letter.'

'And?'

'An anonymous letter.'

'*What?!*' He stared down at her. 'Saying what?'

'That I deserve to go to prison.'

He was bereft of words.

'I'll get it. You can see for yourself.'

His heart was pounding in his chest as he watched her. All his own doubts crowded in, rebuking him.

Perching gingerly on the edge of the chair, not touching him, she passed him the note and sat twisting her fingers together while he opened it, read the three sentences four times.

I KNOW YOU'VE BEEN HARMING YOUR LITTLE GIRL.
PEOPLE LIKE YOU DESERVE TO BE LOCKED
UP IN PRISON.
I'M WATCHING YOU.

CHAPTER 43

'Who on earth would send something diabolical like this? I mean, *who*?' he managed.

'I have no idea. But it has to be somebody who knows us quite well. Where we live. Gypsy's history.'

'Somebody who has it in for you.'

'Or you.'

He startled. 'Me?'

'Yes. Could be somebody who wants to get at you through me.'

She had taken the rug from under him completely, she couldn't know how completely.

Oh yes. There certainly were people who'd like nothing better than to see him destroyed. The same person who'd put him in court this very week; had him in limbo now. But ... how would anyone down south know about ...? – wait a minute ... it was a family firm .... his brothers were fellow directors. The manager, Bill Broadbent, knew. His PA, Sally Ford, knew. How else could he have taken time off when Gypsy was in hospital? Who else might any one of them have told in confidence, or as part of a necessary explanation?

'I take your point, but whoever it is, this has to be a real psycho.'

'Claire thought I ought to take it to the police, but Tiffany said best ignore it.'

He stared at her. 'You discussed it with *them*?'

'Well, yes.' The accusation was back in her voice. 'Can you imagine what it felt like, here on my own, opening up something as ... as ... toxic, as this? I didn't want to scare your mother, but ... I needed to tell *somebody*!'

'But not me. Thanks, Anya. That makes me feel a whole

lot better.'

He got to his feet and began pacing up and down the room, his mind in overdrive.

Anya sat bolt upright, indignation writ large, eyes steely.

'Don't take that tone with me, Leon! You ignore me for days. You even tell your PA not to put my calls through … You're the last person to lecture me about communication. Besides, what would you have done? Come racing home? I don't think so. Give me a break!'

'Look, I *can't* keep taking time off. Things are … complicated … at the moment.'

She shot him a bleak look.

'And before you say anything, I *have* to be away next week. I have no choice. But I really don't think you should be here, on your own.'

'So, you think it's a real threat?'

'No! What I think is that there's some bastard out there who gets a kick out of terrorising a defenceless woman … sorry, I don't mean to be sexist, so don't jump down my throat for *that*. But I doubt this kind of coward would have the guts to do anything physical. What I'm saying is, you shouldn't have to cope with filth like this on your own. So, how about … if you don't want to keep Mother up here, you go to stay in Alnmouth with them? I could drop you off on my way down, pick you up again on the way back. Or better still, come down to Thomas and Juliette's.'

'And show whoever wrote this I'm scared? I don't think so! That'd be playing right into their hands.'

'OK, then, what about asking Father to come up and stay here, too, if he's free. Nobody needs to know this is anything other than fond grandparents coming up to see their newest grandchild. And you could all go on day trips, meals out – make it into a holiday.'

Her pupils were enormous, her face so pale she looked positively ghostly.

'It's not your *father's* problem. It's *yours* – ours!'

He gritted his teeth.

'I've got two hundred people to think about here, Anya. Not just you and Gypsy.'

'Well, you just go and play the big I am. Forget I even told you about the letter.'

She stalked from the room and a few minutes later he heard the front door close and her car crunch along the drive. It was left to his mother to inform him that Anya had gone 'to get something from the supermarket'.

When the doorbell rang forty minutes later, his first thought was that she'd forgotten her key. He was surprised to see Tiffany Corrigan.

The olive skin looked almost black with the sun behind her, the dark fleece and jeans could have been a uniform, but there was no mistaking the purple flare even in this light.

'Oh, hello.'

'Hi. Sorry, I didn't know you were at home. I thought you were down south.'

'Well, as you can see, I'm not. This isn't a cleverly crafted hologram.'

He felt unreasonably irritated that this woman catalogued his absences.

She grinned. 'I was just wanting a quick word with Anya?'

'Not here, I'm afraid. I can pass on a message.'

I'm damned if I'm going to fill you in on my wife's movements.

'It was just to ask her, is she free on Tuesday for a day out? Lunch in town and maybe a dander through an art gallery, a bit of retail therapy. Or maybe I shouldn't let on we go on spending sprees to you, huh?'

Leon felt his cheek muscles tighten. *Ignore it. Ignore it.*

'I'll tell her, but I can, on this occasion, answer for her. We have people staying and she'll be totally tied up all week. So, thanks, but not this time.'

'That's fine. Just thought it might cheer her up.'

'I'll tell her you called.'

'Please do.'

He stepped back as if to close the door but she put out

a hand, leaned closer, and under her breath asked, 'Is anyone within earshot?' her wide amber eyes darting to the doorway and back to him.

'No.'

'It's just ... well, she told you about the letter, yes?' Her Highland accent was more pronounced in the half-whisper.

'Yes.'

'Have there been any more?'

'No.'

'D'you think ... is it possible ... I mean, she's been so edgy lately. Sort of... I don't know ... *haunted* almost. Could she possibly ... have written it herself?'

Leon stared at her. 'Why on earth would she do something like that?'

'Well, she was adamant that you shouldn't be told till you got back. I mean, you'd think she'd turn to you first, wouldn't you? But no. She wouldn't hear of it.'

'I'm not sure what you're implying.'

'Well, I just wondered if this could be her way of grabbing your attention. You know, after all the other little things. She hasn't been robust mentally for some time, has she? And it occurred to me that perhaps some of these incidents with Gypsy have been her way of getting attention. You hear about it, don't you?'

'I think you'll find she tries not to distract me when I'm at work. My trips away aren't jollies, you know. And besides, she's much, much better now,' Leon said firmly. 'So please, I'd be grateful if you could leave the past in the past, and let her move forward normally.'

'Of course. I'm only saying this to *you*. I wouldn't dream of undermining *her* in any way. I'm her friend. I think she knows that.'

'Thank you. I appreciate all you've done to support her, and I mean that sincerely. But the sooner we forget all this nonsense the better for everyone.'

'OK. And again, I'm sorry if I've overstepped the mark.'

He nodded. 'I know you meant well.'

Leon watched her walk away, the purple streak in her

dark hair catching the light, like some iridescent peacock strutting its stuff.

Damn the woman! Damn, damn, damn her!

He'd almost managed to put that niggling thought out of his mind and here she was fleshing it out with logic and reason. But ... could *Anya be so disturbed that she would concoct such a scenario, fake such emotion? Was it even possible?*

CHAPTER 44

Leon had left her with little choice: he'd even co-opted his mother to 'make her see sense' – a new low.

Hannah was only four inches taller than Anya, but she had a presence, a reserve, a containment, that Anya found strangely daunting. It was illogical. Her mother-in-law had never once criticised, always encouraged and complimented, the very soul of generosity. Her home was not the epitome of order that Anya favoured: no stacking cookery books by diminishing height, no daily re-arranging of flowers, no weekly dusting the tops of the doors, for her. Her clothes were a fraction of the price Anya's budget allowed, her waist measurement a good six inches larger. Hobo skirts and floaty tunics bought on-line placed comfort above style, and she'd never shown the slightest interest in owning a Morgan & Sons leather handbag. And yet ...

'I really, really don't want to interfere, Anya. You and Leon have to sort out your differences yourselves. But none of us wants to run the risk of them taking Gypsy away, do we? *We* know you don't need me to nursemaid you, and I promise I'll do my utmost to keep out of your way. But it was a condition ... the authorities imposed it. Gypsy's been totally fine since she came out of hospital; they must surely accept that soon. So, isn't it worth a few more days of me staying, just to keep everybody on side?'

'But it's *our* problem. *You* shouldn't be inconvenienced any longer.'

'Leon says it's only another week ...'

'How many times have I heard that?!'

Hannah grimaced. 'I know.' She paused. 'Anya, would you consider Douglas coming up this time? I think Leon suggested it? If you could cope with us both here, we could all do some fun things with Gypsy, but he'd be only too glad to make himself useful as well. He could attack that overgrown patch in the garden, get it ready for you to plant up. It's exactly the kind of challenge he loves to get his teeth into. A week would soon go.'

They think there's a real danger ... we need a man about the house ... but how kind, to give up their time ...

Hannah simply held her as she wept.

Douglas arrived early enough to have an hour with his son before Leon left for Newcastle. Anya, watching the interplay between them, felt something very like envy. They were so comfortable with each other, the affection obvious, the banter built on years of trust.

Would she ever have that with her own child?

There had been no precedent. Her mother had died when she was only nine years old, and try as she might, Anya could summon up little more than a vague memory of a wan face against white pillows, a hustling hand adjuring her to 'Leave your mother in peace.' Her father was already a remote figure in her life, so his departure to foreign parts and the establishment of a completely new family which left no margin for her, barely ruffled the rhythm of her daily life. Her aunts were not cruel like the fictitious harridans who took in orphaned relatives, but neither did they have the capacity to provide the kind of nurturing environment that she dreamed of. Leon, knowing nothing but unconditional love and support, would never understand the internal hurdles she constantly faced to feel worthy of anything approaching what he took for granted. She consciously held herself at a distance lest she somehow alter the dynamics and spoil something precious.

Leon resembled his father to a quite uncanny degree, and watching the older man with his white hair and slight stoop moving around in her home felt rather like seeing into the future. But Douglas no longer did everything at a run, he pondered a question before answering it, he had a gravitas and calm that she found comforting, as if he had seen the folly of life in the fast lane and found a better way. Several times she found his clouding eyes watching her intently and wondered if this hard-won wisdom allowed him somehow to see beyond the façade she had pinned on with her hostess apron.

It was easier to breathe once Leon had departed and she had a clear baseline to work from, no longer any competition for the attention of a single dominant male, at once child and father, son and husband. And she had two major advantages: she was on her own turf, secure with her own rules of engagement, and better still – her trump card – she had a grandchild to offer Douglas and Hannah.

They wasted no time in reinforcing the terms of their stay: they were her guests.

'A little thank you for being such a delightful hostess – all the delicious meals, the lovely little touches,' Hannah said, handing her a beautifully wrapped box.

'Not sure if it isn't coals to Newcastle,' Douglas said gruffly.

Hannah quelled him with a look.

As soon as Anya lifted the lid, the unmistakable scent assailed her. She closed her eyes and inhaled slowly.

'I just *love* that smell.'

'Leon said you did … I'm afraid it's wasted on me.'

She parted the tissue paper reverently. The dark green shopper was part suede, part calf-skin, elegant and capacious, simple lines but classic.

'This is far, far too generous.'

She ran a hand gently over the surface, loving the luxurious feel, turning it this way and that, admiring the subtle gleam of the polished skin, feeling the weight.

'If it's not to your taste, you change it.'

'It's *perfect*!' The colour, the shape, the design, the feel, the distinctive label: *Morgan & Sons. Luxury Leather. Established 1950* – everything! 'Exquisite. But still far too generous.'

'And it's for using,' Hannah said firmly.

'Han's right. Use the blessed thing. No point in giving houseroom to a museum piece.'

She did, taking it wherever they went; beautiful gardens, famous attractions, art galleries, country drives, historic sites. There was always something to report when Leon touched base.

It was late on the Thursday before the opportunity presented and she could summon the courage.

Douglas was dozing in the sitting room. He'd worn his responsibilities well. The still-lean frame, the strong hands now lightly clasped on his stomach, the calm face, bore little evidence of a life of stress, constant decision-making, corporate hospitality, and ambition. Presumably in his day, Douglas too, had sped up and down the country, burned the midnight oil, striven for more. But he differed from his two older sons in one significant aspect: his modest way of life left no room for a restless search for better, bigger, more modern, faster. Would Leon – would *she* – be less materialistic as they grew older? Would Leon ever learn to relax enough to stretch out like this, pleasantly tired by healthy exercise, at peace with the world?

She tiptoed away.

Hannah was perched on a high stool, paring, mashing, packing, as they jointly prepared Gypsy's food for a picnic the next day.

'Can I ask you ... about child care. You had a nanny at one stage, didn't you? Would you recommend it?'

'It took me till after Roger was born before I finally gave in on that front. I was stubborn when I was younger; I wanted to show everyone I could cope with being the wife of a tycoon.' Hannah pulled back her shoulders, held her head high, put on a superior look. 'I might be young and from humble stock, but I could keep a large home running, entertain high-powered contacts, wear posh frocks, play the part. But three little boys represent a ton of work, and Douglas needed me to play my part.

'She wasn't the traditional Norland Nanny or anything grand like that, just a young woman who'd done some training and loved kids. Flexible enough to babysit when there were big company dos, be there for the boys coming home from school if Douglas needed me to traipse around entertaining the wives of his business colleagues, run the other boys around if one of them was sick, that kind of thing. Not so involved as to be bringing them up instead of me.'

'A bit like Solange, then.'

'Except ours wasn't French and half way to becoming a famous model!'

Anya smiled at her expression. 'Probably all the better for domestic harmony then!'

'Oh, I don't think Juliette is the least bit insecure where Solange is concerned. Looks like a model herself, doesn't she? And I can't imagine Thomas is remotely interested in that way. Although, I'm only his mum; what do I know of my sons' romantic or erotic aspirations!'

Something closed its claws around Anya's heart.

'Did you ever resent the demands of the business?'

'Oh yes! When I was shovelling beans and sausages into our bunch of toe rags, one eye on the clock, the other on the washing machine cycle, and he'd be sipping champagne and dining on venison at some exclusive restaurant. And I must admit I did doubt him sometimes when he said he absolutely had no choice, he *couldn't* attend some school play, or parents' evening, or a football match, or whatever, because of work demands. But of course, you have to remember, he was running the show single-handed. If *he* didn't expand it, there was less to hand on to the next generation, and by this time it was divisible by three. It's different with the boys today, they have each other to share the load. I know Thomas does everything he can to be there at the children's performances – thanks to Leon and Roger filling in for him. And I'm sure he'll return the favour when yours get to school age.'

'They do seem to work well together. Leon's down in Newcastle a lot. I just hope Juliette doesn't object to the time

Thomas spends with him.'

'Oh, Juliette's always had a soft spot for Leon. Those two get on famously, always have. I can't imagine for a moment that she has any negative thoughts on that score, so don't worry about that.'

At that precise moment Douglas wandered in, tousle-haired from sleep.

'What're you two cooking up?'

'A cup of tea if you care for one.'

Anya hopped off the stool and returned the kettle to the hotplate.

'Apologies. I've been incredibly rude, sleeping instead of entertaining you,' he said rubbing his arm vigorously.

'Goodness, you shouldn't apologise. After all that heavy lifting this morning! I hope you aren't doing yourself a mischief.'

'It's nothing. Just a muscle or two I haven't used in a while. Do me good to get a bit of a workout.'

He came to stand behind his wife, slipping his hands loosely around her neck. She looked up at him with a soft expression. There may have been jealousies and doubts over the years, but there was no questioning the solidity of the marriage now.

Would she and Leon ever reach such a point? Did they stand a chance?

Even Hannah knew about Leon and Juliette's bond.

What would she say if she knew it was much, much more?

Was *their own marriage worth fighting for?*

Watching her in-laws, her heart yearned for certainty.

CHAPTER 45

On one level Leon understood Anya's hostility. From where she stood, he must appear to be a distant apology for a husband and father, and she knew nothing of the horrors and pressures he faced daily, the prospect of losing everything. Nevertheless, her coldness cut deep. Which made her first offer of an olive branch the sweeter.

They were standing looking down at their sleeping daughter together.

'We ought to enjoy this time while she's little. It's been far too fraught up to now.'

'Well, amen to that.'

'Tell me more about your sister. Your mum mentioned her in passing but I didn't like to probe.'

'Antonia? She came between me and Roger – I only vaguely remember her. She was just eighteen months when she was killed. Mother had parked the pushchair beside a wall and was talking to some neighbour or other. This hit-and-run driver apparently came out of nowhere and smashed into the pushchair, crushing Antonia against the wall. She didn't stand a chance. Mother saw the whole thing.'

Anya shivered, closing her eyes against the images.

'How d'you ever come to terms with something like that?'

'Funny, I don't remember Mother ever talking about it. But I once walked in on Father on the anniversary of her death ... the only time I ever saw him cry. I can still remember what he said: he'd have given up all the money he made, all the success, all the acclaim he received, to have her back.'

'Puts things into perspective, doesn't it? And I guess that's behind something else your mum said to me. Don't constantly wish them past the various stages – crying infant, terrible twos, endless questions, teens, exams. Embrace every moment. Child-care can be relentless and exhausting, but if you think of it as time you'll never get again to build up relationships, it becomes an investment for the future. Made me feel very small.'

'How come?'

'She must have wanted to shake some sense into me when I worried about small things. I wish I could be more like her.'

'Oh help! You'll be giving me an Oedipus complex in a minute!'

It was the spur he needed. Time to lay his cards on the table.

'Look, Thomas, I know I've made mistakes – serious mistakes. And nobody regrets that more than me. But I *have* to spend more time at home.'

Thomas laid down his pen with infinite care.

'I'm listening.'

The catalogue of problems spilled out.

'Anya resents all the time I'm away. Half the time I don't think she even believes I'm *at* work, and of course, I can't tell her why I've been down here so much … It's *my* fault she has to have supervision … It's *my* fault we have social workers sniffing around … And on top of everything else, she's now saying she got an anonymous note while I was down here last week.'

Thomas leaned forward. 'Hold up a minute, Leo. What d'you mean, "She's *saying*" …? You don't believe her?'

'I don't know what to believe.'

'Did you *see* the letter?'

'Yeah.'

'And … what did it say?'

'Accuses Anya of harming her baby; says she should go to prison.'

Thomas swore with feeling. 'But … I don't get it … why don't you believe her?'

'I suspect … she might be doing it to get my attention.

Force me to stay up in Scotland.'

'You're kidding! ... Sending *herself* a foul message ...?'

'I know it sounds far-fetched but .... It's been one thing after another. Crisis after crisis. And what do I do? Drop everything and race home. She gets my attention.'

'Bloody Nora. *Anya?* She's never been the prima donna type, has she?'

'She's changed, Thomas. I hardly know her these days.'

Thomas shook his head slowly. 'Beggars belief. I wish you'd told me this before, Leo.'

'Nobody wants to broadcast the fact that their wife is losing the plot.'

'Well, go home. Take all the time you need, now. Anya's your priority. Sort things out. And for what it's worth, I don't think it's only Anya who needs a break. You used to be ... well, never mind. Just you concentrate on getting things back on an even keel at home. Roger and I'll take care of things here. You're no use to anybody in this state.'

Apart from checking messages at either end of the day, Leon kept well clear of his study for the next seven days, and gradually a superficial peace allowed them to take tentative steps together, Gypsy the innocent focus of their separate efforts. It was not until Friday morning that anything happened to thwart his efforts.

They were almost ready to leave for a trip to Floors Castle – the largest inhabited castle in Scotland, a magnificent Georgian building in the heart of beautiful countryside in the Borders. Anya had done her homework and was armed with historical detail and horticultural expectation.

'It's a fun day out, don't forget, not an A-level exam!' he called as he strode towards the door to collect the mail.

'Philistine!'

'Only three that aren't circulars or catalogues or informing you that you've won a six-figure sum of money.' He passed them to her and slit the only envelope that looked personal, addressed to them both: *Mr and Mrs Leon Morgan.* He folded the envelope to shield it from her view. She hated being 'Mrs Leon'. Dr Anya Carpenter for years in her professional capacity, she always said it was a double insult, robbing her of her independent identity and her status. But it was a private reflection; she'd never flaunted her academic credentials.

The words caught him by the throat. His very breath strangling him, he managed to close the paper and saunter towards his study.

'Just going to switch off the computer. Got side-tracked this morning. Be with you in a jiffy.'

The words were typed, ubiquitous font, no identifying mark of any kind on the paper.

Go to hell, bitch.
Women like you should be stoned to death.
Children are a gift from God,
not status symbols for the rich and idle like you.
Stop harming her or I'll contact the police.
Matthew 18 v 6

He felt physically sick.

As far as she knew, his leave ended today; he hadn't told her about Thomas' generous offer of indefinite leave. *Was it enough to make her stoop this low to keep him here?*

He stuffed the evidence into the drawer of his desk, under several memos.

Long, steadying breaths, Morgan. In ... out ... in ... out ... in ....

Only then did he take the first steps back into their plans for the day. When he did eventually look directly at his wife, she was totally focused on Gypsy, whose eyes were everywhere, taking in the excitement of her mother's directions.

One more day. Can we just have one more normal happy day before Armageddon is let loose. Please!

CHAPTER 46

Lucinda paused for a long moment outside Dr Brownlee's door, taking long slow breaths.

He held up one finger, returning to the computer immediately. 'Sorry. Two secs ... and I'll be all yours.'

She watched him, peering at the screen, typing with two fingers, only three years off retirement but clinging on to the coat tails of technology at a very basic level till he could take his name off the brass plaque in the hall and join the local history club. His wife, Karen, joked that his children would disown him if they discovered he didn't know how to run his own analytics or edit a photograph of a tumour in his surgery. But the receptionists were always ready to bail him out, leaving him free to do the job he *could* do – dispense comfort and understanding along with the prescriptions.

Lucinda might be mildly amused by his laidback resistance to change, but his casual approach to evolving regulations frustrated her. No one, no matter how senior or experienced, could be permitted to put their head in the sand where the safety of a child was concerned. She *had* to report her qualms, somehow persuade him to listen.

'For once the wretched thing hasn't thrown any tantrums!' he said ruefully, patting his monitor as if it were an obedient terrier.

She grinned. 'I know exactly what you mean. After the whole system crashed last week I've been paranoid, saving every last sentence.'

'The price of progress, huh?'

'Bring back the big fat paper wallets, the handwritten notes, yeah?' She'd seen a set of Robert's notes once. He was the only doctor she knew who wrote like a Steiner schoolgirl;

the records had filled several holders.

'You're about a generation and a half too young to even remember those days! But you haven't come here to stroke my ego. How can I help?' He leaned back in his chair, took off his spectacles and massaged the bridge of his nose. Without the glasses, he looked suddenly more vulnerable, the grandfather twice over that he was.

'It's about the Morgans.'

He groaned. 'Oh no. Not again.'

'It's five weeks now since they came out of hospital, and I've only found them at home twice. Jane was with me one time, and there was nothing to ring any alarm bells at that visit. Gypsy was up to speed on all measures. Anya seemed calm and in control. The house was as immaculate as ever. I've been back twice since but got no answer, Jane's called a couple of times too. They haven't been at the baby clinic, or at the hospital – I rang to check. After seeing so much of her before, it seems odd she hasn't wanted reassurance for *anything*.'

'Could just be gaining in confidence as the baby gets bigger.'

'It's possible. But it's the combination: not seeking reassurance *and* out all the time. I mean, before, she wasn't going anywhere *except* to see us, nor was she mixing with other mums. She seemed to be a loner. Would such a woman suddenly turn into a social gadfly?'

'And you're imagining her skulking inside, not answering the door?'

She shrugged.

'Who's the worry – baby, or mum, or both?' he asked.

'I don't even know that. She's a highly intelligent woman and a superb actor. I don't know if I can trust what I see.'

'So, what're you proposing?'

'I can't decide, hence my visit. There's nothing concrete, so my question is, is it all right to give her the benefit of the doubt now? She might be hiding a baby from professional scrutiny ...'

'Or she *might* be innocently out and about, picking up a social life.' Robert spread his hands. 'Another of those impossible conundrums.'

'I might be being paranoid here, only … the hospital had their doubts too, it's not just me. I've documented everything so far and I thought I'd ring, maybe call, leave a message. Put the ball in her court to get in touch with me. If she doesn't respond, *then* start getting more proactive.'

'Sounds like a sensible plan.'

'Can I record I consulted you and we agreed this plan of action together?'

'Sure.'

'And you'll get in touch with Child Protection if …'

'Yes, Lucinda. I. Will. Get. In. Touch. With. Child. Protection. *If* this turns out to be anything more than a mum finally getting to grips with looking after her baby.'

Lucinda walked down the corridor slowly. She'd done the right thing offloading her niggling doubts, but voicing the fear had made it more real.

If Gypsy was lying somewhere neglected or injured … or worse …

She hurried back to her room to check over every step she'd taken, yet again.

Would there be enough evidence to exonerate her in a court of law?

Would there be enough to reassure her in her own mind that she had done her level best?

Was this baby safe?

Like Jane always said, you were damned if you gave these parents the benefit of the doubt and something went catastrophically wrong; you were damned if you took the child into safe-keeping and they could convince others they were innocent.

CHAPTER 47

It seemed a fitting end to their week together when Roger rang to tell them that Huong Mai was pregnant ... with twins! Leon immediately cracked open a bottle of Prosecco.

When a second call came through that evening, Leon took it in his study and was gone so long Anya went looking for him, thinking he'd fallen asleep. But he was still listening and beckoned her in.

'Here she is now, you can ask her yourself.'

He scribbled one word on a scrap of paper and held it up for her: Juliette.

She took the phone and he sat watching her.

'Super news about the baby, isn't it?' Juliette enthused. 'I was wondering, would you be game to arrange a baby shower for Huong Mai with me, closer to the birth, of course, but in principle? With none of her own family closer than Singapore, I imagine she'll feel a bit alone with this, and sisters-in-law have to be better than nothing. What d'you think?'

'That's a lovely thought, and certainly, I'd be happy to pitch in.'

'You could come and stay with us, extend the occasion. Our two would adore having Gypsy to play with, and you and I could have fun doing baby things. Thomas and Leo can do whatever blokes do in these circumstances.'

In the few seconds it had taken to say this, Anya's mind had flitted over the facts: Leon had jumped to take the call; he'd taken it in private; he'd been on the phone for at least forty minutes; he'd had a strategy to divert suspicion if she came into the room; he was clearly expecting to continue his conversation with Juliette.

All the light had gone out of her day, but somehow she dredged up an impassive give-nothing-away voice.

'Presumably we're talking the autumn. Shall we discuss it closer to the time? A lot can happen in six months.'

'Of course.'

'I'll hand you back to Leon.' She emphasised the ending; it had always irritated her that Juliette adopted the abbreviated name Thomas used for his kid brother.

She returned to the ironing with a fierceness that threatened the tiny garments. There had been no baby shower arranged for *her*, and she only had Claire – one tiny step up from Huong Mai.

It was another ten minutes before Leon emerged and offered her a drink, vanishing behind his newspaper, volunteering nothing of his fifty-minute conversation.

Doubt, suspicion, despair, flooded through her; fragile trust splintered like the first thin ice on the garden pond.

She was feeding Gypsy her breakfast cereal next morning when Leon announced that he wouldn't be going to Newcastle that morning after all; he'd be working in the Edinburgh office, popping home at lunchtime to keep the social workers happy. She could cancel Claire coming. No explanation. No eye contact. Anya just knew it had something to do with that phone call; she knew it as if he had pinned a post-it to her brain. She let him go with a perfunctory kiss.

Her thoughts began to circle depressingly, conjuring up scenarios of increasing complexity and severity. A full hour later a ring at the doorbell dragged her back from a very dark place.

'Hiya! Long time no see. You busy ruling the world, or have you got a crack of time for an old pal?'

Anya stood to one side, and Tiffany skipped up the steps and into the kitchen.

'And lest you think I'm simply on the scrounge, I've brought the eats.' She delivered a packet of Biscoffs with a flourish. 'Your favourites, I believe, m'lady.'

It was impossible not to feel the sunshine Tiffany brought with her, and they were soon sharing stories as they sipped coffee.

'You're looking *tons* better, Anya. I take it there've been no more crises?'

Anya shook her head.

'Mum-in-law still hovering?'

'No. Leon took a week's leave. He's staying up here at the moment. But come and see the transformation in the garden. His dad did the hard slog; we just prettied it up.'

'Well, it's certainly done you a power of good. You look fantastic.'

Gypsy was delighted to see their visitor and the morning flew by before Anya realised her own mood had improved enormously. She texted Leon to say no need to come home at lunchtime; she had officially approved company.

'Have a bowl of soup with us ... if you've got the time.'

'You sure? I don't want to outstay my welcome.'

'Sure I'm sure.'

They ate in the garden, a huge umbrella shading Gypsy and Anya, though Tiffany scorned the need for herself.

'No point in having skin this colour and hiding from the rays.'

Her nonchalance and exuberant spirits had Anya relaxing more and more, and she embraced the security of being able to flip in and out for things without that dreaded surge of concern for an unsupervised child. Even in the seclusion of their own walled garden her imagination quickly conjured up nightmare scenarios of returning to find the pram or highchair or playpen empty. After all, if it had happened before ... No one knew of these haunting fears; they weighed the heavier for being borne alone.

She took advantage of the sentry now, assembling food and drink to maximise the chances of Gypsy sleeping well tonight, Freya Trimble-Coleman's *Guide to Natural Weaning* her trusty pilot.

231

CHAPTER 48

Energy renewed, once Tiffany had gone, Anya determined not to let the clouds descend again. She'd put in some effort, make Leon glad he'd stayed up north. A quick jaunt to the supermarket, a few hours in the kitchen, she'd still have time to slip into something more feminine. Gypsy was already drowsy, a good start.

Not until she was in the queue with her trolley did she notice the familiar purple streak in the next checkout aisle. Tiffany was absorbed in stashing her purchases into a second trolley which appeared to have a life of its own. It was piled high and an older woman took the far side and steered it through the narrow space.

'You look as if you're feeding the five thousand,' Anya called.

Tiffany startled. 'Oh hi! I didn't expect to see you here.'

'We shop too, you know!' Anya quipped.

'Rather more delicately than us, by the look of things. Yeuch, look at you. A fiftieth of our quantity and probably not much in it when it comes to the bill! Oh sorry. This is my mother, Janet. Ma, this is Anya ... and baby Gypsy.'

Anya smiled at the older woman, who bore no resemblance to her daughter. Plain face devoid of makeup and heavily lined, hair – thinning and grey – hanging drearily on her collar, rapidly blinking eyes, clothes functional rather than fashionable, crepuscular skin visible above the high neckline and below the three-quarter sleeves, bare feet bulging through the broad supporting shoes. Not a shred of the flamboyance Tiffany exhibited.

'I'm very grateful to you for sparing Tiffany,' Anya said.

Janet gave a faint smile, glancing from Tiffany to Anya

and back again.

'Mother never sees how important she is, do you, Ma? One of life's unsung heroes. But we need to get you to the chiropodist on time.' She shielded her mouth with one hand and mouthed 'ingrowing toenail', before continuing, 'So, if you'll excuse us, we must dash. Enjoy your day. Say hi to Gypsy when she wakes up. Wee soul. Sleeping the sleep of the righteous. Bye bye.'

Anya watched the mismatched pair struggling with the recalcitrant wheels as she followed them out to the car park. Janet bore no resemblance whatever to the paragon of all grandmothers she'd imagined. How could someone as slow and apparently bewildered deal with three exuberant children, two generations rushing in and out, all living lives to a different drum-beat? Maybe she was just worn down by the constant tasks. Maybe it was her puritanical ideas that insisted on dreary. And of course, to Tiffany she'd always be the Ma who'd rescued her from trouble; stood by her in spite of everything.

Gypsy was still fast asleep when they got home so Anya popped her into her cot, slipped favourite Mr Rabbit in beside her, and made the most of the bonus time. Leon loved anything gamey, and this pheasant recipe sounded extra succulent. Add a chocolate truffle cheesecake and she was well on the way to creating exactly the hint of decadence she had in mind.

So much for the food, now the ambience. The table laid, the flowers arranged, the lighting sorted, she was beginning to think that her best-laid plans were destined to go sadly awry. Gypsy still hadn't stirred. At the present rate of progress, she'd be up all hours wanting to play, insisting her parents devote their attention to her instead of the first overtures of a peace treaty.

Anya bent over the sleeping form.

'Gypsy. Gypsy, darling. Time to wake uu-up.'

The child didn't react.

She peeled back the light covers and lifted Gypsy out of

233

the bed. Her head and limbs flopped but she didn't waken.

'Come on, sweetie pie. Wakey wakey.'

Anya laid her on a rug and began stripping off her clothes ... She wiped her face with a cool flannel ... sat her up ... blew into her ear ... tickled the bottom of her feet ...

No response.

'Come on! Come on, Gypsy! Wake up for Mummy. Come on!'

By the time she had exhausted all her options Anya's breath was coming in sobbing gasps.

'You *can't* do this to me. You *can't*! Wake up! Wake up!'

She gave the child a shake.

Nothing.

She shook harder.

Still nothing.

She grabbed her phone. 999.

Please ... please ... please ...

The voice at the other end of the line was textbook: 'Which service?'

'Ambulance, please. Oh, please, please, come quickly. It's my baby. It's happening again.'

The questions rained down on her.

'Is the patient breathing? ...

'Is the patient conscious? ...

'Can you tell me your name? ...

'Anya ... Anya, what's your address? ...

'Can you tell me what's happened? ...

'How old is she? ...

'That's good. Try to stay calm, Anya. The paramedics are on their way.'

She knew she probably sounded unhinged but Anya was finding it well-nigh impossible to wade through the treacle clogging her mind. The pernicious permutations, the possibilities she'd worked so hard to suppress or explain away, slid into all the crevices.

The dismembered voice kept up a steady stream of sound but Anya heard it through a tank of water. Her mechanical responses wailed into the phone in fragmented clips.

'Is she still breathing? …

'Can you feel her heart beating? …

'Is she in a safe place? …

'Is she sweating? …

'Is she cold? …

'What colour is she?' …

She knew. Any minute now … the legs and arms would spasm … the face would go blue … her baby would become unrecognisable … History – that horrible, terrifying history – would repeat itself. They'd be back inside the nightmare. And this time there was no team of nurses to take over. She was entirely, completely, on her own. Alone with questions ricocheting around her like enemy fire.

'Can you hear me? …

'Is the door open? …

'That sounds like a siren now …

'Is that the paramedics? …

'Can they get in?'

A booming male voice echoed in the doorway. 'Hello? Hello? Mrs Morgan? It's the ambulance service. We're coming in …'

The green figures were instantly on the floor dwarfing the tiny immobile patient.

'Can you tell us what happened?' … the nightmare inquisition started up again, but this time there was a safety barrier between her and certain catastrophe. Her brain untangled the sounds; her tongue formed a semblance of answers; her eyes watched their hands moving, the equipment appearing like Mary Poppin's magic flowers; her ears heard the murmured exchange of words which meant nothing to her.

'We're bringing in an eight-month-old female child.' – The older partner kept his mouth close to his radio mike, which crackled exactly as she'd heard in films – 'Unconscious. Comatose. Glasgow scale 4. Not responding. Spontaneous resps. No drugs paraphernalia apparent. ETA eight to ten minutes.'

She followed them automatically. The blue light was still swirling, surreal in her very own driveway.

She clung to the strap as the vehicle swung into the road, careered along the streets, her eyes never leaving her precious daughter, willing her stomach to hang on to its lunch, the sirens to clear the way.

Had she switched off the oven? Had she even locked the door?

Who cared. All the vagabonds in the neighbourhood could ransack it as long as they reached the hospital in time. And Leon would check ... *no!* she hadn't picked up her phone! ... *he wouldn't even know!* ...

Two nurses and a porter were already hovering at the entrance to the Emergency Department with a trolley when the door swung open and daylight streamed into the surreal space.

'OK. Got her. We'll take the baby, Mum, if you could just give the details at the desk.'

The whole entourage vanished ... Gypsy ... *all on her own with complete strangers ...*

The receptionist took one look at Anya and came out from behind her desk.

'Here, love, take a seat. I'll get you a glass of water. You've had a real shock, I can see. Give yourself a mo, and then we'll take down the details.'

Anya dissolved. 'I didn't have time to pick up my phone and I need to let my husband know he won't have any idea where we are and I don't think I locked the door I need to tell him but I don't have my purse or ...'

'It's OK, it's OK. Ssssh, take long slow breaths. You can use our phone. Just catch your breath first, or the poor man will imagine the worst, won't he?'

The worst? What could be worse than this?

The receptionist crouched down beside her, patting her hand, keeping up a steady flow of soothing sounds. Not until she was coherent did the woman ask the essential questions before passing her a phone. 'Want me to put in the number for you, hen?'

'No. I can manage. But thank you.'

He picked up almost at once.

'Leon! Thank God. It's me. I'm at the hospital ...'

'*What?* Which hospital? What's happened?'

'Sick Kids. It's Gypsy. She won't wake up.'

He swore half under his breath. 'Not *again*! Is she ...?'

'I don't know. They've taken her away somewhere. I'm just phoning you, then I'm going to go and find her.'

'I'm on my way.'

'Leon ... I think the house is unlocked ... we were in such a hurry ... oh, never mind, I'll borrow their phone ... ring Tiffany. She'll lock up for me.' She heard his feet thudding on a hard surface. 'Please, *please,* come quickly.'

CHAPTER 49

Twenty-one minutes later Leon screeched to a halt in the car park, cursed the time it took for the machine to spit out a ticket, threw it onto his dashboard, and sprinted into the hospital, straight up to the reception desk.

'Gypsy Morgan? I'm her father. She's just been admitted.'

'Take a seat, Mr Morgan, and I'll find out for you.'

Could anyone move more slowly? He wanted to scream at the plump figure plodding from behind the front desk ... approaching a young woman in blue scrubs ... then a ginger-haired man with a stethoscope hanging from his neck who vanished through swing doors. The receptionist began her careful trudge back to her post.

'Someone's finding out for you. Would you like to take a seat over there?'

She turned immediately to a woman with three children all competing for brat-of-the-year.

'Can I help you?'

'Yeah. It's Danny. Got a bead up 'is nose. *Again*. Will you shut it, Kylie! Mia! Stop that this instant. You hear me? I won't tell you again.'

She grabbed the nearest tot and yanked her back from stabbing a biro pen into the back of her sister's knee. The unfortunate Danny was clamped in her other hand, staring vacantly into space and solemnly poking the bead further up his orifice with an inquisitive finger.

'Mr Morgan?' A young woman in pale blue and a name badge saying *Carol Simmonds. Student Nurse*, was leaning towards him.

Leon leapt to his feet. 'That's me.'

'Would you like to come with me?'

She led the way through the swing doors, along the corridor, to double doors with RESUSCITATION etched into the glass.

Resuscitation? This was serious.

A stiff concertina of curtains obscured all activity from prying eyes. Would-be-Nurse Simmonds led him to the far corner, her soft shoes squelching on the polished floor. Leon tiptoed after her and entered a cubicle already overpopulated with four members of staff, monitors bleeping, fine lines tracing jagged patterns. Anya was huddled in a chair at the top end of the bed, the eyes she raised to him unfathomable. Gypsy lay absolutely still, face covered with a mask, a drip running into her arm, a sheet over her body, at the epicentre of this drama. So, so still.

'Is she …?'

'Mr Morgan?' A tall man of about thirty-five with a shock of black hair, strikingly even white teeth, and a pronounced limp, peeled away from the group and moved lopsidedly towards him, inching him back outside the curtain. The dark scrubs were designed for a person about two inches shorter and a spreading stain on one side of the tunic top spoke of a doctor at the sharp end of clinical practice. 'My name's Dr Archie Prenderghast, ED registrar. We've stabilised your daughter at the moment, and we've sent off some bloods. We'll know more when the results come back from the lab.'

'What's happened? Is she going to be all right?'

'We aren't entirely sure at the moment. Your wife tells us Gypsy was very sleepy this afternoon, but it wasn't until she tried to wake her for her tea that she realised this was something more than an extra-long nap.'

'So, what is it?'

The doctor moved closer and dropped his voice. 'The picture that's presenting to us is of a child who's gone into a coma.'

'A coma?' Leon hissed back. 'What would make a baby of this age go into a *coma*?'

'That's what we're trying to establish.'

Leon bit back a sharp retort. 'So, what possible causes are you considering?'

'I'd rather not speculate at this point, no point in alarming ourselves with possibilities that we'll probably be able to rule out once we get the test results back. One of the consultants is on her way. As I said, we're monitoring Gypsy closely.'

He led the way back inside the curtains.

Leon stared at the screens which told him precious little.

What was the normal heart-rate for a baby of this age supposed to be, anyway?

He vaguely remembered the rapid bleeping he'd heard on the fetal monitor during labour. *But what should it be now?*

One of the nurses shone a torch into Gypsy's eyes but Leon was too far away to see if there was any reaction.

What if there was?

What if there wasn't?

She did something to the soles of the tiny bare feet.

What was supposed to happen?

Who ever thought to do such a thing to a babe of this age?

She filled in an elaborate form, full of dots and lines and indecipherable squiggles.

The whole assembly fell still, the gaze of six adults homed in on the immobile figure, four of them alert for signs he could only dimly comprehend. Elsewhere the sounds of emergency told him women were weeping, babies were hurting, nurses were comforting, doctors were carrying out unpleasant procedures, lives hung in the balance, but inside this cubicle the world seemed to have frozen in time around a princess under a malign spell; his own baby; his only daughter.

A pretty bobbing head appeared from behind the curtains like a caricature in a Punch and Judy show, flaxen plaits restraining tightly-curled hair. 'RTC on the way. Anyone free in here?' The accent was unmistakably Irish.

'I'll go.' A nurse detached herself from the group, vanished without so much as a backward glance. Routine day-to-day work. She left a breathing space behind her.

'If you'll excuse me. I'll be right back,' Dr Prenderghast said, stopping just long enough to peer into Gypsy's eyes, pat her arm.

And then there were four.

Leon glanced across at Anya. Slow tears were sliding down her cheek unheeded. He moved to her side of the bed and put an arm around her shoulders, feeling the tremor, but at least she didn't pull away.

'Can I get you a glass of water?' The voice was steeped in sympathy.

Anya shook her head.

'Water would be good, thanks,' Leon said.

'No problem. I'll get you one,' she smiled warmly. 'You'll stay, John? I'll be back in two ticks.'

'Gotcha. Will do.' They held each other's gaze for a long moment.

And then there were three.

'How long before you know anything? Till the results come back, I mean?' Leon directed his gaze at the junior doctor, John something – no badge so no opportunity to wing it – currently doing his best to give them privacy without turning his back.

'I'm not sure. But feel free to slip out, take a break. I promise you, we won't leave Gypsy unattended.'

Neither of them moved.

CHAPTER 50

The consultant was more direct. Dr Harriet Fritz was an imposing figure in every way: six feet without shoes, easily a size eighteen but perfectly proportioned, thick hair layered with at least four different shades of tawny highlights, heavy eye-liner, gothic lipstick, dressed entirely in forest green from her crepe shirt to her smart loafers, towering over the bed like the big friendly giant.

She nodded in the direction of Anya and Leon.

'Harriet Fritz. A&E consultant. So, what's this little poppet been up to, then?' It seemed rhetorical; at least, no one answered. Her expert eyes raked over the screens, the baby, the charts. She took a manila folder from under her arm and flicked through the contents.

'I see she's been admitted before. Convulsions. Hypoglycaemia. De-dah-de-dah-de-dah. Nothing pathological found.' It was a statement.

'So … is this … related?' Leon asked.

'Not sure yet. Doesn't appear to be, inasmuch as blood sugar is normal. But some conditions can present in different ways. We'll know more when the results come back.'

All the while she spoke, eyes, ears, fingers, probed Gypsy for vital clues. She asked Anya to tell her – from the beginning – exactly what had happened, what she'd seen, what she thought.

It was mechanical by now, a rehearsed speech.

'If you *had* to say, right this moment, what's the most likely cause?' Leon wasn't sure if his dread of the answer was making his voice squeak, or the fact that he hadn't fully let go of his breath since Anya's phone call.

Dr Fritz turned a fixed look towards them and waited a

long moment before she spoke. 'Would you care to come to the relatives' room to discuss this in private?'

Anya shrank back. 'You go, Leon. I'm staying with Gypsy.'

Leon tightened his hold on her shoulder. 'You stay, I stay. Besides you're the one who knows what happened. We need your input.'

Dr Fitz tightened her lips. 'You're happy to discuss this here?'

'Yes. And we don't need you to sugar-coat it. If it's bad news we want to know what we're dealing with.'

The doctor lowered herself onto the side of Gypsy's bed, her bulk making the mattress emit a weird deflating sigh. She held herself steady with a peculiar arrangement of her long trouser-clad legs which made her look like a giraffe preparing for sleep, the sharp creases in the fabric emphasising the acute angles. In a totally even voice she said, 'Well, a couple more questions if I may first, Mrs Morgan.'

Anya held her gaze.

'When you found Gypsy extra sleepy, how did you try to wake her?'

'I cooled her down – took off her clothes, used a cold flannel on her skin ... tickled her feet.'

'And then?'

'I gave her a little shake.'

Dr Fritz nodded slowly.

'I realise this was a terrifying situation, and please don't think I'm criticising you. How hard would you say you shook her?'

'Not hard at all. Just like this.'

'Is that ...?' Leon dragged his eyes from his wife to Gypsy's doctor.

'It's too early to say with any degree of certainty until we have much more information.'

'But if you *had* to say?'

'Well, if you force me to reveal my hand at this precise moment, I'd say the picture is much more one of a drugs overdose than of any underlying pathological condition or head trauma.'

Leon stared at her, only dimly aware of Anya metamorphosing into stone under his touch. He felt his lungs close, the air shallow in his mouth.

'An ... overdose?'

'That's what the symptoms suggest. Yes.'

'But ... it's not ... *possible*. We don't have ... *drugs*. We don't take ... *anything*! Not even headache pills. Nothing.' He took a gulp of air. 'And we certainly wouldn't give anything to *Gypsy*.' He felt Anya wince as his fingers tightened. 'My wife makes every scrap of her food from scratch – has done from the beginning. Pure organic. No additives. No added sugar. Not even the occasional treat – not while she doesn't know what she's missing.'

'Very commendable,' the consultant said – dryly, Leon thought.

'It's true,' Anya confirmed hoarsely.

'So, is there any way you can think of, any conceivable way, that drugs could have got into her system somehow today? We're not here to judge but anything you can tell us might make a real difference to Gypsy's recovery.'

'No. They couldn't,' Anya said flatly. 'It's impossible. I've been with her all day. I got her up myself. I made her breakfast and her lunch myself. I took her shopping myself. I put her down for a nap myself. And I *certainly* didn't give her *drugs*!'

'When you say "drugs",' Leon said slowly, staring at the consultant, 'what kind of drugs are we talking here? I mean, you aren't suggesting ... you surely don't mean ... *street drugs*, illegal drugs ... do you?'

'Not necessarily. But they can't be excluded. Is that something that might factor in here?'

'You are joking, right? Do we *look* like junkies?'

'There are very few stereotypes in our experience, Mr Morgan. We have to consider all angles here. What about sleeping pills? Anything purchased online? Anything to help you relax, help you sleep, give you energy? ... babies can be exhausting.'

Leon's phone suddenly shrilled. 'Sorry. Sorry. I should have switched it off. There. Done. Look, I've told you, there's *no way* Gypsy's been drugged with anything, so you can rule that out, and tell us what *medical* condition would give her these symptoms, and what you can do for her.' He glared at the doctor, who seemed maddeningly unmoved by his suppressed anger.

'Until toxicology get back to us, there's nothing more we *can* do, except keep a very close eye on the baby.' She reached across and peered at Gypsy, felt a pulse, lifted an arm, opened an eye. 'We shall need to monitor her carefully and run more tests before we can give you any assurances. I'll leave you in Dr Allen's capable hands for now, but I'll be back.'

No sooner had she left than the nurse returned with Leon's water – as if she'd been waiting outside for the most propitious moment. It scarcely touched his parched mouth.

They sat in stunned silence, numbed by the enormity of what had just happened. Leon fiddled with his phone, glanced down at the screen, peered closer.

'There's a missed call from Tiffany Corrigan. Did you ever get a chance to ask her to go and lock up the house?'

She nodded, not taking her eyes off Gypsy.

'Shit! What could she possibly want *now*? Could be a problem with the house, I suppose. I'd better go outside and take this. I'll be right back.'

'She probably just wants to know about Gypsy.'

The low sunlight hurt his eyes and he found a shady spot before he rang her back.

'Leon Morgan. What's up?'

'First off – how's Gypsy? Anya sounded distraught. She didn't give me any details.'

'We don't know. Is there a problem at the house?'

'I'm not sure.'

'What d'you mean? Is there or isn't there? You must have had a reason to ring.'

'It might be something or nothing, only ...'

'Look, can you cut to the chase? I need to get back to

Anya and Gypsy.'

'I went into the house – just to check. She left in such a hurry she couldn't remember what was on, or what she'd been cooking, or anything. I switched off the oven but … I noticed one of the drawers was slightly open. And that just isn't Anya, as you know; she always has everything pin neat … it just struck me as … wrong, somehow.'

'And?'

'I found this sachet sticking out from under the napkins.'

'Sachet? I don't follow …'

'A little plastic wallet. With white powder in it. And … well, it seemed an odd thing to have, and with the drawer still not properly closed, putting two and two together, I guessed she must have been there not long before the ambulance came. And … well, I just thought you ought to at least *know*.'

'What drawer?'

'You know the floor unit on the left of the Aga? The one with four drawers one side, and a cupboard and drawer on the other side?'

Damn the woman! How could she be so intimately acquainted with the inside of his home? She had no business knowing how many drawers they had.

Just how much time did she spend with Anya? How much did she know of the inner workings of his family?

'It was in the top drawer of the set of four. The one where Anya keeps the napkins you use for every day.'

Was nothing sacred?

'Where are you now?'

'I'm outside your house. I've just locked up. She *had* left it open. But you can't blame her for that. She must have been beside herself finding Gypsy like that.'

'I'm not blaming her. Where's the sachet now?'

'In the drawer. I put it back where I found it.'

'I'll be there in …'

'Don't be daft. You stay with Anya and Gypsy. If you want it, I'll bring it over. Least I can do. I'll give you a bell as soon as I get to the hospital.'

She had rung off before he could answer.

He slumped onto the first seat he could find.

It was the same drawer where he'd found those white pills. He'd thought at the time it was an odd place to keep tablets ... she'd assured him they were only vitamin and herb supplements ... to boost her energy levels ... perfectly harmless.

Pills ... powder ... oh Anya! Anya!

He stayed in the car park, ready to grab the offending sachet the minute Tiffany arrived; to give himself time to think. If Anya *had* given Gypsy something, there was no time to lose; they'd need to know what it was ... wash the stuff out of her system somehow ... dilute it ... give her some kind of antidote ...

What did *they do in these circumstances? What could they do?*

Oh God, oh God, oh God – don't let her die. Please, please, please. I'll do anything.

In the meantime, how could he get the sachet to the doctors without arousing Anya's suspicions? He was still mulling over the consequences of various fabrications when Tiffany arrived, complete with sachet *and* answer.

'I've been thinking, if Anya *has* done something, it's important not to scare her. They'll likely call in the psych team, and they're the guys who'll know exactly how to handle this. But you don't want her to think *you're* ganging up against her. So, how about I go in now and see her – if you're comfortable with that? – I can distract her attention while you find the doctor and give him the sachet. Speed's of the essence in these kinds of cases. Sooner they know, sooner they can reverse the damage.'

'She'll wonder what's keeping me ...'

'I'll say you've popped in to pick up a drink. Make sure you come back smelling of coffee ... bring a snack back for her, too! I'll grab a peppermint tea for her on the way. Buy you some time.'

Leon took to his heels, the offending plastic crushed in his sweating palm.

He felt like the worse kind of Judas: *Saving his daughter; betraying his wife.*

CHAPTER 51

Dr George Hooper was deep in a report for the mortality meeting. It was always sobering reflecting on the little lives they hadn't been able to save, each name conjuring up distressing memories: ebbing life, distraught parents, harrowing discussions. Occasionally he leaned away from the screen, raked his fingers through his thinning hair, and closed his eyes against the vivid pictures. Concentration on 'failures' always took its toll.

His response was without enthusiasm when someone tapped briskly at his door.

'Room for a little'un?'

He grinned and swung his chair round to face Harriet Fritz, the biggest little'un of his acquaintance.

'Harry! Come in, come in. What brings you away from the high drama of the ED to my peaceful little backwater on this beautiful sunny day?'

'Got time for a pow-wow?'

'With you? Sure thing. You come way above mortality statistics in my affections.'

She clutched a hand to her generous bosom in a mock swoon and plonked herself down on the vacant chair, stretching her long legs out in front of her with a sigh.

'Gypsy Morgan? Ring any bells?'

'Does it ever. Child Protection case.'

Harriet tapped the manila folder. 'So I gather.'

'Am I in hot water? You looking for fodder for a course in communication skills or something?'

'You should be so lucky! Nah. The high heid yins have this weird notion you and I kinda know how the world works.'

'*They* never get within spitting distance of a terrified parent, that's why!'

'No jolly in a magnificent country retreat in the offing for you, m'lad, sad to say. No sirree. No, we've got Gypsy in the ED right now. Unconscious, unresponsive, slow pulse, sluggish pupils. And if I were a betting chap – which I hasten to add, I am not – I'd lay odds on an overdose.'

George steepled his fingers. 'Arghh.'

'Bloods aren't back yet but ...'

'You told the parents?'

'Only because Dad pushed me to say what I was thinking.'

'And, how did he take it?'

'Not what you'd call a happy bunny. Insists I *have* to be wrong – haven't a clue what I'm talking about. Apparently, the kid's intake's as pure as the driven snow. No way drugs could come within sniffing distance of her.'

'And Mum?'

'Shell shocked. Gives a coherent history, consistent over time, but seems totally unable to explain what's happened. Looks like somebody zapped her with 2400 volts.'

'Dead, then?'

'Pedant! Scientific facts related to electrical currents completely bypassed me in A-level physics.'

'Fair enough. You can't be a genius in everything. Back to the zombified Mrs Morgan ... you believe her?'

'Well, I've only just met her, you know her rather better. Prenderghast admitted the kiddie. and he got the same impression as me – conscientious to a fault, extremely anxious, but ...'

A positive reveille of ragged running footsteps, followed by imperative rapping on the door interrupted her.

'Come in.'

The said Archie Prenderghast erupted into the room, out of breath, clutching his chest as if his heart was at that very moment deciding whether or not to fail him.

'Sorry, boss ... Apologies, Dr Hooper ... but this can't wait.'

He dangled a sachet of white powder in front of them, gulping huge mouthfuls of air.

'Mr Morgan's … just given me … this … Hidden in a … drawer … in their kitchen … apparently … I've sent a … sample off for testing …. Could be … what we're looking for.'

Harriet Fritz patted a seat beside her and took the sachet from him. 'Take the weight off, Prenderghast. George's mortality stats are high enough without you adding to his woes.'

She opened the packet gingerly, sniffed it.

'Anything recognisable?' George asked.

She shook her head and passed it to him.

'Any change in the babe, Archie?'

'Obs stable.' He was looking and sounding more like himself.

'Parents still there?'

'Mum is. Dad's going back now he's given us this.'

'Hold on a minute …' Harriet froze on the spot. George could almost hear the cogs turning. 'Mr Morgan … he's been here in the ED, yes?'

'Yeah.'

'So, how did he suddenly produce this stuff?' She waved the packet in the air. 'When I talked to them he was totally insistent there was no way on God's earth anything noxious could have got into Gypsy's system.'

'Well, their story is … Mrs Morgan phoned a friend, asked her to go around and check the house was locked, cooker switched off. It was a 999 job and she'd left in a big hurry. The friend found this hanging out of one of the kitchen drawers and rang Mr Morgan. She drove in from Dalkeith, met him here, and he brought it straight to us. The friend went to sit with Mrs Morgan to cover for his absence.'

'Why would a *friend* be rootling through drawers in somebody else's kitchen?'

'Seems Mrs Morgan's a bit OCD – sorry, boss, I know we shouldn't use these labels as shorthand – I mean, super, uber, nth degree, tidy. The friend found the drawer slightly open and thought it was out of character. So, she investigated.

And found this.'

'Holy cow! I'd *kill* any of my friends who snooped in my drawers!' Harriet snorted. 'But then, nobody'd ever in a million years accuse me of being – apologies, Archie – OCD!' She turned to Dr Hooper. 'Looks like you could well have been right about the last time, George. Want to join me in our little chat with the aforementioned parents?'

'If Mr Morgan allows me to. We didn't exactly part on the best of terms.'

'Probably choking on his humble pie as we speak. I'll give psych a ring, get their take on the best approach. And get back to you.'

'And I'll ring Diane Moore. Can't say I'm looking forward to it, but you can count me in.'

Harriet strode off with the registrar in tow, now breathing normally for a fit man in his thirties, but needing an extra skipping step to keep up with his senior colleague's long stride.

Leon Morgan was on his own when the three consultants entered the relatives' room.

'Mrs Morgan joining us?' Harriet asked, almost casually.

Leon held her gaze – almost defiantly, George thought. 'She refuses to leave Gypsy.'

'Well, that's her prerogative. She will, of course, be involved at some point.'

Leon shrugged.

'You remember Dr George Hooper, the consultant paediatrician you saw when Gypsy was admitted last time?'

Leon gave a curt nod.

Didn't look like the humble pie had been absorbed into his system yet awhile.

'And Dr Moore from Child Protection.'

Another incline of his head, lips set in a grim line.

Harriet adopted a voice of calm authority. 'I've asked them to be here because, as I think you'll understand, we have a serious situation here, and there are procedures that have to be followed in such cases.'

Leon kept his gaze trained on Harriet as if she was all he could cope with right now.

'Toxicology tell us that it is indeed the contents of the sachet that have caused your daughter to go into a coma.'

'What … is it?' The eyes were staring, the body braced.

'A mild barbiturate and a pain-killer, mixed in with baby milk powder.'

Leon's Adam's apple rose and fell twice in quick succession.

'Can you give Gypsy something – to counteract it?'

'We can, and we have. Naloxone. And I'm happy to tell you, she's already responding. Not out of the woods yet, but definitely responding. So, we very much appreciate you bringing this substance to us.'

It was as if a stiff hanger had been slid out of his shirt, leaving him to crumple.

Harriet gave him a moment. George had space to register how compassionate she was beneath that bluff exterior. It was rare for him to see her in action as a clinician, their encounters were much more likely to be at committee level, when she brought all her bombast and wit and mockery to bear for maximum effect. He'd always been relieved that she was on his side of the battles, but never took it for granted; she would be a formidable opponent.

'Mr Morgan, are you all right to continue?' Her deep voice was gentle.

'Yes. Thank you.'

'Dr Moore? I think you have a couple of points for clarification first?'

'Yes, thank you. Mr Morgan, did *you* know this sachet was in your house?'

'No.'

'Have you any idea how it got there?'

'Well, obviously, there are possibilities, but I'm certainly not going to implicate anybody without any evidence whatever.'

'I can fully understand where you're coming from but,

as I'm sure you would accept, we have a professional duty of care towards Gypsy. To keep her safe. You do understand that, don't you?'

'Of course.'

'You're aware, I know, that there have been concerns in the past. Hence the involvement of my team. How d'you feel your wife's been lately?'

'Much better. Gypsy's sleeping through the night now. Anya's not so exhausted. And she's accepted help – my parents, her sister, a friend. She's been getting out more ... but you can vouch for that, surely? It must be in the records. Your lot have been monitoring us. They *said* they were satisfied she was doing well.'

'Indeed. On the face of it, things have been going well. But what do *you* feel, Mr Morgan? Have you had any reservations yourself?'

George could see the internal struggle in his face.

'We aren't here to judge,' Diane said softly. 'We just want to get to the bottom of what's going on here. Anything you can tell us – in confidence ...'

'I didn't want to believe it but ... well, it makes a kind of sense ... warped sense.' He swallowed hard, fighting with himself. 'These things always seem to happen when I'm away. The crises with Gypsy and the ... there've been a couple of anonymous letters.'

'Letters? Saying?' Diane was strung for every tiny vibration.

'Whoever-it-was knew she'd harmed her baby and she should go to prison for it. And that's what our neighbour, Tiffany Corrigan, ... well, she'd already put the idea in my head ... that ... maybe Anya was doing things deliberately ...'

'Because?'

'To get my attention.'

'This neighbour ...'

'She used to be a nurse. In fact, she works here, in this hospital.'

'And she's a bit of an amateur psychologist, by the sound of things.'

'Anya trusts her judgement anyway. So ... are you saying ... she might have been right about the attention-seeking ...?'

'It's possible.' Diane gestured to Harriet to take over, although George noticed her eyes never left Leon Morgan's face.

'Mr Morgan, have you heard about a condition called Fabricated or Induced Illness?'

'No.'

'Munchausen's Syndrome by Proxy?'

'Rings a vague bell, but I couldn't tell you what it is.'

'It's where a person fabricates an illness in order to gain medical attention.'

'And you think ...?'

'We think it's *possible* that Anya has been creating scenarios involving *Gypsy* rather than herself, in order to gain attention, yes. It's an illness. The symptoms are made up, either fictitious – like saying the child has ailments or even a rare condition when they don't – or induced – as when the child is given a noxious substance to generate symptoms.'

Leon's face was ashen. 'You mean ... like *insulin*? ... Like this powder?'

'Exactly like that.' To George's ears Harriet's tone was as soft as a comfort blanket, but this man was clearly beyond gentle help. His worst suspicions, doubts he'd been doing his best to suppress, were being reinforced; his world was disintegrating around his ears – visibly.

The voice was leaden. 'I thought she loved the baby.'

'I think she does,' George spoke for the first time.

'So, how could she hurt her ... *deliberately*?'

'It's a very complex and rare psychological condition and way above my pay grade,' Harriet said. 'So, with your wife's permission, I'd like to call in a psychiatrist to get a proper evaluation, and assess how best to proceed. In the meantime, we'll keep Gypsy here, under careful observation, until we know she's recovered from the drugs.'

Leon shuddered. But it must cut deep to hear such a harsh reality spelled out. No longer '*whatever this might be*';

255

bald and unqualified *'the drugs'*. Then, suddenly, he shot upright as if a current of electricity had flashed through his chair.

'She's with Gypsy now!'

Harriet put out a restraining hand. 'She is, but have no fear, there has been a member of staff present at all times. We've had this in mind from the outset – given the history and the presenting symptoms.'

George could see the dawning realisation in Leon's face. 'I see now …'

'We couldn't afford to take any chances.'

'Thank you … thank you …'

'This is an unpalatable suspicion to take on board – especially when it's someone close to you,' Diane said. 'Would you like some time to yourself?'

'A few minutes, maybe. But then I need to get back to Anya. Do you have to tell her …? Can I …?'

'We'll be adopting a multi-agency approach here. But let me assure you, we'll be approaching it with extreme caution. And compassion. There will almost certainly need to be a psychiatric evaluation. And we all feel that the psychiatrist would probably be the best person to talk to your wife. But in any event, their findings should help to guide us as to the best way to proceed.'

CHAPTER 52

Whatever was keeping Leon this long? You'd have thought wild horses wouldn't have dragged him away from Gypsy today.

Dr Fritz had gone back down the corridor ages ago.

What could he be doing? Dealing with work stuff? ... Phoning Juliette ... again?

Why hadn't he gone to Newcastle this morning?

It was on the calendar. It was after that long conversation with Juliette that he'd announced it. Just as he was leaving for work. It was as if he *knew* something was going to happen ...

His face was a mask of impassivity when he eventually returned to Gypsy's cubicle.

Guilt? Fear? Dread? Bad news?

His eyes went straight to the baby, who had pinked up, eyes open, staring at the flickering lights on the monitor. The facial muscles relaxed a fraction and a half smile curved Leon's mouth. Anya willed the nurse, Hilary, to leave but she showed no sign of doing so. They probably *had* to monitor Gypsy continuously for a set time; there'd be a protocol somewhere spelling it out. She didn't even turn her back to give them privacy, and it was obvious Leon wasn't about to talk in this public space.

'Hello, Twinkle-toes,' he said softly, stroking one baby cheek with his forefinger. 'You're looking better.' There was a long pause as if he were trying chit-chat out for size and finding it wanting. 'Pretty lights, huh? Beep, beep, beep. Just like your little red car, huh? Beep beep beep.'

Gypsy managed a sleepy grin in recognition, but the fascinating machine soon took precedence.

'Is she …?' Leon glanced briefly at Hilary.

'She's beginning to take an interest in her surroundings.'

As if she understood, Gypsy shot her arms into the air. The intravenous solution waved above her head and she startled, her dark eyes widening as she followed its rocking movement.

'See, you've got your own little kite, sweetheart!' he said. 'Wheeee. There it goes, floating in the breeze, up into the clouds. Wheeee. See it shining. Wheeee.'

The baby stared. The nurse smiled. Leon grinned. Anya watched.

'What did the consultant say, Leon?' Anya asked. 'You've been ages.'

'I'll tell you later.' Without so much as a look in her direction.

'Tell me now. I want to know. Is she going to be all right?'

'I said, I'll tell you later. Not here.'

Anya felt a wave of rage sweep through her. 'Typical!' ground out between her teeth.

'Right. Have it your own way.' His voice was taut as an elastic band stretched to its limit. 'Come with me.'

'I'm not leaving Gypsy.'

Hilary laid a hand on Anya's arm. 'It might be best if you take this outside,' she said softly. 'We need to keep Gypsy as calm as possible. She'll be feeling quite groggy still. Why don't you go to the canteen? You must be ravenous. I'll be here. And, I promise, we'll call you immediately if there's any change.'

Still she hesitated.

'I'll turn up the volume on the monitor for a minute so you can slip out without her noticing, OK? Gypsy! Gypsy! Listen, sweetie.'

Beep beep beep …

The arms thrashed with excitement, the 'kite' caught the light. Gypsy had eyes for nothing but her personal sensory playground.

Two against one.
Besides she had to know what the consultant had said.

Leon led the way to the canteen in silence; even in a queue of customers waiting to be served, the divide felt unnerving. Here they were, joint parents of a child who'd been admitted to hospital unconscious and unresponsive, who was even now sick enough to be under constant scrutiny, and there was no connection between them.

Claire and Ronnie sprang unbidden into her mind. Traumatic experiences opened up all the cracks, exposed all the weaknesses; it was a well-known fact. And communication was one of the first casualties. Claire had told her: 'We were in different places; we just stopped being able to reach each other.'

'Why didn't you go to Newcastle today?' she said abruptly. Anything to break the deadlock. 'And do me the courtesy of an honest answer.'

He paused … long enough for her to taste mounting suspicion.

'Honestly? Because Juliette advised me not to leave you alone.'

'Juliette!'

'Yes. Juliette. As in sister-in-law Juliette.'

'So, she's pulling your strings now, is she? And what does Thomas make of *that*, I wonder?'

'It was Thomas who freed me up to stay up here with you.'

'Well, well, well. So *he*'s not so keen on you spending all your days in Newcastle either. I wonder why.'

'Nobody's pulling my strings, Anya, but sometimes I need permission to neglect one responsibility in favour of another.'

'Why did Juliette think you couldn't leave me on my own? You've just been at home for a whole week.'

'She thought I should make the break more gradual so you got used to my absence gradually.'

'Like a kid with separation anxiety!'

He didn't answer, his eyes on the diminishing queue. 'Listen, what d'you fancy? We'll grab something and take it somewhere quieter.'

'I don't want anything. I'm not hungry.' She sounded like a petulant child; she didn't care.

He leaned slightly towards the girl behind the counter who looked as if she should still be in school multiplying fractions. Totally bored, chewing on gum, she tilted her ear to catch his voice in the hubbub.

'Two sandwiches, wholemeal bread, one ham and salad, one egg and cress, one bar of plain chocolate, one black coffee, one peppermint tea, please. To take away.'

Clutching the paper carrier, he guided Anya out of the busy cafeteria and into a deserted corridor. For all the world as if it were an ordinary family picnic, he divided the spoils and peeled back the cellophane on both sandwiches. 'If you don't eat *something* you're going to be flaking out, and what good will you be to Gypsy then?'

'It's as if you *knew* something was going to happen today.' She threw it out before taking her first bite.

'How could I have known?'

'Good question.'

'Now you've lost me completely.'

'If you somehow had something to do with her coming into hospital.'

There. It was said.

He stopped chewing and stared at her. *'Me!'* She could see the faint glisten of his scar catching the light as his upper lip moved. *Or was it sweat?*

'Who else has access to our kitchen? Who else watched me putting the ingredients for her lunch together first thing this morning? Who else had the opportunity to doctor it? Who else changed their plans at the last minute?'

When he eventually spoke, Leon's voice was eerily calm, like a counsellor echoing a client's words for effect.

'What makes you suspect there was something in her food?'

'They said it was most likely a drug overdose. She was

fine up till lunchtime. How else could it have got into her system? It *had* to be in the food.'

'So, give me one good reason why *I* would do something like that?'

'To make me look like I'm a disturbed person not fit to take care of a baby?'

'And why would I want to do *that*?'

'To break us up.'

He sat for a long moment, before leaning in a fraction closer.

'Anya, this is all a figment of your imagination. You're ill – more ill than I realised. Juliette was right.'

'Of course. Juliette's always right.'

'She suspected. Tiffany suspected. But I didn't want to believe it.'

'Believe what?'

'That you're having some kind of mental crisis.'

'Well, that's a classic, if ever I heard one. Make out the wife's mad. Lock her up, so the husband can waltz off into the sunset with his lover and nobody would blame him. And I very nearly fell for it. Taking a week off. Going places with us. Assuring me you wanted to try again ... everything conspiring to lull me into a false sense of security. I even had a special meal prepared for you for tonight – all your favourites. How could I have been so naïve? Well, I'm wiser now, and I can tell you this for nothing, Leon Morgan, there's no way you're going to take my baby away from me. Absolutely. No. Way.'

'No, you're right, *I'm* not.' He paused, looked directly into her eyes. 'But I can tell you this much, there are others who're contemplating doing exactly that at this precise moment.'

'They can't. She's my baby. I won't let *anybody* take her away. Not *anybody*. I haven't done anything wrong.'

'Listen, Anya. This has been coming on for ages. And the evidence is overwhelming. They've given you the benefit of the doubt for all this time, but today's a step too far. Gypsy *has* to be their top priority. You'd want that, wouldn't you?

You'd want them to make absolutely sure she doesn't come to any more harm, wouldn't you?'

'What d'you mean? What evidence?'

'The stuff in the drawer in the kitchen – underneath the napkins? Why on earth would you take something like that?'

'Freya Trimble-Coleman recommends it.'

'Who the hell is Freya whatever?'

'A natural remedy guru. It's a new product; she brought it out last year.'

'*Sleeping pills*? And *painkillers*? For a *breastfeeding mother*! Anya! You can't be serious.'

'*What*? Don't be ridiculous. Of course it's not! I told you before, it's vitamins and herbs and minerals, specially mixed for lactating women, guaranteed not to harm the baby, but give the mother energy. You dissolve them in expressed breastmilk. Fair enough, I have increased the dose lately – I was feeling so shattered, but ...'

'Where did you get it from?'

'I sent away for it. Freya has this website and you order direct from her. It cuts out the middle-man.'

'I bet it does!'

A thought suddenly struck her.

'Look, you haven't told me ... what did the consultant say?'

'Consultants plural, you mean. There were three of them. Dr Fritz – the big lady doctor who's in charge of Gypsy this time. And remember, Dr Hooper – from the ward? And Dr Moore – from Child Protection.'

'And? Is Gypsy going to be all right?'

'They think so.'

'So, we can take her home soon?'

'Not so sure about that.'

'What d'you mean?'

Leon took a maddening age chewing his mouthful of ham and salad, swilling it down with coffee. 'They'd like you to speak to a psychiatrist.'

'What for?'

'Because they think a psychiatrist would be able to

explain things better than they can.'

Enlightenment dawned. 'This is *your* doing, isn't it? You've convinced them I'm unhinged.'

'Oh, believe me, they didn't need any input from me to convince them! You've done that very successfully all on your own.'

She cowered away from him. 'I will never forgive you if they take away my baby, Leon Morgan. *Never!*'

'It's not *my* fault you can't cope. It's not *my* fault you're taking drugs. It's not *my* fault you're an unsafe mother.' Never before had she seen him so hostile. 'And for what it's worth, I'm not prepared to pussy-foot around you one minute longer. Gypsy's my daughter too. And her safety's a damn sight more important than your bloody ego!'

'Ego? *Ego!* You have the gall to sit there and preach to me about *ego*? *You* – the big I am, the indispensable executive, the arch wheeler-dealer, single-handedly bringing in the millions, king benefactor to hundreds of lesser mortals slaving away in your little empire to …'

'*SHUT … UP*, Anya!' Leon was on his feet, white-faced, fists clenched. 'Thanks to you, the firm's pretty much bankrupt. Thanks to you, I'll be lucky if I'm even *in* a job by the summer. Oh, what's the use … I've had enough of this. I'm going back to Gypsy, but I'll tell you this for nothing … I'll fight for my daughter with every breath in my body. You might be an unsafe mother, but nobody's pointing the finger at *me*.'

CHAPTER 53

She avoided even looking at Leon.

Everything now screamed DANGER. Gypsy in an open area, close by the nurses' station, in full view of everyone coming and going; a surfeit of staff; constant vigilance; insistence on hospital food and drink only. There was to be no possible chink of opportunity for any harm to come to this baby.

But at least she wasn't excluded. Everyone might be treading on eggshell around them, but they were both permitted to visit as they pleased and spend as long as they wished playing with their daughter ... just as long as they were supervised. George Hooper had given them the option of changing to a different consultant if they felt uncomfortable with him personally, but whoever was in charge of her care, there could be no relaxation of this rule. It was non-negotiable. *So, better the devil they knew.*

Anya did her best to focus on Gypsy, to ignore the trappings of prison, but Leon's very presence kept the accumulated doubts and accusations seething. Pride and the circumstances stopped her asking him for clarification, but he was clearly labouring under some kind of misapprehension ... he *had* to be ... or ... *was it ... could it be ... all part of some extremely calculated plot?* He was certainly doing his utmost to derail her for some reason, with his threats of taking Gypsy away, getting her sectioned, ruining her ... idle threats surely ... *how could she possibly have damaged Morgan & Sons?* ... but it was natural to lash out when you were scared and angry ... she'd done it herself ...

It was a relief when he left to 'get some work done'.

She was lost in thought beside a sleeping Gypsy, when

the soft approach of rubber soles caught her attention. Another sentry taking over. She glanced up hoping at least for a familiar face, no necessity to engage in polite small talk.

But no, this was no uniformed nurse. Hannah Morgan, swathed in an olive and chestnut ethnic dress, rows of matching beads draped over her generous bosom, spread her arms wide in greeting. 'Hello, my darling. I just *had* to come.'

Anya jumped up and into her mother-in-law's warm embrace. 'There's no one I'd rather see.' The floodgates finally opened.

Somehow, Anya found herself in a quiet room, sobbing out her anguish in private. She felt an overwhelming need to convince this wise woman who had earned her respect and affection, of her innocence. Incoherent and garbled at times, desperately clawing at shreds of logic, she searched for understanding. Hannah listened and soothed, but offered no false platitudes. Anya wept again, until she had no more tears to shed, before, mutually drained, together they tiptoed back into the ward, to find Leon reading a story to his daughter. He nodded to them, without breaking stride. Not till she had fallen asleep for the night did they leave her, and drive home.

'I want to hear the whole story, from the beginning,' Hannah said, as they toyed in a desultory fashion with lasagne and fruit salad. 'But it's far too late to rake over anything tonight. I'm exhausted and I'm sure you both are too. Most things are better for mature reflection and a night's sleep, so, let's talk tomorrow. And, somehow, we'll find a way through this nightmare. We will. We will.'

She hugged them both, and left without another word.

It was Hannah who suggested that Anya should write down the details of every inexplicable happening, every troubling experience, since Gypsy's birth – including the things she wasn't proud of. What she'd noticed, what she'd thought, who she'd told, how she'd felt, what she'd done, what had happened, how it had been resolved. No holds barred.

'This will be totally up your street, Anya. With your attention to detail, your logical researcher's brain, your powers of observation; they'll all stand you in good stead here. And if I know you, you'll have kept some kind of notes – yes?'

'Dates and the basics. Not how I felt, what I thought.'

'Put down anything at all connected with each one. Let's see what pans out.'

'What are you expecting to find, Mother?' Leon wondered.

'To be honest, son, I have absolutely no idea. But none of this makes sense to me, and I'm not about to watch my family fall apart without a fight.'

They spent as much time as they could with Gypsy, taking it in turns to entertain her, careful not to overlap for long. On the surface, it was all perfectly civil if not exactly amicable, but it was easier to be free to do natural mothering activities with Gypsy without the dread of Leon's comments or looks. So, when he suggested taking his mother for a drink on the third evening of this new regime, she encouraged them to go. She shut out from her field of vision the nurse appointed to watch her, and set herself to lulling Gypsy to sleep – not easy in a ward with other lively children distracting her, so much activity all around her.

The dark eyes were growing heavy and she was on her sixth round of a favourite nursery rhyme sung under her breath, when an unfamiliar figure approached. Anya felt a surge of annoyance. The woman was in her fifties with a face prematurely aged by stress and an excess of sun. Her back-combed hair, mouse-brown and streaked with grey, looked as if she simply added an extra layer of lacquer each day, so that it resembled a solid helmet protecting her brain from the next irate person who came at her with a hatchet. Her nondescript beige acrylic jumper and skirt hung loosely on her gaunt frame, and the eyes that peered over wire-rimmed glasses were an indeterminate colour, sunk in dark sockets as if they were already trying out death for size.

Brenda Brooks. Social Worker.

Not another!

Ms Brooks seemed as gauche in her manner as in her appearance. She made no attempt to moderate her voice in the interests of confidentiality or a baby's drowsiness. Impervious to the vibes Anya was sure she must be emitting, she made no secret of her mission: to watch mother and daughter interacting. But Gypsy hadn't been fed her lines in this drama and, rudely roused from a twilight zone, rebelled at every turn. Anya felt her own tension ratcheting with every false move as her score out of twenty fell exponentially. And when the nurse on sentry duty finally stepped in to calm the fractious child, she knew without a doubt that she had failed the spot test.

Even Hannah could find no words of solace for her.

CHAPTER 54

After thirty years of marriage to a hardworking general practitioner, Karen Brownlee had learned to take her husband's erratic schedules and tentative promises very much in her stride. However, some personal appointments took precedence in her book, and a date with their daughter Sierra, bringing a new 'serious' boyfriend to meet them for the first time, was one of those sacrosanct events she rated above the minor ailments of the good people of Dalkeith. Robert knew he was in for a chilly reception when he still had three patients to go at the time he was supposed to be extending a warm welcome to Kenny Robertson, primary school teacher and ardent green campaigner, who had summoned every ounce of courage to meet the legendary doctor rated two rungs down from a deity by his daughter.

The trouble was, Robert simply couldn't say, No. He'd known Sam McGovan since he was a five pound three ounce mewling infant; he was well aware of the struggle it had been for the man to snatch an hour out of an extremely busy week on his family farm to present his recalcitrant pilonidal sinus at the surgery this evening. He'd heard enough of the rattle in Catriona Ford's lungs on Monday to want to reassure himself as well as her that he could safely keep her here under his care rather than dispatch her to the Infirmary where she'd be completely disorientated in the terrifying world her dementia conjured up in times of stress. He had himself insisted that Mary Bourne should return today to check that her cardiac arrhythmia had settled and she was not in imminent danger of throwing off a life-threatening embolus.

He sent another apologetic text to Karen and called for his next patient. But it was the receptionist, Wendy, who popped her head round the door.

'Sorry to disturb you, Dr Brownlee, but there's a Dr Diane Moore from Child Protection on the phone. She wants to know if you're free for a chat after surgery. Something about the Morgan family?'

'Can you take a number, Wendy? I've still got three patients waiting. Will it wait till the morning? If not I'll ring her when I've finished.'

She withdrew, Sam McGovan entered, walking like a man with a red hot poker up his rear end. By the time Robert had dealt with the cyst … explained five times to Mrs Ford about the importance of finishing her course of antibiotics and written out an instruction in capital letters on a Post-it to stick on her kitchen cabinet … and given Mary Bourne enough reassurance to allow her to close her eyes for sleep without the expectation of never opening them again in this life, Robert knew his own coffin was well and truly nailed shut at home.

He took a long swig of tap water and dialled the number Wendy had procured for him.

'Dr Moore.'

'Robert Brownlee. So sorry to keep you waiting. A long surgery this evening, I'm afraid.'

'My apologies for keeping you back; I imagine you're more than ready for home. But I'd very much welcome your input on this difficult case with the Morgan family. The baby's just been readmitted – did you know?'

'I didn't. But the family's health visitor was just consulting me about them a day or two ago, wondering why we hadn't seen them and why she couldn't get an answer at the door.'

'Well, I'm afraid it's not looking good. Hence my call.'

'What's happened now?'

'You'll have the local consultations in your own records, and may I suggest you bring them up on your screen now … and perhaps it would help if I recap the history after the first hospital visit – give you a context?'

'Please do.'

'Briefly, the baby, Gypsy, has been seen at Sick Children's five times now. First time: three months old. Outpatient. Recurrent diarrhoea.

'Second time: four months. Blood in the nappy. Query intussusception.

'Third time: July. Seven months. Unnaturally drowsy. Suspected infection. Nothing isolated. Not admitted.

'Fourth time: couple of weeks later. Diarrhoea and mini-convulsion. Admitted and observed for a week. Nothing abnormal discovered. But the day before she was due to be discharged, found limp and unresponsive. Full-blown convulsion on the ward. Blood sugar very low. Suspected insulin overdose.

'The paediatric consultants did a thorough check on all their wards, and could find no evidence of a pattern in the hospital, so the finger seemed to point at the family. That's when Child Protection were called in.

'On balance we felt that, though the mother was struggling, the baby was best kept with her parents, so we sanctioned discharge with extra support and increased monitoring. You and your staff picked up there I know, and kept a check on them.'

Had they? Had they properly acted on the risks?

Robert scanned the screen. 'Yes, our records show the paternal grandmother moved up, and the health visitor and social worker did extra house-calls and monitored the situation.'

'Any thoughts up to that point?'

'There's nothing in their reports to ring alarm bells .... Child thriving ... mum more settled and confident .... Well ... until a couple of days ago when the health visitor flagged up that nobody had seen them for some time; they weren't at home on four separate occasions. We felt this was out of character, so we agreed she should send a formal appointment.'

'Well, they're back on the radar again now, with a vengeance!' Diane Moore said. 'Mother reports finding the baby floppy and unresponsive. She rang 999 when she couldn't wake her. The husband subsequently gave the ED staff a sachet of powder found in the kitchen at their house. Toxicology reported barbiturates and painkillers – same drugs they found in Gypsy's blood. Looks like a deliberate act.'

Robert groaned aloud. 'The team were doing their level best to support this family; keep them together.'

'I think we *all* hoped it wouldn't come to this.'

'Doesn't make sense. Well-cared-for kiddie. Immaculate home, highly intelligent parents, plenty of money. I just don't get it.'

'I think you did yourselves consider FII at one stage, am I right?'

'We did – vaguely in passing, but not seriously. Let me just check … yes, there it is; in July.'

'That does seem to be the logical conclusion, I'm afraid. We've asked for a psychiatric assessment.'

'Could the early neuroses be a prelude to the more serious condition?'

'We're still gathering information at the moment, so it's difficult to answer that. Although if this *is* attention-seeking in origin, it makes intuitive sense. Obviously, our first concern is for the child, but none of us wants to take her into care unless we have no other option. So, the question is, who is giving her harmful substances and why? Is the mother mentally well enough to take care of her? And until we know the answers, we can't in all conscience send her home.'

'So, she's still in Sick Kids at the moment, yes?'

'Yes. Under constant supervision.'

'How's the mum coping?'

'Not well. And she's adamant she's innocent; sees herself as a victim here.'

'What an appalling mess. I only hope the papers don't get hold of this.'

'Don't we all.'

By the time Robert finally reached home that night, Sierra had given up waiting, and gone into town with the new boyfriend.

Her text message was terse: *Thanks for nothing, Dad.* His own leftover portion of vegetarian lasagne had dried at the edges, and his wife's reception was nearly as frosty as the lemon dessert he dredged out of the freezer. No one was remotely interested in the burden he carried.

He had ample space to dwell on the ramifications for the practice if they were found to have failed to protect Gypsy Morgan. The fact that four visits had drawn a blank ... the health visitor had been agitating ... he'd personally still taken a softly-softly approach ...

CHAPTER 55

They made a strangely ill-assorted quartet. Dr Diane Moore studied them surreptitiously as they helped themselves to biscuits and coffee. Ten years in Child Protection had given her an instinct for good team players.

Brenda Brooks was a new-comer, drafted in in response to the Head of Social Work's reservations about her predecessor – '*too personally involved. Unable to form dispassionate judgements.*' Pity. Jane Carver's knowledge and experience, her understanding of the specifics of this case, her calm approach, had been impressive. Brenda Brooks didn't have the same empathy. Nor charisma. On the other hand, viewed dispassionately, her assessment of the family dynamics and interactions squared more nearly with the external evidence. She was unlikely to be swayed by emotion.

DS Craig Leverhume was solid in more ways than one. She'd worked with him on previous cases and trusted his instincts. He'd have the courage to remove a child if it came to it, but he was a family man at heart, not one to rush in prematurely with an axe. Though he hadn't met the Morgan family personally as yet, he knew the rules and regulations related to child protection inside out. His voice would add real gravitas.

Marjorie Hoffman represented the health visitors, and Diane knew she'd been listening closely to Lucinda Devonshire's detailed account, her personal misgivings. Lucinda herself was a key figure in this case; not only lynchpin but Achilles heel too. Intimate knowledge of the family; known to have had concerns from early on; but vulnerable. Her judgement, her actions would be under intense scrutiny if this case went belly-up. She couldn't afford to miss so much as a whisper of danger now. And Marjorie was fiercely on her side. She knew first-hand what was at stake here.

'Right, let's get down to business, shall we?' Diane assumed the chair at the head of the table. 'You've all received the documents – strictly confidential, as usual. We've had input from a lot of people here, medical, family, community.'

'Sorry to interrupt,' – Marjorie held up one finger – 'but I don't see a psychiatric evaluation here.'

Diane sighed. 'I know. Apparently, the best person for such an assessment is currently snowed under with referrals. Their sense is that, since Gypsy's currently safe in hospital, this is one job that can wait.' She spread her hands in a what-can-you-do shrug.

'Difficult to make an informed decision without that.'

'Agreed. I'll do what I can. For now, I think, the best we can do is to draw up two plans – if this *is* FII; if it's *not*. What we *do* have, however, is the information gathered from interviews and submissions. I've amalgamated the data and put initials against items so you can see what's reported by more than one witness, and what's uncorroborated. Let's start with the facts and suspicions relating to Anya Morgan. Summary 1. I'll give you a minute or two to refresh your memories.'

Four pairs of eyes trawled through the list.

ANYA MORGAN
1. High anxiety about the baby's health from the outset.
2. Frequent consultations with GPs and health visitors.
3. Five visits to hospital; two admissions.
4. Wore earplugs sometimes to block out baby's cries.
5. Inexplicably heavily asleep, unaware of child crying, on several occasions.
6. Unaccountably moved or mislaid or lost objects in the house contrary to normal fastidious ways and ultra-organised habits.

7. Convinced that her husband wants out of their marriage. (He vigorously denies this.)
8. Resentful of his frequent absences.
9. Socially isolated.
10. Insists on her innocence.
11. Almost all acquaintances/friends find the idea of her guilt incomprehensible.
12. In the house when her baby niece died 6 years ago.

SUSPECTED:
Taken sedatives.
Administered sedatives to child.
Administered insulin to child.
Administered barbiturates and painkillers to child.
Unreliable witness.

'Anything to add?' Diane gave them time. 'No? Right. Comments, thoughts, suggestions.'

For the next thirty-five minutes the four professionals charged with Gypsy Morgan's safety, considered and reflected, surmised and debated.

'You don't need me to remind you of the weight of responsibility the professionals at the coalface carry here. My door remains open for them, but I took the liberty of itemising the doubts and fears expressed to me so far – anonymised this time. I refer you to Summary 3.'

The document spelled out a powerful sense of anxiety.

PROFESSIONAL CONCERNS
1. Were they seduced by the wealth and luxury? or by the high intelligence and charm?
2. Had they been sufficiently vigilant?
3. Did they miss vital cues?
4. Did they dismiss early concerns too readily?

5. Should they have tried harder to find the mother and child when there was no response at the house?
6. Could they live with the prospect of Gypsy returning to her home on their watch?
7. How will they know when to act?
8. Will they be implicated, censured, vilified?
9. What would they declare in a court of law?

Diane fleshed out some of the points more graphically; underlined the prospect of lurid headlines in the tabloids that so clearly hung heavily over these people charged with the practical care of this troubled family. The sombre faces around the table told their own story and she found herself praying devoutly her Protection team would have the wisdom to steer a careful course here, and minimise that risk.

CHAPTER 56

The endless questioning and scrutiny had exacted a heavy toll, but it took the combined pressure of family and staff to persuade Anya she had to take care of herself if she was to be any use to Gypsy. Hannah quickly became a key player, trusted, non-judgemental.

Knowing she was at the hospital, Anya lingered over a long shower after an hour on the treadmill. She was just towelling her hair when the doorbell rang. The strong smell of cheese greeted her as Tiffany held out yet another pyrex dish.

'I won't stop if you want to be alone, but I needed you to know that I'm still here, still your friend, still totally behind you. I can't begin to imagine what you're going through, but I suspect preparing food isn't top of your priorities, so hopefully this will at least give you a bit of nourishment. It's freshly made and fully cooked so you only need to reheat it.'

Anya remained in the doorway.

'That's kind of you, Tiffany, but I'm afraid I'm not good company at the moment.'

The sunlight from the window over the door irradiated Tiffany's purple quiff, but her face was in partial shadow.

'I take it Gypsy's still in hospital?'

Anya nodded wearily.

'Any word of her getting home?'

'No.'

'You must be exhausted traipsing back and forth all the time. Is there anything at all I can do to help?'

'There's nothing *anybody* can do to help. Until the powers that be come to their senses.'

277

'What are they saying *now*?'

'That somebody deliberately tried to harm her.'

Tiffany recoiled.

Another hypocrite.

The knife was out before Anya could check it for sharpness. 'But you know that. You brought in the stuff from my kitchen.'

'I didn't have a choice, Anya. What else could I do? The drawer was open. It was just lying there.'

'When have you ever known me to leave a drawer half open? Why would you think for a second, a) it was me? or b) it was sinister?'

'Normally I wouldn't. But it was in *your* kitchen. You'd just found Gypsy unconscious. You'd rung 999. The last thing on your mind would be how tidy your kitchen was.'

'And if I'd deliberately poisoned my daughter, the last thing I'd be is careless about the evidence.'

'Rationally speaking, yes. But this isn't a rational thing, Anya. You can't blame yourself.'

'Everyone else seems to.'

'No, they aren't *blaming* you. They're trying to find a way of helping you.'

'Funny idea of help.'

'I *know* those people – Dr Hooper, the ward staff, everybody – they wouldn't hesitate to take Gypsy away if they had a cast iron case against you, if they thought you had any kind of malicious intent against her. Believe me, I've seen it happen; kids removed in the early hours, taken into care. The fact that they're keeping her on the ward, you've got full access to her, that's all positive. They know it's a temporary blip. You're just not well at the moment, and they're looking to see if there's any way they can keep you all together and draft in support to make sure everybody's safe.'

'And you agree with them too. *You* think I did this.'

'I don't *want* to think it, Anya. I really, really don't, but … Hey, look, there's one hugely encouraging aspect to this whole business.'

'What's that?'

'In all these incidents, Gypsy wasn't given a big enough dose to do lasting damage. Some women who do this kind of thing go overboard and the baby actually dies.'

'So, I'm a clever titrator of drugs as well as a deluded baby-harmer.'

'I'm trying to be positive here, Anya. You *are* a clever woman. You're also going through a difficult time. But in spite of the illness, your brain's functioning sufficiently rationally to calculate the dose of sedation, insulin, barbiturates, analgesics, that will induce symptoms but not be lethal. That takes a degree of controlled thinking that's reassuring.'

'Damned with faint praise. Look, I can see you're trying to scratch some remnants of hope from this mess, but tepid support's not what I need right now. And I'm struggling to be with people who're suspicious of me.'

'Fair enough. But, remember, I'm only a phone call away.'

That afternoon Gypsy was particularly grizzly and disgruntled, hating the constraints of her limited environment, too tired to play, too wound up to sleep, but the ward sister was adamant: she could not be taken out of the ward, no, not even with a professional escort.

The baby spat out the fish dish sent up from the kitchens, she threw her feeding cup out of her high chair repeatedly, she batted her favourite flashing-light pull-along truck out of the way without a second glance, she clawed her mother's face so hard she left red wheals down her cheek ... By the time her grandmother appeared, Anya was close to tears.

'She's in a terrible mood today.'

Hannah took in the situation at a glance and dispatched Anya to have a good long walk outside in the sunshine, refusing to countenance any reluctance.

It was such a relief to walk away – a thought that cut deep into Anya's soul.

Was she an unnatural mother?

Was she somehow working through deep psychological hurts?

Was she actually harming her daughter by keeping her close?

She was certainly bone weary and the mind plays tricks when it's desperately in need of rest.

Tiffany's ready-made savoury was particularly welcome that evening.

How ungracious she'd been. Tiffany'd be perfectly justified in steering well clear of the Morgans in future.

Anya's mind flitted over this friendship that had developed in spite of her own reservations; a relationship predicated on compassion. Had Tiffany not noticed her tears that day in the surgery, she'd never even have made the first overtures. And somehow her relentless optimism and good humour placed her above the petty irritations that preoccupied Anya's mind, made her the better woman. Even now, excluded from the inner circle, marginalised by Anya's resentment, she was generous, ready to bring her professional knowledge to bear, to give Anya hope in all the turbulence of doubt and suspicion. She forced herself to re-live the doorstep conversation without the hostility that had coloured it that morning.

Tiffany had the benefit of distance; she could achieve a perspective denied to Anya. Somehow, she could grasp the essentials and follow through the ramifications to the kernel of the issue. But then, that was part of her modus operandi. She understood, she listened, she took on board the detail. She had a practical wisdom borne of experience. She was most probably a remarkably good nurse; what a waste to give that up when she had her own family.

The thoughts and memories scrambled over one another.

02:15. She padded to the kitchen and made a cup of tea. Sitting in the soft light of a summer night, she was lost in thought when Leon startled her. He'd emerged from his study, still fully dressed.

'Thought I heard a noise.' He filled his mug and perched on a high stool further along the counter top. 'Bad night?'

'No worse than usual.'

The fridge hummed softly in the background.

'Why did you tell Tiffany what was in those pills?' She did her level best to keep it even, non-accusatory.

'What pills?'

'My Freya Trimble-Coleman pills, what else? The stuff I'm supposed to have fed to Gypsy.'

'It wasn't pills. It was a powder.'

'You sure?'

'Of course I'm sure. I took it from Tiffany. A plastic sachet thingy with white powder in it.'

'Well … leave that aside for the minute … why did you tell her what was in it?'

'Look, don't start! I didn't tell her anything. I wouldn't. The less anybody outside the family knows about this whole sorry business the better, as far as I'm concerned.'

'So, how did she know they found barbiturates and analgesics?'

'Not from me, that's for sure.'

'And I haven't even spoken to her till today. Besides which, I *definitely* haven't told a soul.'

'She knows people in the NHS, doesn't she? Maybe somebody let it slip.'

'But if one of them *did* talk to her, that's way out of order. Patient confidentiality and all that.'

'Fair point, but the Child Protection people have been quizzing us all, maybe it came up in the course of asking questions for clarification.'

'Even so, it's completely out of line.'

They sat in silence for a long time.

It was Leon who broke it next. 'What're you thinking?'

'About the mix-up. I'm trying to recall our exact conversation – yours and mine, I mean, that time when you told me the doctors suspected Gypsy'd been given drugs deliberately. I think you said something like "the stuff in the drawer", and I automatically assumed you meant those pills. But now you're telling me it wasn't them at all. This is the first I've heard of any sachet.'

'It was one of those wee plastic wallets with the press-shut top – like a miniscule freezer bag. It was the powder in that they said had the barbiturates and paracetamol in it.'

'And that's what Tiffany found in the drawer?'

'Yes. When she was checking everything was switched off, before locking up the house.'

Anya sat perfectly still, her mind in turmoil. How easy it was for an error in understanding to completely colour a conversation, and how hard to unravel a thread back in order to reconstruct the sequence and comprehend it accurately.

'Listen, don't bite my head off,' Leon interrupted her thoughts. 'I'm not having a go at you, but ... is it at all possible those pills could have made you ill in the first place? You got mixed up about what you ordered?'

'Hardly! With Trades Description and everything, Freya's not going to be selling something powerful enough to alter the mind of lactating women.'

'Although some people do have idiosyncratic reactions to things, don't they?'

She shrugged. 'Pursue it if you want to. I've nothing to hide. I bought them in good faith. The transaction will still be online.'

'So, why didn't you tell me until I discovered them by accident? Why keep them hidden?'

'Because you'd only scoff. You always do when I mention natural remedies.'

Leon sighed deeply, shaking his head.

'You know ... blaming everybody else, it doesn't help. They're doing their best to get to the bottom of this. If you start casting aspersions, accusing them of breaching confidentiality ...'

'"*Casting aspersions*" ...? So, it's fine for *you* to blame *me*, accuse *me* of bankrupting the firm because you aren't such a free agent as you used to be, but it's a completely different kettle of fish if *I* dare to suggest ... Oh, what's the use?'

She rose and stalked out of the room.

Safe in her own company she took out her lists and looked at them through a different filter. There *had* to be a connection somewhere, *something* that would illuminate this impenetrable maze. After an hour, she consigned the thoughts to a back burner and allowed sleep to reclaim her.

The mind is a wonderful thing and she'd always believed in the power of the subconscious to sift and sort problems. When she'd been faced with pages and pages of statistics in her career, she'd often left the analysis unresolved and gone to bed. Almost invariably the morning brought fresh insights and not infrequently a viable solution.

This time a brand new theory presented itself, but she was not about to share it with anyone, not even Leon. Let it not be said she had single-handedly precipitated Gypsy going into care.

CHAPTER 57

George Hooper had made a point of seeing Anya every day and examining Gypsy openly in front of her. Instinctively he liked her; intellectually he reserved judgement. Why was she now requesting a meeting in private, just the two of them? A plethora of possible complications and compromises raced through his head, but one look at those haunted blue eyes and nervous tics was enough to make him at least consider it.

Was she about to confess?

Pledge him to secrecy?

Should he refuse?

Should he insist on a chaperone, a witness, an independent arbiter, someone from Child Protection, a psychiatrist?

Should he record their conversation?

Whatever he did, he was in danger of losing her trust.

'It's delicate. I don't know who else I can trust …'

'Then, certainly, you can talk to me.'

One look at her hunched in the chair in his room was enough to tell him what an ordeal this was.

'Just take your time, Anya.'

'I don't want to put you into a difficult position …'

'Try me. Sometimes it helps just to share a burden.'

'I've been going over and over what's happened … I can see how people would think I must have been responsible, but … I *know* I didn't do those things!'

'Right.'

'So, since it wasn't me, it must have been someone else.'

She drew an A4 plastic wallet out of her bag and laid it on her lap.

'I've catalogued every single weird happening, who was around at the time, who could have been involved, and one possibility keeps cropping up.'

George kept very, very still.

'I just want to say, Dr Hooper, I've agonised over this … whether I should say anything to anybody. It's a terrible accusation to make. But … if I don't … I could lose Gypsy.' Her voice broke and she roughly brushed a hand across her eyes.

Still she hesitated.

'D'you want me just to look at your notes?' George said quietly. 'Or would you feel able to talk me through what you're thinking?'

'I'd need to explain it.'

'Just when you're ready then.'

She was like a robot in slow motion. 'It started when Gypsy was just eight weeks old …'

The record was meticulous, the argument plausible – the work of a fine brain, capable of marshalling facts, drawing inferences, substantiating claims, with such precision and logic even, apparently, in the face of deep anguish. A highly-trained researcher's mind … clever enough to manipulate and invent … this was *her* account, *her* experience, *her* perception, *her* analysis. No one else could verify it. Apart from … one person.

The question was: was this enough evidence to risk destroying another life? – several, if her theory was correct.

Long after Anya had returned to her cot-side vigil, George remained tensed over his desk, raking through the photocopy of her theory. He knew Diane Moore was currently out of the country. *Could it wait till she returned? Should he contact someone else on the Protection team?* He was still no closer to a decision when another tap on the door roused him.

'Yes.'

Rosemary only half entered his room. 'You sound busy. Want me to come back later?'

'No, come in, come in. Sorry. I've just had Anya

Morgan here and she's given me a lot of stuff to ponder.'

'Well, there's a coincidence. I wanted to have a word with you about the Morgan case. In confidence.'

'Fire away. And if you have any cast iron solutions, I'll personally fund your bonus.'

Rosemary hesitated.

'Before you do, though, what d'you make of her ... of *them*, Rosemary?'

'I'm not sure about *him*. I don't feel to know him really. I get a sense that he's maybe not quite as charming at home as he seems with us, but it's only a hunch. I do like *her*, though. And for what it's worth, I believe her. She's talked to me a fair bit and something doesn't add up. The external evidence points to her certainly, but she simply doesn't fit into the mould that evidence has created.'

'That's a good way of putting it. And strictly twixt thee and me, I'm inclined to agree with you.'

'D'you have an alternative hypothesis?'

'As it happens, as of an hour ago, I do. But that's for your ears only.'

'One that means the Morgans get to keep Gypsy? I so much do *not* want to see this family split up.'

'None of us do, but can we *prove* she'd be safe at home? We can't keep her here indefinitely. But Child Protection are still worrying away at this one. Social Work in particular are twitchy. No way do they want a case of negligence, or a dead child, on their patch.'

'But once they get their hands on Gypsy ...'

'Precisely.'

Rosemary groaned. 'I must admit I feel a bit of a hypocrite here.'

'How so?'

'Well, my partner, Shay, and I are wanting to adopt a kiddie, and we'd absolutely *love* a little girl like Gypsy. But when you know about the heartbreak behind some of these cases, it feels decidedly uncomfortable to think you might benefit from someone else's misery. Could you ever be totally sure it was for the best? I mean ... imagine you were offered

Gypsy! You'd be over the moon. She's absolutely gorgeous. But if you knew Anya, you knew how *she* was feeling ... you'd be sick at heart. And then, say Anya couldn't prove her innocence. Time goes on, the foster-bonds are getting stronger. Protection, Social Work, the courts, say this kiddie needs stability. She's completely integrated into our family by this time. We love her to pieces. And we're offered the chance to adopt her. Once you get to that point, there's no going back. The Morgans have lost her for ever. It's just too horrific to contemplate. Enough to send any mother stir crazy.'

George grimaced. 'And she's a highly intelligent woman. I'm sure she's completely aware of the dangers. So much so, that she's desperate to come up with an explanation to reverse this momentum.'

'And you say she has?'

'She's given me one perfectly plausible scenario, yes. Trouble is, I can't pursue it without pointing the finger at somebody else. If I share this information, I think Child Protection'd be duty bound to investigate it. But if the person turned out to be innocent, there'd be hell to pay.'

'The devil and the deep blue sea come to mind.'

'Exactly so. But that's not what you came about. How can I help you?'

'This might be something or nothing, and I may be totally over-thinking things, but it struck me as relevant, and I feel I ought to at least mention it to somebody. It's about Anya's sister. Something she said. About the night her baby died.'

George didn't move.

'Anya was there. Staying the night.'

'And?'

'Claire didn't suggest anything untoward ... but I'm wondering ... with all that's happened to Gypsy ... could it be significant?'

'Thanks, Rosemary. A legitimate concern. I really appreciate your giving this case so much attention. In point of fact, the Morgans' GP had the same thought and he chased up the records. There was nothing untoward found at postmortem and it was certified as a Sudden Infant Death. But the coincidence of Anya being there has been duly flagged up.'

'Oh. Sorry.'

'No apology required. You did the right thing to mention it. I sincerely hope it was nothing more than a coincidence. And I know I can rely on your complete discretion. I haven't shared Anya's theory with you because it's currently unsubstantiated, and no good can come of speculating at the risk of ruining reputations. At the moment, you're the only person who even knows Anya came to me today, and I'd hate to undermine her trust.'

'I totally understand. And I'm sure you won't mention what I said about adoption.'

'Absolutely. However,' – he smiled at her warmly – 'for what it's worth, I very much hope things work out for you. You'd make a wonderful parent.'

'So would Shay. She's a natural with children.'

CHAPTER 58

The days dragged by, and the hours spent with Gypsy in the confines of the hospital felt interminable at times. A playpen offered limited scope for movement but not nearly enough for Gypsy's energies. Anya's patience was stretched paper thin at times; knowing she was under constant scrutiny forced her to walk away more than once, seeking respite in furious exercise. Claire came more frequently, Leon called in most evenings, his parents became stalwarts in providing invaluable diversion. Hannah was an inexhaustible mine of counting songs and hide'n'seek, while Douglas treated Gypsy to the spectacle of an elderly dignified gentleman impersonating every animal in the zoo. Other small patients were equally entertained and he soon had an appreciative audience as he prowled and roared and stalked and mewled around the playpen, pretending to push a paw through the rails, gobble up a discarded pillow, hide behind a chair before pouncing on a clockwork mouse.

Anya found herself actually laughing. It felt good. It could almost pass for normal family life.

The grandparents' visit was extended.

'Would you be all right with my parents if I popped down to Newcastle for a meeting the day after tomorrow?' Leon's whole body language screamed unease. 'I'd only be away one night and one day. I'd drive back as soon as the meeting finishes on Wednesday. But I won't go if you don't want me to.'

'No. You go.'

But that night, sitting companionably in the garden watching the shadows lengthen across the lawn, Hannah was direct.

'You aren't happy about him going really, are you, Anya?' she said softly.

Anya shrugged. 'I don't know how he can bear to leave her.'

'I don't want to interfere, but is there anything I can do to help *you*?'

She shook her head, her throat tight. *Who knew what she might divulge if she once started to share her doubts about those secret phone calls, the emails, the swish hotels, Leon's secretive behaviours.*

'You've been through a terribly traumatic time. Things like this put a big strain on relationships. Men aren't always good at sharing their emotions. I'm sorry if Leon isn't supporting you enough. I suspect he's terrified of saying the wrong thing, causing more pain.'

Anya said nothing.

'I'm not making excuses for him, but it's not exactly stimulating for *either* of you, is it, being cooped up in a hospital ward playing with a baby for hours. It's artificial being forced to focus on *any* patient in hospital to the exclusion of everything else.'

Anya nodded.

'Plus he hates putting more work on Thomas and Roger. It's bound to create tension.'

'I know.'

'I've mentioned this to Leon, but you might feel differently … I was just wondering … and please don't take this as an insult … would the hospital agree to Gypsy coming to stay with us, meantime – and you too, naturally. How would you feel about that? Would it be the lesser of two evils?'

'You'd do that?'

'Of course I would. I don't want to push in or …'

Anya reached across and laid a hand on her mother-in-law's arm. 'Thank you. Thank you for *all* your support. And understanding.'

'So … would it be all right to ask?'

'We'll speak to Dr Hooper tomorrow.'

For the first time since the terrible accusations against her, Anya slept through the night.

As it happened, George Hooper was away examining medical students that morning, so the suggestion had to be postponed. Now she had a possible get-out-of-jail card in her grasp, Anya found it impossible to suppress her growing sense of frustration and impatience; she was like a coiled spring. When Gypsy eventually fell asleep cuddling a stuffed tiger, Hannah suggested they pop out for something tasty to eat, her treat. Anya seized the opportunity to check out a sale of baby clothes while they were in town and it was 4:30 when they eventually arrived back in the ward.

As they entered, Anya eyes went instinctively to Gypsy's space. Odd. No familiar mobile … no favourite bed-cover … no toys … *no child*! Only a freshly made bed.

Where had they moved her?

And why?

The ward clerkess approached.

'Sister Young wants to speak to you. I'll get her for you.'

Nicole Young was her usual self, immaculate, inscrutable, but there seemed to be something particularly stiff about her posture today.

'Hello, Anya. Could you come into the relatives' room for a moment, please?'

Hannah hung back, but Anya beckoned her to follow, mouthing 'Come with me'.

The ward sister entered the room carefully, shut the door behind them extremely gently, and perched her starched figure on the very edge of the chair. She placed her hands meticulously on her lap and seemed to actively compose her features.

'Anya, I'm afraid I have some bad news for you.'

Anya felt the blood drain from her face, her limbs. Her hands moved of their own accord, covering her mouth.

'I'm sorry, but Gypsy's gone.'

Seeing Anya beyond words, Hannah leaned forward. 'I

291

don't follow. We were with her only this morning. She was fine.'

The nurse nodded and for the first time something like sympathy creased her features.

'So … what happened?' Hannah persisted.

'I'm afraid Social Work have decided the risk is too great and they've taken her to a place of safety.'

Anya found her voice. 'But they *can't*! She's my baby. Dr Hooper knows I haven't harmed her …' She felt the trembling gathering pace.

'Unfortunately, they weren't happy with what they saw of the situation. Dr Hooper wasn't here at lunchtime when they came, and we had no jurisdiction to countermand their order to take her into care.'

'This can't be happening! You've been watching us all this time. You *know* Gypsy's been fine.'

'Our evaluation is only part of the overall appraisal, I'm afraid. And we're only responsible for what happens *here*. The decisions about sending children into the community in these cases are made by the multi-disciplinary Child Protection team. And, in light of the facts, and your husband's frequent absences … the conclusion was that Gypsy would be safest in foster care meantime.'

'*Foster care?!*' Anya exploded. 'My daughter has been placed with *foster parents*?'

'It's a next step. We can't keep children in acute care wards indefinitely. In fact, if I'm honest, I'm surprised that Gypsy's been in hospital this long.'

'*You're* surprised? How d'you think *I* feel. I'm her mother – her *mother!* And I've had to traipse up here day after day, be subjected to all sorts of scrutiny, undergo humiliation after humiliation, even though I know, and I believe Dr Hooper knows, I'm completely innocent.'

'Is Dr Hooper in the hospital now?' Hannah broke in. 'Might it be possible to speak to him?'

'I'm not sure. But I'll check.'

'Please do. I think this requires immediate action, don't you?'

'She'll be so bewildered ... alone ... with strangers ...' Anya broke off, the pictures too awful to contemplate.

But an unseen protocol had to be followed.

'First, can I just ask, Anya, is your husband up here at the moment?'

'He's in Newcastle for work today, but he's coming back tonight.'

'Ah, pity. It would be better if he was here for you. And I think Dr Hooper would want to speak to you both together.'

'And Leon would *want* to be here, but we can't wait till he gets back. We need action *now*. Who knows what psychological damage you're doing to a poor innocent baby. She'll be terrified out of her mind.'

'I'll see if Dr Hooper's back, and if not, I'll call the registrar. If you'd just like to wait here ...'

CHAPTER 59

Back at home, crazed with no baby to visit, no idea of her whereabouts, no progress to report, Anya wasn't sure who she was maddest with. Leon for not being there. The hospital team for not preventing this. The social workers for daring to remove her daughter without consent or even warning. Herself for having taken that fateful lunch break. Hannah for having pressured her into leaving the ward. Nicole Young for not resisting. George Hooper for being away all day and inaccessible. Dr Prenderghast for not being Dr Hooper.

Leon added to her fury next morning by refusing to take her with him to see the hospital CEO to begin the process of complaint and appeal.

'You're not exactly my best ally, the mood you're in.'

Hannah was taking an afternoon rest, Douglas was outside venting his feelings on another patch of wild garden, when a ring at the door sent Anya rushing to see if someone had seen the light and returned her precious baby.

The disappointment felt like a body blow.

Tiffany held out a large box of strawberries.

'Ah, I didn't expect to find you in ... till I saw the window open. I was going to leave these in your porch and vanish. But since you are, you'd be doing me a massive favour if you could let me in. I'm expecting to be arrested any second. At a rough guess, I'd say Maribel and Jude have eaten their combined weight in the wretched berries, and the owners will issue a writ to get me clapped up in jail. I hope you like strawberries?'

'We do, but ...'

'Then take them, for mercy's sake. I never want to

touch another one as long as I live!'

Tiffany slid inside, shut the door, and leaned heavily against it, panting and fanning herself.

Anya stood uncertainly, not sure how to proceed but praying her mother-in-law stayed out of sight.

'How's the gorgeous Gypsy? It's ages since I saw her. And boy, do I miss those cuddles and chuckles. But hey, look at you ... gosh, you've lost even more weight, young lady. There's nothing to you. Best pile the sugar on those berries. You'll fade away completely at this rate and there'll be nothing left but a puff of air.'

When Anya still said nothing, still didn't move from the hallway, Tiffany's expression became more guarded.

'What is it, Anya? What's wrong?'

Anya stared straight at her. 'How did you know there were barbiturates in the powder, Tiffany?'

There was a sudden stillness in the air. Tiffany maintained steady eye contact, her voice soft, careful.

'Somebody must have mentioned it ... probably one of the nurses. I don't just remember. I know a fair few of them, and lots more by sight from the canteen or the corridors or the grounds. I'm the muggins who gets sent to retrieve missing notes, stuff like that. I didn't want to bother you, reckoned you had enough to contend with in the ward, so I asked occasionally how Gypsy was doing. I hope you don't mind. You know how much I love that little girl. I just wanted to know she was out of the woods.'

'Medical details are confidential. They had no business telling.'

'I'm sorry. But they didn't mean any harm, I'm sure. So please, don't go on a witch-hunt. If anyone's to blame, it's me; I shouldn't have asked. But in my defence, I only enquired *in general* how she was doing. I didn't ask for inside information.'

'There's so much about this whole thing that's suspicious. I'm fast losing confidence in everybody.'

'But you know you can trust *me*. And honestly, I can promise you, hand on heart, I never mentioned what was in the powder to a living soul.'

'You mentioned it to Leon.'

'Well, that's different. He knew already.'

'Have you "mentioned" other things to him too?' – she tamped down the simmering anger – 'When you "found" the powder, maybe? Did you plant the idea in his head that I'd put it in Gypsy's food? That I might be unhinged?'

'Look, if it helps to find a scapegoat, by all means use me. I understand. My shoulders are broad. I won't take it personally. I've seen it all before. Go on, load it all onto me.'

'What exactly *do* you understand, Tiffany?'

'That you're struggling with everything that's happened. And you're mentally and physically exhausted. It's only natural. All those crises over the months. Just trudging up and down to Sick Kids every day. It's exhausting. It takes a heavy toll. Never mind the other stuff.'

'What other stuff?'

'The anxiety, the suspicion, the psychological trauma. You know.'

'So, was it you who sowed the seeds in Leon's mind? Have you been hinting I was mentally ill for ages?'

'Only to help him understand that you weren't responsible for all these things that kept happening. It was the illness, not the real you. And to alert him enough so he could make sure Gypsy was safe.'

'Why would you *do* that? Undermine me.'

'Because my nursing instincts told me ages ago you were struggling. And I was worried about Gypsy. I did my level best to help you see for yourself you needed help. I could have reported things to the authorities, but the last thing I wanted on my conscience was breaking up a family – a lovely family. I was glad you trusted me with Gypsy, that you confided in me. It meant I could intervene and keep you out of the radar of the professionals more than you would have been.'

'Was it your idea to have a key to this house?'

'No. I swear. Leon got a real scare that time when we couldn't wake you, remember? Gypsy was beside herself and the door was locked? It was his idea.'

'Was it you who suggested I'd taken drugs to make me sleep like that?'

'No. It was the GP.'

'And did you tell them what *you* thought?'

'No. I had my suspicions, I grant you, but I kept them to myself. *They* were the ones who made the diagnosis, not me.'

'And what about all those times Gypsy had loose stools, all the times we went to the doctor or the hospital, was it you who told Leon I was making it all up, attention-seeking, or even inducing the symptoms myself?'

'Anya, Anya, Anya. You're adding two and two and making eleven. Paranoia's part of the illness too. I've seen it before. You know what? I think you're paying the price for being referred to the one doctor who's slowest to act on this kind of thing. I'm sure he's hanging back for all the right reasons – I don't doubt his integrity – but I honestly don't think he's done you any favours. You were supposed to have a psych consultation, weren't you? But where is it? The sooner you get treatment, the sooner you can start to be a normal family, looking forward instead of back. Living with all this suspicion, the distrust, the constant harking back to perceived conspiracies, it's destructive. I don't suppose you want advice from me, but as a friend who's been round the block a few times, I think it's only fair to tell you, I honestly think you should consider asking for specialist help yourself. Don't wait to be referred.'

'Dr Hooper's been nothing but supportive.'

'I'm sure he has. On the surface. But is he moving heaven and earth to chase up *your* treatment so that Gypsy can come home? What exactly *is* he doing?'

Anya said nothing.

'I rest my case. Sometimes medical people have to be cruel to be kind. They can't always be Mr Nice Guy.'

CHAPTER 60

It had been another hellish meeting for both Leon and Thomas. The lawyers hadn't minced their words: whichever way the decision from the Employment Tribunal went, the options all looked humiliating. The financial statements put together for today's executive meeting made depressing reading, and Thomas was talking redundancies and staff cuts through tight lips. Add to that another long drive home, and Leon was in no mood for more acid.

But Anya was wired. Her words spat out, laden with pent-up fury as she recounted her exchange with Tiffany. She might well be ill and not in full control of her actions, but this trail of destruction must be stopped by some means. Alienating yet another person would serve no useful function, and in this case, it seemed like a poor return for all the help and advice Tiffany had given them.

'I'll need to go round and apologise. What's her address?'

'I don't know.'

'Come on, Anya. You must. You've *been* there.'

'I have *not*.'

'What, never?'

'Never. Are you deaf or what?'

Leon gritted his teeth. *Poor woman probably felt she couldn't live up to your impossible standards.*

But at least he had a surname and a phone number.

The house was exactly the same as its neighbours, nothing to distinguish it from the outside. Twenty-first century standard issue; less imposing than those nearest the road certainly, but neat, functional, low maintenance. The lawn looked dry and under-nourished but a narrow border of flowering shrubs broke the monotony and gave some form and shape to the space. The powerful scent of choisea assailed Leon's nostrils as he waited for someone to answer the door – one of Anya's staples for flower arrangements. He'd never found apologies easy; saying sorry for his wife was no better, and this time there were no professional or work barriers to keep it impersonal and formal.

He was on the point of leaving when the door swung open and a tall man in a sleeveless tee shirt and khaki shorts disarmed him with a profusion of apologies of his own. The sun glinted on rings in his left ear, and Leon couldn't help glancing at the beautifully crafted dragon etched over the shoulder and down the right arm. In a dark alley the man's bulk could have been intimidating, but his warm smile, crinkled chocolate brown eyes and low husky voice took all the threat out of his appearance.

'Sorry, mate. Out the back, disentangling the hose. Had a gang of kids keeping cool in the paddling pool earlier, and the place was a positive death trap. How can I help you?'

'My name's Leon Morgan.'

'Dan Corrigan.'

'Our wives know each other and I've come to apologise to Tiffany. I think my wife might have got a bit carried away today.'

'Come in, come in. Tiff's not here but good to meet you. Heard a lot about your wee one.'

The open-plan living area was dominated by a pool table and massive screen; the floor and surfaces were strewn with discarded clothes, half-finished jigsaws, piles of games, table tennis bats … evidence of children and activity everywhere. Dan whipped a faded tartan rug off an armchair and gestured to his guest to take the seat.

'Sit down quick, if I were you. Best chance you'll get of avoiding white hairs on your trousers. Damn cat's *permanently* in moulting season, seems to me.'

Leon sank into the deep sagging seat which seemed to swallow him.

'Can I get you a beer? Soft drink. Anything else?'

'Cold water'd be fine, thanks.'

'No probs.'

Dan, can in one hand, stretched his long frame along the settee, heedless of the damp towel draped over one end. He kicked a sandal from one foot and tucked it underneath his other knee.

A man totally at ease with himself and his surroundings.

'Listen, I'm sorry to intrude,' Leon said. 'Are you expecting Tiffany back soonish? I don't want to keep you from whatever you were planning to do.'

'You've just missed her as it happens. She's taken the kids to the flicks and then for fish and chips. Won't be back for a couple of hours yet. I'm supposed to get this lot cleared up before they get back.' Dan waved one hand expansively round the room, and grinned at his visitor. 'No hurry s'far as I'm concerned!'

'Did you see her when she got back from visiting my wife this morning?'

'Yeah.'

'Was she upset?'

'Not that I could see. Mind you with all the stuff going on in this place, we pass like ships in the night much of the time. Half the kids in the neighbourhood were here today. But don't fret yourself, she's not the kind to get hot and bothered about things. Takes life as it comes. And she was straight into organising snacks for the entire gang.'

'Well, I hope she didn't take Anya's comments to heart. I'm afraid my wife's not well at the moment, and part of the illness leads her to say and do things she wouldn't normally do. Making false accusations seems to be part of that. I'm very much afraid she's antagonised rather a lot of people recently.'

'Poor woman. Sounds bad. So, what does she reckon Tiff's done?'

'Betrayed her trust, I guess, about sums it up.'

'Really?'

'As good as accused her of conspiracy to … well, never mind the detail. I felt I had to come and explain. And apologise. If it's any consolation, I'm being accused of far worse crimes, so she shouldn't take it personally.'

'She didn't mention anything about it, so I guess she knows it's nothing to take offence at. She used to be a nurse, you know, so she's seen a fair bit of mental illness in her time.'

'But it feels particularly offensive given everything Tiffany's done to help her. All the times she's given her advice, run them to the surgery or the hospital.'

'Has she?' Dan was staring at him with a frown. 'I didn't know about any of that.'

'Well, your wife must be a very modest woman. She's rescued Anya any number of times and normally Anya respects her knowledge and experience hugely. But now they've taken Gypsy away from us, I guess it's the straw that broke the camel's back. She's lashing out because she's powerless to put this right – we both are. We're fighting for her, of course, but I think Anya's trying to put the blame anywhere else but on herself.'

'Hold up a minute. Did I hear you right? They've *taken Gypsy away from you?!*'

'Yes.'

'Who?'

'Social Work.'

'*Shit!* – excuse my French. That's terrible. What on earth for?'

'Because they think she's not safe in her own home.'

'No wonder the poor woman's looking for someone else to pin it on. Who can blame her? Seriously, mate, I'm truly, truly sorry to hear this. You must be going out of your tiny mind.'

Leon gritted his teeth and nodded.

Dan shuffled himself upright and leaned towards Leon. 'Can you bear to tell me about it? I work with deprived and disabled kids and know folk from the Social Work department. If there's anything I can do …?'

His genuine concern was empowering and Leon found

himself outlining the incidents that had led to this impasse. It felt good to emphasise Tiffany's positive role; humiliating to expose the extent of his own wife's unacceptable behaviour.

Dan sat in silence for a long moment before he replied. His first question was unexpected.

'If you don't mind my asking, do *you* think your wife was responsible in some way?'

'Given the evidence and what the doctors say, I can only conclude she *must* have done what they say; there's no other logical explanation that I can see. But was she responsible? No, I don't think she was. I think her mental illness led her to do what she did to get attention.' Leon dropped his head in his hands and ground out, 'Hell, it kills me to say it out loud.'

'Well, I reckon any guy'd feel the same. It's a helluva thing to believe.'

'It certainly is.'

'And you say Tiff's been there most of the times Gypsy's gone to see doctors?'

'She knew when it was serious enough to seek medical assistance. I was usually at work, so she ferried them. She's been fantastic. And she could fill the doctors in on symptoms and everything, too, and explain all the medical stuff to Anya.'

'I guess her nursing qualifications would help there.'

'And her experience as a mother. Anya really valued that. She was always so calm in a crisis. Anya's more highly strung and it's our first. Tiffany sort of took control and reassured her. It made a world of difference.'

'Good to hear.'

'So, you can see why I felt sick when I heard Anya had had a go at her. She's brilliant with Gypsy. And Anya – the real Anya – trusted her more than anyone. So, I hope she can hang on to that.'

'What a bloody awful mess, mate.'

'You could say that.'

'Listen, like I say, if you think I could help with the Social Work squad, say the word. I'll give you my number.

Glad to do anything I can.'

'I might just do that. This whole thing is way outside my comfort zone. Closing ranks seems to have a whole new dimension where a kid's safety is at stake.'

'Has to. You wouldn't believe how grim some of these cases can be … not yours, of course. I'm quite sure you've got a lovely home, and you aren't in and out of prison, and you aren't hammering the living daylights out of each other, or abusing your kids, or …' He gave an eloquent shrug. 'Some of these families? – you wouldn't put your geriatric tortoise in their care for a weekend.'

'And even I can see it's a no-win situation for the social workers. If they take our child away and we're innocent, the public will hang them out to dry. If they don't take her away, and something bad happens, they'll be dragged through the courts and lose their jobs. I wouldn't have their choices for all the tea in China.'

'Yep. Don't envy them one bit myself. But I genuinely feel for you, mate. Can't begin to imagine what it feels like for an innocent father to lose his kid. I'd die for any one of mine, and I guess you would too.'

CHAPTER 61

Lucinda Devonshire felt physically sick. She'd been staying in close touch with the staff caring for Gypsy, and she knew Child Protection had taken on this case, but word was, they were feeling their way cautiously on this one. What could possibly have come to light to make them take *this* course of action?

Piecing the facts together from a distraught and almost incoherent Anya, she'd got straight on the phone to Jane Carver, but Jane was equally bewildered ... no, more than that – incandescent.

'This is what comes of side-lining me! Putting someone "more dispassionate" on the case. *Brenda blinking Brooks* of all people! About as much feeling as a pogo stick!'

'I know ...'

'You know what the Vine weevil said when I protested? The powers-that-be felt I was "too personally involved, too soft, too cautious", to take the necessary difficult steps. Apparently, according to her, concerns have been expressed for some time about my general reluctance to remove children from danger, so much so that there had been talk of taking me off child-custody cases altogether! Typical! The woman's life's been ruled by legal and professional guidelines for a hundred years; she's incapable of independent thought, of any kind of common sense appraisal.'

'Was it Sharon Vine ...? or would it have been Brenda ...?'

'In this case, I've no idea. It shouldn't have been any of them on their own. It should have been a committee decision by Child Protection.'

'And not to even tell the family ... warn them ...'

'It's a scandal! A disgrace! Exactly the kind of thing that gives social workers a bad name. I'm absolutely livid about this.'

'I had kind of got that impression.'

'In fact … yep, I'm going to go and have it out with her. Nobody, no matter what, should be treated like this.'

'Want me to come too, moral support, and all that?'

'I don't need moral support, but it'd be useful to have you there to give your side of things.'

A tight-lipped Sharon Vine sat rigid behind her desk, the Morgans' file in front of her, angled to prevent Jane seeing it.

Lucinda could feel the hostility between the two women before either spoke.

'What on earth's going on here?' Jane started without preamble. 'I *know* this family. Lucinda here's been visiting them from birth. How could somebody just waltz in and take this kiddie into care when she's perfectly safe in *hospital*?'

'I'm not obliged to tell you *anything*,' Mrs Vine sniffed, 'but since you're clearly *determined* to make an issue out of this …' – she consulted the document – 'information came to light that put a very different complexion on the situation. In light of this new development, the social workers involved agreed that the risk of further harm to this child had increased to a level that necessitated removing her from danger immediately. This action was duly implemented by taking her to a place of safety. I'm sure you would agree that her welfare must come first.'

'"The social workers agreed"? Were Child Protection not in on the decision? I understood they were responsible for decisions now.'

'There was no time to waste. Again, I don't owe you any kind of explanation, but I'm told the social workers were unable to contact Child Protection. Some kind of computer glitch, I believe. In the circumstances, they felt they had no choice but to act at once.'

'What were these extreme circumstances? Gypsy was safe, in *hospital*, for heaven's sake! What couldn't wait till the whole Protection team could consider the case?'

'I'm not at liberty to divulge the detail.'

Jane choked back an acid rejoinder. 'But it's correct, then – Dr Moore didn't sanction this?'

'She didn't do so before the event, no.'

'And has she done so now?'

'Errrr … not so far.' It was a mutter rather than a response.

'Well, this is outrageous. And I fully intend to take this matter up with Dr Moore in person.'

'May I remind you, Jane, that you are officially off this case. You are not entitled to receive confidential information. It's not your place to interfere in situations you don't understand.'

'But Lucinda's *not* off the case. She's still their health visitor. And nobody told her either.'

'Miss Devonshire is not a member of my team. If she has issues with this, she should take them up with her own superiors.'

Superiors?! *Sup…!!!*

Jane strode from the room before she could explode.

Lucinda plied her friend with coffee and waited for her to calm down sufficiently to put her own imminent resignation to one side, and reflect on the best way forward for the Morgans.

'Can I ask you something, Jane. It may be a bit off the wall, but …?'

'As long as it's not to go cap in hand to that imbecile, Sharon No-use Vine!'

'Is it at all possible that someone other than a social worker could have removed Gypsy?'

'Huh? What?'

'I've asked around the folk I know up at Sick Kids, and nobody seems to know anything about it. Or who exactly came to the hospital that lunchtime and took her away. I know one of the senior staff nurses, Rosemary Stewart, pretty well, and she said there'd been nothing said about Gypsy going anywhere in her hearing. But, as I understand it, Rosemary's been quite close to Anya, and maybe they were trying to minimise the risk of an almighty scene or a major protest or anything. Certainly, Rosemary wasn't on at all that day – which might also have been a planned thing; the day was chosen because of who was or was not on duty.'

Jane stared at her, her brain clearly absorbing the question.

'She *had* been on the day before though, and as far as she was aware, there were no plans for anything to happen imminently. Dr Hooper'd declared Gypsy medically fit for discharge, but they were waiting for guidance from Child Protection. In the meantime, she was safe in hospital, so Rosemary wasn't particularly concerned.'

'Heck! You're thinking … maybe somebody with a personal agenda … snuck in, masquerading as a social worker, and just waltzed out with the kiddie! You been reading too many thrillers, Ms Devonshire?!'

'No, seriously. It was Anya who put the thought into my head, actually. And I couldn't be certain. So that got me thinking.'

'Well, the Vine-weevil seemed to know all about it, didn't she? And I know Brenda Brooks *was* drafted in to assess Anya in the ward. But I can double-check if you like.'

'Would you? I'd be hugely grateful.'

'How's Anya bearing up?'

'In pieces, as you'd expect. Alternating between utter despair and raging fury. And I feel so helpless. I can't tell her anything; I don't *know* anything.'

'Would it help if I called in to see her, d'you think?'

'Would that cause trouble for you?'

'Don't see why. I'm not interfering in the process of protecting Gypsy; just supporting a parent I've been involved with. And man, must she need all the friends she can get right now! But in any case, at this precise moment, I don't care if it *does* get me into hot water. I'm sick to the back teeth of these morons.'

'Well, if you're sure, I'd really, *really* welcome your

input. I've arranged to call at their house tomorrow at 2. Any good for you? I could reschedule if …'

    'I'll be there.'

CHAPTER 62

Jane sat in complete silence, eyes fixed on the carefully ordered lists of dates and incidents: Anya's accusations.

Lucinda watched her face. She gave nothing away. A consummate professional.

When she eventually spoke, her voice was hushed. 'Who else knows about this, Anya?'

'Dr Hooper at Sick Kids. Rosemary Stewart on the ward. And now you two.'

'And what do the others think?'

'I don't know. They listened and they took copies of my facts. But then ... Gypsy was ... taken away so I haven't seen them since.' Her face crumpled. 'And now I'm wondering ... was that ... *why* they took her away? Was it all my fault?' Tears slid slowly down her white cheeks unheeded.

Lucinda knelt beside her, covering her thin hands with her own. 'I know both of them and I'd stake my life on them not doing anything underhand. But if you're happy for me to talk to Rosemary about this, I'd be more than willing to find out what she thinks. And see if either of them have followed up on your theory.'

'Would you? She was always so kind.'

Lucinda glanced across at Jane. Her expression remained inscrutable, but she looked directly at Anya as she finally spoke.

'It's a very serious accusation, Anya. Everyone would be treading with extreme caution. I can understand them proceeding very slowly and carefully.'

'But it makes sense. It answers all the questions,' Anya said, impatience barely restrained.

'What does your husband think about it?' Jane asked

almost casually.

Anya dropped her gaze to her fingers, twisting, pulling, shredding a tissue.

'He hasn't seen this, but he thinks it's another manifestation of my mental illness, accusing everybody.'

'You've accused other people too?'

'Not to their face ... well, except him.'

'You thought ... think? ... *your husband* might be behind it?'

'Yes.'

'Why?'

'To get out of ... our marriage.'

In the long silence a blackbird emitted a full-throated warble.

'Anya, does Leon know about *these specific* suspicions?' Lucinda said quietly.

'No ... he was mad enough when I challenged Tiffany about her blabbing to the staff. He even went round to apologise on my behalf. To *apologise* ... for *me*! Like I'm some kind of irresponsible kid! I ask you!'

Lucinda watched Jane rapidly considering her options.

'I'm sorry, Anya. I'm sorry this has happened to you – no, I'm appalled, frankly. I'm sorry you feel you're on your own against the whole battalion of professionals here. But you aren't. Lucinda and I are here today because, whatever the rights and wrongs, we think you've had a raw deal, and we want to help if we can. At this moment, we don't know exactly what might be possible, but if we're to do anything, we need all the facts, warts and all. Can you bear to tell us everything.'

They listened without interruption while Anya went over every action and circumstance that had led her to the conclusion she'd just handed them.

'So, can I summarise where we are at this moment?' Jane spoke slowly as if still thinking. 'You feel there are two possible explanations behind what's happened with Gypsy over the months since she first developed diarrhoea ...'

'And for the times when I was unaccountably out of it,'

Anya chipped in.

'Point taken.'

Anya grimaced. 'Put so baldly, I can see why nobody takes me seriously. It sounds like some totally implausible cheapskate novel. It's much more believable to go for the third option, that I'm bonkers and insecure and an unfit mother.'

Lucinda heard the quiver in her voice.

'Let's go back a few steps. Earlier on, the hospital suggested Fictitious Induced Illness, didn't they? Presumably they called in somebody from the psychiatric department to do an assessment. What did he or she say?'

'It was never done. They had one scheduled but the woman was sick herself the day we were meant to meet. I'm still waiting. Leon did jump up and down a bit at the time but nobody did anything as far as we could tell.'

'Well, in my limited experience, I'd say that's an essential step in the process.'

'I agree. Maybe if somebody official ruled it out, they'd stop looking in my direction, and we could start getting somewhere.'

'In that case, I think Lucinda and I need to discuss our next move. It's only fair to say, we can't promise you anything, but we'll certain do our level best. So, our first step: contact Dr Moore. You happy if we share all this with her?'

'Certainly. But whatever the outcome, I can't thank you enough for listening … for taking my concerns seriously.' The blue eyes filled with tears again. 'And can I ask one more favour? If it's possible, could you … get Gypsy's favourite soft toy … to her? It might be some consolation to have something smelling, feeling, familiar.'

She left the room precipitately and Lucinda felt prickling behind her own lids.

The precious Mr Rabbit wrapped in a muslin square, was tucked securely into Lucinda's bag.

They drove to a layby and stopped.

'What are you thinking, Jane?'

'Something's just not right. But I can't for the life of me put a finger on what's bugging me.'

Silence filled the car, each woman lost in her own thoughts.

'I'd dearly like to speak to this neighbour, Tiffany,' Jane said. 'The one who first flagged up a mental health issue. Get her take on things.'

Four phone calls and three internet searches later they were sitting outside the house in St David's Avenue, watching children scampering in and out, listening to the sounds of innocent fun. Lucinda's heart quailed.

'I'm not sure …'

'Let me do the talking; my kind of encounter.'

Lucinda was only too happy to stand to one side on this one.

Dan Corrigan appeared at the second ring, draped in a crimson curtain with a blonde curly wig perched on his head and a smear of livid red forming an improbable scar down one side of his face. He grinned quite unselfconsciously.

'Sorry, guys, this lot make enough din to block out a nuclear explosion. Hope you haven't been waiting too long.'

'Sounds like everybody's having an exciting time,' Jane smiled back.

'Enough of them to make their own fun. I'm just here to keep the peace. And be everybody's stooge.' He indicated his bizarre apparel.

'Brilliant. Sorry to take you away from your ogre's lair but it was actually your wife I came to see. Is she in?'

'Nah. She's taken her mother to some appointment or other.'

'Leaving you in sole charge of a hundred little people, huh?'

'Aye. Must be mad.'

'Or a saint!" Jane laughed with him. 'Sorry. I probably should have rung first.'

'And you are?'

'Jane Carver. Social worker.'

The smile vanished instantly.

'Was she expecting you?'

'No. I was visiting a family a few streets away and thought I'd just call on the off-chance.'

'What's it in connection with?'

'I believe she's been really helpful to a local new mum? Mrs Morgan? And I just wanted to have a quick word, if I might.'

A sound as of two king-sized wardrobes falling rocked the building, followed by an eerie silence. A baby wailed. At least five childish voices blended in a chorus of suppressed reassurance and hissed instruction.

'Look, you'll have to excuse me.'

Dan shot up the stairs instantly and his appearance clearly had the desired effect. Lucinda and Jane could hear his deep level voice restoring order amidst the juvenile protests and explanations.

When he eventually reappeared the wig and curtain had gone and he seemed somehow less genial. The livid red 'scar' unrelieved by the rest of the disguise, the dragon tattoo snaking from beneath his sleeve, his scraped back ponytail emphasising the impressive dome of his head, gave him a disconcerting hint of menace.

'Look, as you can see, I've got my hands pretty full here. Can you cut to the chase and say what you've come to say before all hell breaks loose up there.'

'I was just wondering when I might call by to have a wee chat with Mrs Corrigan.'

'About the Morgans?'

'Yes.'

'Well, listen, I've already had her husband here. I know that babe's been taken away, and I've been involved with too many broken homes, damaged kids, to have any appetite for more. Tiff was just being a pal. She's pretty cut up about it. So, if you don't mind, I'd rather you left us out of this. We're in the business of giving guys a happy childhood, not breaking up families.'

A gale of laughter followed by cheering seemed to verify his statement. At least a dozen voices began singing,

'*I'm the king of the castle, get down you dirty rascal.*' A pillow fell with a soft ppphht on the paving beside them. A row of painted faces peered out of an upstairs window, stifling giggles.

Dan let out a huge roar in their direction, and assumed a shrill penetrating Irish accent. 'The monster is coming to get you! To eat you alive!'

The faces vanished, screaming with delicious fear, the sound of thudding feet spread like a mushrooming cloud overhead.

'I'm a man of my word,' Dan said firmly in his own voice. 'So, you'll have to excuse me. And I'd be grateful if you could take Tiff's name off your list of enquiries. We don't want to have a bar of this. I've told her she should stay well clear of that family in future.'

Not waiting for an answer, he dropped to all fours and began to growl menacingly as he re-entered the house. Lucinda and Jane heard the squeals of delight and the scamper of innumerable escapees as they walked to the car.

'What kind of a bloke babysits the entire neighbourhood of kids on a sunny afternoon?'

'Alone.'

'And has *a baby* in the house.'

'Did you see his reaction when I said I was a social worker?'

'Yeah. Probably thought you'd come to see why a guy on his own has a houseful of minors playing in *bedrooms*.'

'Or ... Would you be happy with me talking to my fiancé about this?' Jane said. 'He'd know the legal position, at least.'

'And whether we ought to involve the police.'

'He *is* the police!'

'Officially, I mean.'

'This feels to be getting way, way, outside my comfort zone.'

'I know. Imagine if we end up being responsible for the authorities taking the *Corrigan* children away next!'

'There was something delightfully innocent and genuine

about him, initially, didn't you think? Until he heard "social worker".'

'I agree. But imagine if that was all just a cover for …'

'Doesn't bear thinking about.'

CHAPTER 63

How could he? How could he? As if work mattered a jot with Gypsy gone, every hour that rolled by erasing vital memories of her real family.

'Gordon Bennett, Anya! What more d'you want?!' Leon stormed, slamming his hand down on the table. 'I've been chasing every single lead I can unravel to try and get information about her. I've been to the *top*. And the Child Protection people, the police, *everybody* assures me they're doing their level best to sort this out. But it won't happen overnight. I can't just kick my heels at home when I'm needed at work. Thomas and Roger've been bending over backwards to allow me to stay up here and sort out our bloody mess, but there's a big old world out there. It can't always revolve around *you*! Other people are fighting for their *lives*! *I'm* fighting for *my* life!

'I *ought* to be in Newcastle this very minute; I can't *believe* I'm not. But for your sake, I told them it was impossible. This conference call's a compromise; Thomas arranged it just so I'm not left out of the discussion. I don't have a choice: I *have* to be in on it. It's our whole future on the line here! So, I'm going in to the office for 10, and that's final. I have no idea how long this'll take, so expect me when you see me.'

He hadn't waited for her response.

She maintained her frozen silence until he left and then vented her rage on the larder, throwing tins, jars, bottles, packets, into bags for the food bank indiscriminately; the noisier the impact the better.

It was Claire who brought the post in from the vestibule floor when she arrived at 10:45.

At the sound of the door opening, and the predictable 'Hi, only me', Anya closed her eyes and sent up a prayer for patience. Her sister's intentions were entirely good, but conversation was so stilted. She would avoid any mention of Gypsy; Anya wanted to talk about nothing else.

Claire dropped the envelope on the table, and a cautious kiss on her sister's cheek. Her basket was full of courgettes, marmalade, and roses, the scent instantly filling the room.

Anya took her time brewing tea, arranging four Viennese fingers on a plate which neither of them would touch, finding serviettes; automatic undemanding tasks that gave a semblance of normality in the void that was now her reality. She made a production of waiting on Claire. Anything to defer the inevitable question: 'No news, I presume?'

The blank envelope looked untidy, she tucked it underneath the photograph of Gypsy on the side table, quickly averting her gaze from the lopsided smile.

'Would you be interested in going fruit picking this morning, Claire?'

'Sure. If you're up for it.'

'Might as well. Thought I'd make some jam for the coffee morning in the local church. They're fundraising for Syrian refugees.'

'Great. I was listening to a programme about all those unaccompanied children ... oh, sorry. I didn't think.' She pressed her fingers against her lips with a stricken look.

It was so much easier to work companionably down either side of the rows of raspberry canes than to sit' artificially making polite conversation in an empty house. Anya pictured Tiffany trying to control two lively children amongst the strawberries, and then sharing the lean pickings with her. It was a physical effort to force her attention back to her sister's account of a new recipe she's been given for a raspberry bombe which she would try making tomorrow after work.

It was 3:15 before she picked up the envelope and slit it

open.

Her fingers froze.

It was typed in pillar-box red ... *blood-red* ... bold text, block capitals, Helvetica font.

I KNOW WHERE YOUR BABY IS.
SHE'S NEVER COMING BACK TO YOU.
SHE DESERVES BETTER.
CALL OFF YOUR SPIES OR
YOU'LL FORCE MY HAND.
GENTLE DEATH IS BETTER
THAN A NEUROTIC LIFE.

Anya slid down the wall and slumped in a heap on the floor. Claire was at her side in an instant, all concern and enquiry. Anya handed her the note.

'You absolutely *have* to call the police this time,' Claire urged. 'They need to ...'

Anya screwed up her eyes and raked her nails against her scalp. 'Stop, Claire. Stop! Stop! *Stop!* Give me some space to *think*.'

Claire froze. Anya rocked back and forth for several minutes.

'OK. OK,' she muttered. 'Calm ... calm ... calm. Who *needs* to know? Leon? Dr Hooper? Lucinda? Social Work? Child Protection? No, I can't tell everybody. I'll ask Dr Hooper. He'll know what to do.'

She leapt to her feet and ran for her mobile phone. Her fingers shook, making the task even harder.

'Can you put me through to Dr George Hooper, please? It's urgent.' ...

'Anya Morgan. The mother of one of his patients.' ...

'I'll hold.'

Claire slid a chair under her sister and pressed her shoulder till she was sitting down.

The silence seemed to go on for ever.

'Dr Hooper? Oh, thank God! I didn't know who to call. I've just had another anonymous note and ... I don't know what … to do.' Her voice crumpled and she took in a huge gulp of air. 'I'll read it to you.'

The familiar voice urging her to remain calm, seemed to come from under water. When did … where was … who said … what happened …???

She answered as cogently as she could but everything seemed unclear.

'Mrs Morgan – Anya – I'll need to take some advice on this. Could you keep your phone with you? As soon as I have anything to report, I'll ring you. Can you do that?'

'Yes. And you'll check Gypsy's safe?'

'I'll get on to Social Work immediately. Is anyone with you?'

'My sister, Claire.'

'Good. I don't think you should be alone right now.'

'She's got a shift later this evening.'

'What about your husband?'

'He's at work.'

'Does he know about the note?'

'Not from me.'

'Could he come home?'

'I don't know …'

'Try to stay calm. I'll get back to you as soon as I can. I promise.'

Claire was insistent. This was far, far more important than any stupid waitressing job; she would stay as long as she was needed.

Anya took her time composing a text to Leon:

> Had another anonymous note.
> Told Dr Hooper. He's dealing with it. Claire here.
> No need for you to leave work.

It was twenty-six minutes before he rang.

'What the hell's going on, Anya? I've only just got your message. Why didn't you call?'

'You said you needed to concentrate on work … your life depended on it.'

She heard him curse under his breath.

'What does the note say? When did you get it?'

Anya read it in a voice devoid of expression.

'Damn it, Anya! One minute you're hysterical over nothing. Next minute you're making light of a death threat! What's the *matter* with you?!'

'Always in the wrong,' she said under her breath.

'What did you say? I didn't hear you.'

'Nothing.'

'So, what's Hooper going to do? Call in the police?'

'And risk whoever it is killing our baby? I don't think so!' she spat out.

'Well, Gypsy's my number one priority, and I'm hanged if *I'm* going to soft pedal on something as serious as this. So, I'll ...'

'Hold on, Leon,' Anya interrupted. 'That's him ringing now. I'll call you back.'

It was indeed Dr Hooper.

'Anya, I've spoken to Child Protection, and they're making absolutely sure Gypsy's safe. They've also arranged an emergency appointment for you with a specialist. Her name's Dr Gabrielle Fournier. She's a psychiatrist. She'll want to see your notes and all the anonymous letters you've received, and hear about everything that's happened, and your hunches – anything you can tell her. I know you're finding it hard to trust people now – that's perfectly understandable – but you can totally trust Dr Fournier. It's safe to tell her everything you know and what you suspect. Is that acceptable with you?'

'Oh, thank you, thank you. I'm going out of my mind here.'

'I know. But Dr Fournier's really good. She'll be able to advise us on what to do next. So, can your sister take you to the Royal Edinburgh ... the psychiatric hospital ... in Morningside Place ... straight away? You know where it is? ... Just go to the main entrance and tell them you have an urgent appointment with Dr Fournier.'

As she scrambled into her jacket, a truth hit Anya foursquare. For months now her first port of call had been Tiffany. Whenever she was worried, uncertain, afraid, her friend had been there with wise advice, a calm presence; saving her from making an issue of a small blip, supporting her in seeking medical help when there was real cause for concern. Had she totally alienated her now?

A malevolent tidal wave of doubt, fear, despair, flooded back into her life. It reminded her of the molten lava of last night's dream. She'd been lying in bed in a house at the foot of a volcano and the deadly river had been flowing stealthily down the slopes. Cracks were appearing in the ground all around her, opened by the sheer force of the inferno below. No one knew the volcano had erupted after years lying dormant; no alarm had sounded; the whole village slept. Everything, everyone, she knew and loved, would be engulfed in this liquid fire.

She'd woken bathed in perspiration. Served her right for watching footage of the Hawaiian volcanic disaster before bed. But she couldn't rid herself of the thought that heat of that magnitude was always burning deep beneath our feet, always there, an invisible pressure cooker, at the centre of this world we inhabit. Just waiting for that sliver of weakness somewhere in the earth's crust to explode into the atmosphere and devour everything in its path. It was a scientific fact.

And her life now was like that. A tiny chink in her control created by one new vulnerable child, and suddenly everything she knew and loved was in jeopardy.

Was the dream an omen?

Was this latest anonymous letter the crack that would release the full power of evil and finally destroy them all?

CHAPTER 64

While Gabrielle Fournier was studying Anya's non-verbal cues, analysing her responses, assessing her mental state, Leon was pacing up and down, phone pressed to his ear.

Why the devil didn't she answer? Was this yet another way to torture him?

Why would no one grasp the iniquity of him being punished for his wife's problems?

One almighty conspiracy of professionals against the laity!

And if one more person said 'It's in the hands of Child Protection' …

When Anya had still not picked up after three hours he abandoned the pretence of working and drove home at a furious pace.

Silence greeted him. Equipment for jam-making was lined up beside the hob … two mugs sat on the draining board … the cushion in his chair bore the imprint of someone else …

He raced through the house … not a sign of her – or anyone else – anywhere.

But her car was in the drive …

The click of the front door brought him galloping down the stairs. She was alone.

'Where have you *been*? I've been going crazy …'

He stopped dead. The face she turned to him was ashen and streaked with tears.

'What's … happened?'

'Somebody really listened. That's what's happened.'

'Meaning?'

'I've been talking to a psychiatrist.'

'*What?* Who? Where?'

'A lady doctor called Dr Fournier. At the Royal Ed.'

'How did you get there? Your car's here.' It spilled out before he had time to vet it.

'Claire took me.'

'So, where's she now?'

'She dropped me off. She's gone home. She's on a late shift. Text her if you don't believe me.'

'I didn't say …'

'You didn't need to.'

'So, what did this doctor say?'

'She said my story isn't that unusual. Lots of women have difficulty adjusting to motherhood. Maybe I've been more anxious than most, but I've had more to contend with than most mothers.'

'You told her about the crises?'

'I told her everything, Leon. *Everything.*' It was a blatant challenge.

'What did she make of all the trips to doctors, Sick Kids? The poison pen letters? Your conspiracy theories?'

'She didn't say exactly, but she did tell me my verbal account was lucid and coherent and consistent. And she read my entire summary. It indicated clear thinking and a logical mind perfectly capable of detaching from the emotion and recording and analysing facts.' She might as well have added *so there!*

'So, does that rule out this Fictitious thingy?'

'I don't know. She said these decisions aren't made by any one person. Next step is to speak to the others involved in our case. She puts forward her assessment, but it's one part of a bigger discussion of everybody's experience and opinions. And then they consider Gypsy's best interests. It won't be decided overnight. Once they have a child in care …'

The reality suddenly and visibly hit her, the fragile façade crumpled. She folded onto the nearest chair and the unearthly sounds she emitted chilled Leon's blood. He dared not touch her, but he fetched a fleece from the airing cupboard and slipped it around her rocking form.

Not until he'd assured himself that Anya was sleeping the sleep of exhaustion did Leon shut himself away in his study. It was too late now to be phoning about Gypsy; that must wait until the morning. In the meantime, he would return to the pressing business of salvaging anything he could from the Morgan & Sons debacle. But how *could* he arrange business trips, meet new clients, consolidate existing partnerships, shoot down to headquarters, when Anya was in this state? Regardless of today's psychiatric evaluation, she was frighteningly brittle.

She might be pushing him away, but he had responsibilities here. She needed *someone* with her. Besides there was this latest death threat. If Anya didn't write it, then who did? And was she herself in danger as well as Gypsy? He had to be sure she was safe from any outside evil, as well as from herself.

There was nothing for it. He'd have to throw himself on Thomas' mercy yet again, tell him about the threat. It'd be easier if he had the psychiatric evaluation as proof, but until that materialised, at least he could say it was pending, things were moving. And as soon as he could ... well, what *would* he do? Maybe ... give Frank Fowler something himself? It might salve his conscience somewhat ... although ...it would go against every grain to give the rat a bean. But at least Fowler wasn't getting off Scot free. He'd be smarting big-time at the comments made, not only by his ex-bosses, but by erstwhile colleagues, not to mention the tribunal panel. No, he certainly hadn't had it all his own way.

'*Given the complainant's rejection of all offers of reconciliation, we do not believe it to be incumbent on the employer, Morgan & Sons, to reinstate him as an employee.*' Imagine if they'd had to live with the blighter ponsing about in the yard, thumbing his nose at them day after day after this fiasco! '*We find that the complainant acted vexatiously, abusively, disruptively, and otherwise unreasonably in the bringing and conducting of the proceedings ...*' And because of his behaviour, they'd even required the wretched fellow to pay costs to his employer '*in respect of the wasted time spent preparing for and attending the preliminary hearings'*. A high price indeed for stubborn pride.

No, Fowler was old news, and once this was all settled ... once Gypsy was safe ... once Anya was herself again ... he'd work all hours to recoup the losses of that disastrous Irish deal ...

But would *Anya recover from all this? Could their marriage survive?*

On the face of it the psychiatric evaluation sounded positive, but this was only *Anya's* interpretation, and no caring professional would leave a vulnerable patient in pieces and just walk away without putting them back together in some way first. She hadn't categorically said Anya was in the clear. *Was she just placating a volatile woman?* She'd admitted her opinion was only one of many. She'd let slip that once a kiddie was in care there was a huge burden of proof on Child Protection's shoulders before the decision could be reversed.

And what if there really was a maniac out there moving in stealthily, hell-bent on killing Gypsy? A sick fiend who wanted to destroy them?

Now they had Gypsy in a place of safety, were the doctors and social workers just humouring Anya to prevent an escalation of her illness and paranoia? Didn't the fact that they'd removed the baby in the first place indicate they didn't trust her?

Whatever, all this time Gypsy was among strangers, forgetting her biological family. He couldn't just let that happen. He *couldn't*!

He'd find the top dog, Dr Moore, drag it out of her if necessary. He was a boss himself; he wasn't about to be intimidated by bureaucracy; he'd go to the *Cabinet Secretary* if he had to. The *First Minister*! Gypsy was *his* daughter, she shouldn't be taken away from *him*; he wasn't going to lie down under a miscarriage of justice like this.

He was still sifting and sorting the options at ten that night when the phone rang. He grabbed it quickly before it woke

Anya, still dead to the world … he was starting to wonder if she'd taken something …

'Mr Morgan? Leon?'

'Yep. Who is this?'

'Dan. Dan Corrigan. Tiffany's husband?'

'Oh, hi.'

'Is Tiff with you?'

'No.'

'OK. Sorry to disturb you.'

'Something wrong?'

'Only that … she hasn't come home. Expected her for tea but there's been no word. Not like her. It was a long shot. I daresay there's a perfectly innocent explanation. I'll try a few more places, but it's getting too late to be ringing on the off-chance.'

'And you're at home with the kids?'

'They're all safely in their beds, and Tiff's Ma's here, so if I needed to go for her I could. No worries. Sorry to disturb you.'

'Shout if you need help.'

'Thanks, mate.'

Bizarre. But everything seemed curiously inexplicable these days. It was as if the normal laws and accepted behaviours of civilised society had somehow been suspended.

CHAPTER 65

It was a struggle to even crawl out of bed. Anya peered at her wan reflection through puffy eyes and abandoned any attempt to repair the superficial damage. Just assuming an upright position threatened to derail her.

Against a rising tide of nausea, she did her best to be grateful for the efforts Leon had made to nourish her, but at best she could only pick at the yogurt, eggs and toast, and accept his stricture that there would be no answers to any questions until he was satisfied she was not going to keel over.

'And before you have another go at me, no, I'm *not* going to work this morning. And that's flat. Non-negotiable. Mother's on her way back up. She insisted. And I can promise you, her scrambled egg is in a different league from mine!'

Anya shrugged. She had absolutely no energy to fight any more battles.

Seeing Hannah again threatened her composure even more, but the older woman had the intuitive sense to simply hold her and say nothing. What, after all, was there to say? They were united in their grief and frustration; mother and grandmother bereft of a child.

Anya kept it level. 'Did you get anywhere after I'd gone to bed, Leon?'

'Not last night, but this morning I made a bit of progress. I got through to Dr Moore. She's the head honcho in the Child Protection team, Mother. She assured me the social workers are confident that Gypsy's safe. They can't tell us *where* she is, of course; only a handful of people are allowed to know that.'

Anya closed her eyes against the vision of her baby in a

strange home.

'I also got out of her *why* they took her into care without any warning.'

'And why did they?'

Leon's gaze was suddenly riveted on her. 'Apparently Social Work got some new information … Dr Moore wouldn't tell me any details, but it was enough to force their hand, and she reckoned their action was commensurate with the perceived risk. She only heard about it herself after the event. Seems there was some kind of network breakdown so the message didn't get through to the rest of the team.'

'This just gets crazier and crazier.'

'Oh, and for what it's worth,' Leon added, 'apparently Tiffany Corrigan's gone awol.'

'What d'you mean?'

'Her husband phoned here to see if she'd come round to see you. Still no sign of her this morning apparently. She's never done this before.'

'Why that look?'

'Well, it's a bit of a coincidence, don't you think? You have a go at her and next minute she's disappeared.'

Anya felt a terrible sinking sensation. 'You think … it's my fault? She …'

'No, no, no!' Leon put up a hand to stop her. 'I didn't mean it like that. For goodness' sake … I just thought maybe … perhaps you pricked her conscience.'

'Excuse me butting in,' Hannah said, 'but what did you have a go at her about, Anya? I'm getting lost here.'

But Anya had suddenly frozen.

'Leon … I'm just thinking … why did Tiffany come round that day with strawberries – the very day Gypsy was taken into care? She'd been out picking for hours with two of her kids, and she admitted they'd been a handful. She *said* she hadn't expected to find me home, she thought I'd be at the hospital; she was just going to leave the berries and go. But … what if she *did* know? What if *she* was the one who tipped off the social workers? She admitted to you she thought I was losing it. What if she *knew* they'd *have* to act? Or … what if she even *had* Gypsy ... and just wanted to see how I was dealing with all this, what I was thinking?'

'That's insane,' Leon shot out. 'How could she *have* her? If she'd snatched her, the hospital would be going nuts trying to find her.'

'Not *snatched*. Made a case for fostering her. After all, she can be totally persuasive, can't she? They *know* her. They've seen her back and forth at the hospital, even being one of only three nominated people we trusted to stay with Gypsy. She's a whizz with children; so's her husband. Her house is always knee-deep in youngsters. Gypsy loves her to bits. She's got three kids of her own. She's a qualified nurse. What's not to like? It'd be the perfect solution ... with one proviso. We – or at least, *I* – mustn't know she had her. But provided she kept Gypsy indoors, why would I? I've never ever been to her house .... but ...'

Leon direct gaze held hers.

'*You* have. So, now she knows her home isn't a safe haven any more ...' She broke off abruptly, fresh horror surging through her brain. 'She ups and offs ... with Gypsy ...'

Leon shook his head. 'This is *so* far-fetched, but for your peace of mind, I'll speak to Dan. The guy seems genuine enough. I didn't have him down as the devious kind, but ... I suppose, it's remotely possible Tiffany spun him some tale about it all being for Gypsy's security and welfare ...'

'She's very, very plausible,' Anya added slowly, her voice barely above a whisper, the images scrolling through her imagination. 'And once she knew you'd been to the house ... she might think it prudent to take Gypsy somewhere else ...'

'... without telling Dan.' Leon gritted his teeth. 'I'll ring him, now. You fill Mother in.'

Leon's face was a mask when he returned.

'He categorically denies ever having Gypsy in the house.'

'So, could Tiffany have her somewhere else?' Anya's mind was in overdrive. 'Maybe got somebody else to care for her, while she went through the motions of being daughter, wife, mother at St David's Avenue ... then gone off to take care of her full time without telling Dan.'

'Sorry, but ...,' Hannah said slowly. 'I thought you said Social Work had reassured the consultant, Gypsy was safe in foster care.'

'They've never told us *who* she was with. But they'd think Tiffany was as good as it gets in the circumstances.'

'Right, well, I'll ring Dr Moore, get her to check. Tell her about Tiffany going missing ... see if anyone anywhere will tell *her* anything.' Leon moved towards the door again, adding, 'But it sounds so totally implausible, I'm fully expecting them to laugh the whole idea out of court.'

'They don't know what she's like!'

Dr Moore was unavailable but her gatekeeper assured Leon she would leave a message.

CHAPTER 66

Anya was insistent: it was her turn to be M'lady Bountiful.

'Those poor children'll be completely bewildered. Scared too, I should imagine. Whatever's happened, they're the innocent parties.'

She rustled up an enormous dish of macaroni cheese and a plum crumble and chocolate chip muffins and sent them via Leon to the Corrigan household.

Red-rimmed eyes, distracted look, flat voice, met him. Even the dazzling dragon was hidden by Dan's crumpled maroon shirt, the ponytail lifeless on his collar.

'Still no news?' Leon said, as he handed over the dishes.

'Nope. Listen, thanks hugely for this. The kids'll love it. Mac cheese is one of their favourites.'

'I think Anya knew that.'

'Please thank her for me. Very good of her – specially with everything that's going on in *your* lives. I was going to call you tonight, actually. Got a minute?'

Leon followed him into the dishevelled living room.

'Perch yourself on that bench and I'll get us a cold drink.'

The 'cold' was interpretive but Leon sipped it without comment.

Dan focused on the liquid swirling in his own glass.

'Look, Tiff's a terrific mother, heart of gold, but .... I wasn't going to say anything at first, but then I got to thinking, if this was one of my lot taken away from me ...' He shuddered. 'And nah, the welfare of your baby trumps my loyalty to her.'

Leon's eyes were pinned on Dan.

'After you'd gone last time, I got to thinking about all

the comings and goings, all the little things, the stuff you told me that I didn't know about. And bits and pieces didn't quite add up. So, when Tiff came home, I asked her straight up. She wanted to know exactly what you said, but I only told her part of it. I could see she was being evasive ... like ... like she was afraid of incriminating herself. And ... well, long story short, I asked her what the hell was going on. She didn't say a thing; just took herself off to bed. Next morning, I tried again: "Look, Tiff. An innocent wee tot's been taken away from her parents here; if you know *anything* about it, for the love of God, you've got to come clean. You can't stand by and let a family be torn apart. You *can't*!"'

Leon held his breath.

'But ... still nothing. And if you knew Tiff like I do, that'd tell you loads. She's *not* the buttoned-up, silent type, my wife! Of course, with our three all over us, demanding attention, and the place going like a madhouse, I couldn't exactly challenge her directly. Youngsters pick up on far too much as it is. But I gave her a hug, and I said, "We'll talk tonight when I get in from work." Only ... she didn't c-come home ...'

'You must be going out of your mind,' Leon said quietly.

'I just don't know what to do for the best. If I report her missing and there's a police hunt, publicity, posters, appeals, and she's just holed up somewhere thinking things through, she'll kill me. On the other hand, if she's in trouble somewhere and I don't go all out to find her ... well ... it could be ... too late.' His voice broke completely and he pursed his lips tightly.

Leon felt the nails cutting into his clenched fists. It took all his restraint to remain on the bench, watching the man.

'We've never had secrets, Tiff and me ... leastways, I didn't *think* we did. But this time ... it's different ... she's hiding *something*.'

'But hopefully not Gypsy.'

Dan gave a mirthless laugh. 'Hardly.'

'D'you think ... she's *capable* of stealing a baby?'

Dan stared at him. 'I thought your wee one had been taken into care.'

'That's the official line, certainly, but *someone* is threatening Anya. And Gypsy.'

'*Seriously?! Jeeez!* Well, I'd stake my life on Tiff not *hurting* a baby. Adores them. Always has.'

'But mental illness changes people. This whole business has affected my wife hugely. I've seen her change out of all recognition ...' Leon stopped abruptly. No need for this guy to know the extent of his disloyalty.

'Tell me about it! I've worked with disadvantaged children all my adult life. I've seen what human beings are capable of. But ... not ... she wouldn't ... hell ...'

He stopped abruptly, coughing to cover his language, as a skinny grey-haired woman moved into the room.

'Sorry, Janet. Didn't know you were there. This is Tiff's Ma. Leon Morgan.'

They shook hands, and Leon was surprised at the strength in the slight fingers.

'You're Gypsy's dad?' she said. 'I couldn't help over-hearing, just now.'

Leon nodded.

'Then, I need to tell you something. You too, Dan.' She sat down gingerly. 'I'll get straight to it. Years ago, before she met you, Dan, Tiffany had a wee girl.'

'I know about that. She told me when we met,' Dan said.

'About Charlotte?' Janet Baker frowned. 'You knew?'

'Charlotte? No, Tiff said her name was Holly Justine.'

Janet shook her head. 'No. No. Holly was before that. Tiffany was only fifteen when she had Holly. I'm talking years later. She was twenty-one, twenty-two. Just finished her training. Got herself pregnant with Charlotte. She moved up to Aberdeen. All I knew was the wee soul was sickly. It wasn't till it was all over that I found out the truth.' She paused, twisting her fingers together, eyes down. 'God forgive me ...' – she crossed herself – 'I promised to keep quiet about it just so long as she behaved. And she's been fine. I thought she was over it. She's been such a good mum. She has. She has.'

Neither man moved a muscle.

'But … maybe … now …' She raised her eyes, imploring Dan to understand. 'It was Tiffany who made Charlotte sick … did things … deliberately.'

Leon felt icy fingers clutching at his heart. 'And she's been … with Gypsy … when all these incidents …' – he stood up suddenly – 'She might even have her now …

'I swear … on my kids' life … I had no idea … Janet's never said …' Dan was clawing at his hair. 'You should have *told* me. You should have …'

Leon glowered down at him. 'You've *got* to find her, man! Call the police. Find her before she …'

He left precipitately, leaving the door wide open behind him.

Leon found his mother and Anya in the shade of the big apple tree. It took every ounce of restraint not to blurt out the truth immediately.

'Dan said thanks a lot for the food.'

'Is he going to the police?'

'I've told him he *has* to.'

'What's he think has happened to her?'

'She's upset about something. Possibly gone somewhere to chill out; possibly in trouble …'

'Nothing to do with Gypsy, though?'

'He doesn't know … but …'

Leon sank onto a seat.

'Listen. There's something you need to know.'

They both listened in stunned silence.

'I've rung Dr Moore, filled her in.'

'And?' Anya's face was bleached of colour, her fingers endlessly plucking the silicone at her wrist.

'She listened. And she'll factor that in to the decision about us getting Gypsy back. But she *assured* me, she was *certain*, Gypsy's perfectly safe – with bona fide foster carers. She's one hundred percent sure. There's no way Tiffany has her.'

Anya closed her eyes, let out a long shuddering breath. 'Thank God. Thank God.' Her eyes when she eventually opened them were widely dilated. 'But … all those times … before …' Her voice was totally devoid of accusation or emotion. '*Now* you believe me …?'

'I'm sorry. I'm sorry. But how was I to know …? I'm going to ring Social Work now, this minute, and get them to review our case immediately.' He thumped the garden table so heavily that Hannah's elbows jerked violently. She winced. 'I don't care if I'm persona non grata with every authority in Britain, I'm *not* going to stand feebly by while my daughter is being traumatised. I'll damn well find *somebody, somewhere,* who can set the wheels in motion to put this whole ridiculous charade right.'

'And I'll call Lucinda. She'll make sure they take this seriously, now!'

It proved much more difficult to press his case without mentioning Tiffany to gatekeepers – 'new evidence has come to light' … 'good reason to believe' … just didn't have the same clout as concrete facts … besides … there was still nothing watertight. Just because Tiffany had hurt her own child, didn't mean she'd done anything harmful to Gypsy. *What if she'd merely sown the seeds in Anya's mind …?*

No surprise. He met with a solid wall of resistance: equivocation … firm dismissal … vague references to people at meetings or unavailable or out on community business. But sheer dogged persistence brought him eventually to the PA to the Head of Service, a Ms Kahn – 'spelt with an h, as in Imran, as in Jemima' – who assured him she would personally pass on the message and get someone to phone him back before the end of the day.

And what exactly does 'the day' mean to you, Ms Kahn with an h? Probably not what I mean by it.

Yes, she gave him her word. Yes, she heard him: a child's safety was at stake. Yes, she too read the papers; she knew that Social Work were sometimes too slow to act. But she was a woman of her word, she would indeed act.

He didn't care a tuppenny toss if she spelt her name with or without the entire bloody alphabet, but he did care if her word counted for anything. What was the equivalent of 'an officer and a gentleman' in this context?

'But before I go ...'

He pressed the phone back to his ear.

Her voice gradually hardened. Mrs Schoolmarm. Mrs Boss lady. Mrs Standing-on-my-not-inconsiderable-dignity. Could she please ask him – nay, *implore* him, not to persist in phoning anyone else. Interference from outside could only hamper professionals in their work. These were delicate situations, requiring careful handling. Everything was predicated on extreme caution and confidentiality. Broadcasting the difficulties and issues far and wide could only jeopardise the operation. It was imperative that everyone trod very softly and gently in these cases. Fragile people were apt to do unexpected things if cornered. There was often mistrust, distorted perceptions, high emotion, around. Confidentiality and discretion – sometimes yes, even secrecy – were at the heart of good management. And besides, there were always two sides to every story.

By the time Ms Kahn with an h had finished her seminar on non-interference, Leon could only replace the phone with infinite caution as if it too might take umbrage at brisk handling.

CHAPTER 67

Anya's phone call left Lucinda on the horns of a dilemma, a dilemma too heavy to bear alone.

'What d'you think, Jane? She says Leon's been on the phone to Dr Moore, but …. is that enough? Should *we* do something? This death threat they've received …'

'I don't like the smell of this one little bit,' Jane said grimly. 'I vote we pile on a bit of pressure … in person.'

Dr Moore listened without interruption, her gaze steady. It was several moments before she spoke.

'I completely understand where you're coming from, and I'm grateful that you came directly to me rather than taking this elsewhere. I know you have the Morgans' best interests at heart, and I hear that you're looking for action. Because of your close involvement with this family, I'm actually going to give you some confidential information which might help you to understand why we're still treading very cautiously in this case.'

Lucinda felt herself tense. *Surely, surely, surely, there was enough to go on now …*

'First and foremost, Gypsy is safe. You have my word on that. I'm well aware of the speculation about exactly who removed Gypsy from the hospital, but I can categorically confirm that it was a genuine social worker who collected her, with all the required documentation, and that she is currently with an approved foster mother. In light of the doubts expressed, I've had this checked and double-checked. And the Morgans have been reassured on this point again and again. The exact whereabouts of the baby are known only to those who need to know – and for what it's worth, I'm personally not among them. I don't need to know the specifics.'

Lucinda heard the soft release of breath beside her.

'I'm well aware that some people are unhappy about the child being taken into care in the first place. She was perfectly safe in hospital, they say. And this is where I'm prepared to go out on a limb and give you confidential information; I know you will respect it as such.' She paused for long enough to gain their nods of assent. 'The social worker most closely involved in this case received an anonymous tip-off from "a well-wisher". It basically said that the writer knew that Anya Morgan had been harming her baby since birth, and had evidence that she was planning to actually kill her next time. If Social Work didn't act fast, it'd be their fault; or more precisely, "her blood will be on your hands". Understandably this panicked the social worker, who went straight to her manager and obtained permission to remove Gypsy to a place of safety immediately. And I have to tell you, that in her shoes, I would have sanctioned exactly that too.'

Lucinda and Jane both nodded again.

'Act first, deliberate afterwards.' Jane's voice sounded tight.

'In these circumstances, yes. I'm well aware that there are rumours about high-handedness circulating, so let me fill you in with the true facts of the matter. Social Work *did* try to engage the whole interagency team at the time, but unfortunately there was some kind of network failure. However, the Child Protection team approved their action retrospectively, so please don't assume this was some officious knee-jerk reaction. It was not.'

'Do the Morgans know about the anonymous tip-off?' Jane said abruptly.

'Not from us. Just that new information came to light.'

Jane raised an eyebrow, but said nothing.

'As you both know, there's been some suggestion that Anya Morgan's been behind the poison pen letters she's reported receiving. One theory is that attention-seeking lies at the root of this whole case. I know you're not going to like this, but we can't rule out the possibility that this latest threat is more of her handiwork.'

'But she'd *know* that would lessen the chance of getting Gypsy home.'

'Possibly. Rationally speaking. But she'd also know it would increase the attention from a number of quarters.'

'It just doesn't ring true …' Lucinda shook her head. 'She's beside herself with grief at losing her little girl.'

'And this is certainly one picture we've been given – from Mrs Morgan herself, and from relatives and professionals who know her. In our defence, I have to say, we've done our level best to listen to *all* the reports and speculative theories and concerns – some of which are conflicting. We've bent over backwards to be as sensitive and reassuring and supportive to the parents as we could be. We've also sought advice from various experts at different points over the weeks since this case was brought to our attention.'

'And you still aren't convinced. What about this latest piece of information – about Tiffany Corrigan's history?'

'Mr Morgan contacted me directly this morning with this story. I can perfectly understand that, in his thinking, this feels like evidence that Mrs Corrigan is responsible for the escalating harm that has come to Gypsy. But my team have deliberated carefully and, whilst we accept that this is certainly one possibility, it's by no means categorical evidence. It could, for example, be the case, that Mrs Corrigan in some way influenced Mrs Morgan – maybe sharing her story, maybe encouraging her to think along these lines, maybe even collaborating with her – but that it was Mrs Morgan who actually gave the noxious substances to her daughter.

'And you have to bear in mind, that our decision to keep Gypsy in care at the moment is based on more than just suspicion. It's a fact that the social worker responsible for assessing Mrs Morgan's relationship with her child in hospital, had good reason for concern. Her detailed report is on file.'

'But Anya's been under enormous pressure,' Lucinda chipped in. 'Jane and I saw her far more times at home, and yes, she's a tense kind of a woman, granted, but we had no doubt that she loved her baby and wanted only the best for her.'

'And didn't you also see Mrs Corrigan engaging with this child?'

'Yes.'

'And did you ever have cause for concern there?'

'Well, no.'

'Indeed, the overall picture is of an exceptionally patient and understanding friend, a perceptive nurse, who bent over backwards to be some kind of ministering angel. Furthermore, one with no apparent motive for harming someone else's baby.' Dr Moore sighed. 'Please believe me when I say, I sympathise with your frustration. It must be incredibly difficult to be with these parents and feel powerless to give them what they want. But *our* job is to make sure this child is safe. And at the moment, with the evidence before us, we don't feel confident that she should be released back to her parents. We shall continue to review the situation, and I sincerely hope that, in due course, the family can indeed be reunited.'

Once outside, Jane and Lucinda collapsed into the car.

'It kills me to say it, but, galling as this is, you *can* understand where they're coming from,' Jane broke the silence first.

'And yet ...'

'Exactly.'

'We *know* Anya.'

'And we've had longer to think about her suspicions. Her explanations all made sense, didn't they?'

'I know there's no cast iron evidence but ... I just have a nasty feeling about this. Tiffany's a devoted mother – why would she suddenly desert three children she adores ... and a husband who loves her ... with no word to them ... unless ...'

'Exactly.'

'Where is she? What's she up to? You know more about the mechanics ... is there *any* possibility she could discover

340

the whereabouts of Gypsy? She has contacts ... What d'you think?'

Jane sat without moving a muscle for a long moment, mulling over the question. 'I'd say it's unlikely, but not impossible. Particularly if the placement's been fairly local.'

'Would they have warned the foster parents of a possible danger?'

'I can't answer that.'

'So, what do we do now?'

'Good question. I could have another chat with my fiancé, Jeremy, unofficially,' Jane said. 'If you're agreeable. With some experience of child custody cases ... he might have a take on this.'

Lucinda laid a hand on Jane's arm. 'Good thinking but ... I've just had the germ of an idea. Tiffany Corrigan has an Achilles heel.'

CHAPTER 68

Jane's fiancé was unequivocal: 'You're not doing this without police backing. And that's non-negotiable, so don't put on the puppy-dog look with me!'

'But if *you* were in the next room …?'

Jeremy stared at her. 'Blimey, Jane. Will I ever be able to trust you again? Crafty Cruella, Devious Dervla, or what?!' He grinned. 'Maybe I should think about re-writing the wedding vows.'

'You'll get your reward. Besides, there's every chance it won't come to anything, in which case, none of your lot need to know anything about it.'

'The first hint of danger … you're out of there, right? Promise me?'

'I'll be all meek and submissive and let you gallop valiantly to my rescue. Promise.'

'Fat chance!'

The schoolroom was empty of children but evidence of them crowded every available space. Miss Clark was clearly a dedicated teacher, bent on encouraging application as well as enterprise, persistence as well as aptitude. Pictures, models, writing, show-and-tell … the surfaces were covered. Worms wriggled their way through layers of soil in a spotlessly clean tank. A piebald guinea pig scrabbled gently in fresh wood-shavings. Flags seemingly of every country known to man – or at least Miss Clark – hung as bunting from high fixtures. Colour, activity, life, youth, radiated from every angle.

The inspiration behind this mini-paradise was herself not out of place on the pint-sized seats Class 3 had so recently occupied. But there was nothing juvenile about her intent.

Jane took her phone and dialled the number before passing it back to Fern Clark.

She could hear it ringing.

'Hello?'

'Mrs Corrigan?'

Jane moved closer the better to overhear responses.

'Speaking.'

'This is Miss Clark, Jude's teacher.'

'Is there something wrong?'

'Nothing serious, but I would like to have a wee chat about him – face to face, if that's possible. I'm happy to come to you, if that would suit you better.'

'Oh,' – a pause – 'I can't manage today but ... would tomorrow be all right?'

'Absolutely fine. We finish at 3, as you know. Any time after that.'

'3:30?'

'Perfect. Where shall I meet you?'

'I'll come to the school.'

'Fine. Just come straight to Jude's classroom. We can be undisturbed there. I'll alert the receptionist so she's expecting you. But please, don't worry – it's nothing to lose sleep over.'

Miss Clark ended the call and put her phone down on the desk. Someone had gouged out a daisy in one corner and another hand had neatly coloured in the grooves with a glittery pink pen.

'Twenty-four hours to dream up a plausible problem for young Jude Corrigan. The lad's no angel, but I'm no snitch!'

'We'll keep you out of this, don't worry,' Jane said. 'The story will be, we saw Mrs Corrigan by chance entering the school premises. But thanks, thanks a lot for your assistance. You were our best hope.'

'They're good parents.'

'I know.'

'Exceptionally so.'

'And that's precisely why you could succeed where we would fail. Her children's welfare comes first. Every time.'

Precisely at 3:30 the following afternoon, Tiffany Corrigan sidled into the school gates complete with large sunhat and glasses, a loose sundress and over-blouse shrouding her figure. Unseen eyes followed her ... acknowledging the receptionist ... collecting a pass ... making her way along the corridors ... shedding hat and specs ... entering the classroom. The screens went blank.

Miss Clark was her usual friendly self. Jane had helped set up the chilled juice at her elbow, a pile of Jude's drawings in front of her.

'Good to see you, Mrs Corrigan. Warm, isn't it? I've left the fan on, say if it's too cold.'

'It's fine, thanks.'

'I'm sure we can sort this out together. Do have a seat. Help yourself to a cold drink.'

Listening on an earpiece Jane could only marvel at the young woman's calm and ease. A story unravelled. A particularly plausible one.

'Jude loves drawing and painting ... as you can observe in these pictures. Lots of colour, happy scenarios.'

Tiffany's voice sounded pleased. 'He's never happier.'

The teacher's tone changed subtly. 'But lately ... well, can you see? Much darker. Even this one, all black ... And notice here ... he really *digs* the pencil into the paper. Fiercely ... As if he's angry about something ... I've tried gently probing. But ... I wonder ... have you seen any change at home, maybe?'

'Not especially.'

'No? Nothing out of the ordinary?'

'Not that I've noticed. But ... I'll look out for signs. Thanks for bringing it to my attention.'

'Best to pick up on these things early. Prevent them developing into anything worrying, I always feel.'

'Absolutely. I will look into it. Promise.'

A scrape of chairs echoed in the empty room.

The door opened.

'Thanks, again. Bye.'

'No problem. Thanks for coming, Mrs Corrigan.'

The purple flare caught the harsh light from the overhead fluorescents, the cover-all hat swung loosely in her hand.

Jane stepped forward as if just that minute strolling up the corridor.

'Mrs Corrigan! Tiffany! It *is* you! Wow! That's a piece of luck. I *thought* I recognised you coming into the school gates. Could I have a quick word about Jude, please? Remember me? Jane Carver?'

Tiffany nodded.

'I was going to pop out and see you, but then I glimpsed you as I drove by just now.'

'Miss Clark's just filled me in.' She was clearly itching to get past.

'She's coming from the educational side of things. I'm more interested in the broader picture.'

'Well, OK. But please, make it quick. I have places to be.'

'Shall we go …' Lucinda made a show of peering into the adjacent room.

'Feel free to use my room,' Miss Clark said cheerily from behind Tiffany. 'I'm done for today. Off to catch some rays while I still can. Bye everyone.'

'Thanks for that.'

Jane held the door open and to her immense relief, Tiffany entered.

'Good grief, these seats are way too small for my rear end,' Jane said. 'I'd never get out again! Let's use the teacher's chair. You have hers. I'll grab another one from over in that corner.'

Tiffany was giving nothing away. But at least she hadn't bolted.

'Now, as I'm sure you know, this school has a really good reputation for taking care of its pupils. Holistic care. So, if a child starts behaving out of character in one area, showing signs of disturbance, they try to get to the bottom of it. Nip it in the bud.'

Tiffany was listening, a guarded expression on her face,

but silent. A far cry from the woman who'd taken the lead so often with Anya.

'The school nurse thinks Jude's not as happy as he was. Have you detected that?'

'Not especially. They all fluctuate. Maybe it's his turn to have a wee strop. He's not as keen on learning as his sisters. Could be just that. Kids don't like to *admit* they're struggling, do they? But I'll keep an eye on him.'

'And I'd say, you're the very best person for the job. You know your boy better than anyone at school – everyone has a high regard for both you and your husband. Sounds as if half the children in the school come round to your house!'

'We've always loved a noisy, busy, home, lots going on. They entertain themselves if there's enough of them.'

'That's fantastic. So, will you be returning home today?'

'What d'you mean?'

'Well, I've called a few times, and I understand you haven't been home for several days now.'

'Flaming Nora, what is this? The Stasi police?'

'It's my job.'

'Did *Dan* tell you that? Well, fair enough. Haven't *you* ever got to a point where you just need a bit of space?'

'I certainly have, and *I* don't have three children making demands day and night.'

'Exactly.'

'But this is more than just needing a little bit of breathing space, isn't it, Tiffany?'

'No …'

'I think it is.'

'Look, what's going on here? Why am I *really* here?'

'Because I want to help you. I know what a brilliant mother you are, how much you do to help other kids. And I especially know how much you did to help Anya Morgan. Now it's *your* turn to get the help *you* need.'

'I don't need help. I'm fine.'

'I think we both know that's not true.'

Tiffany rose to her feet.

'I don't have to sit here and take this. I don't know what crazy ideas you've got in your head, but I'm just going home. I'm late as it is.'

'Home? As in St David's Avenue home?'

'Yes.'

'In which case, I'm very much afraid this whole thing will escalate into something none of us wants to see.'

CHAPTER 69

Jane held her breath.

'What d'you mean?' Tiffany let the words out completely devoid of emotion.

'A lot of people are involved in this. The safety of a child is at stake. Nobody takes that lightly. We have a solemn duty of care for *all* the children on our patch.'

Jane paused to let this sink in.

'Your husband ... the doctors ... the hospital staff ... the social workers ... the health visitors ... we *all* want to resolve this without causing any more damage. Nobody wants to see your three lovely children taken into care. They're a credit to you. Fair enough, Jude's having a blip at the moment, but I suspect he's picking up on the things that aren't right at home, don't you? He doesn't fully understand them, but he knows his mum's not herself, and he certainly knows you haven't been there for him. And that's not like you, is it? Wee soul. He's only seven. He needs you. So, let us help you get back to him ... to them all, huh? Talk to me, and I'll do my level best to keep your family together. I swear it.'

Tiffany shrank back, but remained standing.

'If you walk away now, you're going to force us to take this to the police.' Jane held her gaze. 'It'll spiral completely out of our control. We'll be powerless to contain it.'

Tiffany's gaze dropped to her hands twisting the sunhat.

Jane pressed her advantage. 'We already know a lot of what's happened – not all of it by any means, but most of the what and the how. And we believe you really, really need help, Tiffany. It's nothing to be ashamed of ... but you know that. And the more you can explain to me, the better I'll be able to support you … and the children. You want to do the best thing for your three, right?'

Tiffany seemed to crumple onto the chair.

'What d'you kno … *think* you know?'

'That you've been feeding Gypsy harmful substances. That you've been drugging Anya.'

The look remained defiant, but there was no denial.

'That you've been sending letters, threatening harm to the Morgans.'

No change.

'What I don't follow is … why, Tiffany? Explain to me. What have they done to make you want to cause them harm?'

'No *lasting* harm. Just enough to teach her a lesson.'

'Well, I have to say, that's debatable, but in what sense, teach her a lesson?'

'Look at her! Plenty money. Good jobs. Grand house. Successful husband. Lovely kid. Everything falling into her lap.' A faint sneer accompanied the words. 'And she couldn't even cope with *one* … *little* … *baby!*' She threw her eyes to the ceiling. 'Always fretting. Always fussing. Always pestering the doctors. As if they haven't got better things to do.'

Jane felt her tongue dry in her mouth, but she didn't dare reach for the glass.

'I was in the surgery, right? waiting for a prescription for my mother, the first time. I watched her. Fuss, fuss, fuss. Jig, jig, jig. Check, check, check. What chance has a kid got, huh, trapped in that kind of smothering atmosphere? I wanted to snatch her away, give her a normal rough-and-tumble life. And when they came out of the doctor's room, you could see she'd been crying. At first I felt sorry for her: new mum, probably never had much to do with babies before. I thought I could be a bit of a pal. But it never stopped. If it wasn't one thing, it was another. And it really got to me. People like that shouldn't have children, they should stay in their smart offices, wearing their designer suits, making their executive decisions.'

She stopped, and Jane could see her thoughts tracking back. She forced herself to keep absolutely still.

'She's got a million grey cells for every one of mine, degrees to her name, publications, but when it comes to babies ... not even on the first rung. So, when Gypsy was poorly, *I* was the one she consulted. And, of *course*, I knew what to do! Heck, pretty much every other mother in the country knows what to do when a baby gets diarrhoea. But, yep, I confess, it felt good having someone like *her* turning to *me*. Being valued. So, I slipped the kiddie a little bit of salt. Only enough to give her a wee tummy upset for a couple of days. Give Anya something to really get her teeth into, get a bit more kudos myself.

'It was only a couple of times. But no surprises, Mrs Uber-Anxiety must go roaring up to the doc.

'I knew they'd find the salt if they started tests; but I also knew it was the bewildered Mummy they'd start looking at, not clued-up, experienced, trained-nurse, me. Anya was already pretty neurotic; this just made her look worse.

'You can't keep giving a kid salt, though. So, then I thought, what if the diarrhoea was actually from a bowel complaint? That'd be a bit more dramatic than the common or garden runs. Let's up the ante a bit. So, one day, I pricked my finger, dabbed blood in the nappy. I wasn't to know her sister would call in, but it played out even better. Mummy leaves Aunty upstairs to change the nappy; I'm far away, in the kitchen by this time. All unsuspecting Aunty – also clueless – she shouts for the mummy. Mummy's soon shouting for me. Up I go. And it's the easiest thing in the world to look all professional, calm-in-a-crisis, know-more-than-I'm-letting on; offer to run them to the doc. Nappy's long gone – I saw to that. Couldn't have them testing it. But Mummy needs me there to give an accurate account, doesn't she? So, I'm in pole position, ready to drop the odd hint, let them know I've been thinking intussusception all along. You'll know what that is, but of course, *she* didn't. And you could see the staff up at the hospital are looking at me with more respect now. This woman knows a bit about medicine. Spot-on differential diagnosis. And I'm in there, in the thick of it. I'm the one who can give the accurate history, keep them on track. And Anya's clinging to me; I'm her saviour.'

She stopped abruptly.

Jane took a long silent breath, steadied her voice, controlled the volume.

'And the insulin?'

'Easy as ABC. Gypsy's been cleared for discharge. Mummy's in the playroom all excited about getting home. "Off you go and get yourself some food," I say, "I'll stay with Gypsy." She's still got her cannula in. No need even for a puncture mark. Slip the insulin in. Slow-release.' Tiffany was actually smiling at the memory as she mimed the injection. 'Sweet.'

'But how would you get hold of …?' Jane allowed a hint of disbelief to colour her question.

'Collected my neighbour's prescription that very day, hadn't I? Had it in my bag.'

Jane sat completely still, a terrible chill creeping along her spine.

'By the time the blood sugar drops, and the kid's having a convulsion, *I'm* nowhere to be seen. But Mummy and Daddy are. Finger waggles round once again to this going-bananas mother.'

'Was that what happened with the convulsion at home, too?'

Tiffany actually grinned.

'Nah. I just made that one up. Nobody even thought of doubting me. I could describe a mini-fit perfectly. All the attention, all the kudos, none of the risk. Neat, huh?'

'But the barbiturates, they were real, weren't they?'

'You *do* know your stuff! And before you ask, my Ma takes them, and painkillers. Gets them on prescription. Tra-la, it didn't even *cost* me! How poetic is that? It only took a tiny amount of both in her food, and bingo, Gypsy's out cold. Won't have done any lasting damage. Then, once Gypsy's back in the hospital, all I have to do is offer to check up on the house. She *had* locked it actually, but I had a key, I could *un*lock it. Nobody'd ever know. Mix the crushed-up medication – in baby-sized doses, naturally – with a bit of formula feed, whap it in a plastic wallet and "discover" it in Anya's drawer; the drawer where she kept her ridiculous, useless Freya Trimble-Coleman pills ... bingo again! Anya's in the frame BIG TIME! And I'm watching from a ring-side seat. Because, of course, everybody wants my version of the story.'

'And you were only topping up the suspicion. You'd already discredited Anya by sedating her before.'

'Only two or three times, actually. I didn't want her out of it so she'd *actually* put Gypsy in danger. If hubby wasn't there or me, I couldn't risk it.'

'But it was convincing enough to make Leon believe she was drugging herself.'

'Anybody would. She brought it on herself; obviously unhinged. It only needed a wee hint and he fell for it hook, line and sinker.'

'Speaking of being out of it, one bit of the story I'm not sure about ... the time in the park. Was that anything to do with you? Or was she genuinely so exhausted she forgot to put the baby in the pram?'

The look on Tiffany's face made Jane's blood run cold.

'I couldn't believe it! I'd met up with one of my *real* pals for a cuppa in the Restaurant Yard Café – you know it? It's quite nice actually, since they did it up. Anyway, there's her high-and-mightiness sitting on the park bench, absolutely fast asleep. I couldn't resist it. I just lifted the baby out, tucked the sheets back neatly, and off I went plus babe to their house. I even had time to feed her, pop her in her cot with the favourite soft toy, and lock up again. I knew she'd be fine for hours. And I could always call round on some pretext or other later if it became necessary. But of course, there was no need. Anya woke up and all hell broke loose!'

Tiffany was staring into space, reliving the excitement.

Jane sat for a long moment watching her. *Thank God Jeremy was next door ready to take this woman away.* Not till Tiffany's eyes returned to her did she speak. Her voice was calm and gently enquiring.

'So, why the letters, Tiffany? Wasn't it enough to cast doubt on her suitability to mother Gypsy? To show yourself as so much more capable?'

'You lot were still giving her the benefit of the doubt. I couldn't believe it! Drafting in extra help. Encouraging, reassuring.' Her tone hardened.

'So, I see the rationale for the first one. You were making it seem that Anya was so far gone she was writing anonymous letters to herself. Threatening letters.'

'And everybody believed it. Even her husband did!'

'Encouraged by you.'

'Didn't take much persuading.'

'So, why the last one? I don't get that.'

'What don't you get?'

'Threatening to *kill* Gypsy.'

'I knew she'd have to show it to *somebody*. She wouldn't be able to just keep quiet about a *death* threat. They already suspected she'd written the other notes. Needy mother, seeking attention. Why not this one too? It'd be the final step. They *couldn't* ignore a direct threat to the kid's life, could they? Gypsy would be taken into a normal happy family, allowed to grow up naturally. Nobody'd risk returning her to a mother so far gone she'd contemplate killing her own child. Gypsy'd be free at last.'

'You said in the letter, you knew where Gypsy was. Is that true, Tiffany?'

'*That* is for me to know and you to wonder, as somebody famous once said, only I can't just recall who.' She stood up abruptly. 'Look, I need to be somewhere.'

And she was gone.

CHAPTER 70

Jane sagged in the chair and took long steadying breaths. It had worked ... no, *exceeded* their expectations. And the end result would surely justify the irregular process. Even so, best not to be present when Jeremy actually took Tiffany into custody.

Time to listen to the whole recording again ...

Still no sign of anyone coming to find her. Maybe he'd texted her ...

> Sorry. Called away to emergency.
> Suggest you abandon interview for today.

A terrible coldness enveloped her. What time was ...?
3.20! He hadn't been there at all!
'Think! Think!' She forced herself to calm down.
If she took this straight to Dr Moore ...
If she waited till Jeremy was free ...
If she contacted the police – officially ...
If she went round to the Corrigan's house ...
If she alerted Sharon Vine ...
The only safe ears were Lucinda's.

Two hours and twelve unanswered text messages later, Jeremy rang.

'Hiya. You've been looking for me?'
He listened without interruption.

'I just let her walk out!' Jane wailed. 'It never entered my head you weren't there. I thought you'd pick her up at the front door.'

'I couldn't ignore a major incident, Jane. The fight was

actually in progress. Knives involved. That *had* to take priority.'

'So, what do we do now?'

'Prioritise. First make sure the baby's safe. I guess they'll need to move her – just to be sure. Then find Tiffany Corrigan. Then check out her kids – make sure they're being cared for.'

'But … won't you get it in the neck … being involved in something …'

'Too bad. These kids are more important. Leave it with me. Can you get that recording to me? I'll make sure it gets to Child Protection, and alert my lot. We'll sort it.'

'Thanks, Jeremy. Sorry to have dragged you into this mess.'

'Just don't make a habit of it! Oh, and … how are *you*? Must have been hellish listening.'

'Yep. But worth it to nail this once and for all.'

'Pity the Morgans won't ever know how much they owe you.'

'A family reunited's all the reward I'm needing. What that woman's done …'

She was deep in a report on a problem family riven with drink- and drug-related problems when the call came.

'Hi, Jane.' It was Lucinda. 'I've had Child Protection on the phone. Seems they've authorised us to take Gypsy back to her parents. Apparently, I'm the obvious choice because Gypsy knows me. But we need a social worker too. So, you free to come with me?'

'You bet.'

'We'll collect the documents on the way.' Lucinda couldn't keep the lift out of her voice.

The house was a neat stone cottage, pretty garden, lace curtains at the windows giving privacy even in this quiet back street.

In her late forties, the woman who answered the door was plump, motherly, comfortable; nothing like Anya Morgan.

'Mrs Sanderson? Mrs Agnes Sanderson? My name's Jane Carver; social worker. And this is my colleague, Lucinda Devonshire; health visitor.'

Both professionals offered their identity cards.

'Yes …?' She looked from one to the other with raised eyebrows.

'We've come to collect Gypsy Morgan.'

'Gyp … Wait … can I see your identity again, please?'

This time she took the cards and examined them minutely.

'I'm afraid you've had a wasted journey. Must be some kind of a mix-up. Another social worker came a wee while ago and took her.'

'Another social worker?' Jane kept it even.

'Yep. I wasn't here, but Pearl – that's my daughter – she was minding the baby. She's sixteen; she's perfectly capable. I was only away fifteen, twenty minutes, getting more nappies. And she … I'll get her. Come on in.'

The house was tiny but cosily furnished and welcoming.

'Pearl?' she shouted up the stairs. '*Pearl*!'

'What?'

'Can you come here a minute, please?'

A blonde overweight teenager in a rather violent magenta fleece and tight black leggings thumped down the narrow staircase, stopping suddenly when she saw the two strangers.

'Can you tell these ladies about the social worker who came for Gypsy, pet?'

'What's to tell? She showed me the papers. She said Gypsy was going back to her mum.'

'Was she on her own?'

'Aye … I think so, anyways. I only *saw* one person.'

'Did you see her car?'

'Nah. Didn't want to watch, did I? S'not nice when the babies go.' She shot a darkling look at her mother, responsible for these repeated traumas.

'That's perfectly understandable. You become attached

356

to them, don't you?'

Pearl nodded, eyes veiled.

'Did this woman show you any form of identification, Pearl?' Jane asked gently.

'Yeah. She had a thingy like yours round her neck, and this letter – authorisation, she called it.'

'D'you, by any chance, remember her name?'

'Nah ... errr, wait a minute ... B ... something beginning with B anyway ... Brea ... Bren something, maybes?'

'Brenda?'

'Aye.'

'Brenda Brooks?'

'Aye, that was it.'

'And you say she had some kind of letter of authorisation? Did she show it to you?'

'Aye. She said I ought to read it. You can't just hand over a baby to any Tom, Dick or Harry, that's what she said.'

'So, can you remember the heading? Was it an official kind of document?'

'Social something, it said. I don't just remember exactly. But it was proper headed paper.'

'What did it say underneath the heading?'

'This social worker, Brenda whatever-you-said-just-now, she was authorised to take Gypsy Morgan away and return her to her parents.'

'Can you describe her, Pearl? Anything you can remember.'

'Taller than you' – to Lucinda – 'not so tall as you' – to Jane – 'pretty much Mum's height, I guess. Only thinner. Same sort of age.'

'Hair? Complexion? Eyes? Accent?'

'Grey hair in a kind of bun thingy. Complexion? – dunno, sort of darkish, not Indian dark, not African dark – just tanned, sort of. Eyes ... dunno. Didn't see. She had on these big glasses – the ones that go dark in the sun. No accent. Just ordinary.'

'You're doing very well, Pearl. Anything else you can

tell us?'

Pearl shook her head, eyes flicking from one to the other.

'Am I in some kind of trouble?'

'No, you're not. You did well, checking the woman's credentials.'

'Can I go now, only I've got homework before my music lesson ...'

'Of course. Thank you. If you do think of anything else, let your mum know and she'll contact us. Good luck with the homework.'

As soon as she'd gone, Agnes Sanderson turned back to her visitors. 'Is there something wrong?'

'We're not sure,' Jane said cautiously. 'We'll check with our bosses, but here's my card. Please ring immediately if either of you thinks of something that might help to identify our colleague.'

'Did the woman who called take all Gypsy's things away as well?' Lucinda asked.

'Aye. Everything.'

'Well, thank you for taking care of Gypsy up till now. Someone will be in touch with you formally to thank you.'

'I hope she does well. She's such a bonnie wee lassie. Good as gold.'

Lucinda smiled and nodded. 'She certainly is.'

As soon as they were outside, Jane rang Dr Moore.

It was no surprise: Brenda Brooks had definitely not been officially deputed to collect Gypsy Morgan. The real Brenda Brooks didn't look at all like Pearl's description. Yes, she would report the missing baby to the police immediately; she promised, *immediately*.

For good measure, Jane rang Jeremy, who swore fluently.

'What the devil have you got yourself mixed up in this time, woman?!'

'Just you find this kid alive and well, boyo! We'll talk about my mix-ups another day.'

'Unlawful abduction of a baby? They don't come much more high priority than that here!'

Dr Moore understood completely why both Jane and Lucinda wanted to be the ones to support Anya when the news was broken to her. Leon Morgan should be there too.

There was nothing but the hum of the engine to distract their thoughts as they drove to destroy a woman's life.

'God help us all,' Lucinda muttered as the car swung into the drive.

But there was no sign of Anya. No sign of her car. No sign of anyone.

The policeman patrolled around the outside of the house peering in the windows, tapping, calling. Nothing. He was ringing the bell persistently when a dark Audi crunched to a halt and Leon Morgan leapt out, demanding answers.

'Could you calm down, sir. And maybe we could take this inside?'

Leon listened with mounting horror.

'And my wife knows nothing of this?'

'Not from us anyway.'

'I'll call her ...'

'Best not to tell her without someone present to support her ...'

Leon glared at the officer. 'What d'you take me for? I'm not a complete moron.'

But Anya's phone was switched off.

'Could you give me the details of her car, please, sir? Make, colour, registration? And perhaps a recent picture of her?'

'Are you ...? You think ... *she* might be involved with Gypsy's disappearance?'

'We aren't ruling anything out at this moment. But a baby is missing. And so, it seems, is your wife. We need to find her so she can help us with our enquiries.'

CHAPTER 71

Anya had been pacing up and down, up and down the garden, heedless of the beauty, the heady perfume, all around her, going over and over and over everything that had happened in Gypsy's short life, desperately searching for some sense in it all, when her phone rang. A name flashed up on the screen: *Tiffany Corrigan!*

'Hello?' It took every ounce of control to keep it neutral.

'Listen carefully, Anya. If you want to see Gypsy alive again, you'll do exactly what I say ... Are you there? Are you listening?'

'Y... yes. But ...'

'Shut up and listen. Is anyone else with you?'

'No.'

'Where's your husband?'

'At the office.'

'Up here or in Newcastle?'

'Up here.'

'Is he due home soon?'

'Not till sixish.'

'Good. What I'm going to say is for your ears only. If I find out you've told another living soul, it's curtains for Gypsy. You hear me? Not ... another ... living ... soul.'

'I hear you.'

'I've got Gypsy – right here.'

Anya clapped a hand to her mouth to stifle the scream.

'We're standing on a bridge with a river running underneath it ... a very cold, fast river. It's what? ... thirty, forty feet below us. If you bring anybody else with you, I'm going to drop her all the way down into that icy cold water.

OK? You got that?'

   'Pleeeeease, Tiffany …'

   'Did. You. Get. That?'

   'Yes.'

   'Good. So, this is what you're going to do. When I've finished talking, you're going to go outside, get into your car, and drive. Get onto the M8, then the M9 to Stirling. There's a roundabout at the end of the motorway; take the B8033 signposted to Dunblane. Remember Dunblane? The massacre of all those little children? *That* Dunblane. Poetic, huh? About half a mile along, you'll see a road on the left up from the station. Don't go down there, go straight on, and immediately you'll be on a stone bridge over the Allan Water, with parking on both sides. Park there. It's free for two hours so you don't need to bother with a ticket. Are you still with me?'

   'Yes.'

   'I'll be watching for you. I'll be sitting on the bench on that bridge … holding your baby. Don't come any closer than six feet. And like I say, make sure there's nobody with you … and nobody follows you. As soon as I tell you to, switch off your phone and keep it switched off; if anybody tracks you, it's bye bye Gypsy. Got that?'

   'Yes! Yes! *Please* don't hurt her, Tiffany. I'll do anything you say.'

   'Will you, Anya? *Anything?* We'll see about that. Right, just so you know I *have* got Gypsy, I'm going to tickle her toes and make her laugh. Remember those little pink toes, Anya? Remember how she scrunches herself up when the punch line's coming? Remember that laugh?

   'Gypsy! Gypsy! Look at Aunty Tiffany!

This little piggy went to market.

This little piggy stayed home.

This little piggy had roast beef.

This little piggy had none.

And this little piggy went...

"Wee wee wee" all the way home!'

   The gurgle of merriment was unmistakeable. Anya closed her eyes and pressed the phone hard against her ear.

'Gypsy ... Gypsy ...' The whisper echoed around inside her head.

'Believe me now?'

'I believe you ... please, please, *please*, don't hurt her, Tiffany ...'

'Stop snivelling and listen. I haven't got all day. The clock's ticking. It's ... what? 12:11 now. Just under two hours till my free parking runs out. So, you've got till 1:30. Remember? M8, M9, B8033 – you can do it easily in just over an hour. See you, on the bridge, by 1:30 latest. Switch off your phone ... *now*!'

It was like cutting the umbilical cord to her precious daughter, but she had no choice.

Fingers clenched on the steering wheel, heart racing, sweat running down her spine, Anya could feel the tremble in her knees as she raced along the motorway, careful to keep the needle exactly on seventy; she absolutely couldn't afford to be pulled over by the police today.

1:30 ... latest ...'

Please God! Please God! Don't let me be late. Please keep her safe. Please ... please ... please ...

M8 ... M9 ... Every mile was bringing her closer ...

She slowed at the roundabout ... There it was: B8033 ... Dunblane ...

Just seeing the name, with all its connotations, made her muscles spasm.

The roof of the station ... straight on ... she was on the bridge ...

She pulled in, parked ...

But ... there was no one on the bridge, not a soul ... no one sitting; no one standing; no one walking. Cars, yes, a steady stream in both directions, but absolutely no pedestrians.

She jumped out, ran to the edge. Water, glistening in the bright sunshine, swirled by, forty feet below. She tracked back to the cathedral in the distance ... this definitely was Dunblane ... She darted from side to side, ran from one end to the other. Four people walked past during that time, none of them carrying a child.

She checked her watch yet again … 1:23. *Surely … surely …*

1:27 …

She dropped her head in her arms and leaned onto the rail at the apex of the bridge, blotting out everything except the sound of that hateful voice giving her instruction. *Could she possibly have misunderstood …?*

'Stand perfectly still, Anya.'

She froze.

'I'm right behind you. Don't turn until I tell you to. Remember … fast cars on one side, long drop, cold cold water on the other side … rushing along, ready to carry her away …'

Every second felt like an eternity.

'Now, turn around slowly. No sudden movements, no running at us; stay exactly where you are.'

Tiffany was standing feet from her with Gypsy perched on the rail above the capping stones, her little feet inches from empty space. Anya felt her stomach plummet in fear.

'See, Gypsy,' Tiffany cooed. 'That lady over there, remember her?'

Gypsy's head was craned round, mesmerised by the cars zooming by behind her, head swivelling as she followed each flash of metalwork. She hardly glanced at her mother.

She wore no sunhat; nothing on her chubby arms, legs, feet; nothing but a flimsy sundress and a bulging nappy.

'Please, Tiffany … can we go into the shade to talk?'

'Why? Have you got an army of policemen hiding in the bushes?'

'No, no! Honestly. Nobody knows I'm here. I swear. It's just … the sun … on her skin … she'll burn …'

'You haven't learned a single solitary thing, have you, Anya? Fuss fuss fuss. Worry worry worry. That's precisely why we're where we are.'

Anya stared at her.

'I was prepared to give you a second chance, you know

that? Surely, I thought, she *must* have learned something out of all this. She *must* have. But no. Can you imagine what kind of a girl Gypsy would be if *you* brought her up? Scared of her own shadow? Seeing danger in everything? No, she's better off dead.'

Tiffany bent Gypsy at the waist so her head was hanging over the edge of the bridge.

'No!' Anya clutched her own head in her hands. '*Please! Please!* I'll do anything …'

'Don't make a scene or I swear …' Tiffany hissed, jerking Gypsy over the drop as if she were falling.

'I won't!' Anya managed through her constricted throat, putting her hands down immediately. 'Just tell me what you want me to do.'

Tiffany lifted the child back up to the stone ledge, and let the rail take her weight. She stood completely still while a couple strolled past, stopped for a moment to admire the view, smile at Gypsy, never taking her warning gaze from Anya.

Anya let her breath squeeze out in tiny gasps.

'What do *I* want? I think it's more what does *Gypsy* want.'

'What does she want?'

There were no cars passing now and Gypsy turned towards the voice, dark eyes studying her unblinkingly … Anya didn't dare give her any encouragement … bored, the child turned away and peered over at the light glistening on the swirling water far below.

'I gave her a choc ice for lunch today,' Tiffany said conversationally. 'I couldn't bear to think she'd go to her grave never knowing the simple pleasure of chocolate.'

Anya felt her stomach clench.

'Spinach … curly kale … organic carrots … home-grown broccoli …' Tiffany sneered, 'Have you any idea how other kids would jeer at her if she'd gone to school with your regime instilled into her? Life's hard enough for them these days without obsessions written all over them.'

'I'll change. I'll give her ice cream …'

'And what about when she starts climbing up on your perfect furniture, putting sticky fingers on those spotless marble surfaces, licking those magnificent floor-to-ceiling mirrors? You can't keep her in a playpen for ever, you know. What about when she wants to have little friends to play, little people who don't understand priceless when they see it?'

'None of that matters ...'

'You say that now ... you'd say *anything* at this moment ... just to stop me doing what you know I'm going to do.'

'Please, Tiffany. Imagine this was Maribel ... or Jude... She's an innocent *child*. Hurt *me* if you want to hurt somebody, but not her.'

'Hurt *you*? Why, you crazy woman, can't you see? This is the most exquisite hurt a *real* mother could ever feel. But you're not a *real* mother, are you? You're an obsessive, paranoid perfectionist, going through the motions of conforming to society's expectations. Giving your precious ridiculous Morgan & Sons another generation to carry on their empire. You should never have had children. Once this is over, go back to your statistics, where you belong.'

Gypsy suddenly arched her back and bounced her bare feet against the stone.

Anya froze.

'Oh whoa!' Tiffany laughed, grabbing the child. 'You wanting to jump already, poppet? You in such a hurry to get away from her? A few more minutes, honey. Mummy needs to see it's all her fault.'

A solitary man walked by, glancing curiously at the two women, but not stopping to admire the view. A local presumably. Neither spoke till he was out of earshot.

'I thought you were my friend,' Anya whispered.

Tiffany gave a hollow laugh.

'I looked up to you. I admired you – as a mother.'

'Past tense?' Tiffany said. 'Interesting.'

'The Tiffany I know wouldn't ever ... ever ... *ever* harm an innocent baby ... the Tiffany I know wouldn't risk spending the rest of her life in prison away from her own beloved children.'

'The Tiffany you know is a figment of your imagination. A delusion. You never knew the real one.'

Holding Anya's gaze, she lifted the child high above her head and held her out over the sheer drop.

CHAPTER 72

'Someone's coming!' Anya hissed.

Tiffany jiggled the child above her head as if it was all part of a game, and lowered her until she was sitting on her hip.

Anya felt the breath shudder through her parched mouth.

A young couple strolled along on the far side of the bridge, looking from side to side, pointing, exclaiming, questioning.

'Oh, honey, look at that darling little house,' the woman gushed. 'Gorgeous. Wait while I snap that. Lattice windows even!' She angled her phone this way and that to capture the steep roof highlighted by its white fascia boarding, lifting the brim of her large sunhat to see what she was doing.

Her partner moved to peer over the opposite edge.

'Some bridge, huh?'

The woman shuddered. 'I'm no good with heights.'

'Come this side; you get a good view of the cathedral from here.'

'In a mo.'

Both cameras clicked. Tiffany kept her eyes trained on Anya, only once putting a finger to her lips in the universal gesture of silence.

'Excuse me. I wonder if you can help me?' the young man said, smiling at Tiffany, ignoring the baby. 'I understand there's a memorial garden somewhere for those children killed in the gun massacre? Where will I find that? Sorry, are you local? I should have checked first. Only my cousin's wee boy was at the school when Hamilton went berserk. They moved away – too many bad memories. But I just thought I'd pay my respects.'

'I'm not local, but I know Dunblane. I believe there're two memorial gardens; one on the site of the gymnasium, one in the cemetery where the children are buried. But your best bet's probably the cathedral – over there. See that spire on the horizon? There's a standing stone in the nave there marking the tragedy.'

'Brilliant. Thanks a lot. Hard to take it in, huh? Pretty little place like this. Something as horrific as that.'

'Yep.'

The young woman crossed over to join him, still snapping.

'Hear that, darling? There's a monument to those primary school children in the cathedral. Shouldn't get lost finding that, should we?'

But the woman was captivated by the living child in front of her.

'Hello, Beautiful.' She bobbed her head from side to side, gaining Gypsy's full attention. A big smile spread across the baby's face as the smiling face vanished behind the strange man, and then popped out. 'Here I am again!'

Gypsy squirmed on Tiffany's hip.

'What's her name?'

'Look, I don't mean to be rude or anything, but my friend and I are trying to have a conversation here.'

'Sorry, sorry. Didn't mean to intrude.' The young man put up both hands and moved as if to walk past.

At the same moment the woman reached out to stroke Gypsy's hand.

It was over in a flash.

Gypsy was in the arms of the woman; Tiffany had her hands pinned behind her back by the man; Anya screamed and fainted.

'Tiffany Corrigan, I'm arresting you for the unlawful abduction of a minor. You don't have to say anything, but anything you do say may be written down and given in evidence against you.'

Within minutes Jeremy Tait had summoned the police who'd been stealthily infiltrating the area and restraining Leon Morgan from rushing to the bridge.

His was the first face Anya saw when she came to.

CHAPTER 73

Medical confidentiality ran in Dr Gabrielle Fournier's veins, but so did discernment, and this shrewd and compassionate woman knew intuitively that the people who had gone out on a limb, and contrived to bring to an end Tiffany Corrigan's reign of terror, deserved to know something of what they had surmised, guessed, feared and prevented.

They met in Dr Moore's office, the door firmly closed.

If anyone of superior intellect and razor sharp wit could ever be described as nondescript, Gabrielle Fournier was that person. Average height, androgynous figure, monochrome tailoring matching the raven bob, neutral make-up, the only memorable feature a slight lisp. She had long ago extinguished the last shockable touch-paper in her body.

'I'd like to begin with a huge commendation, guys,' she began, gaze resting on each in turn. 'Tiffany Corrigan's one complicated and troubled woman. We'll draw a veil over your rather irregular methods – they're really not my concern – but I don't doubt your motives, and I hope your superiors don't give you too hard a time; I quite see desperation drove you. And because of your insights and careful handling, you've given this woman a chance to work through the baggage of decades.'

'I echo that, Dr Fournier.' Diane Moore nodded towards them.

'You don't need me to tell you that what happens between trick cyclist and client is confidential, but you chaps must have a whole heap of unanswered questions, and Dr Moore and I have agreed we owe you some kind of closure. Strictly twixt thee and me. Not a squeak outside these four walls. Deal?'

Nods all round.

'Jane excepted, naturally. You're official, and I understand you're involved in the ongoing care of the Corrigan children – yes? You'll be thrashing this stuff out on that committee. And I reckon your fella deserves the bare bones, too.'

'Thanks.'

Gabrielle shuggled herself into a comfortable position and began.

'Apologies if I repeat stuff you know already, and if your version deviates from mine in any significant detail, feel free to chip in. No history's free from some distortion or reinvention. Tiffany Corrigan's been living and breathing a weird double life for some time. She's also been concocting an immensely sophisticated and cunning plot. Even she won't be aware of exactly where the boundaries between truth and lies are. This is my first exposure to her particular brand of story-telling, so I'm sure to have been treated to some embellishments and embroideries along the way. We will, of course, be meeting with her many times in the future and checking up on some of the facts, but the sooner we get to unvarnished the better, so any insights you can supply will be notched on your slate and receive bonuses come the day of reckoning.'

Diane saw shoulders relaxing, facial muscles softening, frowns easing. This woman was good.

'You don't need the detail, and for professional reasons I'm going to stick to the issues that explain the *why* of what she did. The old familiar need-to-know that's been drilled into our tattoos since we entered our respective noble professions and were allowed within sneezing distance of real live people.' She paused and surveyed them solemnly. 'Here goes. Serious face. In summary ...

'Hester Tiffany Baker is born in Paisley, Renfrewshire on 1 April 1981.

'She's the eldest of five – three boys in the middle; another girl last. She has a strict religious upbringing, lots of guilt and punishment.

371

'Aged thirteen: Father dies suddenly – aortic aneurysm. Mother takes part-time work. Tiffany has to assume more domestic responsibility, especially for the youngest sib – Isla, a sickly kid. She resents all the preferential treatment Isla gets. In her mind? – illness equates with attention.

'Aged fifteen: Hester Tiffany becomes pregnant. She's sent away to Northern Ireland to an aunt. The baby – a girl, Holly – is given up for adoption.

'Aged eighteen: She trains as a nurse in Glasgow.

'Aged twenty-one: She's pregnant again. She keeps this one – another girl, Charlotte – and moves up to Aberdeen.

'Aged twenty-three: She's pushing a really ill-looking child – Charlotte – around in a pushchair saying she's terminally ill, needing some kind of rare treatment only available in the States. In fact the symptoms are all induced by her mother. She gets lots of sympathy and publicity, and the community raises a stack of money. Six months later they both vanish. As does the money.

'Aged twenty-five: She's in Edinburgh on her own – she *says* Charlotte died in an accident falling down stairs. No record of that so far. She's now calling herself Tiffany Baker. She meets Dan Corrigan, they marry and have three children – currently eleven, nine and seven. He knows about the first pregnancy, nothing about the second one. Shortly before their first child is born, her mother comes to live with them – renting her own house out. Dan's told it's to give Tiffany help. In fact, the grandmother's threatened to tell Dan about the previous child, Charlotte, if Tiffany refuses to have her there as a safeguard.

'Dan and Tiffany thrive under this regime. The granny is much less harsh with the next generation; her presence frees Tiffany up to have a life of her own. She gets a job as a part-time receptionist in Sick Kids, so she's back in the medical environment but not hands-on nursing. And she's a natural mum.

'Two years ago: Granny sells her house and they invest in a much larger property in Eskbank which, apparently, is always full of children and a very happy home.

'January this year: Tiffany's now thirty-seven. Enter Anya Morgan. In Tiffany's eyes, she's got it all, but she doesn't appreciate it. And motherhood doesn't come naturally to her. It starts off as liking the kudos of being looked up to. Then the attention. Then the thrill of being at the centre of medical crises. You all know the story of what she did to escalate the drama.

'Nothing's written in tablets of stone yet awhile, of course, and it'll get a whole lot more complicated before we see a clear pathway through to wellness, but she's now in the system and we'll do what we can. The whole family will need ongoing support. Jane and her colleagues will take care of the youngsters.'

'Presumably the granny and the husband didn't know anything about all this?' Lucinda asked.

'Apparently, the granny was getting suspicious, but Tiffany slipped her enough barbiturates to keep her slightly woolly and dropped enough hints to make her doubt her own cognitive functioning. More plaudits for Tiffany, caring for her "dementing" mother. When Tiffany went missing, no barbiturates to Granny; that's why she was with it enough to alert the husband to the past history.

'Any questions?'

'How did Tiffany find out where Gypsy was being fostered?' Lucinda asked.

'She saw the foster mum with Gypsy in TK Maxx out at Fort Kinnaird, followed her home. Then planned her next move. Chance in a million.'

Lucinda and George Hooper shook their heads. Diane grimaced. Jane had read the report.

CHAPTER 74

Two years later

Anya stopped dead in the doorway surveying the multi-coloured chaos. Two pairs of eyes peeped out from behind the dolls' house ... instantly vanished. An ominous silence reigned.

'Gypsy Lysette Morgan. Come here, please. ... Now ... *this minute*!'

Gypsy shuffled out from her hiding place on her bottom, back to her mother, rainbow fingers high above her head.

'What did I say about those Smarties?'

'Phoebe did get them.'

'Got them. But that's no excuse, and you know it. You are responsible for your own actions. You *knew* you were not to touch them. Now, sit there. *And don't move.*' She softened her voice. 'Phoebe! Come out, honey. I need to give your hands a wash too.'

The two little people listened solemnly as Anya spelled out the price for their wilful disobedience.

By the time Leon arrived home from work, the Morgan-Templeton edible work of art had been scoured from the playroom wall, Phoebe had gone home in her friend's borrowed onesie, and a subdued Gypsy was in her own Minnie Mouse pyjamas ready for bed.

Thirty minutes later Anya crept upstairs to find Leon still reading *Thumbelina*, his daughter fast asleep, one arm curled around Mr Rabbit.

They stood together looking down at her.

'Holy hooligan one minute; melting moment the next,' Anya whispered.

'Terrible threes, feisty fours, sassy sixes ... roll on twenty-five!' Leon grinned, guiding her to the door. 'Tell me all about today's horrors while we eat. Do we need to call in a psychologist yet?'

'For me, maybe!'

'You? You're doing brilliantly ... and I'm so proud of you, darling.'

'Thanks, but Tiffany was right. I'm not cut out to be a full-time mum. I'm not. I accept that now. Getting back to work, a smaller house, babysitters ... I needed that to keep things in perspective.'

He gave her a hard look. 'D'you miss Eskbank Road? You never mention it.'

A vivid picture of their lovely home flashed into Anya's mind. It was she who'd insisted they had to sell up but, in truth, not a day went by without her comparing then and now.

'I miss the space; I miss the garden. But I *don't* miss the work involved in maintaining it. It's no effort to keep these new-build houses ticking over, gives me way more free time – even with going out to work.'

'I shall be forever in your debt. I can never forgive myself for letting you down so badly. One day ...'

Anya put a finger to his mouth. 'Don't, Leon. One step at a time. This is where we are. I could never have looked your staff in the eye if we'd maintained that lifestyle. And before you bring it up again, no, I am *not* going to that Country House Hotel with you for our anniversary.'

'If I cancel for a *third* time ...'

'I don't care if your name is in their little black book for the next twenty years. I need to be able to sleep with a clear conscience. Spending ridiculous sums of money on luxuries when the guys on the factory floor have had to take *basics* off their list of groceries ... no, I won't, and that's flat. Non-negotiable.'

'At least the name was Frobisher the first twice I booked ... or to be more precise, Juliette booked on my behalf, because you were far too suspicious for your own good!' He gave an exaggerated sigh. 'Come to think of it, it's always been hard to give you a treat.'

'There are treats … and there are disproportionate expenses. Besides, it hasn't been all sacrifice. There are bonuses to down-scaling, moving to Newcastle. Gypsy has lots of little playmates; I've got new friends; we're part of the community here …'

'And you're doing a fabulous job with Bill Broadbent's wife.'

'Gertie? She's a sweetheart. And just seeing her face when Gypsy trots over for a hug … you can actually *see* the dementia receding.'

'Bill's always singing your praises. And there's no more talk of him resigning – thanks largely to you.'

'I'm glad. They don't need any more upheavals. But it's a joy to spend time with her … and her daughters – they're all so lovely with her. That's what I call a real family.'

Leon nodded.

'I'm glad the atmosphere's easier at your place,' she said. 'It's another bonus, being down here, you being close to work as well as at home far more.'

'And the company *is* growing again, now we've paid off our debts.'

'And things really are less tense between you and Thomas now?'

Leon nodded. 'They are. He's not looking over my shoulder the whole time now.'

'Juliette's been so lovely too. It's such a comfort knowing she's on hand if I do need somebody. I can moan to her about things and it stays in the family.'

She felt Leon's sidelong glance.

Still work to do there.

'I wonder how Tiffany's doing,' she said slowly. 'All this time on … those kids … Maribel will be a teenager now …'

'Best not think about it – only brings back horrible memories.'

She held up a hand. 'Not all horrible. I can't forget she tried to support me initially.'

'*And* tried to kill Gypsy, *and* ruin your life!'

'Because I was being such an obsessive mother ...'

Leon shook his head. 'You can't ... you *can't* take responsibility for everybody else's faults, Anya. *Tiffany* was the one who tried to break up our family; *I* was the one who made colossal mistakes in the company. Not you.'

'All actions have consequences. Relationships are a two-way street. But it was Tiffany who forced me to hold up a mirror to my own failings. When she had Gypsy hanging over that bridge, I knew it for sure. I *was* "an obsessive, paranoid perfectionist", I *wasn't* "a real mother." I vowed then – and I renew the pledge every day – I'd learn from that lesson. I admit, it isn't easy; I'm always going to have to fight my natural inclinations. When Gypsy smeared Smarties all over the wall today, I had to *make* myself take it one step at a time. But, well ... it's not the same ... chocolate over the walls *here*. Imagine that at *Eskbank Road*!' She mimed an explosion.

Leon grinned and nodded. 'It *was* rather fabulous, wasn't it?'

'And too perfect. But Tiffany was right. I absolutely *have* to give our children space and freedom to spread their wings, learn about what's really important. The little toe-rag won't be painting the walls with sweeties again in a hurry – not because she's afraid to put a mark on the walls; but because she knows there are boundaries – reasonable understandable boundaries – and she's not a precious prima donna who can do exactly as she pleases.'

'Well, I can only admire your capacity for finding a silver lining in the Tiffany fiasco. I'm still grinding my teeth.'

'Actually, Leon, there's something I need to tell you, and this is probably the right time to do so.'

'Arrgghh ... why do I get a sinking feeling here ...?'

'And I want you to stay calm ... not blow a gasket ... Promise?'

He compressed his lips and pressed a hand down on the top of his head.

'I wrote to the Corrigans this week.'

Leon stared at her, saying nothing.

'I wanted to let them know I've moved on, forgiven Tiffany. Learned from the experience. Give them something positive to hang on to. They must have gone through purgatory themselves since all this happened.'

'You've … *forgiven* her? You mean that?'

'Yes … I think I do. It's taken me all this time but … letting go of all that baggage … I feel so much better in myself. And sending the card sort of put the seal on it.'

'You're something else, you know that?' Leon said slowly. 'I wish I could say the same, but I can't. What she put you through …' He shuddered. 'And yet … logically speaking, *I* ought to be one who's *more* ready to forgive. *I* needed *your* forgiveness … still do … I very nearly wrecked our marriage; I doubted you; I guffed up. I ought to sympathise with weakness and frailty in other people.'

'You'll get there. And I guess it's easier for me – it was *me* she had it in for. I think it's harder to forgive when someone hurts the people we love. Speaking of which … *that's* the biggest incentive for getting rid of all the toxic stuff.'

'What is?'

'This new little person.' She cupped her hands around her growing abdomen. 'I want him/her to have the best start possible; not be soaking up negativity and resentment.'

Leon slid his fingers over hers. 'It'll be a new start. For all of us. This one won't ever know the kind of life I *wanted* for my family; but he … she … will certainly have a wiser father.'

'And who knows … maybe one day …'

Acknowledgements

This book took me into uncharted and challenging waters. Without the support and guidance of many people, I would have floundered at several points. I'm hugely grateful for their input but take full responsibility for any remaining infelicities.

Warm thanks to –

Emeritus Professor of Neonatal Medicine, Rob Hume, who plotted and schemed with me when this book was at an embryonic stage; and authenticated the medical consequences of giving noxious substances to babies. After so many years working together saving real little lives, who'd have thought we'd devise ways to harm them!

Paediatrician, Patricia Jackson, who put herself into Dr Hooper's shoes, and brought my information about safe practice up to date. She also introduced me to a real expert in child protection.

Lead Paediatrician in Child Protection, Jacqui Mok, who so generously read the whole manuscript and introduced me to the role people like her play in keeping children safe. Thanks to her Dr Diane Moore came into existence.

Sandra Hayles, who gave me the benefit of her vast experience as a health visitor and answered a long list of questions with patience and understanding.

Jonathan McHaffie, who painstakingly read several drafts, gave me super-helpful feedback and shared every stage of the writing of this book. He was able to call humbug by its proper name without the necessity for flannel - invaluable!

Alan Smith, Charlotte Smith and James Polanski, who bailed me out when I fell into the opaque waters of accounting and accountability in small businesses.

'Sandy' at Dalkeith Laundry Service, who gave me such an effective map to guide my own reconnoitre for Anya's escape route in the opening chapter.

David McHaffie, who tramped beside the River Esk in January, shadowed me down the streets of Dalkeith and

Eskbank, painstakingly checked the final draft for typos and inconsistencies, and put up with my ridiculous work schedules and absences and preoccupations with his usual fortitude.

Rosalyn Crich, who is always positive in her feedback.

So many friends and relations who supported me with their ongoing belief in my ability to bring this off.

Tom Bee and Senga Fairgrieve, who worked their usual magic on the cover.

I salute you all.

Discussion Points for Book Clubs

•Anya Morgan is a competent, intelligent, career woman, but she struggles as a new mother. What elements of her background and personality do you think have contributed to this? In her shoes, whose support and advice would you have found most helpful? Do you agree that modern career women think in terms of targets and outcomes, and can find the uncertainties of motherhood difficult, as Dr Brownlee suggests?

•Leon Morgan is torn between his domestic and work responsibilities. How much of what goes wrong can be laid at his door? What part do the Morgan & Sons business problems play in this story? Leon decides not to tell Anya about them; to what extent does this influence what happens?

•How would you summarise relationships within the whole Morgan family – senior parents, the three sons and their wives? Compare that to Anya's relationship with her family – her father, sister and Claire's partner Jim. What light does this shed on Anya's actions?

•At one point Anya says to Leon, '*I think your definition of loyalty comes out of a different dictionary from mine*'. How much do a) perceived disloyalty, b) refusal to discuss issues, c) both of them talking to others 'behind their backs' and d) lack of trust, contribute to the deteriorating relationship?

•How would you describe Tiffany Corrigan? Her medical knowledge, current post in the Sick Children's Hospital, and diagnoses and hints, all help to generate suspicion of Anya with both Leon and the medical team. Is trust in health care professionals instinctive? Tiffany has a plausible medical/psychological explanation for everything; how does this add to the suspense of the story?

•Health visitor Lucinda Devonshire is the first to have doubts about Anya's ability to cope. To what extent do the different personalities, status, and degrees of involvement of her professional colleagues, play a part in decision-making? Why do you think they dismiss Lucinda's qualms initially?

•Jane Carver's boss thinks she's too soft; Lucinda thinks she's safe and mature; her fiancé thinks she's a maverick - what do you think of her as a social worker? Was Brenda Brooks a better substitute? Should resources be allowed to dictate clinical responsibility in these sensitive cases?

•A number of senior doctors – both community and hospital – become involved in this case, each with their own inclinations, experience and areas of expertise. In this case, how much did this spread of responsibility help or hinder an accurate diagnosis? Tiffany repeatedly refers to paediatrician Dr George Harper as slow to act. Would you have trusted him? Was his caution justified?

•Why do you think the author chose to make this story a domestic psychological thriller?

•When did you first suspect what was really threatening Gypsy? What alerted you?

•When the social workers are brought in, both Leon and Tiffany say that the family don't fit the usual profile, the GPs feel it's a waste of resources which are badly needed elsewhere, and Anya sees it as a slur. Has this book changed your own perception of the kinds of families who might require additional social support?

•Professionals have a duty of care to ensure children are safe. At what point do you think they should have decided Gypsy could not be left with her mother? Was anyone negligent in this case? Was anyone too precipitate?

•It's commonly said that social workers at the coalface are damned if they do and damned if they don't. What do you think the consequences would have been if Gypsy had been a) taken away sooner, or b) left with her mother? How would you have felt about the authorities in either circumstance? How might the press have reported things?

•The Child Protection system involves medical staff working alongside social services and the police. No organisation is infallible, and at several points in the Morgan case, anomalies result in procedures not being followed. Were the professionals appropriate in their responses? If not, what should they have done?

•The authorities agree to Anya taking Gypsy home after the convulsion provided she has assistance in the house and monitoring by the professionals. Were they right to regard this level of supervision as adequate in the circumstances? Would such an order to considered sufficient in a more disadvantaged family? If you were Hannah Morgan in Chapter 40, how would you have felt when Anya decided she'd take Gypsy for a walk outside on her own?

•When should a woman's right to parent a child as she sees fit, be overridden by the authorities?

•In Chapter 57 Staff Nurse Rosemary Stewart describes her ambivalence about adoption. What do you feel about the rigorous processes couples must go through to adopt children? What differences could you identify between adopting Holly Justine, daughter of the teenage Tiffany, and Gypsy Morgan? Should a child like Gypsy ever be permanently removed from her biological family, do you think? How would you decide between so many competing rights and interests?

•Why do you think the author introduced poison pen letters in the escalation of threat to Gypsy?

•Gypsy is detained in hospital under constant scrutiny and yet harm still comes to her. Do you think there is ever a case to be made for electronic surveillance – either overt or covert – in such circumstances? Would the potential benefits of gaining evidence of high risk behaviours outweigh the invasion of privacy and circumventing of choice and consent?

•Frustrated by the lack of official action, Lucinda and Jane concoct a plan to establish the truth. What did you think of their actions? Were they justified in hastening the process? Were the Child Protection Team in any way to blame?

•Confidentiality plays a major role in these cases, but it can bring its own problems. At what points do you feel that greater openness would have been beneficial here? Once Gypsy is safe, the psychiatrist, Dr Gabrielle Fournier, feels that those closely involved deserve to know the facts. Is she justified in sharing confidences at this point?

•Why do you think the author leaves certain longer-term storylines unresolved?

If you are interested in further information about medical ethics or the issues raised in Hazel McHaffie's books, visit her website and weekly blog.

www.hazelmchaffie.com

By the same author

Listen (A novella)
ISBN 978 0 9926231. 4 2   eBook

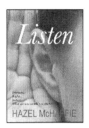

Professor Jocelyn Grammaticus is a renowned expert in medical ethics. But as the train pulls out of Aberdeen station, she has one thing on her mind: murder! A fourteen-hour journey lies ahead of her; awaiting her in Cornwall, the hardest decision of her life

She forces herself to spend the time preparing for a keynote presentation due the following week, but the conversations of her fellow-travellers distract her. When it comes to real life experiences who decides what is right? An ash-blonde adulteress; an anxious granny; a single-minded career girl; a postmenopausal mother; an overweight pasty-lover? And is Jocelyn herself making the right choice for her family?

Over my Dead Body
ISBN 978 0 9926231 0 4   PBK and eBook

When her daughter, Elvira, and three year old granddaughter are fatally injured in a car crash, Carole Beacham, is passionately opposed to their organs being donated. She has been haunted for thirty years by a dark secret and will do anything in her power to keep it from shattering their lives. But unknown to her parents, Elvira has been in a close relationship with a man they have never met, and he insists her wishes were clear: their organs should be used.

Eventually, reassured by the safeguards in place to protect the identities of donor and recipients, Carole is reluctantly persuaded to give qualified consent. But no one has factored in the aspirations of a budding journalist and a young poet. As the family struggle to deal with their crippling loss, barriers crumble with potentially devastating consequences.

Saving Sebastian
ISBN 978 1 906817 87 9   PBK and eBook

Sebastian Zair is four years old, but a rare blood disorder means that he won't live much longer unless he gets a stem cell transplant.

His mother is determined to save him. With no one in the family a match, she appeals to the Pemberton Fertility Centre for help to create an embryo the same tissue type as Sebastian.

But will her resolve falter as her fortieth birthday approaches? When hormones play havoc with her confidence and control? When the Pemberton becomes the focus of a major inquiry following the birth of a white baby to black parents? When an unscrupulous journalist starts to invade the family's privacy? When militant pro-life campaigners protest against the wanton destruction of life?

It's a race against time, and time is not on Sebastian's side.

Remember Remember
ISBN 978 1906817 78 7   PBK and eBook

Doris Mannering's secret has been safely kept for 60 years, but now it's threatened with exposure.

In her early twenties during World War II she made a choice that changed the course of her family's life. The evidence was safely buried, but now, with the onset of Alzheimer's, her mind is wandering. She is haunted by the feeling that she must find the papers before it's too late, but she just can't remember …

Jessica is driven to despair by her mother's behaviour, but it's not until lives are in jeopardy that she consents to Doris going into a residential home. As she begins clearing the family home ready for sale, bittersweet memories and unexpected discoveries await her. But these pale into insignificance against the bombshell her lawyer lover, Aaron, hands her.

Right to Die
ISBN 1 906307 21 0 PBK and eBook

Naomi is haunted by a troubling secret. Struggling to come to terms with her husband's death, her biggest dread is finding out that Adam knew of her betrayal. He left behind an intimate diary – but dare she read it? Will it set her mind at ease – or will it destroy the fragile hold she has over her grief?

Gripped by his unfolding story, Naomi discovers more than she bargained for. Adam writes of his feelings for her, his career, his burning ambition. How his dreams evaporate when he is diagnosed with Motor Neurone Disease, as one by one he loses the ability to walk, to speak, to swallow. How he resolves to mastermind his own exit at a time of his choosing ... but time is one luxury he can't afford. Can he, will he, ask a friend, or even a relative, to help him die?

Vacant Possession
ISBN 1 85775 651 7 PBK and eBook

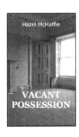

Following a serious accident, Vivienne Faraday has been in a persistent vegetative state, looked after in a residential home, for years. How can she suddenly be pregnant?

She can't speak for herself so who should decide what happens to the unborn child? Who knows what's in her best interests? Her father, her brothers, her estranged mother who is now a nun, the medical director, the police, all have different opinions as to the best way forward. They also have their personal interests and values.

As events gather momentum, and the baby grows, someone must make medical and moral choices on Vivienne's behalf, choices beset with uncertainty, which profoundly affect their own relationships and futures. And all the time suspicion mounts: who exactly is the rapist?

Paternity
ISBN 1 85775 652 5   PBK and eBook

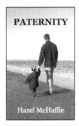

When Judy agrees to marry Declan Robertson his happiness knows no bounds. But from the very first night of their marriage cracks appear in their relationship, which only widen until Judy finally reveals the demons that haunt her.

Then tragedy strikes, threatening their new security: a child dies. Questions follow, questions that rock their foundations to the core. A history of deception and half-truths masquerading as love begins to unravel, challenging their very identities. Who are they? What have they inherited? What are they passing on to future generations? Do they have a future together?

Declan has always lived by a strict moral code; now he must ask himself just how far he will go to protect his wife from the consequences of her parents' actions.

Double Trouble
ISBN 1 85775 669 X   PBK and eBook

The Halleys are a close-knit, successful, loving family. Relationships become strained when identical twins, Michael and Nicholas, fall in love with the same girl, Donella, herself a twin. On the rebound from Nick, Donella eventually marries Mike, but their lives become entangled again when Nick returns from work overseas. His new wife, Heidi, is Swiss, reserved, and haunted by her past; she finds it difficult to find her niche within the demonstrative Halley family.

But Donella's three daughters gradually break down the barriers and a new order is established. Later, when Heidi finds she can't have children of her own, new tensions emerge. Fresh alliances are forged; old feelings return; jealousies develop; mental illness and a surrogate pregnancy threaten the delicate peace the couples have established. Will the family survive intact?

Printed in Poland
by Amazon Fulfillment
Poland Sp. z o.o., Wrocław